The Swallows of Monte Cassino

The Swallows of
Monte Cassino

Helena Janeczek

Translated from the Italian by Frederika Randall

Washington DC

Published by New Academia Publishing 2013
English translation, © 2013 Frederika Randall
Italian edition, *Le rondini di Montecassino,* © 2010 Ugo Guanda Editore, S.p.A.

Printed in the United States of America

Library of Congress Control Number: 2013949963
ISBN 978-0-9899169-0-5 paperback (alk. paper)

 An imprint of New Academia Publishing

 New Academia Publishing, LLC
P.O. Box 27420, Washington, DC 20038-7420
www.newacademia.com - info@newacademia.com

For my father and my son

Contents

Before the Battle

Segrate, the outskirts of Milan, autumn of 2007

Everything that takes place anywhere in any moment is the past.
   —Gustav Landauer, anarchist philosopher, culture minister of the Bavarian republic, stoned to death by rightwing troopers in 1919

War is the father of all things.
   —Heraclitus

My father fought at Monte Cassino, he was with General Anders in the Second Polish Army Corps. He was wounded near Recanati while they were battling their way up the Adriatic toward Bologna. While he was convalescing in a farmhouse there, he met a girl from the Marches. My mother, the reason why he remained in Italy.

Italy, the reason why, more than sixty years later, I have to spell out my surname over the phone. Hearing me repeat it, the taxi driver has just asked me if I am Polish, as he is.

"Did you know that Polish soldiers, if they married an Italian woman, gave up their rights to British citizenship, the prize the British offered those who had fought alongside them against the Nazis?" I ask him, looking down toward the end of the street, the overpass that marks the end of Milan already in sight.

No, he didn't know that.

Poles, went abroad with their wives to the furthest ends of the earth, to Argentina and Australia, I tell him. Only a few, about two hundred, stayed in Italy after the war, apart from the one thousand buried under the Benedictine abbey. For half a century those few veterans have looked after the cemetery, passed on the memory of the battle, kept ties with Poland alive.

"Have you ever been there? Do people in Poland still remember *Czerwone maki na Monte Cassino*?"

The day had begun badly: the train late, a taxi to get to work on time, an argument with the phone provider, but things seem to be looking up. When we get to Via Corelli I'm singing the song about the red poppies on Monte Cassino, the taxi driver joining in on the refrain.

"Do widzenia!" I say, handing him a tip slightly larger than usual, humming on my way to the office.

That's how it might have gone that autumn morning—if any of this
had come to mind. Instead I didn't tell the taxi driver my father
had fought at Monte Cassino. I merely told him that he came from
Poland and various other things, it doesn't matter what, in answer
to his questions: "Where did your father come from? How long has
he been in Italy? Does he still have family in Poland? Where do they
live? Do you ever see them? Why is it that you don't speak Polish?"
    I struggled to provide credible answers, paying with clumsy,
extemporaneous lies for that first sincere reply. I had only given
myself an Italian mother to justify my scant knowledge of Polish; I
hadn't counted on further questions. Entangled in my half-truths,
I learned that invention is not very successful when it's forced and
purely casual lies can be ugly indeed. Maybe the man who dragged
them out of me didn't even notice; maybe only I did. Noticed what
an abyss there was between what I was saying and what I was hiding, and how fragile was the shield of words I'd put up before me
without really needing to.
    Just two words—Monte Cassino—were all I needed to seem to
him fully armored with weapons and uniform. It would have been
enough to really have known the song about the red poppies, when
I had merely heard it sung by Adam Aston in a film about the Polish conquest of the ruined abbey. A tenor already famous before the
war, Aston is immortalized in romantic films where the hero takes
the hand of the heroine to the languid melody of a tango sung by
a man in a dinner jacket, standing before his little gypsy orchestra.
It would have been enough to know that his real name was Adolf
Loewinsohn, and that he was born a Jew in Warsaw, ended up in
a theater in Lviv in 1939, and left the Soviet Union in 1942 with
General Anders' Army. But his greatest patriotic act was to have
recorded, in 1944 in Rome, a song in memory of his fellow soldiers
fallen among the poppies.
    My father also had a nice voice and was a Polish Jew, as were
my mother, my grandparents, my aunts and uncles and all my relatives who did remain in Poland, but only among the ranks of the
dead. It was this that I did not want to tell the curious taxi driver;
even less, when he told me where in Poland he came from.

Kielce: the native city of Gustaw Herling, a deportee to the Soviet gulags, then a soldier in the Second Army Corps, a veteran of
Monte Cassino. These were also things I could have told the taxi
driver, but instead the name of that city brought to mind one thing
only.

Kielce: where the first great pogrom of the post-war period
took place, where some eighty Jewish survivors were murdered—
leading my parents to pack up and leave Poland forever.

My father too, like Adam Aston, answered to a name that was not
the one he was born with. It wasn't a stage name, though, but one
he had taken for the sake of survival.

Had he given it up and taken back his Jewish name, the Polish
taxi driver from Kielce would not have asked me any questions.

But my father's false name is my surname. I was born and raised
with it. I've explained its origin a thousand times. Still I often end
up being taken for a recent immigrant, a minder of elderly ladies,
and even a hooker, because here in Italy, today, I bear a Slavic surname. How can I count as false something that has put its mark on
me? False, a name to which my father owed his life and I, mine?
What is a fiction when it is incarnate, when it has real power to
change the course of history, when it acts on reality and is itself
transformed? What does a lie become when it saves a life?

And what stories, I ask myself, can I tell faced with this? What
can I possibly invent, myself a witness in flesh and blood to the slip-
pery confine that separates truth and fabrication, fiction and reality,
life and death? What can I say knowing that before a life saved because of false papers, there is a giddy void of real names, forgotten
names, names lost and names disappeared; families exterminated
right down to the last, civilians of every nation turned into black
stumps by bombings, bodies exploded until they are unrecognizable, corpses never recovered from the battlefields, unknown soldiers.

I, Helena Janeczek, born in Munich, Bavaria, resident for more
than twenty years in Italy, of Polish origin because my Jewish parents came from Poland and all the more so because I have a Slavic
name, one autumn day found, without even knowing I was looking
for it, a place. A corner of the world that turns out to be far more

than a pretext, an excuse to make of a string of graceless lies, a story so potent, so grand, that it cuts all questions short.

At its heart is an abbey, the first monastery in the West, four times demolished. Beneath it, not far away, the Polish cemetery. Further down the valley, just outside Cassino, the Commonwealth cemetery. The Germans are buried at Caira, the Americans at An- zio, the French at Venafro, the Italians at Mignano-Monte Lungo. These are the soldiers who died in the Italian Campaign, and above all in the Battle of Monte Cassino, the name by which we call the four Allied offensives that took place between January and May, 1944. The abbey has been rebuilt, leaving visible the foundations of a Roman temple brought to light by the bombs; the bluff on which it sits is covered by thick green vegetation hiding the last detritus of the war. The dead were more than all those who lie in the nearby graveyards, more than 30,000. Thirty thousand among millions. Millions of men swallowed up from faraway places and spat out into the neck of a valley ringed with mountains.

Among the millions was one of my mother's cousins, Dolek Szer. And a close family friend, Emilio Steinwurzel, also fought there. Both in the Second Army Corps. But in Italy only someone like the taxi driver from Kielce can be expected to know that the Poles took part in the country's liberation. Nobody even bothers to mention the New Zealanders and the Canadians when the Anglo- Americans—or just "the Americans"—are spoken of. Even those Italians who fought as regular soldiers on the Allied side, and not in the Resistance, have been forgotten. And so it's no surprise that almost no one remembers the Indians, the Nepalese, the Maori, the Algerians, the Japanese-Hawaiians, the Brazilians, the Senegalese, the Jews from Palestine with the Jewish Brigade, and all the other soldiers from around the entire world who ended up in Italy. And fought in Italy and often died in Italy, because the whirlwind that caught them up was not just War but the Second World War.

It is from the Second World War—the dates go back to a false passport—that I trace my origins. The Second World War, one and indivisible. A single vortex that engulfed just about every place on earth, every animal, every landscape, and tossing them crazily around, united and divided people. Too enormous to capture all at once, the actors too distant to grab hold of without the vehicle of invention. And yet too real were their lives and deaths now grown faint and half-forgotten, not to adhere as much as possible to the sources that follow their tracks and document their passage from one continent to another, from the past tense to the present.

My father never fought at Monte Cassino, and he was not one of General Anders's soldiers. But into that channel through the mountains and valleys and rivers of Ciociaria, something of mine perhaps went. Something that was lost and found in a place on the map, a place that contains us all.

The First Battle

January 12-February 12, 1944

Sergeant John "Jacko" Wilkins, 36ᵗʰ Infantry Division "Texas";
enlisted San Marcos, Texas, June 15, 1939—died Cassino,
January 20, 1944

There's a yellow rose in Texas, that I am going to see,
No other soldier knows her, no soldier only me.
She cried so when I left her it like to broke my heart,
And if I ever find her, we nevermore will part.

She's the sweetest rose of Texas this soldier ever knew,
Her eyes are bright as diamonds, they sparkle like the dew.
You may talk about your Dearest May, and sing of Rosa Lee,
But the Yellow Rose of Texas is the only girl for me.
—*Popular song*

Sergeant John "Jacko" Wilkins—and someone like him certainly did exist—was the fifth son of a family of small ranch owners from San Marcos, Texas, who had been hard hit by the Great Depression. He was just over nineteen years old when he left home. Not because he was starving, for the Wilkinses had never actually gone hungry. But memories of straitened circumstances had left a dusty, humiliating pall over his childhood. Things were improving now, but four young men were still too many to make a living off a herd of fifty longhorns, and it was right to leave it all in the hands of his oldest brother, Henry Jr. And so, when Jacko announced to the family that he wanted to enlist in the National Guard, they were proud, and approved. Glory, and above all, suffering, belonged to the past: Fort Alamo, the Civil War. His fellow townsmen who died on the Marne in 1918 were long gone; "France" was a word used to sell perfume or silk stockings that nobody bought. The nation was now large, united and fortified and "serving one's country" often meant battling the fires rushing through the plains grass. Whether the fires were caused by drought or human greed (so often invisible and inextinguishable) was another matter. In any case you had to fight for every acre of Texas land.

His mother embraced him, and feeling herself close to tears went off to get him some dried beef and homemade jam. His father said "God bless you, son." Henry Jr. gave him a ride to Austin in the green truck. It was 1939.

When John "Jacko" Wilkins came home for Thanksgiving, he told them he had met a girl named Sally, and after hesitating just a moment pulled out a photograph in which Sally was smiling broadly, showing a row of upper teeth that were none too straight.

A photographer from San Antonio had signed the picture down at the bottom, where you could make out a studio set of a Western landscape. Sally was wearing a little flowered dress, her legs in a pair of Texan boots. Jacko alone looked stiff and unnatural in his uniform, right in the middle like a pillar but somehow extraneous, and from this his mother deduced that the affair was serious. Unfortunately Jacko didn't make it back home for Christmas, either alone or with his fiancée, and by Thanksgiving the following year it was too late. On November 25, 1940 the entire Texas National Guard was called up as the 36th Division of the U.S. Army.

It was in the air. It had been since June, where the capital of silk and perfume fell and the Blitz hit London; it had been from the time, after the summer, when President Roosevelt got approval for the first ever draft call-up in times of peace, for men from twenty one to thirty five years old. But down in San Marcos they liked to think that their son and brother had been called up to defend Texan soil.

At Christmas time Jacko Wilkins and the 36th Division were transferred to Camp Bowie, Texas. The day they arrived, the area was hit by the worst hailstorm ever recorded in local history. Some thought it was a bad omen; but most, among them Wilkins, responded to the challenge of the elements in a spirit of military defiance. Then there were months and months of training and maneuvers up and down the country, in Louisiana and South Carolina, at Camp Blanding, Florida, and at Camp Edwards, Massachusetts, not so far from where the pilgrim fathers landed. The months became years marked by furloughs, to be divided between Sally and home, with the visits to San Marcos becoming briefer and briefer once everyone had got together to celebrate their wedding.

Not long before he shipped out of New York on April 2, 1943, Jacko wrote to his family:

> I am proud and happy to have gotten to know the whole of the United States. I've seen the ocean, I've seen palms and pines, I've spent my days with fellows who talk in a way I find strange and hard to understand, just as how I talk must seem to them. I've gotten used to the fact that many

of them are black folk. This country is so huge you can't
imagine; I don't think there's anything in the world like it.
We are so strong and so much in the right that we will soon
be home with victory in our pockets. Don't worry about me,
just know I am doing my duty and that I'm doing it with all
my heart.

Crossing the Atlantic, Jacko was seasick many times, he even vomited bile. When they got to Arzew in Algeria where they would
train up for the European landing, many of his fellow soldiers collapsed in the heat and were ill with diarrhea, but Wilkins held out,
swallowed dust, wet his chapped lips with saliva. In Rabat, Morocco, they promoted him. Jacko had known how to shoot from the
time he was a kid, he had even finished off a few sick animals, but
his talent with a pistol had manifested itself in the National Guard,
when he had hit a rattlesnake on the head at his first try. A good
shot, a soldier capable of endurance and discipline, a positive per-
sonality with a real patriotic commitment to the mission. America
had forged a gigantic force of war, but in that huge, dirty-green
river anyone who could occupy a place of command was valuable.

Big news: I've been promoted. Haven't even seen a Kraut
yet and I'm already sergeant. "Try to live up to it, kid," said
Major Stratford, but I took that as a compliment. We went
into town to celebrate, to a place where they do belly dancing. There's one woman for every twenty men over here,
veiled head to foot, and usually you can just see their eyes
and sometimes some tattooed designs above them. Tribal
customs, they told us. Be careful of the men, don't fool
around, they said. But I mean, I feel for the boys. There they
were, in front of these dancers naked from the bottom of
their brassieres down to their belly buttons, moving their
hips and bellies in an unbelievably provocative way, and
our fellows were going crazy. We'd been drinking, too, obviously. The boys were going up and putting their dollars
in the bra tops or down the girls' pants: that's how you do
it here. Then they wanted me to come along to the cathouse,
but I said no.

I'm sorry, I shouldn't tell you these things. It's just to say that I think about you, and that I missed you a lot that evening. You can't imagine the nostalgia and the feelings of loneliness that get to you sometimes. Like at night lying on your cot, when you're completely wiped out with fatigue but can't get to sleep right away. You wouldn't believe the world we've fallen into here: poor, old, dirty, people who yell at you in this incomprehensible ugly language, children who buzz around you like flies begging, dust, the sun beating down. At this point I just hope they ship us off soon to fight the real war so I can stop thinking all these foul thoughts. I love you Sally, that's all I wanted to say.

The Moroccan summer, though, never seemed to end. By August, Jacko was no longer able to pretend not to see his men, one by one, go off with the local boys, usually the same ones, Faid, Cherif, Mohammed, while he kept them at a distance, giving them too many cigarettes for a few handfuls of ripe dates. He held upset, furious conversations with the photo of Sally from San Antonio. "Sally, they're trying to make us into good soldiers here," he told her, "and they're making us into faggots," and sometimes he jerked off desperately until he fell asleep.

They finally drew closer to war on September 9, 1943. The sea was so flat, the night so peaceful, that when the voice of General Eisenhower came over the loudspeakers to announce that the Italians had surrendered, the soldiers began to dance like couples on a cruise ship. There was no trace of the enemy on the beach at Paestum where they landed before dawn, but as they advanced and the sky began to grow paler, they saw the enemy's bloodless presence: barbed wire on the dunes, mines, then some fighter-bombers, fire from tanks hidden and lying in wait, German mortars and machine guns pitched on the town's medieval towers. His eyes burning with smoke, Jacko saw in passing the ancient temple to the Greek god of the sea that had spat them out there, not even surprised that it was still there, intact. In the end they took Paestum, tired and giddy from the fighting. Those of them who came back to these parts again—several months later, or half a century on—would feel the same wonder before the Temple of Poseidon, the place that marked that moment when, unawares, the status of veteran was forever written on them. Just then, however, Sergeant Wilkins could do nothing but run and look straight ahead, not seeing the fallen, ignoring the shudder he felt when his boot struck one of them, the obscene slackness of a human corpse. He signaled to his men, loaded and fired.

Two days later came the counterattack, very intense, from both land and air. Hit by machine gun fire in the chest, Jacko went down during one of the charges to retake Altavilla Silentina. His boys got to ground in time, and the next day they advanced on their target and took it. During his convalescence Wilkins heard all about the city of Naples, where war and poverty seemed to have overthrown all semblance of order, and if those tales seemed a mite exaggerated, the way stories told to buck up a patient's spirits can be, he had no choice but to accept the news from the front. Two of his men had died attacking the village of San Pietro, one fell on the slopes of Monte Lungo, another had stepped on a mine along the Volturno Line. These were the days of the winter holidays, between Halloween and Christmas.

Jacko took it upon himself to write to the relatives and girlfriends of the dead, and that made him sink into a state of helpless homesickness. But it kept the boredom at bay, boredom that became dejection, boredom mixed with anxiety for the battles he couldn't take part in. He kept going over that moment in which his war had nearly ended just as it was beginning. His memories were very confused, but in the end there wasn't much to comprehend. He did understand he had been saved by being wounded, and went back and forth between feeling guilty and very grateful to God. He tried to focus on God, exhorting himself to be patient, aiming for optimism, oblivion. But then one day one of his boys from Indiana came to tell him that during his leave he'd caught syphilis from a Neapolitan prostitute in Pallonetto, she was pretty, beautiful, but—and here he started sobbing like a baby—she was a *he*, and now he was so ashamed he thought he was going to die. Sergeant Wilkins tried to make him feel better, but afterwards he found he had a raging desire to fight this damn war, win it and go home—to fight and win with his eyes firmly on their goals and on Hitler's great evil that had fostered them, never once stopping to let himself be contaminated by this old world decomposing in poverty and madness.

In January John Wilkins left his camp near the Allied headquarters in the royal palace of Caserta, traveling with a backup convoy. They were headed toward the American lines to the northeast, just over the border into the Lazio region, now that the last line of defense, Monte Trocchio, had been wiped out and overtaken. It was raining. It rained almost all the time and on the mountain roads the rain often turned into sticky sleet and then to snow. It was a lot colder than he had expected of a country called Italy, much colder than Texas, and the trucks often got beached in the mud, especially on the uphill stretches. But Jacko was in a hurry to finally reach his regiment, the 141st regiment of the 36th Infantry Division, and his morale matched his physical condition, now fully restored to health. Rested, well fed, shaved, he joked aloud with his fellow soldiers. Still, something of what passed before him was being deposited at the back of those blue eyes: the villages reduced to piles of stones, the groves of olive tree stumps, the shoeless children and the ones with rags on their feet, their mothers carrying babies in their arms and large bundles of something on their heads. You couldn't figure out where these people were going, or where they came from, only that they were moving along the road with the measured tread of people who still have a long way to go.

It was cold, Italy, cold and narrow and dark, all dark: eyes, hair, faces, ragged clothes, burned out camps, low grey houses, low grey skies, winter darkness. And the bare feet of those children, the feet of children under the rain who slapped the mud with an apathetic thud, a thud Jacko couldn't help thinking he would take home with him. He might be able to leave behind the dead seen at night while they ran and fought, but not those feet that passed them as the convoy struggled to slide forward, feet that when they approached he chased away with chocolate or chewing gum or a couple of cigarettes saying *toma, amigo*. Only then, just for a moment, he surrendered to those big, dazed, serious eyes, as the offering was grabbed by a filthy hand and a pair of cracked lips muttered something like *tenk-yoo*, and the bare feet took off, sending bigger splashes of mud than before. And then everybody laughed. Each time Sergeant Wilkins looked around for someone to whom he could say that those children were worse off than the poorest campesino kids down his way, and each time he remembered he was the only Texan on that truck. Did the others on their way toward the "Texas" Division think his Spanish sounded comical?

That day when he got to camp, Wilkins had a glimpse of how he looked like from the outside. Like the hero of a comic book he had loved since the days of the National Guard, like Flash Gordon on another planet. The men in his platoon—besides the four dead, two others had been gravely wounded in action—were beginning to take on the appearance of the place they'd invaded, with their unshaved faces, the dark circles under their eyes, their faces marked with the signs of a poor diet and exposure to the elements, with a patina of dirt, soot and something else that hadn't disappeared even after going on leave. He would soon look like them, it was his duty. It was also a privilege to have come from Planet America to this critical position to attack the Gustav Line, the last line of defense on their path toward Rome. That night, however, he couldn't sleep. In three months the faces of these buddies who had been with him since the landing at Salerno had aged more years than he could say. Jacko tried to tell himself that Billy Morrison, Stanley Laughlin, Richard Gonzales and Jeff McVey had become men, as was inevitable in a war, but he could feel the hand with which he'd slapped their backs in greeting weigh on his chest, it felt alien, marked. Luckily he fell asleep before he realized that it was fear.

The morning after was very cold but sunny, and the weather reports said those conditions should hold for the next few days. After a breakfast of coffee and powdered eggs, Wilkins and his platoon were sent out to reconnoiter from Monte Trocchio. The view was excellent; the Germans were down there in the Liri Valley below, but he couldn't take his eyes off the building on top of the mountain before him. The abbey of Monte Cassino rose out of the rock in a massive, perfect oblong, so beautiful, white and immaculate that it seemed the "mighty fortress" of that celebrated Lutheran hymn made manifest. The Germans had taken it upon themselves to protect this cradle of Western monasticism—established by St. Benedict in 529 before even the Vikings had even reached the shores of the New World—and they had declared a safety zone around it. The officer who informed them about the abbey's strategic and cultural significance had spoken in a neutral tone, but Jacko thought he'd caught a note of annoyance in his voice. Or maybe it was he who was feeling an entirely new hostility toward this enemy who'd taken the lives of so many boys so quickly, and was now going to such trouble to keep these stones intact.

There was no time to ponder this, however. They had to go back down the valley and prepare for the attack. The Allied offensive had begun a few days before with the French storming the mountains to the northeast and the British crossing the Garigliano River, southwest, but nothing definitive was going to happen before the Americans joined in. The onus, and the honor, of breaking the Gustav Line was going to fall to the 36th Infantry Division.

They sent some patrols ahead—and those patrols came back safe and sound. At this point the sappers went out to remove mines and stretches of barbed wire, and trace the newly cleaned-up trails with white tape. On the evening of January 19 the soldiers of the 141st and 143rd Regiments got steak for dinner—one steak each, and at least in principle something like the stuff they ate back in Texas. Jacko watched as his boys, now used to tins and powdered food, chewed silently.

"Not exactly like steak from home," he said trying to sound cheerful, to Gonzales, who was sitting next to him and came from somewhere near Houston.

"No sir," said Gonzales, who put his head down and ate another bite.

"Every time you send some down, it makes you homesick, doesn't it? Isn't that right, Rick, that we'd all like to go home soon?"

"Right, sir, but I'm not sure that's going to happen, because every time they give us this stuff, the next day they send us out, and every time, there's somebody who doesn't come back."

"Hey, at least they bother to let us croak on a full stomach!"

The remark came from Jeff McVey, who was looking toward the sergeant hoping to get his agreement.

"You know what I say, Jeff? If we were eating the meat of our own animals here, we would have already sent those Krauts to the devil!"

And on that comment from Sergeant Wilkins, they finished their last supper.

They left the following day after nightfall, on orders from commander in chief General Clark. They had to reach the River Rapido, wait until the engineers built a bridge, cross the bridge to the other side and go forward in two columns, one above and one below, to Sant'Angelo in Theodice where the enemy was dug into the ruins. The land next to the river was fertile but soft and muddy, and the Germans had built a dam to flood it so that it was impossible to get not just a tank through, but any motorized vehicle. And so it was up to them, the five thousand soldiers of the 141st and 143rd to push through the mud with their munitions on their backs: four hand grenades, 136 bullets, canteen, mess-tin, rations, and the rubber rafts and dinghies for the crossing. They advanced hunched over under the weight of the boats, silently and in single file, following the white tape that was disappearing into the mud under their boots. Had it occurred to them, or had they been Germans, they might have recalled the little boy abandoned in the woods who had marked the way back with bread crumbs. But then the birds flew down to eat them and Hansel and Gretel got lost and ended up in front of the gingerbread house. With the dark and the fog that rose from the river, they also got lost, and strayed off-track into a mine field, and one of them got blown up, and the explosion of that first mine told the Germans they were on their way and how far they had gotten.

The Germans opened up heavy fire with mortars and grenades, they fired from bunkers well-prepared for their arrival, they were down in their trenches, they were everywhere, on high and underground. John Wilkins saw Billy Morrison go down but he couldn't stop to figure out whether it had been a mine or something shot from the other side of the river, because now he had to duck a Nebelwerfer rocket, a so-called Screaming Mimi, with that girl's nickname to exorcise the terrible howl. Billy Morrison was also screaming, and therefore he was still breathing. Good. They advanced on the run, crouched over, tripping and slipping on the chill, wet earth, falling, getting up again, crawling, slithering. One after another they lost their battered rafts, they lost man after man as they stopped, trying to reply to the enemy fire, without the Germans ever stopping or weakening on any side. They reached the river right where the bank jutted out over the water, it wasn't easy to jump into their rafts already half deflated by all the bullet holes from all those German machine guns that were now tearing up the waves. Some of the rafts capsized and soldiers began to drown in that river that in fact was called the Gari but which was cold and swollen and rapid — to be inscribed forever in American memory as the Rapido.

Richard Gonzales died of a shrapnel wound in the neck that tore open his shoulder; his head, mouth open, fell back off the edge of the raft as it tipped under the weight of his dead body. Stanley Laughlin ended up in the river; he tried to swim but couldn't with all that equipment on him. Sergeant Wilkins yelled at him to grab on, then watched him borne away by the current as he threw off his backpack and gun and swam for his life. Sergeant Wilkins had other things to think about, other commands to bark out to the boys in the rafts. Sergeant Wilkins was the first to set foot on the other side and aim his weapon toward that dark minefield while Jeff McVey held the boat steady on all fours. Sergeant Wilkins was hit in the chest and collapsed backward, falling into the water. He disappeared in the Rapido the night of January 20, 1944.

The soldiers who hadn't yet crossed and the few who managed to swim back to the other side, now blocked with heaps of bodies to wade through or hide behind, were reassigned to other units. A second attack was ordered on January 22. When this failed too, pretty much in the same way, the Germans agreed to a truce to let them collect the bodies. The body of John "Jacko" Wilkins was never found. Between the dead, the wounded and the missing, the casualties amounted to 1681. That was the official figure announced by General Clark, that *goddam Yankee* who in order to land the rest of his Fifth Army at Anzio simultaneously, had sent those boys from Texas to take a fall, and it didn't matter that there weren't many Texans left in the 36th Infantry Division. It was as if they were all there on the damned Rapido River, as if the f-ing Gustav Line had sucked up the f-ing Mason-Dixon line and they had all ended up in the South, those boys from Illinois, Maine and New Jersey, all of them Southerners to butcher, while in the North, where victory was taken for granted, there was no one at all but their goddam f-ing Commander in Chief. Private Jeff McVey, ever since he had crawled back to the starting line, baptized in that freezing, red water, had started to revile him in those terms, instinctively broadening his Texan accent. He was the only one who'd been left alive, and would survive the rest of his other battles in Italy always aching to make Clark pay.

Let it therefore be recorded that the men of the 36th Division Veterans Association, meeting in Brownwood, Texas, intend to present a petition to the Congress of the United States to open an investigation of the Rapido disaster and to undertake all necessary measures to correct a military structure that permits an inexperienced and inept officer in high command (such as General Mark W. Clark) to destroy this country's young lives, and to stop soldiers from being sacrificed in this pointless way in the future.

Exactly two years later on January 20, 1946, McVey was among the veterans who signed that petition. Sharing mesquite-grilled steak with them, Jeff thought about Wilkins and the other boys dead at the river, cherishing in his anger and sense of betrayal, the hope that perhaps this meal consumed in their memory might strengthen the case against that damned Yankee Mark Wayne Clark.

But the Congress of the United States absolved the general.

The Second and Third Battle

February 15-March 24, 1944

Charles Maui Hira, 28th Maori Battalion, left Hopuhopu, Waikato,
N. Z., Oct. 1939, returned Wellington, 1946

His grandson Rapata Sullivan, left Auckland, N. Z., May 15, 2004
for Cassino, May 18-21, 2004

The call of the desert
And the call of Point 209
Have summoned us here from afar
In the sixth month of the Maori Calendar
In the sixth season
In the sixth heaven
The outward visible sign of an inward spiritual grace
The celestial canoe of the 28th Maori Battalion
Haere-rā, Haere-rā, Haere-rā
Farewell to you who laid down your lives for your brothers
The sacred mountains of Greece, Crete, North Africa, and Italy
Will forever stand watch over you.
My heart believes that you have cleared the pathway to enable
Me to stand on Point 209 and say farewell
Job said: we brought nothing into the world
We take nothing out
The Lord gives, the Lord takes away. This is the power of God.
I still see you all: the children of the war god Tumatauenga
Your people still weep for you
Your people still grieve for you.
You have fallen: we ask why
But we'll always mourn your loss
Haere-rā, Haere-rā, Haere-rā
— *Prayer by Canon Wiremu Te Tau Huata*
  Point 209, Tebaga Gap, Tunisia

Charles Maui Hira was just a few days past the enrollment age of twenty-one when he signed up for the 28th Maori Battalion, and he wasn't yet twenty-two when he sailed from the port of Wellington aboard the Aquitania on May 1, 1940. By the time he got to Monte Cassino he was just about the same age as his grandson Rapata, who many years later was about to board the Auckland-Dubai flight in his place, on the first leg of the long voyage that Charles the New Zealander had once made over four years. Four years, of which he spent the first months aboard that ship heading toward a destination that in the middle of the ocean seemed infinitely far off, not to mention that for a long time they did not know their destination, except that they were destined to go to war.

It was the first time Rapata Ihipa Sullivan had ever left New Zealand and when he got to the gate he began to think about his grandfather, and tried to convince himself that the twenty-seven hours in the air that awaited him, if all went well, were nothing in comparison with the sea haul. So he tried to control his nervousness about the flight, and his fatigue. He had slept badly, packed quickly, and might have been just as happy not to be there. But Charles Maui Hira had booked the flight—the best one there was, on Emirates with just one stopover—many months before and he had been setting aside money for that trip his whole life.

It wasn't right that his grandfather had died like that, from one second to the next, like a refrigerator, or the radio he himself had repaired so many times. It wasn't right that he should die just when he was finally ready to return to Italy. The medal that Rapata gripped in his hand while he waited for take off, tensed up in his Arab seat famous for being wider and more comfortable than all the others, Charles Maui Hira should have been wearing that medal the day they celebrated the sixtieth anniversary of the battle. Instead, he wore it for the last time in his coffin: for two days, there on his chest, before they closed it, before someone who had the right to touch him took it away and handed it to Rapata.

His father had turned up on the last day of the funeral service; he found Rapata in the *marae* where the body of Charles Maui Hira was laid out. There had been traffic at Auckland, he told him. It had taken him an eternity, he added, to make his way through the crowds, for the entire village had come to the place of prayer. "There are even some *mōrehu*," he went on, "all decorated up." Rapata too had seen the veterans. They were people he didn't know; only the uniforms, hung on bodies that time had shrunk, not filled out, told him who those old men were. Rapata said nothing to his father, grateful that for the *kiri mate*, speech was *tapu*. Forbidden: to speak, to touch the body, to touch food for the duration of the service, but only forbidden to direct kin. The others were permitted, even encouraged, to laugh and jest. So what could you expect from his father but that he should make fun of his grandfather and his fellow veterans? It was already a lot that he had even come.
    Rapata watched his mother by the bier in her mourning dress, a crown of *kawakawa* leaves on her head, his mother who had cried so much there beside the body that now she could observe her ex-husband with eyes that were reddened, but hard and dry. His father had stayed for the banquet and got drunk during the wake on the final night, but the next morning, when they left the cemetery to purify Charles Maui Hira's house with their prayers and offerings, he had disappeared. Rapata had not seen him since then. He had no idea how his father had come to know he was about to leave for Italy, and was still kicking himself for having answered the phone when he called.
    It was the money, that was the problem. Rapata was spending his grandfather's money to travel, when instead it was the government's job to shell out for the trip, and his to cling to it, gamble it, spend it on whores, buy a Harley, even sign up for a Masters in Economics—or, if he really couldn't think of anything better to do, give some to his father, a man of *mana* worthy of the true Maori, not

like the old man, who continued to think he was a hero for having served the British Crown a half a century ago on the other side of the world.

"Forget it," said Rapata with a bitter smile.

"You're an idiot," said his father, and Rapata saw him turn toward what he supposed were his mates, that bunch of hooligans and delinquents he went around with, and heard him say, in the stentorian tones of the drinker, "My son is an idiot, he kisses *Pākehā* ass like his grandfather did, he's half a man, a *kūpapa*." He could hear them laughing, hear that shitty pub where they went every night filling up with their lewd, self-confident laughter.

"Okay, Dad, you've done your act with your friends, now drop it," he said, and put down the phone.

From the time his father had left, and above all from the time he had ceased being a father Rapata could believe in—despite his legendary youth when he was a rising star with the All Blacks, despite his years as a militant in the Maori rights movement, things that had already happened before Rapata was born but which his father went on grandstanding about—the boy's compass had become Charles Maui Hira. And it was this that his father, whenever he remembered he had a son, couldn't tolerate: that Rapata preferred that old man in his tweed jacket and pomaded hair who had stayed in his native village on the Waikato, to himself who had gone out to conquer the city and wore the proud designs of the *moko* on his back, his chest, his legs and buttocks. And that was what Rapata, for his part, could never forgive: having discovered that all that stuff that seemed genuine, virile, the marks of a warrior's *mana*, like those tattoos on his massive body, was really false and as flimsy as a puff of air, as the infinite quantities of bullshit his father continued to spout, impressing those who didn't know him, because that was perhaps his only talent, his one real quality.

Kūpapa. The insult came from the times when Maori sold themselves to the *Pākehā* to fight against other Maori, but there had been no collaborators among the Waikato peoples, who beginning in 1863 had held off the colonial troops for two years, and there were scarcely any in 1916 when Princess Te Puea Herangi decreed her people must not to go to war for those who had plundered their ancestral lands. The Waikato followed her lead until the *Pākehā* passed a law obliging them to enlist, and anyone who resisted was hustled off to the trenches of Flanders or to the Dardanelles. But in 1939 Te Puea relaxed the ban somewhat and those who wanted to join the 28th Battalion were allowed to go. Some went because they were starving, some because they wanted to get out, some to see the world. Few, very few of the Waikato people signed up to honor the ideal on which the Maori Battalion was founded. It hadn't been easy for the Liberal deputy Sir Apirana Ngata to get parliament to approve creating an all-Maori unit, who, fighting alongside the *Pākehā*, shedding their blood along with that of the *Pākehā*, could pay a tribute that would earn them the right to be considered New Zealanders like the others. To pay "the price of citizenship" as Sir Apirana Ngata had called it: that was what Charles Maui Hira had in mind when he enlisted, and the reason he'd at times been called *kūpapa* in his village.

And despite his contempt for his father, that word hurt Rapata like a brand, it hurt a lot more than when he was eighteen and had the *moko* tattooed on his arm, more than his grandfather's remark the first time he saw it, scrutinizing his barely adult torso. "Very well, Rapi, I see that today it's become the custom again. However, don't forget that even in ancient times the bravest warriors were the ones who relied on the *mana* inside themselves, not those who tried to show off their armor plate of ink. We were warriors, even Feldmarschall Rommel recognized that, and none of us wore tattoos."

"Right," said Rapata, angry and let down, although he had known that was what his grandfather would say. "But at least you could admit that the reason you avoided the *moko* was because the *Pākehā* had convinced you it was a savage, primitive thing, and you didn't want to be savages and primitive, you wanted to be like them."

"That's probably true. But we did fight."

Charles Maui Hira had spent his life trying to show they had been warriors, not collaborators, not *kūpapa*. Now, high over the Pacific, Rapata asked himself whether that was why he had raised his grandson so devotedly. Was it because he needed someone of his own kin to absolve him, someone to vouch for him on the tombs of their ancestors who died fighting the *Pākehā*, someone to visit his dead companions, someone to whom he could pass on his role as witness. Merely to pay the price of an air ticket, rather than be offered it by the state, was evidently not enough. The price of citizenship was higher than that, it was the price of the one sacrifice that had not been paid with blood, a debt that all the privations, the denials, the scraping and saving of the post-war years had not been enough to extinguish.

Maybe it was the airplane—the air conditioning, the belt that tethered him to his seat, the Arab sitting next to him reading the *Financial Times*, invading his space with each page he turned—but as Rapata flew toward Italy he felt himself deflating, collapsing into a sense of loss that he hadn't experienced before. At the funeral, he'd been protected by his rage against his father, and also by the presence of all those *mōrehu* in uniform who remembered Charles Maui Hira as he wished to be remembered, and the love of people Rapata had known since he'd been a child, and the embrace of the very *marae* where he'd attended weddings, celebrations, banquets, where even the wood smelled of family.

He closed his eyes for a moment; he squeezed them shut. Then he turned to look out the window, where there was nothing to look at but the sky.

Before that blue void, Rapata Sullivan had never been aware of Charles Maui Hira's hurt. Not because his grandfather had concealed the dark side of his years at war, but because he had behaved as if it was secondary, bearable, in the face of that glorious experience, so that Rapata saw any troubles as a mere contrast that made the feats of the 28th Battalion all the more exalted. And in any case, he had been a child. What could he understand, if even now he was just a young man, the same age as his grandfather when he fought at Monte Cassino?

"We saw the world, Rapi," he could hear him say, as he had so many times, "we fought at Mt. Olympus, at Thermopylae, in Crete, in Egypt. Know what there was in Crete? The Minotaur, a monster who was half-man, half-bull who ate the little boys and girls delivered to him by the king of the island who kept him locked up in a kind of palace called a labyrinth. Until one day there came a boy who was braver and more cunning than the rest, and he killed the Minotaur."

"How did he kill it, *koro*? With a gun?"

"No, there were no guns back then, this was many years ago, centuries before the Maori came to Aotearoa from the islands nearby. With a dagger, or a sword; I don't know."

"Was this before they built the pyramids in Egypt? Like the one that's in your picture on the kitchen wall?"

"Could be, Rapi; I don't really know. But they made sure we savages from the other end of the world knew those were very ancient monuments, the cradle of civilization. Only, to tell the truth, I liked the palace of Crete better; inside there was a great wall painted with blue dolphins that made me feel at home."

"The house of the monster, *koro*?"

"No, the house of the king who was the Minotaur's master."

"But he was evil! Who cares if he had a beautiful palace if he was evil!"

"I believe it wasn't that king who had the dolphins painted, but someone who came after him. Maybe even several centuries had passed. And then, you know, Rapi, probably they were not all true, the stories; like the ones we believed before the *Pākehā* brought us Jesus."

"Like Tumatauenga who so he could have space and light wanted to divide Rangi and Papa and kill them even if they were his parents? Like Maui? Tell me the story of Maui, *koro*?"

"Another time. Now I think I told you that our first operation was on Mt. Olympus, where the ancient Greeks thought their gods lived: the god of the heavens, the god of war, the god of fire, even the god of the sea. And they also thought that when they went to fight, the gods would watch them from up there and intervene on behalf of one or the other. When we went up though, we didn't come across anything but mines and barbed wire and Germans."

"And did you kill a lot?"

"Not all that many. It was just the beginning, Rapata. At night in camp Major Dyer, who was the only *Pākehā* among our commanders, would tell these stories. After the war he became a teacher. You could tell it mattered to him. But we were tired out, and too excited to be at the front at last. We asked him stupid questions, silly things that irritated him. Why was it, Major, that those old *Pākehā* used to get their gods together on top of a mountain that wasn't even that high? We thought it was ridiculous, or anyway, weird. We were a pretty undiciplined bunch but very tight-knit, which is something very important for company morale, and Major Dyer knew that. There was a kid, and this I remember, the kind of kid who was at most sixteen when he signed up, and as they always did they pretended to believe he was twenty-one, and he asked the Major, "Did the ancient Greeks also believe they were descended from Tumatauenga, or what did they call their god of war?" Major Dyer said no, and then he thought for a minute. "I don't know whether the Greeks had a specific idea of who they were descended from," he finally said.

"And we're the savages, are we Major?" somebody shouted, but it was dark and you couldn't see who. But the Major, who was deep in thought, paid no attention. "However," he went on, "I can say that they believed that war is the father of all things." Whether anyone besides me was still listening I don't know, and probably I myself would have forgotten those words if Major Dyer hadn't repeated them in Crete, as the Germans were coming down like rain from the heavens in their parachutes. We fought that invasion with all our might, but we had to retreat, and we suffered many losses. That was when the Major once again said that war was the father of all things for the Greeks, who used the word *mortals* to describe themselves. That was the first time one of my companions died right near me."

"How did he die, *koro*? Did blood pour out of his mouth?"

"Never mind, child, that's no business of yours. That's enough, now; time for bed."

Why hadn't he ever noticed, even when he was older, said Rapata to himself, that his grandfather's stories always ended there, in the shadows, and then he would fall silent? Were even the most glorious tales clouded by that gloom? How had he not noticed that there were things that his grandfather mentioned, yes, but of which they never spoke? Prison, for example. At school he had learned that in camp E535 of Milowitz in Poland, Kiwi prisoners put out a newspaper called the *Tiki Times*, that all New Zealand was still proud of; but Charles Maui Hira never talked about it. The gloom brushed everything: the Minotaur that gobbled children, the gods lined up on Olympus like the capricious, eternal commanders of rival armies. Or when he spoke of Thermopylae where the Spartans had halted the immense Persian army, noting that three hundred was the number of Maori soldiers that had fallen in Italy. "We were like that, Rapata, we were far more united than the *Pākehā*, we would give up our lives for one another without a thought, and when they chose us to lead the attack on Monte Cassino, well, they knew that."

Crap, thought Rapata, his eyes lost in the blue void, his vehemence a surprise to him. The truth was they had fought in vain at Monte Cassino, they hadn't even earned a defeat that helped to achieve a victory. The truth was: who do you think was sent to head up the second offensive? The Maori and the Indians, mostly. Among them the Gurkhas from Nepal, who according to Charles Maui Hira were also very brave. This was what having dominated half the world with your empire was good for: to send the good indigenous soldier ahead to be slaughtered. But in all the BBC footage he'd looked at on the web, Rapata had never seen an interview with even one veteran of color. The price of citizenship the Maori had paid was sixty percent higher than that of the *Pākehā*. And what had it got them? Some plaques and monuments and some words in the *marae* and in the schools every April 25, ANZAC Day, when the dead from all the wars were remembered. That, and the fact that more than half of those who ended up in New Zealand's army continued to be Maori. That's what we earned, *koro*: the privilege to die first, and in greater numbers. Your health, *koro*! *Kia ora*, all the best!

They had served dinner and Rapata, following the example of his seat-mate from the Gulf, had asked for a whiskey, which they gave out free; Rapata, who contemptuous of his father and obedient to his grandfather, drank no more than the occasional beer. But now, having devoured his chicken breast with spiced rice and carrots, he raised the glass in a toast and swallowed it neat, and the alcohol he wasn't used to flamed in his throat, right up to his eyes.

Getting ready for the trip, Rapata had felt he ought to prepare himself with some reading, but now the words of those books about the 28th Battalion and about Monte Cassino, books that were in his backpack, threatened to erase the stories Charles Maui Hira had told him. In truth, he was afraid that once he got to Monte Cassino, all that his grandfather had been for him might be demolished.

Maybe he should have done things his own way, not go to hear the speeches and the prayers, but use the money to search out what was left of that coal mine in Poland where his grandfather had been a prisoner, a place Rapata knew nothing about, apart from the name of the most precious coin of exchange, the *papiroski*. "Cigarettes," he had told the boy, but only to explain that he already knew that word, which he had heard in Libya, where alongside the Poles they had defeated Rommel and his Afrika Korps in the siege of Tobruk.

Yes, maybe Rapata should have done the opposite of what Charles Maui Hira would have done. Follow the darkness rather than take part in ufficialdom's glorification. Betray his memories in order to save them.

Maybe his father wasn't wrong: maybe Rapata Ihipa Sullivan really was half a man, a man divided in half: half the son of a rebellious, then rabid father who had slapped Maori names on him while raising him on the edges of Auckland; half the son of a grandfather who kept him in the village but made him study, keep his room in order, and speak proper English , punishing him with stubborn calm each time he violated the rules.

He must have been about twelve that time when, one school morning, he went out to fish with his friends and came back quite late. "If you ever do that again," Charles Maui Hira greeted him, "if you think you can confuse your duty with having fun, I will have to send you back to your mother in Auckland." They never spoke of it again. Not that night, or ever.

He could still recall the insults he had hurled at his grandfather, his mouth sealed shut. Could he really not understand that once, just once, he didn't want to say no to his friends? And yet Rapata Sullivan was the only one among his friends in the village on the Waikato (or from the old neighborhood in Auckland) who had gotten a university degree, and just about the only one who had ever set foot in a university at all. But who was forever jeering at him for having studied sociology, specializing in "post-colonial studies"? Not his grandfather; his father.

The Arab in the next seat was sleeping with his mouth wide open, his head bobbing in Rapata's direction; the cabin was dark except for a reading light here and there. Now that his thoughts had returned to himself, had slid away from private Charles Maui

Hira, Rapata too was tired. He would try to sleep until the plane landed, and the next day, on the Dubai to Rome leg, he would have all the time he needed to go on reading, if he really felt like it.

Ward 4
NZ MOB. CCS
10 March 1944

Lt-Col R. R. C. Young, Officers, NCOs and Men of the 28th (Maori) Battalion,

I have received with pride your message. It will always be one of my most treasured possessions. Further battles lie ahead of you, but mine are finished; no more will I share in planning your battles and it will fall to others to help you in your tasks. I will still, from a distance, glory in your deeds, and grieve over your losses. I know that you will always re-member that in the hands of each one of you rests the fame of your great battalion and the honor of your people. It has been one of my proudest privileges to have had the Mao-ri Battalion under my command in so many battles. Now the time has come to part. I thank you and those who have served before you and wish you well. I thank you with all my heart.

> H.K. Kippenberger
> Major-General

When he saw that letter, Rapata was touched. He had opened the book on the Maori Battalion at random, or rather, the pages had parted where a bookmark had once been inserted by his grandfa-ther. He still had almost two more hours of layover at Dubai air-port, and didn't know what to do with himself. He had walked through kilometers and kilometers of Duty Free, bought an unbe-lievably expensive Coca Cola, and sat down at the end of a long av-enue marked by two rows of palms, whether real or fake it wasn't clear, but in any case almost as tall as the ceiling. For a moment he tried to think what Charles Maui Hira would have done had he had a stopover in the Dubai airport. Nothing, he decided; he would merely have tried to find the gate he was supposed to depart from and sat down nearby to wait, paying no attention to anything or anyone, something Rapata was unable to do.

Maybe this huge, ostentatious beehive of glass and steel had something to do with why that major general's letter had disturbed him so. The man who wrote it, out on a routine patrol, had stepped on a land mine that had sheared off one foot and reduced the other to pulp. The place where Rapata now sat was utterly alien to himself and his grandfather, and even to Howard Kippenberger, although he'd been white and the major general. This place was for fat sheikhs trailing flocks of wives and rowdy children; for blonde ladies on tall spike heels who must be tarts, at least in part; a place through which men of every color moved, all alike in their grey suits, ties, laptops and briefcases. In a flash Rapata was certain of one thing: it was to build and spread places like this that they had once embarked thousands of Maori soldiers, among them three hundred who died in the country he was headed to, where an Allied general of German origin lost his feet on a German mine. It was for places like this. Places of exchange, places of peace: peace founded on the worldwide exchange of goods and assets, that sort of world peace. He went back to his reading, stubbornly.

On the flight to Rome he was seized by that sleep that felt like oblivion, and when he woke he saw they were about to show *Master and Commander* with Russell Crowe, who had become a New Zealand idol after *Gladiator*, and even though that costume drama about a ship's captain during the Napoleonic wars bored him, he watched it from start to finish, and decided that the Galapagos iguanas weren't bad.

And so Rapata Sullivan, when he arrived at Rome-Fiumicino airport, was exhausted, drifting, docile and disposed to do what he must, that is, to find the train to Termini rail station and from there, the train to Cassino. What he saw from the windows of the train looked almost familiar. Mountains, flocks of sheep. Roads with normal cars, with gas stations. Feed silos. Kids eating potato chips, with iPod and mp3 buds in their ears like Rapata when he went back to the village to see his grandfather. That, however, was a coach ride and it took nearly five hours. Here students and commuters traveled on trains that looked like their coaches at home;

here the scale of everything was smaller; the mountains less high, the slice of pizza he'd eaten at Cassino station thinner, but the way they put it on your tray and gave you Coca Cola on tap in a red paper cup was the same. Sure, he had said *this*, pointing at the pizza he wanted, and had said *Coke* to a guy who although he replied *okay* did not seem to know how to say anything more, and even the price he had figured out by looking at the number listed on the "Menù" above the counter. Still, it was all very easy, easy as in a dream, and hearing an unfamiliar language spoken around him wasn't sufficient to make it seem real.

"Hotel Eden?"

Even before the manager could look for someone who spoke English, a girl got up from one of the plastic tables nearby and said, "I show you."

She was studying languages at the University of Cassino, came from Caserta, had a few pimples on her face, an accent like the waiters at the pizza shop at home, a largish behind swathed in denim.

"You American?"

"No, New Zealand."

"Oh. You see *Lord of the Rings*?"

"Yes. But I live in Auckland, big city."

She had followed him out the door, repeating *straight* and *third street to the left* and then gone back inside to her girlfriends wearing a victorious look on her face.

At the hotel, even before he opened his mouth, he had been greeted with "Welcome, sir; I hope you had a pleasant journey" and accompanied to his room. It had a perfect view of the abbey, which was pointed out to him along with the small safe in the wardrobe. The day was brilliantly clear, even warm. The white walls of the abbey seemed to reverberate with the light coming from the blue sky; they stood intact, perfectly intact, there atop the grassy mountain. Rapata used the toilet, took off his shoes and trousers, and threw himself on the bed. He kept the abbey in his sights, so luminous and lovely, as if it had always been there. Rapata had made it to Monte Cassino and Charles Maui Hira was no more. The reborn abbey suggested that things could come back to life; people, no, not even those who had survived war and destruction. He felt like swearing in the abbey's direction, but he didn't. He closed the shutters and lay down to sleep until evening.

Under the Abbey's Eye

WARNING: Italian friends!
Until now we have tried to avoid bombing the Abbey of
Monte Cassino. The Germans have taken advantage of our
restraint. But now the fighting has intensified around the
holy precinct. The time has come, unfortunately, when we
are forced to point our guns toward the Monastery itself.
We are warning you so that you can avoid harm. Our warning is urgent: abandon the Abbey. Leave immediately. Respect this warning. It is issued in your interests.
— THE FIFTH ARMY

The leaflets fell from the sky, from Allied artillery guns aimed at
the the abbey, but they fell outside the walls, hidden in grenades
that exploded and sent them flying like slips from the Baci Perugina
chocolates of which autarkic Italy, when it still existed, had been so
proud. It was February 14, 1944, St. Valentine's Day. The Benedictine monks knew it, and they prayed for the saint of the day, the
martyred bishop beheaded on the Via Flaminia more than a mil-
lenium before. The American soliders perched on a hilltop knew it,
and were hoping the British would get there to relieve them before
they ended up with frozen feet or shrapnel in the head, or both.
The English, Scots, Irish and New Zealanders killing time before
battle in their camps writing letters to their wives and girlfriends,
or mocking those writing such letters, knew it; and it all risked
ending up in obscenities, drinking, brawls, that in turn made them
despondent, lonely, longing for home.
    A loneliness plumbed in all its depths when it was time to apol-
ogize, when you realized that jackass beside you — making cracks

about whether she'd been true to you, that girl to whom you were sending your kisses, your promise to return in one piece and take her in your arms—that subliterate jackass you'd never have given the time of day at home, was the person who'd been closest to you for months, the one whose personal smell you woke up and fell asleep with, the one (in the event you didn't keep your promise to her) who'd be the last person you'd see on earth.

"Mate, have some wine, it's all we have to keep us company. I'm sorry. Really."

"It sucks. The weather sucks, our gear's too light, even the wine is so sour that the more you drink, the more comes up. Did it ever occur to you that nobody's going to believe us when we tell them what Sunny Italy was like?"

"No, it never occurred to me. I try not to think more than one day ahead and even so the waiting is driving me crazy. Would you send some things to someone, to my wife, if I don't make it and you do?"

"You mean you're married?"

"Four years. We have a little girl, Deidre. If I haven't lost count, she's two years old."

"Sure. You know what? I'll go there, in person."

"To Belfast? From Bristol? No, don't worry."

"I'll go. That's a promise."

"You promise too much. And we've learned not to trust your English promises. Wait, I'm kidding, right? What I mean is, thanks."

"And now can I finish writing this letter?"

"Mate, listen to me: I'm drinking and you can do whatever you please."

Neither the soldiers of the 4th Indian Division, the *sepoys* and the *naiks* of the Punjab Regiment and the Rajputana Rifles, nor the Gurkha Rifles of Nepal, who had been ordered to advance on the mountain and prepare for a new assault on the abbey, knew of St. Valentine, and their white officers, and the soldiers of the Royal Sussex Regiment, didn't even know what day it was, between the snow, the artillery fire and the perilous trails flanked by sheer cliffs and crevasses that swallowed men and mules whole.

Nor did the evacuees know anything, the ones who had been housed in the abbey and then tossed out to huddle in grottos on the mountain when the monastery no longer seemed secure, and who had begun, in their stone caves, to die of cold, of fevers, of hunger and thirst and fear, an unremitting fear caused by the end-less hammering of artillery that kept them hidden away in their holes and killed anyone who ventured outside to look for food and water. The Liri Valley, their valley, way down there, was now very far away, farther away than the capital where some of them, once, had been taken to see Il Duce high atop the *Altar of the Patria*, altar of the fatherland. Everything was now far away, both in space and in time, for the people of the caves. Maybe their relatives had man-aged to get to the hill on the other side, to Monte Trocchio where the American headquarters was, and were eating American chocolate, not Italian, and if not long before they had thought they could pity those others because *they* had a roof and a saint protecting them, all that had been forgotten in the ancient, interminable time of the caves. Everything was now upside down, and they had gone back to times in which there were no roofs over a man's head or saints to protect him, and yet there were mines, barbed wire, and flying bullets. And when, at the beginning of February, the artillery began to pound so hard they thought they'd be buried alive, they left their caves and forced the monks to take them back, begging, and some-times threatening them. Everything was very far away in time and space, everything except the abbey.

They had been back in that holy place ten days now but they continued to die inside Benedict's walls, no longer of hunger or thirst but of a fever that they seemed to have brought with them, and which ended up infecting even the monk nursing them, don Eusebio, who was among the youngest and who was dividing his time between praying for and tending the sick, and the under-ground carpentry shop where he nailed together their rough cof-fins. *Ora et labora*. That was the rule of the saint in the hour of war: time devoted to the living, time devoted to the dead, and ever more weary time devoted more to the memory than to the glory of God, and his son who had died on the cross as a man. Decades later, it was historians, not doctors, who determined that epidemic was ty-phus. On February 13, during a snow storm that froze the soldiers in the trenches and at the front lines, don Eusebio breathed his last. The nursing monk gone, there were only five Benedictines left, in-cluding the abbot. The next day, the weather was calm, the heavens clear.

Everyone took hope from that bright blue sky on February 14: the soldiers, thinking they might get just dry enough to stave off pneumonia or avoid being locked in a permanent crouch; the refugees, thinking they might go out and find some German to barter with, for food and water had begun to run short in the abbey too; the monks, who would have liked to offer a half-decent Christians burial at least to don Eusebio, who'd been put to rest in a coffin he'd made with his own hands. *Ora et labora.* As they prepared to join a procession toward a chapel just outside the walls, a boy rushed in with—not German provisions—but those Allied leaflets in his hands. The unease created by those messages that had rained down like bombs spread panic among the people who'd taken refuge in the fortress, a fortress that might be a refuge and might be a prison. They didn't know whether to run away or hide inside; whether to believe the Allied message, whether it was a ruse to get the Germans to withdraw, whether the monks who sought to convince them to go elsewhere didn't merely want to be rid of their hungry mouths and their contagious flesh. Panic made them apathetic, cave dwellers huddled in the various corners of the house of St. Benedict, mice stunned and frozen before the snake. The abbot sent for a German officer who came in, read the enemy leaflet, categorically warned the civilians not to go out on the battlefield, promised to open up a protected exit route, and left. The monks decided to stay, and if the monks were staying, the evacuees were determined to stick with them. Their logic was a mixture of guile and faith—if *they* were staying that means we will also be safe—faith dressed up as guile and cunning, and no one bothered to think that this handful of monks and their few servants were all that was left there, and they felt obliged not to abandon the house and holy remains of their founder Benedict.

In their stupor, not wanting to be sent back to the caves, the refugees tried to make a leap toward something vaguely resembling a future, as far forward as they could go, and they made it from the Stone Age to the Middle Ages, instinctively taking shelter with the clergy when foreign armies descended. Present time, however, also went forward, and the monks buried don Eusebio, came back in, recited their vespers, the German officer did not return, the heavens remained clear but grew dark, and outside the walls the gunfire resumed. But the heavens are not the same independently of who's looking at them. The heavens of February 14, finally blue, calm, without a hint of cloud, looked different to the army commanders (who could observe them standing upright and scrutinizing the far horizons, comparing sky and weather reports) than they did to those peering at them from a cave, from stone huts perched where the ribs of the mountain were least steep, from bunkers dug out at the foot of the abbey or in its courtyard, where refugees stuck their heads out like tortoise men to look.

The heavens are not the same independently of who's looking at them. What General Freyberg saw were heavens in any case unstable. The rain was supposed to resume no more than two days later, so the bombing must be moved forward. It was he, just nominated chief of the new New Zealand Army Corps and thus reponsible for operations in the Monte Cassino area, who urged that the abbey be bombed. General Clark was opposed. But the 36th Division had sunk into the River Rapido, and the 34th ("Red Bull") was wedged up on the mountain where more half of its men had died, and it wasn't yet possible to guess how many more wouldn't make it down from there. Two US divisions ripped to shreds in a single battle on a secondary front. Problems at Anzio; the planned landing on the coast of France; Montgomery called back just before Christmas, named commander of ground forces for the upcoming operations on the French coast. He had left the Italian Campaign ("a dog's breakfast," he called it) to General Clark, a second choice commander of a hodge-podge army, and if the troops available to him were the New Zealand contingent and the Indian division, those were the facts, he had to deal with.

But the facts were not all. Beyond the facts, above the facts, like the droves of bombers called to the heavens of Cassino, propaganda's black and white light rained down, and Clark, who had created his own press office to make sure that the papers referred to all military actions as "carried out by the Fifth Army of General Mark W. Clark" understood this better than the others. He knew he would be made to look like a barbarian come to destroy Europe's artistic and spiritual heritage, he who longed to liberate the capital of this country, reduced to a bone for stray dogs to haggle over, because the only glory he could get out of it was to take Rome, *caput mundi*, so near and yet so far beyond the abbey.

If they razed that holy place to the ground, the great cloud rising from its rubble would arrive there long before the first soldier among his troops, in fact it would spin round the globe on the wings of propaganda, faster than the Allied air forces, and the blast wave would come down and hit him. If only someone else would play the part of the barbarian invader: General Tuker, for example, commander of the Indian Army until a recurrent tropical fever landed him in bed. Or what about Freyberg, who came from some faraway islands where sheep were, are, and would probably always be more numerous than men. Let them insist, those old wasters who'd been scraped up on the fringes of an aging empire, along with Sir Harold Rupert Leofric George Alexander, who was clearly an aristocrat like most British generals, with their hereditary titles or those granted by the King, who merely required a decent military victory to call them to an audience, their heads bowed and shoulders waiting to be tapped by the sword. Let them worry about it, these gentlemen for whom war was merely the continuation of a cricket match by other means.

They would never understand that it was no longer them and their enemy peers facing off on the battlefield; it wasn't them against Fridolin von Senger und Etterlin or Heinrich von Vietinghoff or any of those other high officers who continued to serve *Führer*, *Reich* and *Vaterland*. Because a new era had begun, an era of new people like himself, or like the Reich Minister for Popular Enlightenment and Propaganda, short, gimpy, plebian Goebbels who was more powerful than anyone else although he had not one armed man to send onto the battlefield, because he didn't think in terms of men but in terms of masses, didn't calculate losses, but counted up gains.

General Freyberg—Sir Bernard, Baron Freyberg, wounded nine times in the Great War—he, no, he would never understand. General Freyberg, discussing matters with brigadier Kippenberger, had a sheep problem in New Zealand. The problem was to bring the men home in sufficient numbers to look after the sheep. Kippenberger had grown up on a farm and he certainly knew something about that. And both of them knew what the land their ancestors had come from was capable of when it came to swallowing up its own soldiers and soldiers from every continent, devouring them without letting them go forward an inch, without letting them out of the mud in the trenches, although there on the Somme, where Freyberg earned the highest of military honors, the Victoria Cross, and Kippenberger a badly wounded arm, there hadn't been any mountains at least. That was Europe for them: Verdun and Ypres, the Dardanelles and Passchendaele, the Marne and the Somme, and also the Isonzo, rivers that went on flowing while stark still on their banks, men went on dying. That, and not Rome, or the Abbey of Monte Cassino, or any of those other historical and artistic stage sets that Clark, the typical Yankee seeking cultural refinement seemed to find so suggestive. They had been there; they had come out alive and gone home as heroes, which meant, among other things, that it was impossible ever again to return to a life made of sheep and sons to raise.

The medals they'd earned, medals to be worn on their dress uniforms on ANZAC Day and other official celebrations, were heavy; not literally heavy, but when they were pinned on, they transmitted the cold of the metal, an eternal cold that would outlive them as well. And they had to answer: they had to answer to that metal for their absolved and decorated lives; and when they assembled before the monuments they had to show off those medals with their heads high and their chests proud, facing the fallen commemorated there. For otherwise, if there were no men like themselves, war heroes like them, to come to visit, those soldiers buried in a name inscribed on marble would soon be merely a name and a date. Otherwise their compatriots' sacrifice would be in vain; it wouldn't be sacrifice but just flesh that metal had torn to pieces, flesh rotting in a faraway country, sometimes unburied, sometimes not even identified—and that, a nation such as theirs, or any other nation small or large, defeated or victorious, could not endure.

General Freyberg and Major-General Kippenberger, studying the maps and the sky on February 14, knew all this. Perhaps Clark was not all wrong to think that if the abbey were reduced to rubble, it would make an even better stronghold for the enemy, but meanwhile a month had gone by since the first, disastrous attack, a month had gone by and the troops landed at Anzio were in trouble, a month had gone by and the winter remained chill and rainy, and it was destined to be winter for at least another month. What, then, could they do so that this offensive did not deteriorate into the stupidest, filthiest, longest and most unpredictable ground war? Into a bloodbath like the one they'd already seen, and that the world, the Old World right down to New Zealand, hoped never to see again. They'd been there, they had fought; even Clark had been there, not to mention all those who were now generals in the Wehrmacht. Only Goebbels hadn't, the cripple, the "little doctor": were they supposed to fear some disabled civilian's propaganda more than the shooting that was consuming their soldiers' lives and morale?

The men, the boys, felt crushed by the abbey's eye, exposed in their every action and movement—they should do nothing to put down that immaculate white, looming threat? And what was this hypocrisy, as if anyone had protested when first the British, then the Americans and finally the Germans had bombed Naples, a city older than Rome itself, reducing part of the Gothic church of Santa Chiara and many ancient works of art to rubble and destroying ten thousand buildings and as many human lives. Even Rome had been bombed, even the windows of the dome of St. Peter's, Michelangelo's masterwork, were shattered by the explosives that rained down from a single airplane. What was holier about the abbey of St. Benedict, holier than St. Lawrence or St. Clare? Why was that dozen monks and that unknown number of refugees more precious? Propaganda was the answer. German propaganda had gone to great lengths to show the Wehrmacht transporting codexes and other books and works of art from the abbey of Monte Cassino to Castel Sant'Angelo in Rome. Great care was taken not to photograph the same Wehrmacht exacting reprisal as it set fire to the National Library in Naples, nor did propaganda have the courage to show the devastated cities in Germany where the Allied carpet bombs had struck, a hail of armor-piercing incendiary bombs capable of raising fire storms higher than the highest buildings. The spires of the Cologne Cathedral, intentionally left standing in the midst of a vast field of ruins, evidence of how vile and cruel the enemy was: this was shown, but not one of the fifty thousand corpses that were charred, mummified, fused in the liquified asphalt of Hamburg in July of the previous year. Mourn the stones, not the men: so propaganda demanded.

* * *

Propaganda is like a shroud that covers everything before it happens. Men and stones, doubts and truth, the friction and the contingencies by which the chain of command arrives at a decision. Had General Tuker not fallen ill; had he not, already feverish, thought of sending one of his officers to rummage around in the libraries and antiquarian bookshops of Naples. Had the officer not returned with a book published in 1887, titled *Historic Description of the Monastery of Monte Cassino with a Brief Account of the City of Cassino*. Had Tuker, that is, Sir Francis Tuker, made Companion of the Order of the Bath the previous year, a career in India, school at Brighton, not been an expression of that English military caste that can also read a book in Italian. Had Francis "Gertie" Tuker not held all his superiors in such deep contempt (he thought General Freyberg was "a stubborn ass"; General Clark, "tremendously ignorant," and General Alexander "a lazy spare wheel"). Had he not, in the unbearable immobility of his sickbed between attacks of fever and penicillin injections, come to the realization he would not be returning to his command. Had he not had the time to read and re-read the description of the abbey until he could smell and taste the thickness of its walls, the number and location of its windows, the strength of its door, the only means of access to it. Had that white presence not taken possession of his nights like the ghost of a whale possessed those of Captain Ahab: something to destroy when nothing else remained. Had he not become convinced that the monastery was a fortress, insisting on it to the doctor and perhaps even to those brave Gurkhas and Indians who would now be following someone else's orders.

"It is a fortress; a fortress indeed."

"Yes, sahib. Sahib want his tea?"

Had he not written (or dictated) that irritable, meticulous letter to Freyberg, outlining point by point how the abbey was built, complaining he had had received no assistance at all from the information services in his efforts "to understand the true nature of this fortress, a thorn in our side now for many weeks now." Had he not signed off stiffly that when an army was called upon to bomb something, it must be certain that the target can be destroyed with the means at its disposal, "without having to go to the bookstalls of

Naples to find out what should have been fully considered many weeks ago."

Had Freyberg (albeit annoyed by his native tribe's usual sour smugness) not decided Tuker was right and in turn pressed Alexander to act, warning him that should he refuse he would have to answer to Parliament for having lost too many soldiers, that is, pointing at the risk the New Zealand contingent might be withdrawn. Had Alexander, rather than decide, done nothing but waver and try to mediate; had Clark, as commander of the army in question, not merely said he disagreed but filed a formal refusal, and finally, had he not asked Alexander for a direct order to bomb the abbey. Had the commander of Allied Air Forces in the Mediterranean, the American general Ira Eaker, not insisted he had personally spotted an enemy antenna atop the abbey during a reconnaissance flight; had Eaker not made it clear his fleet would only be available for a day or two; had he not been an advocate of *strategic bombing* which he'd never before been able to try out on one single edifice; and finally had not Clark, perhaps beguiled by the idea that the bombers at least would be Americans, said to Alexander: "You give me a direct order and we'll do it." Had there been, among all these coordinated and subordinated generals just one of them capable of delivering an order, or a flat refusal, maybe things wouldn't have worked out differently, but at least there would have been someone responsible.

But modern war, war as it is conducted by modern democracies, is different. In order to conceal their weakness before a people/army under the will of a single Führer, they had no choice but to rely on their air corps, and on propaganda. Bomb. But not on a limited scale. If the images of this thing were going to be seen around the world, let them at least be momentous, terrifying, witness to the unparalleled powers of the Allied Air Forces, proof that this war would be won in spite of everything, in spite of inadequacies, in spite of the men themselves. They would bomb. But not on a limited scale. They were going to use everything they had.

Our War, which art in heaven, highest of all Wars, appearing with the first squadron of B-17s from Foggia and Sicily, from bases as far away as North Africa and Great Britain. War that unleashes Flying

Fortresses above the fortress of St. Benedict and his faith, that arrives when all is ready, when the cameraman of the Wochenschau, the cameraman of the Pathé News, the BBC correspondent from London are ready, and huddled in the nearby mountains for the last several days, war photographers and correspondents from around the world stand ready—because what is about to come hurtling over the mountains of the Ciociaria is World War made visible. But to make it tangible, to project the people of Chicago and Berlin, of Osaka and Stockholm, into a theater of war as large as the world, the world must be united in the heavens before the spectacle of the bombers and the precision of their bombs. Even Martha Gellhorn, at the time Mrs. Hemingway, was there, and would later recall having gazed upwards from some wall or bridge and waxed enthusiastic like all the other fools: look, there they are, our bombers, in perfect symmetric formation!

It was the morning of February 15, 1944, 9:28 a.m. The great bombers had arrived and everyone knew it, everyone except the soldiers of the Indian contingent who had gone up to relieve the Americans, by now so exhausted, guns clenched catatonically in their fists, that many were unable to get down from the mountain on their own legs. And of course the refugees in the abbey didn't know it; they were still waiting for that German officer to return with his promises he would take them to safety, or they were waiting for a sign from the heavens (which no longer answered to God but to things called, in reverential ignorance, *apparecchi*, "flying devices," things potent, unflinching, and utterly blind). And so when the planes hit their target the soldiers of the Punjab regiment closest to the abbey would be pummeled by a hail of detritis, and those of the Royal Sussex who were busy trying to regain a position that was already supposed to be theirs would lose twenty four men to the bombs splintering off the stone walls.

The first run would destroy the abbey's central floor, showering the lower level and those cowering below with rubble. The dome with its frescoes was hit; the high altar, the beautiful pipe organ made by Catarinozzi, the choir stalls, masterpiece of anonymous Neapolitan wood-carvers of the 17th century, lay in pieces. Split and splintered beams, full-length columns, a white flag run up for nothing, tumbled into the courtyards and cloisters; stones and shards of windows rained down; fragments of bodies and of things, hurled into the air by the explosions, flew by. The Prior's Cloister collapsed on a hundred of the refugees; the Bramante Cloister was but a heap of plaster and rubble. The cries of the buried went unheard; the cries of the wounded were drowned out by the roar of bombers, bombs, destruction. Everything men had built over the centuries was louder than they were, louder than their prayers, their curses, their wails. Death came down hard and deafening; the living inhaled dust and panic, gulped down pulverized frescoes, tried to move, to get away.

After the first run, some of the refugees dragged themselves out, or were dragged: where, they didn't know. The monks, still alive inside their shelter, came out to see what was left, to help the living as they could. They had a little food to hand around, no water. The second run began at 1:28 p.m.: formations of B-25 Mitchell and B-26 Marauder bombers, flying low, now hit with greater precision what was left of their target. When the bombing runs were finished, the abbey sat in the sights of the heavy artillery, which kept on shelling from land and sea until night fell. The tomb and the cell of the saint remained intact: a miracle for which there was no time, no force, no will to give thanks as one should. And that was all.

The German officer returned at about 8 p.m., got the abbot to sign a statement declaring there were no German soldiers in the monastery at the time of the bombing, promised a cease-fire requested by Hitler himself. In the silence, another wall that had remained standing collapsed, and then there was nothing but the cries of the injured and the terrified to fill up the empty darkness. At dawn, most of the survivors came out of the ruins, hoping to be rescued. The abbot and the monks stayed with the few who remained, awaiting the German officer (who did not come back), while the bombs and grenades resumed. The next day they would come out, walking in file behind a cross held aloft by the eighty year old abbot, leaving a few of the worst-injured in the abbey until all was finished. All was finished when the dying died: a legless boy and girl abandoned by their father when their mother expired. It finished in a horizontal blur of grey and red, of grey absorbing red, of red that turned dark brown, the colors of organic and inorganic matter both, colors that preceded any knowledge of the black and white of those images shot from afar that would fill the movie screens of all the world and can still be seen today. Tabula rasa. Nothing. The final estimates spoke of about 200 of the 1,000 civilians present in the abbey when it was bombed; the accounts were made sometime later based on a tally of bones and skulls. With any luck, the results of that subtraction operation may be somewhere near the number of civilians saved.

Mōrehu

Around two in the morning, Rapata realized it was two in the afternoon at home, and that the hotel room in which he couldn't sleep
was as far away as you could get from the room where he'd slept
the night before setting off, his childhood room on the other side
of the world. He had gone back there to get photographs from the
front to show to the *mōrehu* who might remember Charles Maui
Hira, for he didn't see himself putting on the uniform his grandfather hadn't wanted to be buried in.

He had, however, taken the uniform out of the closet, laid it
on the bed and dusted it off energetically, although it didn't need
dusting. Then he had covered it up again with the large black gar-
bage bag (a hole at the top to pass the hook of the hanger through)
and hung it up in its place.

And went out, closing the door carefully, before he could decide whether the room and the house were more empty with the
uniform draped on the bed, or with nothing on it. Using his old
toothbrush that stood next to his grandfather's in a plastic cup, he
brushed his teeth and lay down to sleep in shorts and a t-shirt. He
thought he'd have trouble sleeping but the sound of the Waikato
was conducive to sleep, as always.

Now there was no helpful river nearby, and Rapata lay awake.

A few hours before he had eaten at the hotel restaurant. They
sat him near the door, at what was probably the only free table, because the place was very crowded; a large group occupying several
long tables was celebrating something. Rapata sat with back to the
room; when the waiter came he brought him a menu and a basket
of bread, just bread, but didn't ask what he wanted to drink. He bit
into a slice of bread and studied the menu, which luckily offered

a translation of the dishes they served in English, French and German. The soldiers' languages, he thought; the war there had become a source of income. No more enemies or invaders: only tourists. Nothing wrong with that, he thought to himself. But would that peaceful coexistence of English and German have bothered his grandfather? The question, in any case, made him think he should send a message to his mother.

"Got here; tell *koro* if U want," he texted.

Once, at the beginning, when his mother was still coming back from Auckland every weekend, his father had come to visit him. He turned up at Charles Maui Hira's house without warning one Sunday morning bearing a toy motorbike for Rapata and a necklace of colored beads for his mother. He had been invited to their lunch of mutton and potatoes, and had been on best behavior, drinking Fanta and, when not chewing, serving up the usual questions: school, rugby, girls, did he already have a girlfriend, come on, you can tell your Pa. All seemed normal, serene, except that his grandfather and his mother frequently got up at the same moment, and then said, too hastily, "No, sit, I'll go to the kitchen!" In the end, his mother had drawn the task of washing up, and he was left in the living room when his grandfather took a bottle of whiskey out of the sideboard where it was kept with the good glasses, and poured some for himself and Rapata's father.

"*Kia ora*! Cheers to you Charlie and above all to our Rapata! Want a taste of this stuff, Rapi?" his father had said.

"No thanks. I don't like it. It stings."

"So, they have let you try out some man things. Good work, *koro*!"

His father had burst out in loud laughter, and even his grandfather had laughed a little. Rapata had crouched down, to ride his new red motorbike on the floor and to conceal the lightheaded feeling of the moment. He hoped that his mother would take a long time to put the kitchen in order, and he hadn't even felt ashamed. He bore down with his bike and shot under the table, making "brrmm, brrm" noises.

"There's one man thing I'm really keen to do with my boy," he heard his father's voice boom out above the table. "I'd like to take him around the pubs here before I go home. Hey, you don't have to drink beer, I'll buy you Coke and potato chips, and you can play video games. Will you join me, Rapi?"

"Okay," he replied without leaving his hiding place, but too fast and too loud not to betray himself. "But I have to ask my mother first."

Charles Maui Hira had continued to sip the whiskey that had remained in his glass (and his alone) and when the question was put to his daughter, he merely watched her, calm and serious.

"Fine. You can go," his mother said.

Rapata couldn't say just what happened afterward. Whether his mother grew suspicious and came to keep an eye on him from afar, or whether someone in town had called Charles Maui Hira to tell him that his grandson was all by himself in front of a video game machine, while the guy who had come in announcing he was his father was getting drunk with his mates at the bar. All he knew was that at a certain point he heard his grandfather's voice saying, "That's enough now, Rapata; let's go home." And the voice was so firm, so flat, that he hadn't even dared to ask if he could finish the game he was playing, or what he should do with the tokens still in his pocket. He was grabbed around the waist and lifted up from his stool like when was five years old, or even less, but now he was nearly eight and could jump down if someone simply held out a hand. His grandfather took him by the hand afterward, as they were on their way toward the door behind his father, who didn't stop knocking it back with his friends, and never noticed a thing.

Rapata understood that his grandfather had just one thing in mind: to take him out, take him away. Let his father discover—when? how?—that his son was gone. Supposing he even noticed. In any event: shame him. Without a word, a scene, a fight. With deeds, which hurt much more, and certainly were hurting Rapata: his hand crushed in that of his grandfather, the vivid realization that his father could forget he had come to the pub with him, could go all the way back to Auckland without remembering to look for him. But then that unexpected thing happened. Just before he got to the door, Charles Maui Hira stopped. Something he had heard Rapata's father and his mates say, no, yell, made him stop. And he too shouted, he even dropped Rapi's hand and went back a few steps. "If you ever again dare to say *that* in front of my grandson, if you ever again dare to bring him into the presence of that human shit you brought here with you, I swear to you I'll never let you lay eyes on him again."

Human shit. Charles Maui Hira had never been heard to say anything like that. For a moment everyone and everything froze. His father's friends' faces—they had already frightened him when he first saw them, because some were completely covered with old, blurred tattoos—now stared with drunken, opaque hostility at his grandfather, leaning forward and ready to jump down from their bar stools at the first signal. His father said nothing, did nothing. He merely kept his hands clasped around the bottle, and after a pause had carried it to his lips, whether consciously or not. And so the others also returned to their beers, raising them and clinking them, shouting out a slurred, booming toast that Rapata didn't understand: the words were neither English nor Maori. Probably some language from the Cook Islands, Samoa, or somewhere: he had already guessed that the men his father claimed to have brought from Auckland to meet his son were not all Maori. Just as he guessed then that he must try to grasp the meaning of those words that had turned the hard, cold anger of his grandfather into rage—a furor that made him drop Rapata's hand and transformed him into the dangerous, vulnerable soldier he must have been.

"To Charles Maui Hira, glorious fighter of our heroic Maori Battalion!" his father, wearing an obscenely broad smile, had shouted, and the others all launched their shouted toasts his way.

"Fools," said his grandfather sharply, but now calm again, as if those insults had helped him recover himself. "You think you are men, but you are bastard dogs, and *they*, faced with bastards like you, would have exterminated the lot of you. Come, Rapata, let's go. Your mother is waiting for us."

And as they exited side by side in that hostile silence, no longer holding hands, Rapata understood that his grandfather had won, and he wouldn't see his father for some time, if ever. In the car, he stared out the window at the tall grass tossed back and forth in waves by the wind, and up at the long, ragged clouds racing across the sky against them as they left town.

"Were you afraid, Rapi?"

"No..."

"No?"

"A little, yes. Were they going to beat you up, *koro*? There were a lot of them."

"Yes, there were a lot. Forgive me, Rapata. Those men there meant nothing to you; you were just playing your game."

"It's okay. I still have a whole bunch of tokens. Can I keep them?"

"A bunch of tokens? How much money did your father give you?"

They had almost arrived home when his grandfather said to him: "Shall we go down to the river for a moment? I want to tell you something."

"*Koro*, you know I wasn't having any fun. I'm glad you came to get me. If only you hadn't gotten so angry."

"Did I frighten you too? Eh, Rapata?"

"They could have beaten you up, and you were alone, and you're…"

"Old?"

His grandfather had run a hand through his hair and then rapped him twice on the shoulder, as if to shake off any excess tenderness. His grandfather was old, his hands were lined and his hair was white, but he was real: he had frightened him more than ten men, drunken and black from their leather jackets to the tattooed skin of their faces. It was a vague, boundless fear, both "fear of" and "fear for," and above all, fear for himself, for what would have become of Rapata if a barroom brawl had deprived him both of his grandfather and his father in one go? He was just a child, and a conflict between adults could annihilate him. That he understood only later, at the table of a restaurant in Cassino while he sat waiting and the waiter didn't arrive: that it was he, the child, son and grandson, who had stopped anyone from getting off his bar stool, who allowed Charles Maui Hira to walk away without being beaten to a pulp.

They sat down on the banks of the Waikato and began to throw stones in the water, to see who could throw farther. After ten throws they were equal, and stopped, and just stared at the river banks along which their *iwi*, the warriors of their people, had been cut down by English guns. His grandfather began to speak.

"What those friends of your father were shouting was *Sieg Heil!* The salute of the Germans, although they don't even know how to pronounce it. They think they are big men, because they provoke the *Pākehā*, and ridicule our history going around drinking and beating people up, dressed like that, wearing the enemy's symbols, like English bulldogs with enemy helmets shoved on their heads. But they are the ones who are ridiculous, ridiculous and disgraceful. I couldn't allow them to carry on shouting that: it was an insult to all the boys who died. Do you understand?"

Rapata had nodded, but he didn't know what else to say. "Can we go home now, *koro*?"

"Yes, you're right. We had better go."

On the way home, his grandfather told a story about the Maori Battalion that Rapata had never heard before. It was not yet a war story, because they had just embarked: they were a dozen days out to sea after finally sailing from Australia, and where they were headed no one knew. There were rumors that enemy submarines were standing by to strike even before they arrived in some port or on some front. When the ships transporting the New Zealand contingent approached a coastline, they even saw the lights of a city, Cape Town, and everyone dreamed they might finally be allowed to put to port. But the sea was rough, and a day went by when no one was permitted to leave ship, those ships so large they were anchored far off-shore. Some angry wits penned a sign to the *Aquitania* saying "Prison Ship."

The following day only the white soldiers were allowed to go ashore. Their commanders and other fellow soldiers protested, the government got involved, and in the end the Maori Battalion was hustled ashore and onto buses at the Simonstown military port and taken to Cape Town. They had been told they must not protest if people didn't treat them well or wouldn't serve them in the shops. But there was no problem, or almost none. Charles Maui Hira had walked through the pretty center of the white city with the boys of his company, he had gone into a few shops to get some provisions, he was ever so polite and the shopkeepers were polite in turn, their courtesy almost unreal, as if what was happening wasn't really happening, as if the color of their skin was an oversight, or something caused by the sun. Down there, they hadn't met even the shadow of a black man. But from the bus windows they had seen bodies bent over in the fields, and the shantytowns. Back on board ship, the commander praised them. He said they were the first persons of color ever to be received on South African soil, and they had brought credit to New Zealand.

"It was a historic moment," he said.

That night Charles Maui Hira, sucking on a mint he'd bought in Cape Town, had thought about those Africans he had seen beyond the bus window.

"You know, Rapi, I had never really seen a black African before. The whites were more or less identical to ours; maybe the English they spoke was a little odd. But the blacks were completely different: very tall, very dark, with faces that look nothing like us. This is something you won't understand because today, even if you grow up in the most out-of-the-way place, you can see them on TV, athletes, or singers. But I was asking myself in all seriousness: how can they possibly confuse us Maori with people so utterly different? It was so unbelievably crude that I was pretty much scandalized. It was like we decided that *Pākehā* and Chinese were the same, no, it was even more absurd, because between those two the difference in skin color is minute. I just couldn't understand it. I did understand, though, they they had let us go ashore because our army was fighting alongside the South African army, because we were both on the same side. And in fact, when the war was over, everything went back to the way it had been before. When the All Blacks went out to play the Springboks, they left the Maori players at home. Then, in the 1960s, in the days when your father was playing, the protests began. A lot of people didn't want the team to set foot in South Africa, and they didn't want the South Africans to come here to play either. In 1981, when you were two, the Springboks came to New Zealand and all hell broke out. I thought they were going too far because, after all, rugby is everybody's national sport and those two teams—the All Blacks and the Springboks—were undoubtedly the best. I thought the right thing to do was to let our teams beat them."

"And did we win?"

"If I remember right, the All Blacks won two out of three matches, but our other teams all lost. You would have thought we were on the brink of civil war, and one match was even cancelled, at Hamilton right near here; Waikato Rugby Union was playing. It was *Pākehā* and Maori, fans versus protesters, on both sides. After that there were no more rugby matches between New Zealanders and South Africans."

"So there's no way to ever know if we could now beat the Springboks?"

"No, but there's something else I wanted to say to you. Maybe it will sound strange, but during the war I realized that racism has nothing to do with the color of your skin. Racism is the power to decide who you are. The Germans treated people who were often whiter and blonder than they were as slaves. Like the Poles. Do you understand how stupid your father's mates are, with their Swastikas, their gangs they call "Mongrel Mob" or "Black Power"? They're like naughty children who want to provoke the *Pākehā*, but they have no idea who they themselves are. What do we have to do with blacks? We are Maori, we are New Zealanders. That's why they let us go ashore in South Africa. Because the war was on. The laws of war can bend any other laws.

"Remember that, Rapata. It's easy enough to yell *Ka mate, ka mate! Ka ora, ka ora!* before a rugby match; All Blacks fans do it all around the world. But remember, that *haka* was composed many centuries ago by a chieftain who had just managed to escape his enemies. *'Tis death, 'tis death; 'tis life, 'tis life!* Try saying that in the heat of battle. We used to know how to do battle, we could take the heat, at least we could up to my day."

That night, after a dinner eaten in silence, after being sent to bed and overhearing the inevitable argument between his grandfather and his mother, and the inevitable explosion of tears that with the door closed sounded like a cat howling or a saw screeching, and after he too had wept, face down into the pillow and then with the pillow like a silencer over his head, Rapata understood for the first time that he hated the Maori Battalion. He had no right to cry and wail about his father and his mother; he was born of war, born of it more than other Maoris, offspring of Tumatauenga, and like the god of war, whose brother Tane had stopped him from killing his parents, he too had caused separation and conflict. He had been born to make war. But unlike Tumatauenga who had innumerable siblings (although by the end he had devoured nearly all of them) Rapata was all alone with his pillow, turned dry side up, and the ever-present background noise of the Waikato, and his grandfather the war veteran, whose every audible sign of life was covered by sonorous rushing water, and who slept unmoving on his back in the other bedroom.

In the restaurant, the waiter still did not appear, and he grew thirsty, very thirsty, and his hunger, mixed with the fatigue of traveling, felt like nausea. The spongy bread had dried out the already dry inside of his mouth, and its bitter and burned taste stuck to him. All the waiters were busy looking after the large Italian party, and were ignoring him. But when someone appeared that must have been the owner, because he wasn't wearing a white shirt or a bow tie and was good enough to say, "Excuse me sir, we are very busy tonight," he still hadn't decided what to order.

"Pasta? Some special pasta?"

"Yes, I bring you special pasta. From here, Cassino. Made with chicken, with what is inside the chicken. Very good."

Afterwards, when he opened the menu again and found grilled lamb chops and French fries, he felt like a fool for having ordered some dish made of he had no idea what. A fool and a foreigner. A foreigner sitting all by himself at a table, watching waiters who looked like the unmatched partners of a team of ice dancers as they carried trays, full and then empty, to and from the kitchen; listening to the laughter and loud voices of the Italians and the squeals of their children as they raced from one table to another, and finally understanding that they were celebrating a birthday, an anniversary, or some other occasion for which the entire *whānau* had come together.

The way that word had come forth made him feel alienated. It would never have come to a *Pākehā* mind, or certainly not in this situation, looking at that group of Italians. The whites knew what *whānau* meant, they knew it referred to the Maori extended family. But whites did not have *whānau*. Rapata, instead, had recognized it, that trait of his people, in another people about which he knew next to nothing and of whose language he understood not a single word. And there he was, in full *Pākehā* solitude at his table, while the New Zealand delegation was probably having dinner together in another hotel, and therefore he was even more alone. Alone now, here, as he always had been. A Maori without a family, without *whānau*. Thanks to Charles Maui Hira, who was both cause and cure of his condition. However, when you got to the bottom of it, it was better that way. Better than having to put up with all those other Kiwi, having to sing his part in that opera about the tiny, great nation where everybody knew everybody, and going to the front was more or less like going on a group outing.

This came to him after he had eaten two little spheres that tasted of milk and cowshed, come to him from where, he did not know. He finally understood that the Italian *whānau* had ordered them when they saw him sitting there all alone. His grandfather had told him that the Italians were like the Maori, but that was one of those claims that he had been somewhat skeptical about when he began to understand that war memories were Charles Maui Hira's measure for everything.

Yet after he ate that first dish, children had appeared: two dark-haired boys and a girl who pummeled him with a stream of questions he didn't understand and finally put a Game Boy in front of his plate—something he did understand. He came second playing Super Mario Bros, but he wasn't sure whether it was because of his performance that they went away and came back with an interpreter, a girl who was almost grown up. She, too, asked him if he was "American" and it dawned on Rapata that American didn't really mean American but black, or something like black, and in any case, not white.

"No. New Zealand. Maori," he said.

"What?"

"Ma-o-ri. New Zealand."

"Oh, Maori," she said, pronouncing it more like a Maori than when he said it in English, "we think you have family from here, from Italy."

"No, but my grandfather was here during the war. He was a soldier."

And while the girl translated what he had said to "my little cousins" as she called them, and they signalled they understood in the universal language of onomatopoetic blasts from imaginary bombs and machine guns, Rapata felt so bereft of himself, so far away from the cardinal points of his own place, that he could scarcely say a word.

"You know Maori?"

"Yes, yes. Maori tattoo. My boyfriend has tattoo. Here," she said, pointing to the spot. "You have also?"

Rapata nodded, taking advantage of the momentary solemnity to hide the laugh that threatened to burst out watching the girl stab her ring-becrusted fingers into various portions of her soft arms, arms that emerged from the sleeves of her designer t-shirt on which the word GURU was printed over her breasts. Then his pasta came and the girl sent the children away so that he could eat. He asked her to thank her people for the good things they had sent his way, and added, without knowing why himself, that for his people, too, hospitality and the family were very important, were sacred, but maybe his comment was too complicated, because she replied simply "Thank you" before going back to sit down again.

He ate only half of the pasta, for his hunger had passed, but he could not say no to the slice of cake and the glass of liqueur smelling of lemonade that the Italian *whānau* had sent over. They made a toast from their vast table toward his little one, and although Rapata still had no idea what they were all celebrating, he did make out the words "Maori" and "New Zealand." When he rose to return to his room, and bowed toward them in thanks, the Italians were still eating and drinking, and they looked a long way from being finished. Perhaps it was that lemon-flavored liqueur, perhaps it was his feet swollen with tiredness, but Rapata felt awkward and strange for what his body language had conveyed on his behalf, and when he studied himself in the bathroom mirror searching for something Italian in his face, for an exhilarating moment he thought he saw a hint of *other* there. What, after all, did Rapata Sullivan really know of himself, far away from Auckland, from the Waikato, from New Zealand?

He undressed and stood under the shower, and the water beat down on his head. The touch refreshed him, but as he soaped his arms, he realized he had fewer tattoos than the unknown boyfriend of an Italian girl. There was the one he'd had done at 18, that needed to be refreshed, and the one on the other arm, which he'd understood later he'd chosen more for the love of symmetry than for its meaning, and there was the little spiral on his left thigh, because you must never have an even number.

When he got his university degree he had gone to one of the best traditional tattoo artists, but when, to determine the right pattern, he had to answer a series of questions about the genealogy of his *tūpuna*, he had recited the list of his ancestors in a neutral voice to conceal his unease. Now the pain of the tattoo came back to him as the grief he'd felt asking himself, over and over during that operation, what sense there was in inscribing that perfect but pointless lineage on his skin. When he left, promising to return for the designs to be drilled onto his thighs and buttocks, he felt that even the masks on the walls in the *marae* saw his involontary lie. Acquaintance with that grief, he thought now, might just be the only indelibly real thing he'd been marked with that day.

Toweling off, he stood before the closet naked, hanging up his clothes as they came out of the knapsack. He put on the underwear he meant to sleep in, and lay down on the bed, noticing that his feet were still swollen, and also his stomach. The shower, he thought, had washed away little more than his smell. He thought he might put a pillow under his feet, like an old man with gout or a pregnant woman. The main feature of the Maori, he thought, was their tendency to obesity, but even that they shared with most survivors of other native peoples. Around two, when he realized it was two in the afternoon in New Zealand, he understood that his mother hadn't replied to his text message not because of the time difference or because it was forbidden at work, but because, as always, she did not have enough credit in her account. He would have to scare up a prepaid card tomorrow or the day after to call her, and now he must try to sleep at least three or four hours, beginning as quickly as possible. He turned off the TV and began to read the introduction to the book about Monte Cassino, *The Hollow Victory*. He wasn't wrong to think it would be dull enough to put him to sleep.

The next day, when Rapata Sullivan stopped at the front desk to ask where to get the bus for the Commonwealth War Cemetery, his knapsack with the photo of Charles Maui Hira on his back, they told him there was no bus. He could try to call a taxi. But with so many visitors come to Cassino for the anniversary of the battle, he couldn't be sure to find one.

"Sorry, we are small town. Not too much tourism. Not much

taxis. Only the abbey, and the war. Many people come here now for the war; they are old people, they need taxis. However, we can try."

Rapata had been exhausted when morning came, and despite the wake up call, he had gotten up late. His feet weren't swollen as they'd been the night before, but the orange juice and strong Italian coffee had brought back the nausea, and new burning sensations coursed from his trachea down to his stomach. He just wanted to get where he needed to go quickly and without too much effort, even spending money that he shouldn't for that purpose. And instead it seemed it was going to be very difficult, and it wasn't even guaranteed he would succeed. He wasn't sure what was more discouraging, whether the lack of sleep or this crazy traveling halfway around the world without the least problem and then having no idea how to proceed for the small stretch still ahead of him. Meanwhile the lady behind the desk looked at him, phone poised in her hand.

"And I couldn't walk there?"

Even as he voiced that daring suggestion, he was sure the answer would be no. But the only answer he got was a long interrogative stare, suggesting this was an option never before contemplated. Well, in fact, he was finally told, the British cemetery was outside the center of town on the road toward Sant'Angelo in Theodice. It was, however, the only military burial place you could get to on foot. The German cemetery was out of the question; it was in Caira, another village entirely. The Polish one, at the foot of the abbey, was a long, long walk away, a mountain hike all uphill, following the switchbacks. How long would it take: half an hour? Three quarters of an hour? Sorry, she couldn't say, but a young man like himself could certainly do it. Otherwise he could try to get a taxi, or if that didn't pan out, maybe someone in the hotel would be free to give him a lift.

No thank you, he would go on foot, said Rapata quickly. It didn't matter if he missed the opening ceremonies; in any case he was tired, and maybe a walk in the open air would revive him. He wanted to get out of there as quickly as possible, because he had the impression that he had missed something in that conversation, although the English had been quite clear.

The woman behind the counter, who looked to be the owner of

the hotel—if age and hair style meant anything, and the gold jewelry on her hands and around her neck like only the richest social climbing *Pākehā* at home wore—was she being so forthcoming, so friendly, in order to take advantage of someone who was evidently an alien here, if not visibly, then certainly because of the passport he held? Rapata Ihipa Sullivan. Born in Ngaruawahia, Waikato, New Zealand. So what did she want? To make him pay some further charge, or at least get a big tip out of him? The Italians were known to be dishonest, he remembered, unhappily. The Maori too, in a different way. Unfortunately there was some truth to it; think of his father. But this was not the moment to pursue such thoughts or try to fathom his suspicions, which might even be wrong or exaggerated. It wasn't very complicated, after all: he was abroad for the first time, and all alone to boot, and so he couldn't expect to understand everything. And anyway he didn't really care much about Italy, or the Italians, what they were like. A forty-five minute walk on a beautiful day in the middle of May: what was that in comparison with marching through stifling deserts, under the rain, snow and mud, like Charles Maui Hira had done? Rather than be ashamed even to think of his grandfather, he would just go out and walk.

But now the lady couldn't say which road he should take.

"Oh, that's no problem," said Rapata, who had made up his mind. "I'll just ask for the British Cemetery."

"Yes, but not everyone knows how to get there. Like me."

"Okay, maybe we can find the way with Google Maps."

She looked puzzled.

"With the internet. On the computer."

"Okay. Yes. But I am an old woman, and my son is in the restaurant, for the lunch."

"I could have a look myself, if you don't mind."

"Good. You teach me."

As he typed in his destination and the results began to come up, the hotel lady stood behind him, leaning over his shoulder and making little squeaks and exclamations: "Incredible! Very good! Yes, it is this!" She was so close that Rapata thought he could smell her skin under her spicy, heavy perfume. Finally the map came forth from the printer, marking out an almost straight line in blue, the distance estimated to be about two kilometers distance, less than half an hour away.

Rapata put his knapsack back on his shoulders, thanked her triumphantly, and went out. He felt he had won, he wasn't quite sure what, and so he began to walk fast with his head down, not looking at the city around him, his eyes permanently fixed on the map. After a while he realized that he was keeping up a stiff pace and holding his piece of paper as if it were a field map, and so, to maintain his pace and express his ridiculous happiness, he began to sing:

> Maori Battalion march to victory!
> Maori Battalion staunch and true!
> Maori Battalion march to glory!
> And take the honor of the people with you!
>
> And we'll march, march, march to the enemy!
> And we'll fight right to the end!
> For God! For King! And for Country!
> Au-E! Ake! Ake! Kia Kaha e!

Ten minutes went by and he had crossed the center of town; another ten, more or less, and he found himself in front of the entrance to the cemetery. He took his phone out of the front pocket of his knapsack to see how long it had taken him, but then he remembered he hadn't looked at the time before he left the hotel. There were some messages, however. His mother had tried to call him, she had even left a voice message, but he couldn't call it up. She had tried several times from a number he recognized as that of her office, just when he must have finally fallen asleep. Rapata felt he could see her there before him, felt he understood everything; and a blast of hot, uncontrollable fury hit him, the kind that only someone very close can unleash. He could hear the excuse his mother had come up with to remain late in the office and make her phone calls when everyone had left, calls that if they were discovered could never be traced to anyone else. But she wouldn't have been capable of more deception than that, and if anyone had asked about it she would have admitted it was she who had broken the no-calls rule because she wanted, just once, to speak to her son in Italy. "Wanted to," not "had to": no made-up excuses, no prettified lies, no contrite faces or excessive remorse. She'd be almost defiant, her head held high.

Rapata could feel her waiting on the other end of the line, stubborn, nervous, as the seconds went by and he didn't answer, the apprehension she would never admit to, mounting. And then her giving up, because she couldn't stay there any longer, because she had to go home and make some sort of supper for her companion, the one it still bothered Rapata to have to consider her companion. But what bothered him most of all was the fact that his mother had not even dreamed of trying to call him from home. Because it was not her home, it belonged to the *Pākehā* she had gone to live with when Rapata left home. "There's nothing romantic about it," she told him, "but you yourself can see that it makes no sense to go on paying the rent here. It makes a lot more sense to put the money away, money for you as well, I mean." What could he say but, "Sure, I understand"?

For years his mother had kept them all at bay, and if she ever did go out with someone, he knew nothing of it because she had never brought any strangers home. From the time that Rapata had been old enough to catch the drift of certain remarks, his mother had always dismissed with an impatient smile and a few words those hints from her women friends that she might want to try again, make a new life for herself, not rule out the possibilities open to a woman who was still young, good-looking and capable. "I'm much better off this way," she would say, "I really don't think about it." In fact, his mother was beautiful. Unlike many Maori women she hadn't lost her looks with age; she hadn't let herself go or become faded and colorless. Rather, the more time went by and she continued to live apart from his father and enjoy her independence, the more she seemed to flower. But that was the wrong word. His mother's mature beauty had nothing of a flower's fragility; it was hard and stately, like the wooden figures of the *marae*, of the same amber color, and the same fierce, old-fashioned elegance. His mother had always been a determined woman and a demanding, inflexible mother: the worthy offspring of Charles Maui Hira, the girl who should have been his son. But it was only when she

was finally alone in life that she ceased being the daughter of a soldier who had fought for God, King and Country, and became the
daughter of a warrior descended from one of the toughest tribes of
all his people.

And so Rapata just could not abide thinking of her with her
companion, and he rarely set foot in the new apartment, prefer-
ring to meet her elsewhere, to take her out for lunch at the Chinese
restaurant where her workmates tended not to go, or sometimes
out to dinner, letting her decide where, coming to pick her up and
taking her home. And sometimes, on the doorstep, she would turn
around, and upright as a queen, bid him goodnight with a small
wave of her hand. In that moment, as Rapata too raised his hand
to say goodbye, he was grateful to the windscreen of his car, grateful to the wide sidewalks of this newly built neighborhood and the
distance it enforced between himself and his mother, who otherwise might have seen the fleeting grimace that always crossed his
face—but just a shadow, for Rapata had been raised in his grandfather's school—just a shadow but enough for her to notice it. In
those seconds he was seized by a sudden impulse to put his arms
around her and breathe in the smell of his mother, to be reassured
she was still the same, that the smell hadn't changed although she
had softened enough to pause on the doorstep and wave goodbye
with that hand of hers that was too big for such a gesture. The last
time he had hugged her, really, had been at Charles Maui Hira's
funeral. He had never hugged her so much in all the other years of
his life; that he knew.

Now, as he stood there in front of the Commonwealth War Cemetery trying to read the meaning of those lost calls, Rapata realized
he had never asked himself what his grandfather sacrificed in order
to take in his daughter's son and raise him for ten years. He wasn't
the only child who had ever been brought up by grandparents:
grandparents who to a boy's eyes seemed old and therefore free to
dedicate their time, their "left-over" time, as it were. But for miles
around Charles Maui Hira had been the only old man to bring up
a grandchild without any other members of the *whānau* to give him
a hand. When he first began to live with him, his grandfather had
not even been very old, and he didn't suffer from any particular

aches and pains. He could have gone hunting or fishing; could have taken the car and traveled somewhere, to visit his fellow soldiers in the battalion, who were after all his true family, his real *whānau*, as he often liked to say. He had lost touch with his three sisters, too, in part because when they married they had gone to live in Gisborne, in Otago and the far South Island; in part because they had never really forgiven him for leaving them all behind and going off to a distant war he might never have returned from. Still, without a child to occupy his time and narrow his spatial horizons, who knew whether, sooner or later, he might not have wanted to see them again. To judge by that last surviving great aunt, the one at the funeral with the *kawakawa* wreath around her tiny, lined face that kept slipping off during her gusts of violent tears, he would have been more than welcome. Charles Maui Hira might even have found himself another woman.

It was a stunning new thought for Rapata, and it revealed to him a sort of commandment that had been passed down from father to daughter. *Have no need of any other.* In that light, his mother's extreme pride was not perhaps so absurd. It was pride (and not what seemed to be the opposite) that sent her running home to cook for a man who did not expect her to. Pride that kept her from using the telephone when he did not want her to pay the bill.

And what if there was really something, some serious problem down home there in New Zealand? It would never occur to his mother that he could not connect to his voice mail.

So Rapata was thinking as he punched in his mother's number on his cell phone, even though he could hear the national anthem being played inside the cemetery and didn't have enough credit to make the call. And above all, despite what time it was. He thought he would find her phone turned off, but instead it began to ring.

"Rapata?...where are you? What time is it? Where are you calling from?"

"From my phone. I'm sorry I woke you up. You left me a message, but outside the country I can't access it. Is everything okay?"

"What? We mustn't talk; it's too expensive. Is everything all right? Did you get there?"

"I'm in front of the cemetery, at Monte Cassino. They've already started."

"Good, then go. Go. I embrace you, my son."

"Can I know why you called me a hundred times?"

"I just wanted to say I told *koro* that you went to Italy to pay homage to him."

The pitiless phone message informed him that his credit was now exhausted.

He just couldn't think what had come over his mother. It was probably nothing, he thought, but he knew that his mother was always very reluctant to consider anything to be grave or urgent. The time they found a tumor, a papilloma, Rapata, who had been closed up in his room finishing his doctoral thesis, only heard about it three weeks later. "I just got the test results, and there aren't any malignant cells," she announced to him, dipping a steamed dumpling into vinegar and soy sauce.

"And why didn't you tell me?"

"What could you have done about it?" she said. "Everything's fine, no?" As if the negative result proved her conduct had been correct.

Maybe the tumor had come back, Rapata thought. Yes, that was probably it, or something like it, otherwise his mother would not have made those forbidden phone calls from the office. From the cemetery he could hear a wave of applause; the speeches must have begun. His mother had bladder cancer and Rapata was two whole days away, in front of a military graveyard where he knew not one person among the living or the dead. Except, from the TV, prime minister Helen Clark and (was he there? who knew?) her husband. Tall, blond, glasses, as thin and dry as his subject matter, which was medical sociology, statistics on prevention and cures under the national health service—numbers his mother too would be part of. If right now he were to come across that fellow ("Mr. Clark" they sometimes called him) he would say something like: "Hello there, professor, I don't know if you remember me, but may I ask what your tables have to say on the cure rate for papilloma recurrence in Maori women aged fifty?"

"One moment, what was the name? Morrison? Rapata Morrison?"

"Sullivan. You may be confusing me with the actor of *Once Were Warriors*, the one who played the bounty hunter in *Star Wars*."

"*Star Wars*? You're the student who recently did a master's with my colleague in post-colonial studies, isn't that right? Young people like you are an example to your community. And now you are here, at this ceremony..."

"My grandfather was in the Maori Battalion."

"Oh, excellent. Now as for your question, all I can say at this point is that among Maori women, neoplasms are more frequently diagnosed at a late stage. But you must come to see me at my office and we'll discuss it. I must go now. All the best!"

Rapata had no desire at all to enter the cemetery and find himself in a situation like that he'd just imagined.

If he went back toward town right away, fast, he might be able to buy more credit for his phone in time to call his mother back before she was fast asleep again. No, that was foolish, and anyway she had probably turned off her phone for the night by now. He'd been walking back and forth in front of the gate of the cemetery getting tangled up in memories, indecision, fantasies and other bullshit. Anyway there was no fast way to get back to town. He began to curse out loud, pronouncing swear words that were anything but mysterious to the Italian drivers passing by with their car windows down in the heat. Rapata, too, was sweating, his knapsack pressing on the bomber jacket he hadn't taken off. There were no bus lines in Cassino, and no swear words in Maori. From Milowitz, his grandfather had told him, they wrote their letters in *te reo* so they couldn't be censored; but that was another story. The U.S. army, too, had used the Navajo to send messages in their inscrutable language, and the condition of the Native Americans had always been worse than their own. War rewrote the usual rules, then peace came and put them back in place. Back to the usual hypocrisy by which a woman elected prime minister could deliver a fine speech in honor of the fallen in that sacrosanct horror of World War II, while Maori women still suffered God knows how much more domestic abuse and abortions, even fucking tumors, because not even an excellent health service could make them overcome that shame that passed as pride and go to the hospital when they needed to. And then there were those who, no matter how much trouble they took to avoid it, ended up in those columns of numbers divided by ethnic origin, like his mother. His mother, who was maybe beginning to die while Rapata was here in Italy retracing the steps of a dead man.

When he calmed down, stopped, expelled the air in his lungs which came out in a sigh, he saw that this was it, his fear: abandonment, total abandonment. And like the good Maori idiot that he was, had tried to fend it off with rage, that rage of theirs that made the *Pākehā* sit up and take notice, so that the more the *Pākehā* took notice and acted very concerned about Maori matters, the more the Maori got enraged, with that damned rage that was good for nothing except war, or rather it was only good to maintain white democratic predominance over them. And yet, if they lost their rage, if they discarded their pride, there was nothing left but despair. Maybe not for all Maori, but for him, yes: three generations had struggled against a destiny marked by their origins, and now here he was, all alone and blocked in front of the gates of an imperial cememtery. So what was the meaning of their struggle? The only thing that mattered was what you did for someone else. And he was there for someone else, for Charles Maui Hira, his mother's father. Because he had loved him, his grandfather. And therefore he would go into that cemetery and he would call his mother later, when the stupid ceremony was over and he was back in town, waking her up when it was dawn at home.

What he wasn't prepared for, when he got through the gate and began to walk toward the crowd gathered around the tall white cross planted at the top of a stairway of the same white marble, down at the bottom of the cemetery, was not the fact that there were more people there than he had expected—photographers, TV and press both Italian and from New Zealand—nor that the Kiwi veterans wore their medals not on uniforms but on the pockets of their blue blazers, and wore identical hats marked on the brims with the name of the country they had fought for—Panama hats from some latterday Grand Tour. It wasn't that he actually saw the professor with his thick-lensed spectacles, standing bolt upright and slightly behind his wife, who in a comfortable dark suit was finishing up her speech, nor that nearby Mr. and Mrs. Clark stood a group of Maori in costume. It was something he might not even have noticed if he hadn't felt it underfoot with each step he took.

The grass. Military cemetery grass, grass in which all the little graves, each one just like the other, were immersed, and which felt more like the hard, even surface of a doormat underfoot than like a soft carpet, so insistant that he had to look down at it. A lawn, that's what it was: a lawn made to remain like this not only in spring but in high summer and in winter, a piece of artifice extorted from nature more costly to maintain than any white marble. There in the midst of an Italian landscape of rivers and mountains, not so different from New Zealand, their dead—all the dead, the Scots, Irish, Welsh, Canadians, Nepalese, Indians—were covered by an almost perfect English lawn.

Only when he stopped, his mind wandering from the speeches now being made by some veterans, did Rapata recall that every war cemetery he had ever seen looked the same, from the grass point of view. He hadn't walked on them of course, only seen them in films: cemeteries that almost always contained the dead of the United States. So it wasn't the fault of the English, this time; this was simply how you did it, as if to adequately preserve the remains of soldiers nature itself had to be made to stand to attention.

When Rapata turned his attention back to the ceremony, the Maori group was in the space allotted to the New Zealanders, ready to play their part. They had their *taiaha*, their fighting sticks, in hand, and they thrust them forward and shouted their ritual shouts. Their faces and their bodies bared by their dance kilts bore the *moko* forbidden to soldiers, both the ones whose graves were underfoot and those old men staring at them from beneath their white Panama hats. A group of girls in long tunics and cloaks decorated with feathers stood waiting to sing the funeral hymns that would torment their tattooed mouths. But the tattooes were only painted on their lips and chins, unlike those of the mothers whose sons had gone to fight and die; in the days of the 28th Battalion, women's face tattoos were still a live tradition. They were the New Zealand Defense Force Maori Cultural Group and they were part of the New Zealand army, called *Ngāti Tumatauenga*, the Tribe of the God of War, in Maori. They took part in all official celebrations, but there was no way someone who didn't come from their homeland and was seeing them for the first time, could know that. Right now everyone there was watching those bodies intently. The silence in that cemetery (all else was anyway drowned out by the shouting and singing) had become total, more so than when the veterans, holding back tears that had been held back for sixty years, had spoken. As those bare feet pounded the grass and purified the soil of the New Zealanders' graves, Rapata stole a look at those who were watching.

The faces of the Italians, most of whom must be people from around here, looked dazed, excited; those of some old men with military caps whom he recognized as Germans showed no expression; he tried to get his mouth around the word *Fallschirmjäger* with that tone of reverential fear he'd heard from his grandfather and he couldn't do it, but he did feel genuine rancor watching those men, still alive, observe funeral rites led by the half-naked warriors of his people. He wasn't sure whether he was more uncomfortable watching the German parachutists or the Maori, who seemed to acting out a performance for tourists, rather than a solemn tribal rite. And in fact, anyone who wasn't a New Zealander and had a camera or videocamera, was busy recording. One reporter, filming a Maori who was especially large and heavily tattooed, seemed drawn toward his target as if he were being sucked in, until the man lunged toward him and pushed him back with a sharp stab of his *taiaha*. The stunned photographer withdrew, but by now tensions were running high.

"Behave yourself!" shouted a voice that belonged to a *Pākehā* veteran, but the tone and spirit were exactly those with which Charles Maui Hira had shouted at him when he was small. "Behave yourself, Rapata," and if he needed to go further than that admonition so clipped it sounded like a dog's bark, he would say he would tolerate no "misbehaving brat" in his house. Now Rapata too wished he could disappear beneath that lawn, under the Italian soil sanctified by his grandfather's fellow soldiers. What the hell had he come here for? Two damned days of traveling just to find out that their official warriors were no more than a bunch of clowns, their fine tattoos touched up like a cheerleader's makeup, and that just one old man in a foolish hat worthy of a picnic was enough to put them in their place? That their customs, their culture (in which it was so hard to be sure that corpses would permit souls and spirits to reach the ancestral lands of Hawaiki) would in the end be assigned only to young males, so long as their games were not too wild or violent? Let the Maori play, as long as they behave themselves: that's what it all boiled down to. What am I doing here? Rapata looked at the time on his cell phone, and saw it was still night-time at home.

He began to walk, making his way around the other side of the cemetery, far from where the ceremony was taking place. He knew his reaction wasn't right, wasn't fair; that in his knapsack there were a medal and especially some photos, and that he should wait and show them to the *mōrehu* he'd picked out, maybe beginning with that little old fellow wearing the cloak of feathers over his uniform that seemed to weigh on those bent shoulders like a great stone. Was there something ridiculous, folklorish, buffoonish about that old man too? No, not in the least, but Rapata had no idea how to approach a man who had carried his hardship with him across the oceans in the shape of bird feathers.

Unable to decide whether to stay or go, he stopped for a moment. When he looked up, his eye fell on the gravestone in front of him. There were a pair of crossed machetes carved on it that looked familiar, but in the middle were some words in an alphabet he couldn't decipher. *Jas Bahadur Limbu*, he read further, *7th Gurkha Rifles. February 25, 1944. Age 17.* A chill went through him. The lawn there was less cared-for, frayed and a bit bare where it met the gravel path. He had come to the far corner of the cemetery on the left, where the Gurkha dead were buried. Reading the inscriptions he saw that most of them had died before they were eighteen.

Why so surprised, he asked himself. He knew that many of the young men in the Maori Battalion were even younger, that the age limit existed only on paper, the usual hypocritical fig leaf; all you had to do was show up and swear to a lie; nobody was going to go and check on it. They were volunteers, no? Nobody was forcing them to enroll. So let them come, let them put their bare feet and their boys' bodies into boots and uniforms. They were all volunteers those boys who enlisted in all the far corners of the world to fight the good war of planetary liberation: Gurkhas, Indians, the Maori themselves. Even when they had no idea where Germany was, and had never heard the great dictator's name before they began their training. Just give them something to eat, clothes to wear, a bunk out of the rain, and above all, a paycheck. How much were the lives of those boys worth? Rapata had no idea. Not even when it came to the Maori Battalion had he ever heard money mentioned, not by his grandfather, and certainly not in all the official commemorations: school books, TV programs, newspaper articles, ANZAC Day and all the rest. He realized that if the mention of money was always, in any case, considered squalid, when it came to war, to that war, it was even more so, to the point that the *Pākehā* had appropriated their word *tapu*—"sacred"—and twisted it around to mean "unmentionable." The price of citizenship, my ass! The price of blood—but whose? Thirty pieces of silver or three thousand ducats for our pound of flesh, because if you prick us, do we not bleed? If you tickle us, do we not laugh? If you poison us, do we not die?

His grandfather had told him how, when he went to the camp hospital to see his buddies who had been wounded in the attack on the Cassino station, he had seen a Nepalese boy lying on a cot weeping quietly. His legs, both of them, had been devoured, and there was a stink of old blood and burst flesh despite all the iodine and chloroform on him and in the air, and just splintered fragments of bony remains up to the knee, visible when they came to replace the bandages. Charles Maui Hira thought he was crying in pain, for his round child's face seemed unable to bear it, and so he bent over him and said, "They'll save you; they'll amputate and afterwards you won't feel the pain anymore."

But now the boy's whimpering became loud weeping. "What is it?" asked Charles Maui Hira, "are you afraid? Afraid they'll hurt you even more, or afraid that what I said isn't true? Is that it?" Now the Gurkha shook his head violently, his intact, child's head with those sweet eyes, so awful to watch as it whipped from side to side above that damaged body. Until finally, between sobs and in broken English, he heard the boy say, "They spent all their money so that I could become a soldier and take care of them all with the money I sent home. Now what? How will I take care of them with no legs?"

Rapata wondered if that Nepalese boy had survived, or whether maybe he was right there in front of him, in one of those shabby tombs, Jas Bahadur Limbu or someone, and while he was thinking that he was startled at the memory that had come back. It was pure horror, no courage, no esprit de corps. It must have escaped his grandfather one of the times he had told him about the first attack, and how proud they were that the 28th Battalion had been chosen, and how disappointed when they learned that A and B company, and not theirs, was being sent into action because everyone wanted to show they could break through where the Americans had failed, everyone was already convinced they had the jingle of glory in their pockets. They had seen the abbey, that enemy eye on top of the hill, crumble; they could feel the smoke and dust in their noses, in their hair.

It was the first time, from Greece right through their years of fighting in the desert, that they been able to measure with their own eyes the inexorable might of the military alliance they were fighting for, and no one asked himself why, after three days of aerial bombardment, the ruins of the abbey had not been wiped out. "Avenger": the name of the operation to which they'd been assigned, was enough; it was enough to know that the ones who had been chosen to advance along the embankments of the Rome-Naples railway, cross the Rapido and avenge those almost 2,000 Texans who had drowned there, were two hundred men from the north and east coast tribes. "All we need to show up two Yankee regiments are these boys of ours who know how to scratch the earth to find kauri gum, or dive down from the rocks to pick up a few coins," they would say, in part to mock the Gum Diggers and the Penny Divers, as the boys in company A and B were called, and in part to buck themselves up. They'd taken up the positions of the 36th Division, and they had heard, from the Texans themselves, those tales of the river that had become so red as to merit the name "Bloody", and now there was nothing else to do but accept what had happened there as an incentive to victory.

Other Maori soldiers were supposed to occupy the railway station to allow the engineers to lay down bridges and prepare the way for the tanks, while the Nepalese and the Indians went up top to capture the ruins of the abbey. That was the plan. They were all volunteers, crack troops; that's why they had been chosen for the advance guard. They had already fought side by side in North Africa; they had made themselves known to Desert Foxes and to Rommel. The Gurkha were famous because they cut off their enemies' heads with their *kukri*; the Rajputana Rifles were supposed to be selected from peoples for centuries dedicated to the art of war, and of the Maori, it was rumored they were cannibals, as perhaps some tribes had been many years ago.

"The poor Italians were terrorized just to hear us mentioned," his grandfather had told him. "They cowered in fear, wondering if we meant to eat them, and it made us laugh. But after a while, the Italians realized we were better than we were reputed to be, us and the other strange, dark soldiers in our army. We were more respectful, better-behaved; those Nepalese head-hunters didn't even permit themselves to say one word to the local girls. We, well, we were not quite that restrained, but we never did anything to be ashamed of. We were jollier, and often we would spend the evening together drinking and singing; us singing our *waiata*, the Italians sang Italian songs that I don't remember anymore, but there were some, like our chaplain, who knew them all and had even learned Italian. They were songs about love, the kind they used to have then; tearjerkers, you might call them, I'd call them sentimental; but easy to sing for anyone with a nice voice. When they were a bit drunk, the Italians might say to us: 'But who would ever have guessed that among all these soldiers the real Christians would be you savages!' The Americans were generous, but they were whoremongers and braggarts; the British were arrogant, and according to the Italians they would die first before offering anything to the people, the poor. The way it looked to me, they were just angry and disgusted by that broken-down country, that war that risked costing them, if not their lives, an eye, a leg, an arm. That's why they got so mean, so crazy. Not us. When we weren't fighting we would fill our bellies with wine and the best food we could find, and then we'd laugh, we'd sing, fool around and make fun of each other, and even in this you could see we were made of better stuff; we weren't poor teachers or peasants or office workers who'd had a gun put in their hands. Otherwise they wouldn't have chosen us for that second attack."

Rapata had stopped in front of the gravestone of a head-hunter who had died at age 16, muttering, "you see, *koro*, where those warriors of yours ended up?" Then he turned around, toward the entrance, ready to leave and to let those compatriots of his finish their blessed ceremony, there being not one flower and just a single, dry wreath in the section where the Gurkha remains stood. Some official representative must have come to lay it there in the past few days, he thought, when they were commemorating all the Commonwealth troops. No veterans' delegation on a plane from Kathmandu, and probably none from London either, least of all a few miserable relatives come to mourn before the proof their family members had lived and died. Commonwealth? This was *empire*, without even the duty and the obligation to transport those abandoned in its dismembered far reaches to its funeral celebrations. And where were the Indians? If the world, as it was revealing itself to Rapata in the geometrical hierarchies of a cemetery, made any sense, then the Indians should be on the far side. Seized by a pedantic fury to find out, Rapata walked past the wide swath of British graves without even a glance and stopped on the other side. Same square, same size. Not even a wreath, nothing. On the gravestones, the names of the dead, Ali and Khan, many of them, like those damned Pakistani cricket champions. Inscriptions in Arabic. And the rest? They belonged to different companies—Rajputana, Punjab, Marattha, Punjab, Rajputana, Rajputana—he read quickly as he slalomed among the graves. They couldn't all have been Muslims. He found two graves, not far from each other, one Sikh and one Hindu, both named Singh. Where had the others gone? Had they frozen and been left to disintegrate on the mountain? Only the Hindus? It made no sense. Had they been cremated and sent home? Had they put the ashes on a truck and buried them somewhere else? Too much of an honor to be buried where one had fallen, only a few steps away from the English officers who were their commanders? One thing was certain; some of the dead were missing. The area marked out for the Indian Division contained only a small part of the soldiers who had lost their lives at Monte Cassino.

And this revealed something else: not only was this military cemetery ruled by notions of race and class, it was also fraudulent. It transmitted the message that the men who died in those battles were mostly natives of Great Britain. The others were relegated to the back where they remained invisible unless you went to look for them. Rapata had no idea how many men in the Indian Division had fought on that front; later, he said to himself, he would consult *The Hollow Victory*. Meanwhile a remark his grandfather had made came back to mind, but with a new meaning. "From when they began to bomb the monastery, the Indian Division sent whole brigades up there—two, three, four battalions at a time— while we had to make do with half of one." He began to understand what Charles Maui Hira had meant to say when he spoke of the legless Gurkha. And the memory brought back another.

Rapata had returned to the village for the holidays that went on until just after ANZAC Day; his mother had gone with him to get the bus, so he must have been between thirteen and fifteen years old. It was one of the first times he had gone to his grandfather's on his own. During the last week of his holiday there his mother had called to say that she would come to collect him on a day off from work but they would have to leave immediately because she had an appointment in the city the next day. Rapata had no desire to give up his last afternoon with his friends, and he wanted to show that he was grown-up. "You stay in Auckland, Mum," he had said, "I can come back on the bus the next day and you can come get me at the station in the evening." He had no idea how she would react to this declaration of independence, but having thought about it briefly, she agreed. Perhaps her appointment was a romantic one? That was something that only occurred to him much later.

As usual on ANZAC day Rapata met his old friends; as usual, on account of the mountains of food downed with the *whānau*, they met a bit later than accustomed, and so he was allowed to return home a bit later as well. What did happen for the first time was that his grandfather was alone in the house waiting for him. Where he received a call from the mother of Rapata's closest boyhood friends, who told him the boys had come back not only filthy, but wet to the bone. Could Rapata stay for supper until his clothing was at least slightly drier? Oddly, Charles Maui Hira said he could.

First they had played soccer on some mud-soaked fields, then they went down to the Waikato for a canoe race, and madly paddling away, failed to notice that another downpour was threatening, one of those that burst from the heavens suddenly and with great violence; instead, they just kept on paddling. Feeling invulnerable under the thunderbolts, competing with the thunder to shout even louder, they abandoned all competitive drive in the thrill of being together in the midst of the storm, water all sides. Finally one of them said his father was going to beat him silly if they didn't go in immediately. And so they paddled to the bank, put the canoes on their heads, and headed down the road home. One of them slipped, causing the others to lose their balance (miraculously the canoe hadn't toppled into the river) and so they lost some more time. In the end it was pitch dark, and they were trembling all over despite the effort and the fact they were still moving. The others were used to being outdoors even in bad weather, and if they sometimes caught a chill, that was that. Rapata, however, wasn't supposed to risk coming down with a fever just now, when he had to go back to school in two days.

All this he was going to have to confess to Charles Maui Hira. Not just because he would find out sooner or later anyway, but because Rapata was unable to lie to his grandfather. He was expecting one of those icy tongue-lashings that made him feel like a little boy, for he had behaved irresponsibly and that was what he deserved, but when he got home he found his grandfather in front of the TV, the remains of pork stew and *kūmara* on a dirty plate on the table in front of him. It was odd that he hadn't taken it to the kitchen and washed up, just as it was odd that he hadn't gotten up when Rapata came in. "Take off those wet clothes, put your pyjamas on and go to bed," his grandfather said without looking up, and Rapata felt so guilty he went immediately to the bathroom. Just one remark, in a tired, but not angry, voice, but it was enough to make a boy understand that the very worst dressing-down of all was utter silence. Lying in bed, he realized he would not be able to sleep unless he confronted his grandfather. So he got up and went to the living room, sad and fearful, where he said the only thing that came to mind: "Good night, *koro*."

"Good night, Rapata."

And then? He needed to ask him, "Don't you want to know what happened?" But he couldn't say it, he wasn't strong enough, brave enough, and he had the shivers, a condition he hoped was merely due to weariness. At last he said, "How did your day go?"

No reply. He had moved forward to where he could see his grandfather's face, and he was frightened. Charles Maui Hira's eyes had not even registered his presence; they were fixed on the television screen, which Rapata now also stared at.

It was a documentary about New Zealanders who had been

awarded the Victoria Cross, and they were showing pictures of
Second Lieutenant Ngarimu, who had led his unit up the hill at
the Tebaga Gap in Tunisia, had personally wiped out two enemy
machine gun posts, and although seriously wounded, had resisted
there through the night with his men, only to die the next morning
during the first counter-attack.

ANZAC Day. Rapata had completely forgotten. Or rather, he
had forgotten how important it was, maybe because his grandfather never turned on the TV during the day, maybe because the
heroic tales of the Maori Battalion, which he'd loved so much when
he was small, had begun to bore him.

"Did you know Second Lieutenant Ngarimu?" he ventured.
"Did you fight together?"

"Not directly; he was from the east coast; he belonged to the
Ngati Porou, who were part of C Company. I wouldn't have known
what tribe he was from if they hadn't said so in TV, but I certainly
knew him."

"He was handsome. At least in photos he looks just like the hero
you imagine," said Rapata, feeling he had to say something just to
keep his grandfather looking at him, as he finally had done.

"Young and handsome. Yes he was. He was the only Maori the
English ever gave that medal to, although our generals had proposed a number of others. But the television doesn't tell you that."

"Would you tell me yourself, *koro*?"

"It's late now, Rapi, you should go to bed, because tomorrow
you're leaving."

"I've already packed everything. I wanted to go and say goodbye to my friends tomorrow, but it doesn't matter."

Now that Rapata was remembering that evening again, he
thought about something he had learned about much later, those
fables in which somebody tells a tale, and thereby is saved. But
even if Scheherazade or Esther were not pertinent here, what he
now saw was that he had understood how to drag Charles Maui
Hira out of his spell, terrorized as he was for having understood
for the first time that his grandfather was old. Not old in the sense
that all old people are old for the young, but old in the sense he was
ready to join his dead companions. *Mōrehu:* it meant veteran, but
originally it had meant "survivor."

"Turn off that thing and sit down. No, first go and get something to drink: there's Coke or orange soda."

"Wouldn't you rather have tea?"

"Okay, but that means you've taken a chill; get yourself an aspirin, and put some warm clothes on."

Rapata came back with the tray, and after he had poured the tea and put sugar in it, he sat down on the chair next to the sofa where his grandfather spent the day reading or fixing things, and leaned forward to look at him.

"Who do you want to hear about? There was Haane Manahi who grew up in Rotorua near the lake; he was a Te Arawa who came from the Bay of Plenty, a Penny Diver from B Company. But when we took the village of Takrouna there in Tunisia, we were all sent up there, and Sergeant Manahi even led me up that hill of thorn bushes, dust and rock. He had with him twelve volunteers, eight from his company and four from ours, for that assault, one of many but fortunately the last. So in the end, the Italians surrendered, and afterward we took three hundred prisoners plus five Germans, and we took the village (which had been reduced to rubble by our artillery, but that mattered little to us). Haane was ordered to recover the bodies, which wasn't easy; you had to wrap them in sheets, tie them up like sausages and lower them with ropes down the cliff— all this in the middle of the night. They nominated him for the Victoria Cross right away—Freyberg but also Montgomery—because what he had done was quite incredible: two days under heavy enemy fire on that stony peak where at times they had to scramble up, attack, resist, climb down to ask for reinforcements, bring new men up, and attack again. A miracle that he didn't croak up there. He died a couple of years ago in a car accident, the stupidest thing that could happen to a hero who was never recognized. Sure, they gave him a medal, but not one of the most distinguished, because he wasn't a high officer."

Charles Maui Hira now turned off the television (they were talking about something else) before continuing. The only light now burning was the one in the entry hall, but even though Rapata couldn't see very well, he thought his grandfather looked calm, revived.

"The same thing happened to Charlie Shelford, a private in my company, who unlike Manahi was a hothead, if not worse; he was always drunk and quick to say appalling things. Several times he was put in detention, once for almost a month, but it made no difference. Discipline meant nothing to Charlie; he would be absent without leave for days on end. In Egypt he would go off in one of our trucks to pick up German weapons, then sell them on the black market. He was a legend, for better, and above all, for worse. What can I say: I just tried to keep out of his way. Sometimes he would call me "Charles" like I was his butler, just to provoke me. He had guts, though.

"At Gazala in Libya we were being fired on from two sides, we were cut off. They would have massacred us if Charlie hadn't volunteered to go up by himself and wipe out those machine gunners who were going at us. He ran up there like a crazy man, the Spandau at his hip still firing; we couldn't believe he was still standing, with all the ordnance hitting him. Just a few meters before his target, they hit him on the legs with a barrage of bullets. But he kept on crawling, trying to fire his machine gun, which however had been damaged. Finally, in a final desperate effort, he tossed a hand grenade—a dead hit. He had routed the enemy by now. Charlie, still on those bleeding legs of his, succeeded in capturing the officers and some forty men. They gave him the Distinguished Conduct Medal but he deserved a Victoria Cross. Charlie too came to a bad end; he was hit by a car while (drunk as usual) he was crossing a road on the outskirts of Auckland. But what could you expect of Charlie?"

The need for sleep now hit Rapata hard, yet this last story intrigued him. It was the first time his grandfather had admitted that among his heroic fellow soldiers there had been some wasters, that not everyone had been a saint. He would have liked to ask him if there had been others like Shelford, but he figured he shouldn't. It was already a lot that his grandfather considered him old enough to hear that story without it being censored.

"Okay, and then what?"

"Well, Rapi, I think I've already told you many times. They covered us with medals and decorations, a hundred of them, meaning that we got more than twice those received by the other New Zealand units, so it's not easy to choose. There were many of our men who maybe didn't meet the requisites for the Victoria Cross, which honors outstanding gallantry. Officers distinguished in their courage and dedication, their sense of responsibility toward the troops. Their *mana*. Which isn't one of the criteria by which the King of England gave out honors, but I can assure you it matters. We owe everything to those men, not just our battalion's glory, but our lives. Which we managed to save, while many of them died. Because a good officer doesn't spare himself, he leads his men as far as he can, he's their spur and their shield, and so he's almost always the first to die. I could tell you about Captain Wikiriwhi, for example; he was also company B, a Te Arawa, and he's not dead, no, he's doing fine as far as I know; let's not talk about the dead anymore. The last time I saw him was when your mother was about three or four years old, at a meeting to found the veterans' association for our battalion. We elected him president; it was our way of showing him how grateful we were. He had married and had children, and he had fairly important job in social services, over toward his parts, at Pukekohe. And then I also heard he'd been promoted and transferred to Auckland. He was named Matarehua, but we called him Monty—like the general but not on purpose. Before the war he looked after his *whānau*'s sheep. He, too, had made all the difference at Takrouna, and they gave him the Distinguished Service Order medal, which is a higher honor than the one that Shelford got, but can only be awarded above a certain rank. He was injured two times; the first in some God-forsaken place in the desert, I don't remember the name, the second, badly, at Cassino during the attack on the railway station. But I think I've also told you that story many times."

"Yes, but I don't remember Captain Wikiriwhi."

"You don't think it's time to go to bed? You look feverish."

"No, I feel better, the aspirin's starting to work. It's not even ten-thirty. And tomorrow I'm leaving."

"All right; okay. So, the A and B companies were supposed to take the rail station and hold it until the sappers had repaired the railway embankment, mostly filling up the holes left by the Germans, so that we could move forward with our tanks and the bulk of our infantry. They even considered deploying Combat Command, which the Americans first used during the war. There really

wasn't any other way around, because the whole valley was a bog,
partly because the Jerries had deliberately flooded it, partly because it hadn't stopped raining for a month. Even bombing the abbey was a problem; they had to guess when the only sunny day in
weeks might fall. The railway line was not some neat arrangement
of rails and ties as you'd think, because the Germans had blasted
everything, but it was nevertheless the only path you could travel
on, even if only by foot and in single file, which is why they didn't
deploy more than two companies.

"The action was supposed to take place at 9:30 a.m., which
meant we were on our feet at 6:15. We managed to eat something
and then there was a service conducted by Second Lieutenant
Takurua, the son of Takurua Tamarau, chief of the Tuhoe and of the
Ringatū church, which was pretty strong among the peoples on the
east coast. Many of the soldiers who were picked to carry out the
attack adhered to that faith, which has no priests, no special vestments or symbols, where the services take place mostly in the *marae*
rather than in a real church. Takurua recited some verses from the
prophets that he knew by heart, and then we all recited *The Lord is
My Shepherd* and and the psalm that goes, "Blessed be the Lord my
strength,/ who teacheth my hands to war/ and my fingers to fight:/
my goodness and my fortress;/ my high tower and my deliverer;/
my shield and he in whom I trust." Maybe you'll wonder how I can
remember it. Well, we never finished that prayer. And everyone
felt that was a bad omen. Later, the Italians told us that the 17th (that
was the date) was a very unlucky number as far as they were concerned, although they also said it would have been far worse had it
fallen on the day after, which was a Friday.

"We asked Father Huata to hold a service after the attack. What
else could we do? Nothing. All we could do was sit there waiting
while Captain Henare marched off with A Company, and Captain
Wikiriwhi with B. The artillery fire began around nine, and even
though we knew that our boys hadn't yet attacked, that noise relieved our anxiety some. There's nothing worse than silence on
the front; it's practically never silent, but even when the night is
pierced only by scattered gunshots you feel death at your back.
And there's nothing worse for a soldier than to stand by while his
mates are in action and be able to do nothing, only try to decipher

those messages that barking weapons write on the dark. A point-less exercise, in our case, because we were so far away from the action that we could hear almost nothing except the opening barrage. And we couldn't do anything. Maybe you're wondering if I'm not exaggerating..."

"No, *koro*; I'm listening, go on."

"You know, Rapi, you're not a child anymore, and I'm pretty sure that—maybe not right now, but later, not tonight, but maybe in a year or two—you will ask yourself whether everything your grandfather said was completely true: that none of us, deep in our hearts, was a tiny bit relieved not to have been sent into battle. It's a legitimate question, Rapata, from a young man who has learned how to reason from his own experience, who uses his own head. But my answer is, no. Not in that moment. When the others are out and you are waiting, not one fiber of your being can really think of anything else. The waiting hurts, physically; and that's not a meta-phor, because if you have any wounds on you, they will hurt then. In any case, you know, you feel them when the weather changes. Like today, even though half a century has passed. And you know, Rapata, we had been together for four years, day and night. We were a new tribe put together from the old; and in any case, inside those companies we were all neighbors, classmates, if not cousins or brothers. Men of the same *iwi*. As if you went off tomorrow with half or more of those kids you went and got soaked with today."

"We were on the river under the storm, and getting back was terrible, it was freezing cold, but it was wonderful all the same!"

"Take another aspirin before you go to bed. I mean: go to bed!"

"Come on, it makes no difference at this point, you can't just stop halfway through the story..."

"No, but I can finish it tomorrow. Assuming you don't get a raving fever. I'm a bit tired myself, if you don't mind."

"Please, *koro*, just the story about Captain Wikiriwhi, and then we'll go to bed."

"There's not much to tell. We waited through the night and the day after. At a certain point, C Company was mobilized to go in aid of the others, but at ten in the morning, in full daylight, it was im-possible to proceed along the embankment. You could fire on us as easily as spray insecticide on a column of ants. When C Company came back, I confess I felt a small, mean stab of satisfaction, because it wasn't fair that they should go and not us, before I realized what it meant: that neither tanks nor infantry reinforcements, nothing, had got through. And that our men had done what they had to do, and then they had held out. Because those were their orders, to hold out at all costs. They began to come back the following evening, around 8 p.m., about sixty out of two hundred, many of them wounded. A Company had forty men left; B Company was down to twenty-six. We had never had anything like such heavy losses, and for a complete flop, a defeat.

"Wikiriwhi was missing. Takurua was missing too, and we heard he was dead. Wikiriwhi was wounded right at the end, when they were retreating; actually he had been wounded at the start, gone back to be patched up and then returned to take over the command, which he'd temporarily handed over to Takurua. He had led them to secure the engine shed, and then to the station itself, on one good leg and one bandaged. He had the radio, too, because he was afraid it might go out during a night attack, but it was shot to pieces the first time they were hit. So there was no contact right from the start. Until A Company came back, given that they couldn't reach their objective. When they had called for artillery support, the guns aimed too short; Lieutenant Asher was brought down and Second Lieutenant Crapp gravely wounded. Wikiriwhi had no officers left but Takurua. They had dug in behind the station from midnight until 3 pm the next day. Suddenly they felt the ground tremble under their hole, and then, like a mirage in midst of the smoke screen, the air so thick it made you gag, they watched the wall of a house nearby collapse and an enormous Tiger tank emerge.

Its turret pointed toward them, and they had no anti-tank weapons, which would have been useless in any case, and Captain Wikiriwhi called the command shouting, "We're in trouble," and they must have told him to hold his ground, because he was shouting "Go to hell!" and to the men, "Get out, run!" He was hit on the leg again when he stopped to hustle away a couple of boys who had taken cover rather than run. A really ugly wound, from a grenade. They didn't want to leave him there but he ordered them to get out and even threatened Sutherland with a pistol when he tried to stay by him. Rewi, the only one of the Wikiriwhi brothers to come back with his company, was grinding his teeth in order not to cry. He wept when he saw his brother Te Tuahu, who came in alone in the middle of the night, as the last survivors did. The rest of us were sleeping that leaden sleep soldiers do when they survive by some miracle; but I couldn't. But then I too fell asleep, because you can learn anything, anything can become a duty you must carry out. The following day we had no news of the missing men. We assumed Captain Wikiriwhi was dead. He was found by the 24th Battalion twenty-four hours later. Somehow, he had dragged himself to our lines. We were very put out when we learned that *Pākehā* troops had been sent out to recover our men. In May, when the victory finally came, we didn't let them take away our rights to recover our own dead. Military police, burial by the unit charged with registering the graves, that's what the rules said. Our commander Peta Awatere told the boys, in Maori, to calm down, and then he told the guy from the military police that he could not be responsible for what would happen if they stopped us from burying our comrades, brothers, kin. It was a month and a half before we could take charge of the remains!

In any event when we heard they had recovered Captain Wikiriwhi, we were relieved, but also fearful. We didn't know who else had ended up in the camp hospital, or what shape they might be in. Father Huata, who had to go there, understood our distress, and to be fair to everyone, he determined that a soldier from D Company would go with him. I don't know why he chose me; maybe because he saw me as being calm and under control. He was an odd sort, a warrior priest who always went into battle with us. He also knew I was just about the only one there without close kin or members of the *whānau* among his mates, and maybe he thought that would make the hospital visit easier on me. On the way there, I imagined that our men would stick out, if not for their skin color then because there were few of them, but instead it was the opposite: the white men stuck out. There was a Gurkha lad with no legs who was weeping on his cot not far from where we found Captain Wikiriwhi. There was a Sikh with a deep shrapnel gash that had turned his head cloth red with blood, shouting that no one had better touch that turban of his. A soldier of the Rajputana Rifles swore he had got all the way up to the monastery with his platoon, but then one barrage of artillery fire had wiped them all out and he alone, how he didn't know, had survived, *Allahu akbar*. While Padre Huata and I were there looking for our men, new injured Indian and Nepalese soldiers kept arriving, many of them in desperate shape. Our boys were but a drop in that sea of dark flesh torn to pieces by useless slaughter; throats crying out in so many incomprehensible languages they sounded like the voices of animals; and when we left, after finding out that none of our boys were dying, I couldn't help making a stupid remark to Father Huata. "Even this time, maybe, God hasn't completely abandoned us."

"Why do you say that, Charlie?"

"Because I kept on thinking about Second Lieutenant Takurua's prayers, that they were useless. Or that the handwriting was on the wall when we didn't finish that last prayer. But coming here, I had the impression that God decided to spare us."

Father Huata thought for a moment. "The one who sometimes doesn't help us in battle is the god of war, but the god of love never abandons us...not us, or anyone." Quite honestly, that sounded to me like one of those things priests say. He seemed relieved we could go back with fairly good news about all the boys, none of whom were in desperate shape. And in fact, except for one, they all survived. Captain Wikiriwhi received another medal on top of the one he'd earned at Takrouna, but this time a lesser honor. That is where this conversation began; that's what I wanted to tell you. He did everything he could to obey orders, but who knows how many more men would have died if it hadn't been him commanding. I'm not at all sure that the god of love never abandons us, but I did learn that when the god of war turns his back on us, only men can save us. Whether they be men like Wikiriwhi, or us ourselves. And that is about all. Good night, Rapata."

Rapata, who had stopped on the gravel path, turned and saw there were only a few of his fellow New Zealanders left there in the midst of their section, among them a boy in a dance kilt and a girl with a chin tattoo, paying homage at a grave like all the others, heads down and arms crossed. It seemed somehow unreal to him, not just because they looked anachronistic, as if they came out of the pages of a schoolbook—a pair of ancestors grieving for a kinsman killed by the English in the Land Wars of the 19th century—but also because he realized he couldn't trust his memory. He had feared it would be damaged if he read too much, if he relied too much on an official, objective truth that would alter, and in part replace, his grandfather's stories. He had never imagined that those stories that had grown along with him, tales he considered belonged fully to him, could be so brittle. Okay, he had found the legless Gurkha. But was he sure that the man wept because he despaired he would not be able to maintain his family, sure that his grandfather had told him so? When had that been? Could he have invented it? But how; based on what, where had the story come from?

No, he didn't think he had dreamed that event, although he had no way to trace where it came from. He had to trust his grandfather and himself; he had to put his faith in that tale put together by the two of them, recognize its invisible *moko*. Mataora, "Living Face," was the name of the ancestor who had taught the Maori to tattoo their faces. Although the designs were the same, the *moko* adapted itself to the individual face wearing it, and then the movement of the muscles made it more individual still. That was the difference between a living memory, and a dead one.

No more than a grave stone to sacrifice wreaths and flowers on, while bending your head and shoulders, standing there stiffly upright as if you too were made of stone? His people possessed more than that; they were not just a bunch of survivors from tribes of savages. They were a people of memory, a people of memory generated by the war, thought Rapata for the first time at the Commonwealth War Cemetery of Monte Cassino. Otherwise they would have disappeared. Otherwise gunfire, disease, missionaries and all the rest—civilization, progress, democracy, money, supermarkets and mixed marriages—would have wiped them out. Despite the Maori party in parliament and all those other roles that guaranteed nothing by themselves, just as the warriors in their kilts meant nothing by themselves, and even less his father's gratuitous celebration of Maori pride. Instead, they had succeeded in passing down, invisibly and for centuries, the Living Face, the way Charles Maui Hira had done with him.

Now Rapata approached the New Zealand graves, ready to find his grandfather's comrades in some little corner on the side. Not right at the back, not all the way on one side, because he'd seen the phony old-fashioned *tūpuna* who were now coming down the path hand in hand somewhere over near the center. And then, it wasn't quite right to compare the position of the Maori Battalion to that of the other soldiers of color under the British, because their battalion had been created by a Maori and had Maori officers right up to the rank of commander. And so to bury them together meant something else: was it not right and natural that men who had served and fought together should lie with their comrades and kinsmen in death? And all the more so for a people who called themselves *tangata whenua*, where "whenua" meant both earth and placenta; for a language in which the word *iwi* meant both tribe, and bones; for those who held that wherever Maori were buried was sacred ground, and belonged to them. And that was surely why the government had invited the Maori Cultural Group to today's ceremony. Even if they sometimes looked a bit foolish, that didn't mean they didn't have reason to be there.

If he hadn't seen those Gurkha and Indian graves, maybe he wouldn't have felt so uneasy about seeking out his own dead. But he had walked by those grave plots, they were just a few paces away: ghettos for the dead that pointed to ghettos for the living.

It was in one of those ghettos that Rapata had spent a few years of his adolescence, and had recently gone back to live: Otara, south of Auckland. There were no tall apartment buildings in Otara; there was nothing in those rows of little houses that would really remind you of an American inner city, and yet just about no one but Polynesians and Maori lived there. One evening, on the way to fill the tank of his new Korean rust bucket, he met the younger brother of one his middle school classmates with his mates, all dressed gangsta rap style in oversize T-shirts and sagging trousers, shades and baseball caps. He wouldn't have recognized him but the kid came toward him shouting, "Hey Rapata Sullivan! What you doing here?" When he told him he'd come to live there, the kid said "Brother, welcome back to the underdogs." A remark that sounded all too pat, but it was true. Even the Asians who had just arrived didn't settle in certain neighborhoods. Neighborhoods on the outskirts that were every day more cut off, as were those who lived there.

But there was no special plot for the Maori Battalion in the Commonwealth War Cemetery. It took Rapata a while to understand this, it wasn't what he had expected and furthermore, many of them had English names and surnames. They were all buried together, the soldiers of the New Zealand contingent. It was the price of citizenship, he couldn't help thinking: the price that had earned them the right to be buried alongside the *Pākehā*. Maybe it was too little, maybe it meant nothing, but when Rapata found himself in front of a photo of a soldier in uniform on the only gravestone with a picture on it, and he was a Maori, he felt like crying, although he had no idea who the young man was. That round face with the slightly foolish proud smile in faded black and white, hair parted and slicked with brillantine, posed by a photographer who had charged too much: it suggested that Sir Apirana Ngata had been right and so had his grandfather Charles Maui Hira, who hadn't lived long enough to pay homage to his comrades, to see they had been buried as New Zealand citizens, and to say to his grandson, "You see, that's what I told you."

Maybe it had happened by chance and not by choice, and quite likely it wouldn't have happened that way if the cemetery had been laid out thirty years later, when the Maori rights struggle had grown more radical. Still, it mattered what was there, what it meant in the here and now, no matter why or how it had been decided. For sure the architect or the military official in charge of burial grounds had not thought about the fact that those dead from the 28th Battalion, spread all around like that, had made the entire New Zealand sector a *urupā*, a Maori burial place. That was why the Cultural Group had done the purification rite all around the perimeter. For in the continent they came from, Europeans lay in New Zealand soil (there in that stretch of Italy so like their homeland) thanks to the presence of their Maori comrades in their midst. The *Pākehā* had stolen their lands; they had cheated and killed to have them, but they were not capable of consecrating them. He thought of the expression *salt of the earth*. The Maori, in spite of everything, had remained the salt of their earth. But to find this out you had to go to the other end of the world, where, with further blood and more war, they had taken back a tiny strip of what had been taken from them.

* * *

Only now Rapata didn't know what to do. There were no *mōrehu* left there among the New Zealanders still in the cemetery, and he would have to search out his grandfather's fallen comrades one by one. He recalled some of the names, but not all, and so in order to find them he would have to walk down each row reading the dates of death on each grave stone. How many were there? Even that he didn't know. The only thing he did know was that if he walked up and down, he would certainly not be able to connect with those veterans who were probably now on the bus awaiting the last of them. Anyway, he could hardly climb on that bus and say, "I'm the grandson of Charles Maui Hira who served in the 28th Battalion, and I want to meet the survivors who fought with my grandfather."

He had better find out instead where they were staying or where they were going to dinner tonight, and here, too, he had better hurry up. He had seen a small group of *Pākehā* who were chatting among themselves, no longer in that attitude of prayer he preferred not to disturb. Rapata went over to them and introduced himself, said something about why he was there all by himself, and whether he might join them somewhere. Certainly, they said; maybe he'd like to come along with them now, seeing as how the hotel was outside town and supper was to be at 7 pm, because tomorrow they had to leave for Rome quite early. The prime minister and her husband had an audience with the Polish Pope, and they were going to visit the city with a tour guide.

Rapata was tempted to say yes, sparing himself the money for a taxi and the trouble of finding one, but he didn't feel like waiting for them in the hall, all by himself and wasting a lot of time when he could have been calling his mother. So he took down the name of the hotel and thanked them, said goodbye and made his way quickly out of the cemetery, for there wasn't much time left to do everything he wanted. If he hurried, he might even have time for a shower at the Hotel Eden, or at least change the clothes now sticking to his sweaty self.

He returned by the same road he had come on, walking quickly without looking around until he got to town. "Telephone, telephone card, international phone call?" he said to a bunch of kids on the street who looked as if they had come out of a school or some university. They seemed to understand, because they began to confer among themselves, and finally a girl said to him, "come with us." Some of them picked up bags and knapsacks on the ground, said goodbye with great waving of hands, then began to walk along, still chattering. Rapata wasn't sure he would find what he needed by following them, and began to study the street. Maybe a telephone box would jump out at him, something the students had never even noticed. But he saw nothing except apartment buildings, a car repair shop here and there, a grocery store, advertizing panels. When he passed by a house crowded in between new buildings, a small, old house with a courtyard full of chickens scratching and a dog on a chain howling, he realized that this city had nothing to do with the one that had been bombed before his grandfather was sent to occupy the ruins, the one that had been flattened for no good reason.

Had he wanted to see where Charles Maui Hira had fought to drive the enemy out of the skeletons of the Hotel Continental and the Hotel des Roses (and ended up being captured) he would find no sign of them, maybe not even the street they had been on. Cassino had come back to life by cancelling out what had been, everything but the Benedictine Abbey that looked down on the city from the top of the mountain, half lighthouse, half Disneyland castle: that was the only link with itself and its past he could hope for. Rapata felt tired suddenly, and following those kids who were caught up in their own affairs, laughing and talking in their own language, didn't help. He hadn't succeeded in finding his grandfather's dead comrades, he hadn't spoken with a single veteran of the Maori Battalion, and now he was trotting along behind these students for whom the war that had taken place there was light years away, or maybe not, but certainly further away than it was for him who had come from New Zealand. Like some stupid mutt, he thought; maybe because the dog he had seen on the chain had been medium-sized and of no certain breed, a dog that had probably got lost or been abandoned.

In any case, what were the people of Cassino supposed to do? They hadn't asked those planes to drop tons of bombs on their houses; why should they care about preserving the memory of those who came to destroy them? They could only be happy that their grandchildren could walk among those new buildings as if they had always been there. And anyway, hadn't those buildings been there since they and he were born, or even before?

When they got to a wide intersection with a street light, they had to stop.

"There," said a kid, pointing to the far side of the square. "Now we take the train. You go to the bar and ask."

"The bar?" said Rapata.

"Yes, the station bar; it is to the left. There is the telephone, we think."

Rapata saw a café with outdoor tables and a few people sitting down, most of them kids like the ones who had brought him here. They crossed the piazza together; the kids yelled "Ciao" and "Bye-bye," and were off to get their trains. The station clock said 12 minutes after 5 p.m.; it had taken far less than he imagined to get here.

Inside there was a long bar and a cashier selling cigarettes, but he saw no telephone. He tried asking; it was hard to make himself understood and hard to understand, but finally he gathered that the card they were showing him worked in a nearby public telephone. His mother got up about 6 a.m., which meant he still had time to walk around a bit and see if he found one of those places where you could make international calls. If worse came to worst, he'd come back and use the card, even though it would be expensive. He tried to explain, but they didn't seem to understand, and so he said "Thank you" a number of times before going out and heading for the street he'd taken the day before on the way to the hotel, where he'd had a pizza on the corner.

He pulled out his phone and saw it was 5:19. Without thinking, he turned to compare the time with that on the station clock. In that precise moment, he understood where he was. The Cassino rail station was not just that place where he had got down from the train; it was the place where A and B company had held out for 20 hours. He wanted to see it, that embankment along which the Maori Battalion had marched, and he certainly had time.

He crossed the station and arrived at track 1, looking in the opposite direction from the one he'd come from, in the direction of Naples. And down near the end of the platform he saw them. There were four of them, lined up beyond any other passengers, down at the end. They were looking down, their shoulders bent, white panama hats in their hands. Only the *mōrehu* in uniform still had his side cap on, but he had taken off the feathered cloak. He floated it before him on outstretched arms, and the wind caught it and sent it billowing like a curtain over the empty tracks. He was about to let it fly off, Rapata saw, but his mates stopped him, and they stood there with their hands on each other's shoulders, practically embracing, all of them crying.

The loudspeaker announced the arrival of a train—"Roma" was the only word Rapata understood—and that noisy artificial voice from the present drove him into action; he could not just stand there yards away from his grandfather's fellow soldiers, cut off by the noise and the rush of Italians on their way home.

When he approached them, the soldiers of the 28th Battalion were drying their eyes with the backs of their hands. He waited, and then he said, "Tēnā koutou," and then, taking a deep breath, "Tēnā koutou i tēnei ahiahi." *Good evening.*

"Tēnā koutou i tēnei ahiahi," said the man nearest him, turning slowly toward the Maori-speaking voice. The others turned too, seeming unsurprised to hear themselves addressed in Maori, not apparently curious about this young man they'd never seen before and who he might be, or how he'd ended up at the Cassino train station. Perhaps it seemed natural just then that a strip of earth on which iron tracks were laid was *whenua tapu*, ancestral land, fit for the *tangata whenua*, the indigenous people, the people of the land. Or perhaps it was only because they had wept, because of the emptiness behind those reddened eyes. The lines on their faces were sharp; the *mōrehu* with the cloak, the shortest of them all, the one who looked most Maori, resembled a tortoise.

"I'm the grandson of a soldier who was in D Company," said Rapata. "Tainui-Waikato from Hopuhopu, who sailed on the *Aquitania* and was captured by the Germans right here. Charles Maui Hira."

"Charlie? You're Charlie's *mokopuna*? How's he doing?"

It was the same man who had spoken to him before, but the one next to him shook his head.

"I heard he had left us, but it was too far to come to his *tangi-*

hanga, anyway it was for me. We're all from the east coast; three Cowboys and one Penny Diver, if that means anything to you."

"Sure, he told me everything about the Battalion, and he wanted very much to come back to these parts. It was so unlucky that he left us just a few months ago, very suddenly. I don't know if you heard, but there were half a dozen *mōrehu* at his funeral. I suppose they must have belonged to his company, or lived somewhere nearby."

"Sad to say, young fellow, we are getting older and fewer; otherwise, I can tell you there would have been a lot more than half a dozen at Charles Maui Hira's funeral. It's a fine thing that you came, however, because now we have just about all of the glorious team here. We're missing A Company, but our Gum Digger had to stay in the hotel and rest. By the way, you didn't tell us your name."

"Rapata. Rapata Sullivan. I was actually going to come to your hotel later to find you. It didn't seem like the right thing to do at the cemetery. Or maybe I just don't know how to behave at these official ceremonies. In fact, I've been very happy just to be here on my own, with the money that *koro* had set aside."

"Yes, yes, official ceremonies. We came here before, a couple of days ago with a delegation to lay a wreath, over there below the plaque. But as you can see, we have quietly returned to the scene of the crime. And you were pretty lucky to find us here, because tonight we have decided to do our own thing. Right, boys?"

They smiled, and their faces changed utterly. They were now the soldiers they wanted to be, the "old boys" of the battalion so pleased with themselves for escaping the protocol, with how little it took to feel united and strong once again. They were all around eighty years old, but they didn't look it: really the same breed as my grandfather, thought Rapata, and his remark about what bad luck it was that he hadn't made it to Italy, which he'd said mostly to be polite, went through him like a knife. How happy Charles Maui Hira would have been in his place; how much he would have enjoyed returning to the scene of the crime with his mates. But there was nothing he could do; now it was his turn to grab what chance offered.

"That sounds like an excellent plan," he said, "and if it's all right with you, I'll keep you company, I'd like to offer you something, you know, a beer, to make a toast to the battalion and to my grandfather."

"We told you, didn't we, that you've been signed up, Rapata Sullivan. Just what we need, a Ngati Walkabout. But forget about the beer; we are old men and we can only drink tea or orange soda."

"Fine. So we'll make our toast with tea and soda, how does that sound?"

"They all began to laugh, and if there was a cough or two in the midst of their hilarity, the laughter was still noisy, insistent, alive.

"You don't know us yet, young fellow; we were joking. Soda, beer, no thank you! We'll have a nice bottle of red wine like in the old days, and maybe not just one. But you must let us offer, it's the least we can do, since we weren't able to make it to Charles's *tangi* to bid him farewell."

Was it possible for your head to feel utterly light, floating in an exhilarating euphoria, while from the chest down you were gripped by a suffocating heaviness? Possible to feel intensely happy and very sad at the same time? It had never happened to Rapata; he had never before felt so strongly he belonged while feeling so sharply a loss, and what astonished him was that happiness ultimately won out, not because it was preponderant, but because it somehow colored or embraced the rest.

"Thank you," he said. *Whakamoemiti*. I thank you so much.

"He brought you up well, our Charlie," said the old man who had known about his grandfather's death, and Rapata had the sense that they all knew something about him, although maybe that wasn't the case, maybe that remark was just a chance comment. Still, it comforted him to think that Charles Maui Hira had stayed in touch, even if he, that grandson to look after, had been the greatest obstacle. The strangest thing, though, was how familiar he felt with those men, even though they were very different from what he had imagined. Their appearance—elegant gentlemen—had something to do with it, as did the fact that two of the four didn't look as if they had been part of the Maori Battalion: they were finer-boned, more slender, and age seemed to have molded their faces into that shape that all old faces have. They must have been part-Maori only, people who cared more about their roots in a certain *iwi* than about all the rest, and so had enrolled in the Maori Battalion when they might have been able to enroll in another, people who might have fought in a *Pākehā* unit where they would have risked less, or even taken advantage of their Maori roots to avoid the obligatory draft for the whites, and stayed out of the fighting altogether.

"However, before we get to the enjoyable part," said the tallest, leanest one of the veterans, the one with blue eyes, interrupting his reveries, "we must finish what we came to do here: say a prayer for our dead brothers. If you want to join us you are welcome; if you would rather leave us to ourselves, we'll meet you in front of the station in a little while."

Rapata had no need to reflect on the matter, nor think what his grandfather would have done. He wanted to commemorate the fallen, and said so right off. "If it's not a problem for you, I'll stay."

They smiled, just a hint; but they all smiled. "Well, there's always the risk with a Ngati Walkabout that you'll run into some bother," said the veteran wearing the side cap, while with a little help from his friends, he scaled a low iron fence, "but then, what can you do?" That remark served to let him rid himself of his cloak, which he lay over the wreath like a coverlet, a coverlet that however touched the earth, so that he had to lean down further and bend deeply on his knees, taking the hem in his hand and pulling at it until it was neatly positioned on the grass where the plaque stood. You could see it wasn't easy for him, especially in the way he patted the brown and green feathers many times with his old hand, in a farewell gesture. One of his friends put his hands under his arms to help him rise to his feet again, but when he was standing, he said, "Sorry, Hereme, but it won't do…"

"You're right; we must find a way to attach it."

"We need some stones to hold it down."

"I'll get them," said Rapata, and seeing that there were no trains coming through, he stepped down on the tracks to pick up some of the larger stones. Only when he turned around to hand them to the *mōrehu* did he realize he was bending over the soil where half a century before Captain Wikiriwhi's men had died. One of those old men he handed the stone to had fought under the Captain. Rapata wondered which one he was and whether he would have a chance to ask them later. Now, though, he came back up with the last handful of stones and waited while the veterans lay them on the cloak to hold it down.

"Okay, let's continue," said private Hereme, and they stood in a half circle around the plaque covered by the cloak, with Rapata on the far right.

"We could have used Father Huata."

"Yeah, but he left us all of a sudden."

"Oh, so you would rather vegetate for months and months or even years? He did the right thing: three two one off. That is how a soldier dies."

"What do soldiers have to do with it? Anyway, we don't get to choose. We're in the Lord's hands, you know, boys?"

"Right, we'll leave that to you, Jamie, you're the most acquainted with the Lord."

The old man with the white hair and blue eyes, the one who looked more like a white man that the others, raised his right hand and began to sing a funeral chant that Rapata had never heard before. From the way he held his raised hand, he understood that this must be a chant used among the Ringatū, and he guessed Jamie had been in B Company, because the Ringatū were strong where that company was recruited. But everyone knew that *waiata tangi* and the chorus was not difficult to follow, even Rapata was able to sing it. *E Hori e'*: they were words of farewell to this Hori and his comrades who had left their lives and their bones in a faraway land, but who remained in the hearts of the Tuhoe around the lake and all across the Bay of Plenty.

Rapata tried not to look around or pay any attention to the travelers drawn by that incomprehensible chant who had lined up along the platform, and he avoided the eyes of the *mōrehu*, who seemed to be battling tears with the force of their lungs and the volume of their voices. They came to the end of the chant.

Jamie swallowed and bit his lip, but it was not long before he spoke. "I don't know what to say," he began, in *te reo*, "except that we still miss you. And your presence. Therefore, I will say no more than farewell."

With a slightly trembling hand he took a sheet of paper from his pocket and began to read:

"*Haere-rā*, George Asher."

"*Haere-rā*," said the others in chorus.

"*Haere-rā*, Barney Brass

Haere-rā, John Dinsdale

Haere-rā, Charles Hapeta
Haere-rā, Albert Heke
Haere-rā, Anaru Heke
Haere-rā, Hatu Herewini
Haere-rā, Patrick Kereti
Haere-rā, Leonard Koha
Haere-rā, Raroa Leef.
Haere-rā, Ephram Maaka
Haere-rā, Peeti McCauley
Haere-rā, Samuel Mendes
Haere-rā, Tei Porter
Haere-rā, Roihi Rikiriki
Haere-rā, George Simon
Haere-rā, George Takurua
Haere-rā, Huinui Te Kuru
Haere-rā, John Robert Thwaites
Haere-rā, Pompey Tuiri
Haere-rā, George Warren
Haere-rā, Wipere Wiremu

And farewell to you too, Donald Puke: you who died in hospital some days after. Perhaps it is best that the Lord called you, because it would have have been a hard life, Donnie. *Haere-rā*."

"*Haere-rā*," said the others once more, and with them, Rapata Sullivan.

That last farewell faded out across Cassino station, losing all meaning. In that foreign, open space it no longer sounded like a normal farewell, but like some archaic invocation, some ritual cry not too unlike the enemy *Heil* that Rapata, and most of the Italians watching them, knew only from war films.

"I'm sorry," Jamie began again in a low, uncertain voice, "forgive me for having to use that sheet of paper to remember everyone. Many years have gone by, but for me that day in which I lost you here somewhere is still with me. It's still not over. And I still do not know why I am here. Why me and not you. I want to thank you for that; I want to thank all of those who died to save me. You know who, you know better than I do, because when you are in the midst of battle you can make no sense of anything…"

A train being announced drowned out Jamie's voice, so that it sounded like he was whispering.

"And we want to thank you because you were the best comrades we could have wanted!" shouted the *mōrehu* with the greying hair and thick lenses, who had said nothing up until now. *Kia Kaha!* His deep voice resounded over the repeat of the loudspeaker, and then, in a normal tone, he said, "If you pass me that paper Jamie, I'll continue."

As the old man from B Company nodded and held out the sheet of paper, a train making a great roar of noise and rushing air rolled up on the track near them and pulled out with most of those who had been watching them. While they waited for the train to be off, the *mōrehu* pushed his glasses up over his high forehead, fiddling to make them stay there because his hat was in the way, and put on another pair of glasses.

"We would like to bid farewell to our comrades from C and D Companies with whom we fought to drive the Jerries out of the hotels in March.

Haere-rā, Louis Aspinall
Haere-rā, Frank Rodney Brooking
Haere-rā, Rukutai Haddon
Haere-rā, Komene Kaire
Haere-rā, Richard Matthews
Haere-rā, James Mohi
Haere-rā, Tama Paurini
Haere-rā, Thomas Himona Rakau
Haere-rā, Ruihui Rogers
Haere-rā, Peter Simon
Haere-rā, Matekino Te Keena
Haere-rā, Colin Maurice Topi
Haere-rā, Walter Ratana Tumaru

And how could they forget Robert Turei who had unluckily stepped on a mine a month later, or Barko Rameka and George Perawiti, brought down by a German MG-42 as we were retreating at Mignano."

"*Haere*," came the voices of the others.

"And last, let us say farewell to Charles Maui Hira who had hoped to be here with us today, but who instead has gone back to Hawaiki and perhaps is watching us from us there in heaven along with our other comrades. *Haere-rā*, Charlie, *Haere-rā*, all of you."

The *mōrehu* looked at him as they repeated those words of fare-well, and Rapata took a deep breath and said "goodbye, Charlie" too. He had never called his grandfather Charlie. The veteran who had read those last names stood for a moment with his reading glasses in hand and an absent gaze.

"You've got the other glasses on your head, Ben," said Jamie, maybe to show he had recovered, "but you were good; who would have bet on that?"

"Both of you were good, but we did our bit too. Those buddies of ours must have known we were talking about them!"

"No question about that, Rewi. You open your mouth and even the dead know you're talking about them."

"Okay, let's be on our way. We've earned our bottle of wine. Now all we have to do is figure out where we can get it."

"Never a problem for the men of the 18th Battalion, or am I wrong?"

"Hey," Rapata broke in, "there's a place right out front that I saw before. They have tables outside, so we can feel relaxed and take advantage of this fine day. And there's a telephone nearby, too. I have to call home; it was too early before, which is how I ended up here and found you."

"Great. There's also a taxi rank, so we don't have to go looking for one if we get too loaded to walk," said the veteran with the thick glasses. "And Hereme has some time to consider whether he really wants to leave the *korowai* he inherited from his father here. That is, supposing he's able to find that cloak of his later."

"What's got into you, Ben?" said Rewi, the old man who was silent and near-bald. It was as if they were so sad they didn't know how to release the grief stuck in their throats. Even Rapata, as they began to walk along, felt his legs were heavy, half-asleep.

When they got to the piazza, he turned around to look at the clock. It was five minutes to six; he could sit down with them and order, because his mother would not leave home for another hour and a half. But the urgency he had felt to talk to her was gone now, and the only reason he didn't decide to put the call off until tomor-row was that he had just mentioned it to the others.

They were sitting in a corner by themselves, a sunny corner. It was nice there.

"Good thing they gave us this," said Rewi pointing a finger at his Panama,"or at this hour my bald head would have been blistered."

"Your bald head, okay. Burn what's left of what's inside, and that would be serious," said Ben, but it was a warm-hearted jab and the others just laughed.

When the waiter arrived, they were all studying Hereme, who without his cloak and with his uniform unbuttoned halfway down his chest, looked almost undressed, or disarmed. "Okay, I'll try," he said, and to the young waiter, in his best Italian, said "Un fiasco di Chianti, per favore." They applauded. The waiter too, smiled, and speaking slowly said something that Rapata couldn't understand, although he could see that the *mōrehu* were making a great effort to decipher his words, faces screwed up with the effort.

"*Capiche* boys?" said Hereme, and to help Rapata out, he translated what the waiter had said: they only had Chianti in bottles, no straw-covered flasks; however, he could suggest the house wine, which was better and actually cost less.

"Nothing has changed; you talk to them in their language and right away you get good treatment," said Jamie.

"Okay, you keep it up. Go, Major Richardson! You can do it!"

"Grazie," Jamie spoke to the waiter, "un *bottle* di buono vino rosso, per favore."

Loud applause and whistles of approval. Even the waiter clapped his hands once or twice, and you could see he was amused. When he replied he forgot to speak slowly, but the cheerful faces, the hands pounding on medals, the *Grazie, grazie* sounded out in unison made it clear to Rapata that the young man had delivered some compliments on their Italian and been told they'd learned it while battling their way from Taranto to Trieste during World War II.

The wine was dark and strong, and it set off a debate, because it was called Montepulciano d'Abruzzo, and Montepulciano was not in Abruzzo—they had passed through Abruzzo while coming up the peninsula—but in Tuscany, where they had also been. While the *mōrehu* went on discussing wine and geography—Montepulciano, Montalcino, Monte Cassino, all those damned monte-somethings scattered around Italy—Rapata had taken off his knapsack and removed from it the photos of Charles Maui Hira, most of them taken in Egypt, for all he knew, for among them was the one with the pyramid that had hung in the kitchen.

"Let's see what you have there," said Ben, who was sitting next to him.

The pictures were passed around in silence. Strange, the old men blinked and squeezed their eyes now, yet when they had recited the names of the dead and chanted the funeral lament, they had been dry-eyed. Fighting off an embarrassment that was probably more his own than theirs, those old men softened by the wine, the sun, and the weight of their responsibility, Rapata spoke: "I've never heard the *waiata tangi* you sang today. If I understand rightly, it was written for one of you in the Battalion."

"Yes," said Hereme, "for Second Lieutenant Takurua. It was written by his father, who survived him for a good ten years, although George—Hori—was the last of his many children. His favorite. The father had several wives; he was a chief and a man with influence even beyond his *iwi*. He had *mana*, he fought for the Maori with strength and the intelligence and built alliances with important people like Sir Apirana Ngata, and he had a role in the Ringatū church, which has a lot of followers among our people too. Rewi, for example, who is Ngati Porou like me. George was a gentle, profoundly religious man, who seemed even younger than he was. Thirty years old when he died! But in battle, he was...courageous isn't the word, nor would you say daring. It was as if he always knew exactly what his role and his duty were, and acted accordingly. Jamie here says he saved his life more than once."

"My grandfather talked about Takurua, he told me he held a service before the attack on the station and died during the retreat, when Captain Wikiriwhi was badly wounded. Oh, by the way, Captain Wikiriwhi didn't come?"

"No, young fellow," said Ben. "Age, you know. And the leg. More the damned leg than age: the buses, airplanes, crutches, if you know what I mean. It's already a miracle that he's done what he's done in his life."

Rapata was embarrassed to ask exactly what had happened to Captain Wikiriwhi's leg. Stories with happy endings, the ones he knew, did not involve crutches, artificial limbs, wheelchairs, and such. Two thirds of the Maori Battalion had been injured during the war: he knew that. But he had associated that fact, at the most, with Charles Maui Hira's intermittent pains, normal aches that grew worse with age. As for the rest, a wound was temporary; you were hit and then you healed. In his imaginary accounts there was no room for someone who was neither alive or dead; there was no third case. But it wasn't just Rapata Sullivan who thought that, because he was young and had grown up in peaceful times. Everyone thought that. The dead devoured the wounded; the dead got all the grief and all the glory. Mourning was that managed suffering he had just witnessed; it was still vital after half a century, you could even inherit it, and grieve for men you had never known. Grief for the dead was a hungry beast, and to make it bearable you had to divide it, break it up, spread it around so it could be satisfied. While the wounded, some of them, did not exist except for themselves and as a burden to their families. Rapata thought about the statistics collected by Helen Clark's husband, and mentally inserted a new category under "Injured": those maimed and crippled in war. The words sounded obscene, repugnant, numbers to bury and conceal even more than those malignancy rates among Maori women.

So, 3,500 men had sailed off; one third had died, another third had been wounded, perhaps maimed for life. That was the least you could say. And it would not include other, invisible consequences: bullets lodged under a shoulder blade, lungs riddled with holes, changes in a man's nature, and so on.

Why so serious, young man?" Ben asked. "And what's that you have hidden in your hand?"

He couldn't help smiling as Rapata opened his fist with the medal in it, the medal he'd pulled out with the photographs the mōrehu had passed around the table. Yet it made Rapata feel bereft; the metal that had warmed to his body temperature now felt heavy hanging from his hand poised over the table. Hereme, sitting across from him, took the medal and studied it carefully, although it was just an ordinary War Service Medal, and he probably couldn't even see to read the name inscribed on it.

"What is it you want to know, Rapata? Do you want us to tell you what we remember about your grandfather? Do you want to know who are the soldiers with him in the photos?"

"Yes, but maybe not now. I can come to see you in New Zealand,

I don't know, maybe some of you live in Auckland, that would be easy for me."

"I live in Auckland; Jamie is in Pukehohe, so nearby; and Ben often comes to see us, more or less every time someone in his *whānau* has some business in the city. In Rewi's case you would need to make a nice long trip up to the top of the East Cape. I advise you to go: it's a beautiful spot. However, you could also come to the meeting of our association."

"Sure," shouted Ben, "you might even meet some old Ngati Walkabout who spent his nights with Charlie crushing lice. As I did with this lucky fellow here who didn't have much more hair when he was a kid than he does now; still, it was the height of intimacy. I say no more."

They all laughed, Rapata maybe even more than the old men. He stretched out his legs under the table, knowing in that moment that he was happy, and that was that.

"I want to tell you something, young fellow" Jamie said. "I have the greatest respect for what Charlie did. When we heard from him that he had to bring up a *mokopuna*, some of us made fun of him, called him *māmā* Walkabout. The fact that you are here with us today shows that he did the right thing. Hold on to what he gave you; don't forget. It doesn't matter whether you know the names of those boys, at least half of whom are dead; but don't lose the whole photo, if you know what I mean. The psalm says, 'If I do not remember thee, let my tongue cleave to the roof of my mouth!' But that's enough preaching."

"Lay off the psalms, James Richardson, we still have to make that toast to Charlie. And order another bottle, because this one is used up."

"Yeah, and we have to put that medal on the young man," said Hereme.

"I'll take care of that," said Ben, "before his tongue cleaves to the roof of his mouth, which would be a real shame when we have this red wine of Monte Cassino."

"To Charles Maui Hira," Rewi shouted all of a sudden, "who, just about sixty years ago, ate fire, dust and stones on the front line against the enemy, while we followed behind him!"

"To Charlie! *Kia ora*! And to his *mokopuna*!"

Rapata raised his glass and downed the contents in one swallow, like the *mōrehu*. They couldn't know, but he was already quite tipsy, and the alcoholic fuzz helped him raise his voice and shout "To you and all the men of the28[th] Battalion. *Kia ora!*" but that didn't seem gratitude enough, and so he began to sing "Maori Battalion march to victory/ Maori Battalion staunch and true/ Maori Battalion march to glory/and take the honor of the people with you!" And the old men chimed in, singing *Au-E! Ake! Ake! Kia Kaha e!* at the top of their lungs, and the Italians at the nearby tables all stared at them, and even the waiter came to the door, which made it easy to signal they wanted another bottle.

"Just one thing I need to add," said Rewi, "given that we may not see each other again, and given that I, too, was present that day when right near here, your grandfather's active duty came to an end. And then that's enough for today, we must celebrate. You see, to us in C Company and those in B Company, we who were the great majority and came from areas where the Battalion had a lot of support, the Ngati Walkabout sometimes seemed to be strange folk. You can hear it in that nickname of theirs. It wasn't that easy to come up with a name for the boys in D Company. They came from all over the place, from Wellington, from some God-forsaken village on the South Island, even from the Pacific islands. In short, there was a bit of everything in D Company; there were fewer kinship ties and more men who had signed up for all sorts of reasons — need, spirit of adventure, uncertainty what to do in life, hatred for a parent, a girlfriend who had gone with another guy, and I'm not kidding. You think that when a kid enlists in the army at 20 years old he knows what he's doing?

"Those of us from the East Coast, it mattered a lot to us to follow our brothers, cousins, uncles, and so often nearly all the young males from an *iwi* would join up. While, but this you probably already know, there were few Waikato in the Maori Battalion on account of what had gone on before—the land the *Pākehā* stole, the efforts to avoid the draft and the deportations to the front during the First World War."

Rapata nodded as he poured out wine from the new bottle and Rewi took a sip before going on. "Okay, that you say yes already confirms what I'm about to tell you. I, and all of us, knew your

grandfather, but not well. After the war he came to the first meet-
ings, and then he disappeared. We knew from Father Huata that
his wife was ill, and that she had died. Years later he came back,
and then once again we lost track of him. But it didn't surprise us
all that much. It was pretty much an exception that a Ngati Walkabout, however courageous he had proved himself to be in wartime, would feel that much esprit de corps. We figured you were
a sort of excuse, that Charlie had other things to do, that maybe
he was fed up and even—why not?—that he would rather forget
about it all. That's legitimate, and sometimes even indispensable,
when you have to carry on. In short, after a while we stopped con-
tacting him. Father Huata kept in touch I believe, they were friends,
but then at the beginning of the 70s, Huata was transferred from
Waikato to Wairoa, five hours away. And then, thirteen years ago
when Father Huata died, we lost that channel too. We only sent
your grandfather official association mailings. It never occurred to
us that we could go and see him, maybe not me, but those who had
moved near Auckland. And we didn't even think to put his name
on the list of the *mōrehu* to be invited by the government on this
trip. Did you know that?"

Rapata shook his head, and took a gulp of wine to send down
the knot he felt in his throat.

"Yet Charles Maui Hira came all the same. He came on his own,
with his own blood. I told you, didn't I, that you look like him?
And if you weren't dressed the way you are, if you weren't a young
fellow of today, we might even think it was one of those ghosts
you find in Shakespeare's tragedies standing before us. The ones
that come back to remind you that you are guilty, if only of neg-
ligence, to tell you that your tongue should cleave to the roof of
your mouth. I don't know whether I did well to tell you what I did,
Rapata Sullivan, but I would like to apologize to Charlie, I'd like
you to ask him to pardon all of us."

Rapata did not know what to say. He wasn't used to drinking,
not a heavy red wine like this, and he wasn't used to the heat it
delivered to his stomach and sent to his head, so that the chill those
words cast over him felt even colder.

"*Koro* would have very happy if one of you had gone to visit
him," he said as he slowly raised his eyes from the wine-glasses to

the faces of the *mōrehu*. Hostile eyes, or at least judgmental eyes; it was unjust, he knew. "You know, he often said that the Battalion was his *whānau*." The fact was, he couldn't care less about hurting them.

The silence that followed went on for a while, until the people at the nearby tables looked up to see why those old fellows, who had been so high-spirited, so noisy, had suddenly been struck dumb.

"Our Rewi is better at keeping company with his Shetland sheep than with human beings," said Jamie finally. "Whenever he starts to say something longer than one sentence, you can be sure it will be something hard to swallow. He has a lot of sheep, and he always has had, but I've always preferred the goats. The ones you find grazing nose down at 90 degrees on a sheer cliff."

"It is I who must apologize," said Rapata. "It may be partly the wine that's gone to my head; I'm not used to drinking."

"Well then, you wouldn't make a good soldier in the Battalion."

"Im afraid I wouldn't."

"However, you can continue your training now."

Rapata smiled a faint smile and said, "Yes, sir, Major Richardson," before taking another sip. It should have been up to him to repair the situation, and instead they had done it themselves, with those funny ways of theirs, old soldiers and eternal lads. They were not like his grandfather in this.

"I miss him," he muttered in the direction of the *mōrehu* who had told him the truth about their relations with Charles Maui Hira.

"Sure," said Rewi. "That's right. You're a good young fellow."

"For he's a jolly good fellow, for he's a jolly good fellow," Ben continued, joined by the others with raised glasses, "for he's a jolly good fellow…and so say all of us!"

They went on singing until the incident had been buried under the entire popular repertory of the Battalion. Traditional *waiata* and also American songs that had been given Maori lyrics, some of them cheerful enough to dance to, others quite sentimental.

Rapata gave in to a pleasurable drunken weariness, rousing himself only to wave the empty bottle in the waiter's direction.

"*Moolto grassie*," said Hereme, when another bottle appeared.

"We need a tribute to Italy," said Ben, looking at his buddy who had sacrificed his ancestral cloak of feathers.

Hereme broke into "Che bella cosa na jurnata 'e sole" and when he got to the refrain, "O sole mio", the rest of them joined in, until the nearby tables and even passersby turned to listen. But it was the brown-skinned old fellow in uniform, his tenor voice just slightly scratched by age, who astonished everyone. How had he got down that entire Neapolitan song, never a hesitation, never a mistake?

"Incredible!" said the waiter.

"Enrico Caruso," Hereme explained. "Learned at war." He was radiant, but with that ecstatic glow of a sleepwalker it was better not to wake.

"Most beautiful song. Beniamino Gigli," he said, and Ben told Rapata that his best number was coming up, the song they always called for when it was getting late.

Mamma, how happy I am now,
now that I've come back to you!
Mamma my dream has come true now,
that's what my song means to say.
Mamma how happy I am now,
why would I ever depart?
Mamma, for you alone my song takes flight,
Mamma I'll be with you tonight, always, forever, with you.

The piazza was utterly silent as Hereme intoned that hymn to a faraway mother, his gaze focused on some point in the distance:

The *mōrehu* sat wineglasses in hand, not daring to raise them. Rather, they seemed to be hanging onto them for dear life, the tears beginning to fill their eyes. Jamie brushed them away with his fingers, then let them to spill over and run down his face, so as not to disturb his friend's warbling, and because it was as pointless as trying to stop a downpour.

When Hereme finished, he seemed exhausted. The Italians, who didn't understand, applauded enthusiastically, and Jamie took the opportunity to blow his nose before beginning to speak.

"Do you know who the wounded, the dying, nearly all of them, invoke? Even before they call on God. And even the most devout of them, and the bravest? We were so very far from our mothers, but we had this song to comfort us."

"We had better go," said Rewi, the only one of them who wasn't visibly moved.

He paid, and on a paper napkin wrote down their addresses for Rapata. They made their way slowly, some of them tottering a little, to the taxi rank a few meters away.

"I'll call you when I get back," Rapata promised, and then they embraced in their way, forehead to forehead, nose to nose.

While the *mōrehu* were getting into that old white Mercedes, it occurred to him that he could ask the driver how to get to the Hotel Continental, that is, where his grandfather had fought his last battle. He took out the napkin with the addresses on it and handed it to Hereme who was sitting next to the driver, and waited until it came back to him with a simple map and some written directions. He thanked the man and returned to the center of the piazza, even before the taxi reversed directions and sped off down the wide street to the right.

There was no point in looking behind him; he already felt wrapped in cotton wool from head to foot, somewhat stunned and yet strangely energized. The station clock said 7:15. He could still try to reach his mother, but he would have to do it right away. He went back to the bar, asked for a phone card, and went inside the station where he had seen two telephones. The ring bounced back from the other end of the world with a sort of echo; maybe his mother was already in the car. He had to keep ringing and hope the line didn't fall.

"Rapi, is that you? I saw the number and I pulled over. What's up? Where are you calling me from now?"

"The station. On a phone card. We can talk."

"You know, I'm late already; what is it?"

"Mum, why did you call? Don't pretend you don't know what I mean, because I don't believe you. If you have a health problem, tell me now."

"Health? Have you been drinking, Rapata? Your voice sounds very peculiar…"

"Yeah, I drank; okay? However, you reply to my question all the same! Because I know you wouldn't have called me a hundred times from the office for no reason."

"You may not talk to me like that, all right? Even if you are in Italy, and even if you are drunk. Pull yourself together or hang up, child."

"Okay, but I was worried. I thought maybe the cancer had come back."

"The what?" He heard his mother laughing on the other end of the line. "I hope that's not your excuse for getting drunk. No, son, I don't have cancer. What I wanted to tell you was something else entirely. Do you remember Aunt Kiri, your grandfather's youngest sister, the one who came to the *tangihanga*? She sent me all the letters he had written home, both from prison and from the front, and yesterday morning I found them in the office. I wanted you to have them while you were there, that's why I called. But then I realized that even the fastest courier service wouldn't be fast enough. All right?"

Rapata was silent, his ears full of the oceanic hum of the intercontinental telephone line, so like the buzzing in his head. He was in Cassino, there were five days before his return flight, but if he left right away he could make it, he could get to the place those letters had been sent from.

"Now listen; there is a way to get them to me fast. When you get to the office, you run them through the scanner and send them to me by email. Okay, Mum?"

"I did think of that, only they are not very legible. But yesterday, while I was trying to call you, I copied out the last one on the computer."

"Will you send it to me?"

"Yes, if you will allow me to get to the office."

"Thanks!"

"Rapata, now don't start drinking, at least not on your grandfather's money."

"No, no!" It was he who laughed this time. "Some *mōrehu* invited me out, and I couldn't refuse, if you see what I mean."

"Well, for a fellow who had trouble refusing, you certainly didn't hold back," said his mother, but it was an affectionate reproach, and as usual, she liked to have the last word, and Rapata let her.

Relieved and now very curious, he returned to the hotel, stopping along the way to get a sandwich and a Coca Cola to soak up the wine, but above all to let enough time pass so that the letter could arrive.

At the hotel there was a young man at the desk, the owner's son, probably. His English was not much better than hers, but he was not surprised by Rapata's request to use the email. "Fifteen minutes, ten Euros," he said, getting up to leave him his place, and taking a cell phone and the hotel's cordless with him.

Rapata was annoyed at the cost; he needed to be sparing with Charles Maui Hira's money if he wanted to get a flight to Poland. At least his mother's email had arrived.

"Here's the letter," she wrote, "I knew nothing about this myself until the other day. After the funeral I connected with Aunt Kiri again. I called her a couple of times and the last time I told her you were about to go on this trip. And so she decided to send me these letters which otherwise she would have kept until they passed to you and me. Aroha nui!"

Rapata opened the attachment and decided to print it out without asking permission. Then he began to scan it rapidly, because his time at the computer was scarce.

Landshut, Germany, April 20, 1945

My dear family,
    I am alive! And free. By the time this letter reaches you I hope I shall already be embarked on a ship to New Zealand. Here in Bavaria the Americans have arrived, and to the north the Russians are advancing, sowing revenge and destruction. The Germans flee from them because they kill and rape the women. You cannot imagine what this war has been like; not even the fiercest of our old chiefs ever did anything to match this. All I can do is try to get my strength back. I got to the point where I was almost four stones less than than when they weighed me at my first medical in the army. It's a miracle we're alive. We walked seven hundred miles on foot, in deep snow and storms, over the mountains. Our feet were frozen, forever wet, we kept our boots on even at night to avoid the worst. We left Milowitz on January 19, which is the middle of winter here. At first they made us march up to twenty miles a day so we wouldn't fall into the hands of the Russians, who were so close behind us

we could hear their machine guns. When it wasn't snowing, it was even colder: -15°, -20° Celsius. It's a kind of cold that overwhelms you, annihilates you. It burns out your brain. Yes, cold burns, but in a different, more cruel way; it's hard to explain. It even occurred to me that the cruelty of these people is connected to the cold here. Because at a certain point, you don't feel anything. Not even hunger. You are like a walking dead man. And everything dies, except the lice.

Since they captured me, I've spent a year in the kingdom of the dead. The one the ancient *Pākehā* believed in, the realm of shades, as our commander explained to us when we were in Greece. I feel as if I haven't seen a color on earth since then, just black and white and grey. The ruins of Cassino, the snow, the mine. The most beautiful thing was the sky, those times when we caught a glimpse of it at dawn before going underground, or when during our march it was high and blue. I couldn't help but see Rangi jeering at us and taking his revenge for what we did to his wife Papa and our land, we the progeny of their son Tumatauenga. One day one of my mates pretended he was shooting at a pigeon. We all understood the envy in it. I told him how Maui took the form of a pigeon to go and find his immortal father. They all laughed at me but after a while Jack Gallichan, the one who put together the *Tiki Times* in the camp, asked me to tell him the stories about Maui: how he stole the secret of fire; how he and his brothers had caught and cut up a fish, from which the North Island took its shape; how the South Island came forth from his canoe. How strange; I, the only Maori, was the one to keep nostalgia burning in the *Pākehā* so we could grit our teeth and get home as soon as possible. They started to call me Maui. In the mine where we were working, they defended me against a guard who was badgering me; they said I was a citizen of New Zealand just like them. But it was only when they began to call me Maui that I saw they really meant it.

There is so much to tell you! It was impossible to write during the march and at Milowitz we mostly had no paper.

There is one thing I want to say right off, even though it hurts. Since I was captured, I've had many doubts about whether I did well to enlist. I thought of you with rage at myself, thought you had been right, told myself there was no reason why we should die for this land of ice. Let them tear each other apart, these white men ruled by greed that can survive anything, just like lice. Inside me there was something worse than hatred. I had never felt anything like it. I had killed the enemy so that he didn't kill me; I had hated him when he killed my comrades. That was war. But the Germans I found in Poland were something else again. The guards, the SS who shot the Poles and the Russians from behind the columns of prisoners being evacuated. Not to speak of the *Hūrai* they exterminated. I didn't know there had been so many of them, and in Europe, in Poland. Who knows how they got there from the Holy Land? Although the Tuhoe in the Ringatū church believe their *tūpuna* came from there with their canoes, and certainly Aotearoa is farther away.

I heard about the *Hūrai* from a Polish lad, one of those they sent to work in the lowest, narrowest tunnels. The entire mine was dangerous and unstable; you could break something if a piece of rock caved in, or be overcome by fumes. One day three children died and my friend Marek was among those sent to bring them up. The next day he brought me bread and butter in exchange for chocolates and cigarettes. I asked him if he was sorry about his friends who had been "gassed," that was how we described it. He said nothing, just lowered his eyes. Then he stared at me defiantly. "Deutche make kaput, vergast: Polacken many, Jude, all," he said. And then, miming and using his hands, he told me there was an enormous camp not far away where *Hūrai* had been brought by train from around the world. If they were children or old people, they were *vergast* immediately; otherwise they had to work until they died. Then their corpses were burned. His relatives who lived nearby smelled the stench night and day. If it hadn't been for the hard, hard stare that kid gave me, I wouldn't have believed him for a minute. What sense did it make to bring people in on trains and then kill them somehow with gas and burn them? But one day, we saw them.

The day before we began our march, a column of people wearing ragged grey pyjamas, with wooden clogs on their feet, passed in front of our huts. All around them, SS, guards and dogs. Later I got used to that sight; on the sides of the road we would often see frozen heaps of *Hūrai* who had been killed. Both men and women, although some were so starved that you couldn't guess which from looking at their shaved heads. Dead people who must not be touched, or buried. What kind of human being could invent something like that?

Now all I want is to come home and forget all that I saw and lived through from that day of March 22, when, hiding among the ruins, I heard those mines exploding that trapped and killed my comrades. I knew that if I came out, I might fall into the hands of the Jerries, but I had to go to their aid. Alas, there was nothing left for me to do.

I hope you can forgive me for abandoning you during this awful war. I cannot wait to embrace you again.

Nāku noa,
Charlie

The computer's clock told him he still had a minute or two to send his mother a reply. He wasn't sure but maybe it had been his haste that made him seize on that one fact out of so many new facts that made his plan to travel to Milowitz more workable.

"Sorry," he wrote, "I don't have much time. Could you book a flight for me on the web for whatever airport in Poland is closest to Auschwitz, on the afternoon of the 22nd? I'm heading back to Rome tomorrow morning and from there I'll be back in touch. Thanks! R."

Rapata had already gotten up from the chair and was walking back and forth in front of the reception desk when the kid came back.

"I have to leave very early tomorrow," he said. "Can you prepare the bill and tell me what's the first train to Rome in the morning?"

"Now? Immediately?" the young man asked, but he said no more, and Rapata understood that he must look very tense.

"Later is okay. I'm going out for a walk." The thought came to his mind at the very moment that he said it.

"After supper?"

"Fine, fine," he said, already at the door, sticking the letter in his jacket pocket.

He began walking back toward the station. Dusk was falling, but the shops were still open, and he had to step over crates of fruits and vegetables that a shopkeeper was piling up to remove them from the display tables that covered most of the side walk. INTERNATIONAL FRUIT said the sign, in the colors of the Italian flag. He came to the intersection on a street full of shop windows, bars and restaurants, people strolling about with ice cream cones. He turned right and walked down to the end of the street, where he found himself at the edge of town in front of the stone, at the curve where the SMALL RED BUILDING—so Hereme had written—that had been the Hotel Continental stood. The German stronghold in which neither Charles Maui Hira nor any other soldier of the Maori Battalion or the New Zealand contingent had set foot except as a POW. Prisoner of War.

It had been four days of fighting, leaping over piles of debris, losing themselves in a void of dust, stones and plaster as big as a city, where no military map was of any use; playing hide and seek behind the walls still standing, the bomb craters, the grottos of collapsed houses; playing cat and mouse with life and death and German snipers. Four years of war, four years in which he saw, battle after battle, their *iwi* decimated, saw their bones scattered and dispersed—two brothers in Crete, one in Tunisia, now on the embankment of a railway station or a stretch of dirt threaded with mines some devastated part of southern Italy. He alone. Charles Maui Hira, Tainui-Waikato from Hopuhopu near Ngaruawahia, *kūpapa* of his queen, his people, his *whānau* left behind, was still intact under a pile of rubble, alive.

He'd told Rapata that when he came out in the open hoping to rescue his mates, he had heard the crackling of a machine gun, but by then it was too late. Maybe it wasn't true; maybe the gunfire that had finished them all off had come when his grandfather might still have been able to turn back and save himself. "I knew that if I came out, I might fall into the hands of the Jerries, but I had to go to their aid," he had written. Maybe he was tired of being a prisoner of the war, of centuries of war that didn't seem to want to end. Rapata closed his eyes. There was no hint of tears in them, nothing, apart from a picture of Charles Maui Hira in front of a pyramid in Egypt, a photo taken by the tomb of a Pharaoh dead before their time began. He would liberate the prisoner and carry on their war, their war of liberation; he had no other choice.

From New Zealand

In the frozen foods section at the Lidl, I come across a product that unsettles me. A transparent bag containing a block of mud-colored meat, with the words VENISON/ORIGIN: NEW ZEALAND stamped on it. For months now I've been researching New Zealand, tracing routes and distances on Google Maps, checking timetables for flights and buses, watching documentaries and home-made videos on You Tube, seeking out discussion forums, memorizing the contents of books and articles, grateful to a nation so remote and so scarcely populated as to put whole books and entire encyclopedias on line. I've spent mornings watching Maori Television to get a sense of how the average modern-day Maori looks, I've peered inside their houses, listened to the sound of their language and the way they speak English, tried to understand their gestures and all that is expressed in body language. I have used two Maori-English dictionaries to ferret out the most important words in their hybrid speech. But I have never met a Maori, never been to New Zealand, and for the moment—that is to say for the entire span of time in which I'll be writing this book—I will not be going there.

It's this that the words stamped on the bag of frozen meat remind me. They remind me that something will always escape me, something that betrays my second-hand knowledge. They tell me that the error won't insinuate itself into the heart of the matter, it won't involve the story of the Maori Battalion, nor the backdrop of indigenous life and thought, it will hide in some almost invisible detail, that banal mistake you make because you were not born and raised there.

I had read there were no mammals native to New Zealand; no kangaroos, koalas or platypuses as there were in Australia. I had read about the rich diversity of aboriginal species, especially birds, like the kiwi, that have long been protected because they risk extinction. I had mentally inserted sheep, cows, pigs and even dogs and cats brought over by the British colonists; I had melded them into the daily diet and folded them into the landscape of pastures and houses. But deer? How did deer get to New Zealand? And how many must there now be if they are showing up in the Lombardy branch of a large discount supermarket chain headquartered in Baden-Württemberg? Working backward from this dead flesh, my imagination fills the vales and forests of New Zealand with great, silent herds that are all the more majestic and beautiful because incongruous in that austral hemisphere.

Now, shopping bags balanced on the handlebars of my bicycle, I'm off toward home with visions of New Zealand deer risen from the freezer and a wish to repair this lacuna in my knowledge. Not that it's in any way indispensable in order to write my story, but that no longer matters. What matters is an urgency to know that goes beyond any mere scope, that harbors no illusion it can fill all the gaps and or in any way substitute experience, but which is above all a movement *toward*, a tension with which you try to shrink a distance that no longer involves merely what you know but also what you feel and imagine. Nothing is useless in this light; there are just flashes of facts that must be chased willy-nilly until you get them inside you and can make them real on the page. This is how it always is in any case, whether the places and people are reached through invention, or by dipping your brush into your own life. The reality, the truth you write about is a wager founded on an act of faith and submission to its rules. You believe it's there: in no way interchangeable inside and out of you, but nevertheless a zone in which external reality intersects with what you have lived—something like an Archimedean point from which to extract it and to return to, a grounded electric socket. Nothing human is alien to you, you say following Terence; one story is as good as another, but only in this sense: that you are able to treat it as if it were your own, or as if your own were worth that of another—something you must discover, ask questions of, learn to know.

The deer, in any event, came to New Zealand from England and Scotland, beginning in 1851. Most belong to the species *Cervus elaphus*, commonly called the "European red deer" or "noble" deer. They were introduced for *sport*—that is, for pleasure or for the hunt which had become a sport, and also for a higher purpose: because European deer were proof of the supremacy of European men, and by recreating that supremacy in the image of their own native habitat, they expanded it to all of nature. In the first years some 250 of these animals made the inverse voyage to that of the Maori Battalion—and altogether about 1,000 were brought in. In the woods and vales of New Zealand they found abundant food, a suitable climate and no predators, apart from human beings who, during the permitted seasons and with a proper license, come to shoot at them. And so the noble deer, the European red deer, multiplied. And at the turn of the new century, some people began to notice that these living landscape ornaments, these gentle herbivores susceptible only to firearms, were becoming pests.

They were destroying an ecosystem in which they were not foreseen, invading meadows and pastures, eating the undergrowth and the tender shoots of young trees, leaving the soil to grow thin, at risk of erosion and landslides. And so this protected species was reclassified as harmful, and a great hunt, no longer for sport, began. Squads of armed men were deployed, each getting a government paycheck plus a premium for every animal killed. At the height of the kill—when helicopters were introduced and the deer could be shot from on high by the hundreds every day, not unlike the way Vietnamese peasants were disposed of not very far away—some 50,000 deer were eliminated each year. They were killed not merely by government mandate but in a gigantic hunt not subject to any rules, in which the spoils had become so remunerative as to set off a war between airborne poachers and government regulars with license to kill. In the heat of the deer hunt, when even the helicopters were shot at and set on fire, the exact count of animals culled was lost. Between one and a half and three million are estimated to have been eliminated between the 1930s to the 1970s.

At last, out of this great extermination and its economic returns, a new idea came forth. Rather than hunt for game, why not control and profit from the proliferation of the species? The helicopters would no longer take off to shoot down the deer, but capture them alive. Deer farms were established, expanded, perfected. These were new world factories, conceived on the basis of new world spaces: American-style farm industries in which livestock grazed inside huge, fenced territories. But here, instead of bovines, we had deer, the latest species that men had learned to raise and domesticate. New Zealand, thanks to catastrophe and then slaughter, became the largest producer and exporter of venison in the world.

It hurts to think of those poor animals crowded together in the holds of ships that in the mid-19th century employed three or four months to cross the oceans—and to think of the millions of their descendents who have only escaped the fate of the American bison thanks to the high market price of their flesh. I wonder how many must have died onboard ship, how many had to be captured in England and in Scotland to arrive at that surviving one thousand? Thinking about the deer, I see men. The slave trade: the inverse of this utterly cruel and gratuitous importation. In the one, men are reduced to property, to instruments of work for crude economic gain, the whole legitimated by racist theories. In the other, an animal species is transferred to another continent for no practical purpose at all. An activity that instantly unmasks the ideology of an entire age, revealing the desperate folly at the heart of its rage to dominate.

Deer were brought to New Zealand for one reason above all others, for which all others are mere justification and pretext: to make it seem like home. Because, one day, out cutting wood, someone stopped in the middle of a clearing and saw something that wasn't there, something he missed. And all that landscape which only an instant before had looked familiar, now reminded him he was *thousands and thousands of miles from home*. The whole heavens of his ideology had fanned out over the head of that one colonist to protect him from feeling far from home. Expelling homesickness from that alien landscape made him the master of every place, the measure of every thing, the owner of the right to remake the world in his own image. It meant he didn't have to see that in reality, he was no one: a speck that even on the most up to date maps is invisible, a pawn moving at his own expense on a game board half Risk, half Monopoly.

The European deer restored humanity to those human pawns who also came from England and Scotland, also spent three or four months at sea, all their savings paid out for a journey to a destination from which they could never return. Most were poor peasants, small craftsmen, people who couldn't resign themselves to life in a factory now that machines had deprived them of their livelihood. Later, there were also soldiers. Whether they had to shoot at deer or bison, at Cherokee or Maori, mattered not at all. No one, anywhere, now had the natural right to exist outside the bonds of force and profit radiating out from a single center. There was no more nature, only a citizenship that had to be earned and conquered like a virgin land that must bear fruit, even at the cost of death. The colonists also died: of overwork, of accidents, of diseases that in these frontier places become incurable, or in predatory wars blessed by those who had never set foot outside their mansions, the well-lit houses and libraries of the Old World. Fewer died than did the deer and the Maori, certainly, in a supposed *struggle for life* that was a mystification of a natural law no longer valid. Because the real agents, what rules, the will and the interest of a few individuals, are locked inside minds and bank accounts and have nothing to do with biology.

The last act of this story takes place in the theater where we began. In Italy, on the Gustav Line, where—against those Germans sent to defend with their pure Aryan blood the last gasp of that frenzy of omnipotence that swept every continent for more than a century—the Maori paid their price to be citizens of a land where they were indigenous.

In June, 1940, as the Aquitania left Capetown traveling toward the front, a ghetto was established in my parents' native city, occupied by the Wehrmacht on September 4, 1939, the day after Great Britain, France, Australia and New Zealand entered the war. The Judenrat, under German orders, had to uproot the Jewish population from their homes in the better quarters or in the villages, and force them into the prescribed perimeter. And when, around Christmas, 1941, the Maori Battalion was fighting the Axis troops near Tobruk along with the Poles of the Karpacka Division and the Indians they would meet again in Italy, the ghetto of Zawiercie was fenced with barbed wire, leaving just one entry gate that was patrolled day and night by armed guards. No Jew was allowed out—penalty, death— apart from those 2,500 under police escort who worked as forced labor in a Luftwaffe uniforms factory, and a few, like my grandfather, who was authorized to go on managing the crystal works by request of the new owners. In August, 1942, the Maori serving in the troops commanded by Montgomery had just arrested the advance of Feldmarschall Rommel at El Alamein, when the Gestapo and SS forced 2,000 Jews from their lodgings, herded them into the square and put them on trains for Auschwitz.

In the summer of 1943, when Zawiercie was declared *Judenrein* after the deportation of some 7,000 Jews, the Maori troops were back in camp at Maadi, Egypt, ready for a new destination and for seaborne reinforcements to replenish the huge losses that three years of victorious war in North Africa had produced. On the train that arrived and was registered at Auschwitz-Birkenau on August 27, 1943, were my grandparents, my aunts and uncles, my entire extended family apart from my mother who had escaped the evening before when a guard was distracted, and apart from my father (in hiding with his younger brothers and two nephews aged ten and fourteen), and my mother's cousins who soon after the German invasion, had separately fled toward the Russian zone of Poland, and who were then able to leave the Soviet Union when they were drafted in General Anders' Second Army. While the Maori were landing at Taranto and fighting their way up the Adriatic to the Gustav Line, while they were dying in vain in the second battle of Monte Cassino, the survivors among my family were in hiding, with false papers and bleached hair, lost, hidden, hunted down, one by one betrayed by something or someone, and deported. In March, 1944, when several companies of the 28th Battalion were sent in as reinforcements in a last ditch attempt to dislodge the enemy from their Cassino headquarters, the Hotel Continental and the Hotel des Roses, my mother was captured when she was reported by a Pole who had promised to take her to her father. She remained locked up in a Gestapo prison during the entire battle to breach the Gustav Line. While the Maori, having fought their way up through Tuscany, clustered near the soon-to-be-liberated city of Florence, on July 19, 1944, my mother was being deported to the Auschwitz-Birkenau death camp. "Of the cumulative transport from Sosnowiec and Będzin, 34 men were selected, numbered A-17556 to A-17589, and seven women, numbered A-9800 to A-9806, and were consigned to the camp as *Häftlinge*. The others, among them 276 men, were killed in the gas chambers." My mother, one of those seven women, was assigned to Kanada, the deposit of goods confiscated from the interned and the gassed, even as the Maori were taking Rimini and advancing up the Adriatic with the Eighth Army. In November, while the Maori Battalion was fighting at Cesena, Forlì and Faenza, she was packed into a cattle car headed for Weisswasser, a concentration camp for women in the Sudetenland, where she survived until the Red Army appeared. The Maori soldiers were in Trieste when the war ended for them as well, but they had to wait months before they were sent back down to Taranto to be shipped home. They didn't get to Wellington until January 23, 1946. Only a very few of those who stepped off the Dominion Monarch and were filmed by newsreel crews and cheered by the crowd and met by the *wero* and the *tangi*, the welcome ceremony and that to pay respects to the dead, were among those soldiers who six years before had sailed off on the Aquitania.

When I was a child in Munich, *Hauptstadt der Bewegung*, the "capital of the movement" as the Nazis had called it, I knew nothing of any of this: nothing about the world war set off by the country where I was born, nor about the existence of that people to which I belonged, not to mention the recent catastrophe and how it had left its mark on my family. I was raised in the normality of a comfortable childhood, in a time when peace and prosperity were the only possible future horizons, in a pleasant and peaceful city by then free of any trace of the destruction caused by the bombing. I often listened to the birdsong language my parents spoke to each other, trying to catch words and pieces of it, but without asking myself questions. I knew they were Polish, and that was enough for me. I lived in a house in the center where there were no children, and the tiny nuclear families where I was later allowed to play with other girls gave me no clue that anything was missing. But when we played Cowboys and Indians in one of those girls' courtyard with other children in her apartment block, I was always the only one to volunteer for the redskins' team.

War had entered my home courtesy of my father, who read to me from the story of the *Iliad* at bedtime, and I, hating the Greek woman whose name I bore, grieved for Hector and rooted for the Trojans. I used to draw them too: down below, the mortals divided

in their opposing ranks, and above their heads, the cruel and capricious gods, the lords of war setting one against the other. Even
earlier, I couldn't say just when, I had been given a stuffed animal
that never left my sight, a black cat with a human body, perhaps
in origin a sort of Puss in Boots, although he was dressed in a turban and long brocade coat suitable for a Maharajah. My mother
had made that outfit and left it under the Christmas tree before I
was five. I did not like dolls, apart from one I saw a few years later
in a shop window in Italy and which I absolutely had to have, a
girl-doll with black hair and toast-colored skin wearing a poncho. I
named her Felicitas because I knew that girls from the Andes must
be given Spanish names. Later, when I could read, I chose books
for children set in Amazonia, on the Atlas Mountains among the
Tuareg, in Tibet, Malesia and the Andes. I listened to the radio program "Voices of Foreign Peoples," taping Chinese, Arab and Indian melodies and dirges, indigenous chants and Slavic choruses.
There may even have been a *haka* once, a Maori dance, but then
the cassettes were taped and retaped to make room for Abba and
for American folk and rock. For a long time I dreamed of being an
ethnologist when I grew up, a dream that seems to have come forth
when I learned the word itself.

     None of this could have happened had I not been four years old
in 1968. 1968 was just a time that meant a child got certain particular books and toys; I sensed no direct consequences of the upheav-
als from my family nor even from the city of Munich, not even an
echo. It must have been then—groping and casting about with that
deep intuition that derives from what isn't said and can't be pro-
hibited—that I discovered myself to be the voice of foreign peoples.
Foreign peoples: they were me. It made no difference what threatened, exploited, minority tribe or ethnic group. They were me: I felt
it deep inside. When, my childhood ending, I came to learn what
persecuted people I really did belong to, it was already late. Mere
facts were not enough to reshape a sentiment so huge and at the
same time so precise.

     I knew nothing of the Maori, Nepalese, Indian and Magreb sol-
diers who had come to fight and die on the continent that was anni-
hilating my people. I still don't know whether and how much (beyond all verifiable links of cause and effect, operating more like the

proverbial butterfly that beats its wings and causes an earthquake on the other side of the world) their sacrifice may have contributed so that at least my mother and my father could be saved and I born because they had survived. And yet, here I am at this crossroads, a point of possible, dizzying, terribly objective convergence between my real and imaginary story and that which took place sixty years ago to human beings in flesh and blood. It doesn't matter whether those human beings are my own parents or Maori come from New Zealand; I can only try to unearth their traces by going the opposite way, like salmon going back up river. Set out from information, from documents, dates, bits and pieces; seek to make this accumulated material lay itself out in a map, in knowledge; hope that absorbing it will fill in the blanks and make it all come to life. There's no way to imagine anything real without finding a foothold in your interior life, and yet the marks etched on the soul are in their own way more abstract than a map, as impersonal as any document. And right now I can only think of them as the very image of the *moko* whose scrolls conceal a more recent mark, one of those numbers between A-9800 and A-9806 that after the war, my mother had removed from her arm.

Before and After the Last Battle

Edoardo Bielinski and Anand Gupta, Rome-Cassino, Aug. 2009

Irena Levick and the Szer brothers, Poland 1939—Palestine 1943
Rishon Le Zion, Israel, Oct. 2009

I'd sell my boots and take a cart
just to be with you.
Me without you, you without me,
like a handle without a door,
my kitten, my sweet little bird.

I'd sell handkerchiefs at the railway station
just to be with you.
Me without you, you without me,
like a handle without a door,
my kitten, my sweet little bird.

I'd eat without a table, sleep without a pillow
just to be with you.
Me without you, you without me,
like a handle without a door,
my kitten, my sweet little bird.

I'd sleep at the station, wash the floor
just to be with you.
Me without you, you without me,
like a handle without a door,
my kitten, my sweet little bird.
—*"Di Sapozhkelekh," Yiddish song*

Searching for the Missing

The third day the kid took his place at the gates of the Polish Cemetery of Monte Cassino, he turned toward the list of the war dead behind him, a bit to the right of the folding chair he had been sitting on until a few minutes ago. There were two chairs, actually, strategically placed and in the shade, but the second had been empty for a while. And so he was beginning to grow bored, or beginning to think, think aimlessly, which was more or less the same thing, and possibly risky. He had therefore stood up and begun to walk back and forth around his little encampment, trying to make out the birds he could hear on the high branches, studying the leaves and pine cones on the ground, finally stopping a few inches from the list of the dead. He had his iPod with him, a couple of books, *Corriere dello Sport*, all of them read from top to bottom, a notebook and a pen in his knapsack, plus the day's supply of fliers he'd had printed up in Rome, in that shop where his father had them prepare notes for his students. Just now he had piled his things on the other chair, keeping hold only of his cellphone, with which he'd sent out various texts, the last one reading: "When R U back?" "About 3, Ok?" "Ok" "Need anything?" "Nope." In a plastic bag under the chair there was a large bottle of water, a pack of Vivident Cube gum, and a bag of Chipsters. But he didn't feel like killing time by stuffing something in his mouth, and anyway he'd already had lunch. He'd let himself be persuaded they could leave their stations to eat a plate of pasta for lunch. After the *rigatoni all'arrabbiata*, they'd permitted themselves a *tartufo affogato al caffè*, an adult desert, ice cream with a shot of espresso poured over it.

Now the kid doesn't know what to do with that list of soldiers buried a few meters away, except maybe look under the letter B to see if anyone there has his name, but there's not one Bielinski. That seems odd. He had always thought it was a cheap, second-rate surname, or at least a very common one, although at home they always said, half-joking, half-not, "Now don't sully the Bielinksi name." But even if no namesake of his had been unfortunate enough to die at Monte Cassino, that didn't necessarily mean it was not a second-rate name. Fine, so be it; as if he cared what had happened to the Bielinskis in the war.

The kid had been there in front of the gates of the Polish Cemetery for three days, but he had only set foot inside the first day, out of a sort of obligation to the guy he considered his partner in this matter. He had come there with him in the early morning, when the curved amphitheater of graves was still cool and above all empty, free of visitors and tourists.

They had walked over to the great monument in the center immersed in a circle of white stones, and then further on, to the marble slab below the first step up to the higher tombs, and there they stopped.

"General Anders," he had said. "He died in exile in London, but he wanted to be laid to rest near his soldiers, so he left orders to be brought here."

"Hey, there's a bunch of wreaths and fresh flowers. Cool."

"To you, it's cool. But I can tell you that when they bring you here every two years from the time you're a little kid, you're sick of it up to here."

"Sure, I understand. What do we do now, Edo? Go back?"

"I have to finish preparing. Take a walk around if you want to."

"No, I'm coming with you. Anyway I've already seen this part."

He spread his arms out toward the whole sanctuary, the second kid, but so loosely that you could see it was, in its way, a bow of respect. They had turned their backs on the risers of the dead and walked toward their red- and blue-striped chairs, supplied by the Bielinski family. The other comforts they enjoyed were courtesy of Andy and his family. The car, to begin with, his mother's grey Citroen, which they were able to use because the second kid had recently gotten his driver's license. And there was the room in the bed and breakfast instead of the Bielinski tent pitched at Camping Terme Varroniane, although Edoardo's parents had said: "We'll pay half, certainly. They're right, it's better for you to have a roof over your heads; the weather down there can be unpredictable."

Okay, it was great to have a room. But that comment about the weather betrayed the fact there must have been a consulation between the two sets of parents to agree on the conditions under which they would be allowed to depart, and confirmed the inescapable truth that freedom that is not economic freedom is merely an abstraction. And finally, the excuse being "I'm going to the bathroom," today's lunch had also been paid by Andy.

The first day they had gone off with sandwiches prepared in the salumeria: sandwiches, McVitie's biscuits with chocolate, and fruit: the same provisions they would have taken along on a scooter ride or for a day at the beach. The next day, Sunday, things were more complicated, and so when Andy had said "I'll go and get some pizzas and bring them back" that was okay. When the hour came he found himself alone for the first time. However, the situation had changed. The cemetery had emptied out, but some people were picnicking in the shade in the parking lot; he had seen them when he walked Andy to the car. And so he returned to their chairs and picked up some leaflets that read, all in capitals, ZAGINIENI WE WŁOSZECH, "Missing in Italy" and tried to figure out, as he walked back, who would be most likely to take them.

"Przepraszam," he began, excusing himself more with the women than with the men, and especially with the mothers busy handing our food and drinks. "Forgive me if bother you again; I'm sorry to disturb your lunch. The hand-out we gave you back there at the cemetery, well, I don't know if you looked at it, but it deals with something very important. Many Poles who've come to this country to find work, honest work, have disappeared without leaving a trace. At least a hundred of them. The police in Poland have been searching for them for some years now. However, there are still some eighty of them about whom we have no word at all, no trace. It's a very serious, terrible thing; we need to do everything we can to find out what happened to them."

"Ah," said the Polish mothers, dubious but polite, studying him.

"You see, a lot of people come here to make some money, not much money, doing hard jobs, exhausting jobs, harvesting tomatoes and things like that, and they use them like slaves, they lock them up in old, broken-down houses without electricity or water. Like in the lagers, and the Communist ones where they deported the soldiers you've come here to visit," said Edoardo, who was as surprised as anyone by that comparison that had come to mind, and the attention it received. So, those trips to the cemetery hadn't been totally useless, nor all those stories about that faraway country of theirs that had been sold off cheap, all those speeches to "you children who were the first to be born and grow up with a free Poland, and don't understand what a privilege that is, what a great and miraculous fortune!"

"Like in the lagers. Where you die...pffft. It's intolerable! Poland is a democratic country, a member of the European Union for five years now," he went on, pleased with his rhetorical skills, worthy of his father making a speech at some congress, although he realized he was losing sight of what he wanted to say. But he couldn't stop talking, and the more his remarks focused on principles, the more complicated they became, as he trudged along brandishing the words and damned grammar of that language passed down through some kind of innate patriotism. For the first time, facing those families passing around drinks and bottles of beer from their coolers, so few (compared to the hordes coming out of the buses, where he could only hope to get a flier in hand), Edoardo Bielinski could see who he was addressing, and see, in their faces, something of himself.

What did he look like? How old would you say? He had always been one of the tallest at school, and he had never been asked to show a document in any of those places where you needed to be eighteen to go in. When he went to parties he had begun to give himself a few extra years; the first time, on account of a girl who said she was in her second year at Rome-Tor Vergata University. He liked her, and if he hadn't come back with "Philosophy, Rome-Sapienza" that would have been the end of that. As it happened, the matter had ended there, but in other occasions he had met other girls older than he was, and so now he automatically made himself older, sometimes just for the fun of seeing how far he could push it: from twenty he had gone to twenty-two and then, on occasion, to twenty-four. But standing in front of the gates of the Monte Cassino cemetery trying to find some lost souls who had disappeared was not the same as dishing out tall tales to a girl at a party. Not only did he need to seem adult, or more adult than he was, he had to be something more. A person whom, if you knew something terrible, you would trust enough to tell it to. And he—with his Polish dipped in Romanesco, his curly blond hair in a ponytail so it didn't fall to his shoulders, that mane of his he should get rid of but couldn't bring himself to, his oversized jeans and T-shirt—did he seem to be that person?

It was up to him to get people to talk to him; Andy could do no more than help out with the fliers. But Edoardo had never thought about how Poles might react to his friend, so minute, so elegant, that when they went to parties he sometimes pretended Andy was the son of a maharajah from Kashmir. "Really?" the girls would gush, "Say something to me in Indian." And Andy would recite some rigmarole he claimed was a hymn to Krishna, and in the end he was always the one most likely to score.

What did they look like, these two standing at either side of the gates? Black and White, as Mr. Dowland, their math teacher, called them—like the little fox terrier on the whisky bottle—because from elementary school on up Edoardo Bielinski and Anand Gupta had been joined at the hip. They looked like two kids paid to hand out leaflets; that was the truth of it. How many people threw them away thinking they were advertising fliers? Luckily there were no trash baskets before you got out to the parking lot. The thought made Edoardo feel better, and he began to speak once more about how too little effort had gone into finding the missing, and the fact that others risked the same fate.

"Paradoxically, now that Italy has approved a law making it a crime to be undocumented or to hire an undocumented worker, these criminals may find it preferable to exploit workers with European passports; it's less of a risk. And so we also need to call attention to what has happened to protect those who may find themselves in the same situation in the future," Edoardo went on, battling with words—"undocumented," "legislative statute"—that he didn't know in Polish. The anger bubbling up in him as he struggled to paraphrase them made him stumble over the rest.

"Say it in Italian; we've been living here for years," a young, blond mother said: not real blond but nicely done, and the toenails visible inside her in orthopedic sandals were polished too. The car from which she had just produced some packaged snacks for her childen, a girl and a boy, was an Opel Astra with Bologna plates: far from where the missing Poles had disappeared, and even more unlikely that this middle-class Polish family had ever had anything to do with 21st century slave traders. And if instead some freed slave from the fields of Puglia were to turn up, if someone said to him, "I know a lot better than you what you're talking about; I've been there," what would he do?

"Would you like a beer?"

"No thanks."

"Coca Cola? Not even water?"

"I'm waiting for my friend who went to get some pizzas, but you know, I might just accept a a sip of beer."

"Take a cold one out of the car."

"Oh *pani*, thank you, that's very kind. I just want a sip so I can make a toast."

"Just take one, and we'll finish it."

Edoardo went to get a half-liter can of beer out of the cooler, sniffing the air inside the car perfumed by some chemical flowers over the dashboard. He filled the plastic cup the Polish mother had brought him, and raising it to his lips, he felt his voice begin to tremble.

"Na zdrowie. Na zdrowie Polski I Polaków we Włoszech!" To the health of Poland and the Poles in Italy!

"Na zdrowie," said both husband and wife, taking a sip from the beer cans they had in hand.

"Um, nothing," he said after taking another sip. "I just wanted to ask if I could leave you some of these things, these leaflets. To hand out to people you meet. You know, like in church; I don't know if there is a Polish service where you live, maybe you could give them to your parish priest. There are pictures of the missing and an address to write to if you think you have some news. Also my email and cellphone number," he said, even as he realized he had better say who he was. "Edoardo, Edoardo Bielinski. Edward. I'm a journalist, um, not quite yet but I'm working on it."

"Aha," said the young Polish mother, with a smile that was either incredulous, or convinced, but in any case accepting the flier he held out. "Yes, we can try in church, even though we don't go every Sunday. We live in the country, not in town."

"Dziękuję, dziękuję bardzo. Thank you!" said Edoardo, feeling his hands lighter and not much caring just then whether they believed him or saw him for what he was: a privileged kid, or rather one who been given a privilege when he was born. On that day, March 21, 1990, just after 8:26 a.m., an angel had appeared by his cradle. The angel had come to the Policlinico Gemelli hospital bringing, not a medal of the Virgin of Częstochowa, nor a tiny gold bracelet with coral beads on it, or any of those other large or small, useful or well-wishing presents that grandparents, aunts and uncles, relatives, friends and colleagues had brought to his parents during visiting hours, filling the room with flowers and voices in many languages. It was just a sheet of white paper on which it was written that Edoardo Radosław Bielinski, firstborn of Giorgio Bielinski and Flavia D'Angelo, was a citizen of the Italian Republic. And while the baby was sucking his first milk at the breast, his father headed out into the Roman traffic to put his name down at the Registry of Births.

When Anand came back at 3 p.m. as he had promised in his text message, true to that obstinate English punctuality that was almost embarrassing in Rome, Edoardo was pacing back and forth from one side to the other of the entrance, nervous. There were not one but two groups inside the cemetery, and the first had been there for nearly an hour and might come out at any moment. Alone, however, he would only be able to hand out half as many of his leaflets; elementary mathematics, there was no way around it.

"Whoah, good thing!" he shouted at his associate when he saw him coming down the final stretch of the road, and his hand was already out to give Andy a pile of fliers.

"I told you I'd be here in time. I timed it..."

"Yeah, timed it. I've been here since 2:00. These people eat lunch while we're just finishing breakfast."

"Sure, when they're at home. But around here where do you find a place to give you something to eat before 12:30?"

"Andy, know what it means, an organized tour? It means the organizers make an agreement with the hotel or the restaurant, because it's in their interests too. That way they can serve the group, and then their usual clients."

"Right. I didn't think of that."

"Okay, no problem. Where have you been?"

"Guess."

"Took a nap? Confess, you bastard."

"No, totally wrong track."

"You went online and chatted with friends and relatives far and wide?"

"Okay, that was easy. But mostly something else. You'll never get there."

"Come on, out with it; we've got to prepare for action."

"I found you a beach."

"What?"

"Reading up on the battle of Monte Cassino online—because I said to myself it was dumb to be here and be totally ignorant—I discovered that where the front ended, the sea began. Minturno, Scauri, Formia. Even from here, we can leave and we're there in less than an hour."

"I don't believe this. You leave me here with four busloads of Poles that I have no idea how to deal with, and meanwhile you're thinking about how to get to the beach?"

"So? What's the problem? This place closes at six and when we're packed up, we don't have the right to do whatever we want? Or you think we can't move from Cassino because we might come across the third cousin of some missing Pole? Jesus, Edo, all I wanted to do was arrange something fun after days of being stuck here between the mountains and the tombstones. You do know that that I'm leaving for the Maremma and then in September, bye-bye, I'm off to America? These are the last times we can go to the beach together, you know."

"Okay. I don't know about you, but I didn't bring a swim suit. So, I should go swimming in my underwear? Bad idea..."

"I have a suit; in fact I have several and I can lend you one. And I borrowed two towels from the room."

"Right, so I can see that this plot has been on the boil for a while. Fuck if it just came to your mind this afternoon."

At this remark, the sparks between them by now almost spent,

Anand stared at the ground. Among the many things that distinguished him from this person he considered his best friend—or rather the most important person he knew who was not a member of his family—there were some huge and obvious ones. Different origins, appearance, character, even interests: these he could contemplate quite calmly as facts of nature. And then there were small differences that one tended to forget about, such as the fact that his bag for the trip had been packed by the Filipina housemaid.

"Dolores probably thought I was going to the beach," he said, his eyes on the toes of his shoes: a pair of white Converse All Stars, the one point of contact between his wardrobe and that of Edoardo.

"Yeah, Dolores. Right, I forgot you were a Kashmiri prince. On that subject, maybe tomorrow we'll go and look for your fellow countrymen at the British Cemetery, what do you say?"

Andy understood that this was a big conciliatory gesture and said okay just in time. The crescendo of voices coming from the cemetery now made it clear they should take their positions and hand out their leaflets to the first wave of tourists emerging. At first he was kind of amazed by them; he couldn't quite believe they were still so...so super-Polish in every way, with their acrylic sweat suits and their fake Nikes, those droopy moustaches hanging down, those big women in flowered somethings you didn't know whetherr to call house-dresses or sundresses, that atmosphere of hapless, hopeless Eastern Europe when it was now more than twenty years since Comunism had come to an end. And this was not something he was expecting, because the little that he knew directly about that world made him think of it as a vast land of conquest, a land that began where the Bielinski family came from and kept on going beyond that of the Guptas, a market in expansion for the sector his father was in, luxury goods. Three boutiques in Moscow; one recently opened in Baku, and even one in the old Kazak capital Almaty. And Manil Gupta who came home to report the grumbling about all those magnificent creations ending up on the backs of the wives and concubines of ex-Communist yahoos, Russian gangsters who made the sheikhs look like paragons of good taste. And the designers grumbled too, for they'd so often seen him speak with reverence about a perfectly cut diamond or the glow of a batch of emeralds, and this was something the Bulgari gem manager was so proud of as to talk about it at table with his wife and children.

Poland, so far as Anand Gupta was concerned, was part of that huge nebulous orbit in which more and more people were better off, better groomed and better dressed, or at least more attuned to fashions in the West. He was struck by the way these people looked, though, people who had after all come here as tourists, and therefore were not poor, because the real poor he had seen in India, they were right outside the airport at New Delhi when he went to visit his grandparents. And no, that was not pleasant for a child who had grown up in the opulent heights above piazzale Flaminio, although there had almost always been the windscreen of a car between him and them. Real poverty was something that took your breath away on first impact; it was made of people in actual rags, barefoot, dirty, often lame and toothless people. Real poverty was genuine, the *real thing*. It was so ubiquitous, so absolute that it took on a sort of dignity of its own; Andy didn't know how to explain it, but it was different from these losers with ugly clothes and stupid moustaches.

Such were the thoughts spinning around in Anand Gupta's head, and as they spun they collided with the tiny photographs on the leaflets, shrunk to the size of postage stamps so they would all fit. Moustaches there too. Huge moustaches, drooping moustaches, sad moustaches. Moustaches that looked even more desolate because of the vacant stares on those identity cards, because the wearers were among the missing in Italy, because the flier ink turned the brown to tow-blond hair you saw on the tourists into a uniform grey-black.

"Where do these people come from?" he had asked Edoardo at the end of the first day.

"Got me," Edoardo said, but the question began to eat at him, and he began to note every detail: the license plates on the buses right down to the words on the wreaths brought in to lay on the graves.

"From all over," he informed his associate, and so it seemed that deploying themselves at the gate of the Monte Cassino cemetery had been an excellent strategic move.

"I mean, from the country, from the provinces?" Andy had asked, and Edo, without being certain because he had only been able to recognize the names of the largest cities, said yes. It was an

illumination; according to the book from which he'd learned about
the disappearances, most of the missing came from scattered, remote areas of Poland. He said nothing, however, about his trium-
phant sense he was on the right track, partly out of superstition, but
mostly because he knew his friend was not there because he really
cared about finding any of these lost souls. He knew that Anand
Gupta has come with him to Monte Cassino to do him a favor, to
help him out, so they could hang around together before one of
them registered to study something or other in an Italian university, while the other went off to get an economics degree from the
best department in the United States. He was there out of friendship. It was in the name of their friendship, in the name of what was
and what they feared might be no more and in the dogged hope it
would survive that Andy and Edo were standing on either side of
the gate without saying much to one another about what was going
through their heads.

Anand, for instance, did not share his thoughts about the acylic
sweat suits and the moustaches with Edoardo, not wanting to hear
his friend come out with "Sure, for you the only normal people are
rich and good looking," but that also meant he didn't mention what
he had observed without realizing it, which was that in the scale of
Polish hard luck any visitor to the Monte Cassino cemetery, single
or in a group, must be a lot better off than a missing slave. And
therefore, those routes that wound up in a tomato field or some other God-forsaken plot growing vegetables would never cross those
that led to the remains of General Anders' Army, and so Edoardo
Bielinski and Anand Gupta might as well fold up their camp chairs
and enjoy a few days between the beaches and country fairs from
Gaeta to Scauri.

But no, Andy kept his mouth shut, or rather, he stood there saying "przepraszam"; he'd been saying it since day two, and now,
as he handed out his fliers more or less in march-step with Edoardo, he was also saying "proszę" and "proszę panstwo", and the
first time he heard him Edoardo sent him an amazed and admiring
glance, thinking, hey look at this guy who just doesn't care about
the color of his skin, look what he can do with those good manners
of his, they seem to be the most important thing in the world.

"Hey partner, and if I started to say swear words would you

repeat them after me too just like a parrot?" he said to him when they were in the car, heading toward someplace decided by Andy, Edo was sprawled in the passenger seat, exhausted. Exhausted but quite happy to go to the beach, and that too he didn't admit, or rather he did, but only in the way he made fun of his friend.

"Sure. But I would say them with style," said Andy, adding that it didn't take a genius to repeat two words and understand what they meant when you heard them hundreds of times in a day.

"Okay, if it's so easy, let's see how you do with this. "Trzydzieścitrzy."

"What? Say it again."

"Trzydzieścitrzy."

Andy tried to say it but stumbled, and a "ch ch" came out that sounded like a baby making train noises; he laughed too and asked Edoardo whether he had just screwed up the pronunciation of some particularly filthy obscenity, "because if so, life must be tough for the Pole who wants to talk dirty."

"Nah. It just means thirty-three. I thought of it because when I was a kid I used to trip up on it myself, damn it."

"Well if you want a rematch, I'll give you something to say in Hindi, but for today, I'll be nice and spare you."

"You're scared of losing, admit it. Polish is rougher."

"Well, I wouldn't bet on that, but when you think that it's a language spoken on this same continent, it's pretty crazy."

"Yep. Crazy language, spoken by crazy Polish people. Freaks 'em right out. Remember Chad Jones who used to try to razz me by calling me Radosław? *Hey guys, here he comes, our Rad-o-sław! So you made three baskets, who do you think you are, Radosław Bielinski?* And me like a fool I keep telling him, *My name is Edoardo* when all I had to do was say *Call me whatever the fuck you want, but at least pronounce it right, asshole!* But when you're a kid, you never get there. What ever happened to him, that idiot who thought he was God's gift?"

"No idea, went back to America," said his associate with that supreme indifference that was worse than the worst contempt— perhaps the reason why even the biggest bastards that came through the Rome International School had always left him alone, even when he was no longer sweet little Anand Gupta. Everyone's little Andy, so nice , so diligent, with that milk-chocolate skin and great big eyes, every mother's favorite, friend of all the little girls, teacher's pet because he did well in all subjects and excellently in the most important ones. But too much of a regular guy to end up as a mere grind, and above all, too tight with that eternal renegade Edoardo, whose friendship and protection he had mysteriously earned from grade one.

"Bielinski, get rid of that pigsty under your desk immediately or the next time nobody's going to blink before giving you a demerit, understand?"

"Yes, Mrs. Fergusson."

But two weeks later the desk was once again a mess, and his report card always bore the same comment. "The student shows interest and learns quickly, but is weak on discipline, order and application."

Every time he went to meet the teacher—every time he could make it— Giorgio Bielinski came out more exasperated, he who'd gone to a Swiss boarding school, a choice that had cost his poor parents a lot of extra work, work that he now understood and appreciated. Driving home he would regularly explode "that's where we should have sent him, in fact that's what we're going to do" until Flavia gently touched his arm saying, "sure, calm down," and began rattling off the usual arguments in defense of their son. Probably all that was needed was a "calm down" to restore that attitude of detachment and balance he was so dismayed to be jerked out of, for Giorgio, had he not been born and raised and remained a practicing Roman Catholic, was practically a Buddhist. And therefore Giorgio Bielinksi, on his way upstairs in the elevator, was already once again a father capable of speaking to his son without raising his voice or losing his calm.

"Edoardo, come here a minute. You know better than I do what I have to say to you. In fact, you tell me."

"The usual story, order, the rules must be respected...is that it?"

"Precisely. And will you now tell me what you intend to do about it?"

"Try harder, I suppose."

"No, that's not good enough. You must tell me how, concretely, you intend to face the problem."

"Okay. I'm going to set the alarm earlier so I don't get there late, and remember when the Tipp-Ex is used up because without it, I have to correct by hand and that makes a mess…"

"Ah, Tipp-Ex. You know Edoardo perhaps you don't realize that it's because of just this kind of tomfoolery that your marks are regularly lower than they should be."

"Hey, Papà, it makes me furious too, you know."

"Oh really? Well then perhaps you don't realize that we are not rich like the parents of your friend Anand, who by the way has never had the least problem at school. We're not barons either, although considering those academic barons who run the universities, we're not doing so badly. We're not doing so badly, mind you, because in our day there was still a tiny bit of room for a person of merit with no connections. But you can forget about that today—understand?"

"But Papà, I'm not even in high school!"

"Yes. But you are no longer a child. And you're not stupid. We wanted to give you and your sister a more international education, and that means a substantial burden for us, do you understand?"

At this point Giorgio Bielinski would decide he had done his duty, as usual in vain, and therefore that was enough this time too.

"So when is your next game?"

"On Saturday, against the kids in Tenth, including that cretin Chad Jones who's totally pissed because he's always been the best at all the team sports. Are you coming?"

"Sorry, I'll be in Brussels. But I'll make sure I get there for the finals."

"Okay, but this is better than the finals. This is going to be pure revenge, you know?"

"Mamma will be there; I'll tell her now. I'll tell your grandfather Radek, too, he'll be pleased. And you, champion: keep the Bielinski name flying high."

Edoardo, it was clear, was itching to get in front of the TV to catch the Roma soccer goals and NBA results, and his father, who could see him yearning, let him go.

Maybe that was the moment, on the way to the kitchen to tell Flavia about their talk, that he began to frame a strategy to put an end to this farce that had been going on for eight years. Flavia, stirring the boiling spaghetti, said, "Well, he says it himself; why don't we begin to seriously consider sending him to a good public liceo? He's close to finishing now."

They would discuss it again in the summer, when the kids were off at camp or somewhere and the silence in the evening was unusual, even too much sometimes. It would have taken very little time to come to a decision in perfect agreement had it not been for the fact that the transfer would mean losing a year.

"Let's not worry about it. At least he didn't go to one of those Italian middle schools where the kids can lose their way for ever."

In the end Giorgio persuaded Flavia that Edoardo could study for the middle school exam on his own. If he just procured the textbooks and sat down and studied, he could achieve the dusting of history, geography and Italian literature he needed to pass.

"Still, it would be only fair to offer him some incentive, some reward if he passes. We could invest, let's say, a part of the money we would have spent on tuition in something he likes. Can you think of something?"

It was a perfect political move and it amazed Flavia, who thought, not for the first time: what a shame, if this country were not so hopelessly divided into political fiefdoms, had her husband any choice but to keep his distance from the communists (for he hadn't the least interest in dealing with any of the other parties) that talent of his that emerged even in family administration might have been used differently, for the benefit of all. She could think of nothing to add beyond suggesting the sum that Edoardo might use as he pleased. But that wasn't what happened because Professor Bielinski, returning from a think tank conference on new EU member states, flying across the skies of United Europe, had a revelation: a year's subscription to the soccer stadium. Afterwards he was unsure whether the magical lure of AS Roma had done the trick, or whether having studied for the exam so quickly had allowed Edoardo discover the joy of competition, and although he might not be in shape to run a marathon, he could make a sprint of two hundred meters. But once he got to the Liceo Tasso, things continued to go well. Maybe it was simply that he was maturing, as Flavia had always maintained, or maybe it was that in an illustrious but progressive school like the Tasso, certain formal scholastic deficits could be overlooked. Edoardo himself seemed so pleased with the new school and his new friends that he he even stopped playing baskbetball and making any reference to his previous life, apart from Anand Gupta.

During his high school years Edo kept in daily touch with Andy via Facebook, messenger and texts, and he took him along to a party or two as a "prince from Kashmir." ("Hey, why Kashmir?" Anand asked him, the third or fourth time his friend said that. "We come from Uttar Pradesh, much farther south." "Of what?" "Yeah, I knew it...") At times, in perfect contradiction with his political views, he would disappear like a thief in the reassuring luxury of his friend's Parioli house, returning at supper time with a "Hi, Ma; I'm not eating anything," which made Flavia feel a certain inconfessable tenderness.

"Filled yourself with junk food?" she prodded.

"No, no, I was at Andy's and they filled me up with those stuffed things of theirs, and chutney and various sauces, and it seemed, you know, not polite to refuse."

"Oh, I see," she said, putting her head in the refrigerator ("there's a mozzarella and some fruit if you get hungry") so that he wouldn't see her smiling.

Flavia, when she saw her son and his Indian friend together, had always thought of Tonio Kröger, and then she'd re-read the novel for an article on Thomas Mann and Benjamin Britten and saw that in reality the cards had strangely been reshuffled, and that her tall athletic blond son was in fact the one with the emotional, changeable nature attributed to the artist, while Andy had seemed to be the balanced one from the very beginning, and beneath his dark looks, had a bourgeois soul so solid you couldn't find the like in this day and age. Yes, he really was a sort of complete young gentleman, for whom every value was still in its proper place: duty, money, culture, family, friendships. Anand Gupta's world was as graceful, ordered and fixed as if it reproduced the heavens' starry vault.

Flavia recalled the time she had gone to collect Edoardo who'd been invited for "a sort of Christmas party Indian style" as Anand's mother had put it, for which Flavia the day before had bought a box of Lego to build a Star Wars space ship. She knew the festival was called Diwali, but hadn't expected to see the house lit up in every corner with lanterns and sweet-smelling candles, all those stripes and waves of light that made the colors of the divans and cushions sparkle, all those glitterng fabrics that Anand's mother had brought in, first for herself and then for the ladies of the international community, until finally a brass plaque declared the presence in the building of *Shrila Gupta, Architect. Contemporary designer from India.* On that occasion Mrs Gupta was not the tiny woman in front of the school wearing (apart from some Bulgari jewelry) trousers and low-heeled shoes; she wore a rose-pink sari woven with threads of gold that glimmered in the infinite candle flames, and after she had offered sweets and spiced tea (her hands be-ringed and painted with delicate patterns up to her wrists) she led her out to the terrace, where Flavia found her son lit up by other lanterns and sparklers that he was holding out over the railing and spinning around.

Did you see that, Ma?" Edoardo said when they were heading home in the car. "These guys do Halloween, Christmas and New Year's all in one," and his cheeks were still red in the ruthless hygienic white light of the bathroom when he was putting on his pyjamas. A Polish peasant just come out of *A Thousand and One Nights,* or better, just back from some planet furnished in high Renaissance splendor on a set in Hollywood. They would never be able to provide anything like the equivalent at home, thought Flavia. No amount of unity, domestic harmony and attention could ever compete with something so far beyond the Bielinski virtues and their diligence. It wasn't even a matter of wealth or class; it was that the Bielinskis might be a wonderful family as much as they liked, they could even be proud of themselves and transmit that pride to their children, but they could never rid themselves of all those stories of flight and of mass graves. They could never free the sofa and the dining room table of all those exiled guests, those former soldiers in the Second Army Corps, in Berling's Army, in the Armia Krajowa, the Home Army that led the Warsaw Uprising, of all the deported who, while Flavia took away the *scialatielli* and served the fish *all'acqua pazza,* made the room resound with the word *lager* in all the seven declinations of Polish, without it being very clear, often, what kind of camp it was, whether a work camp, prison camp, concentration camp or death camp and whether it had been built to please Stalin or Hitler. Nor could Flavia prevent them from repeating, like a fairy tale, the story of little Giorgio held hostage by a state hostage to another state while grandmother Dorka, poor woman, wept every night and threatened, "I'm going back, Radek, I'm going back to Poland" until finally grandfather found someone willing to smuggle the boy in return for some expensive American scientific text, and so two-year-old Jerzik arrived in Rome all by himself on his little white legs.

"Grandmother, but really all by himself?"

"Yes, Edzui darling, because if I had gone they wouldn't have let me out again and they certainly wouldn't have given permits to my parents, who had been looking after him until then."

"Why Babcia?"

"Because the whole of Poland was like a prison."

Even on Flavia's side there were memories of bombing raids and police reprisals, great monstrous memories like that of the explosion of the *Caterina Costa*, leviathan of steel flung in twisted slivers from the port of Naples all the way up the hill to Capodimonte. There were high school friends who had died on the Vomero during the Quattro Giornate, and all the bitterness—after Naples became the symbol of a country that would stoop to anything to get by—of how little that sacrifice was honored. Her parents, her mother especially, might never have spoken about it, had they not come together with their Polish in-laws on holidays and anniversaries, when her father felt compelled to throw himself into a suffering-and-hopeless-heroism competiton, or at least to try to save some shred of Italian, or better, Neapolitan honor.

"See Radek," he would say, after riffling through his bookshelves, "this is the photo of those lads, those Italian patriots. It wasn't taken by some nobody; no, it was taken by the great Robert Capa, but nobody remembers them anyway."

No, casa Bielinski could never be made into a place out of time and space, some far, far galaxy. Flavia understood perfectly what Edoardo sought in Andy—even in these times that seemed utterly of the here and now however much a part of history, the present an outpost of the past—but it was far more mysterious to her what tied his friend Anand Gupta to him. For example: why had he agreed to spend a week with him at Cassino, pursuing the dreams of glory and justice that so oddly moved her son?

Did he feel obliged simply because they were friends, was that all? Andy was probably going to be bored stiff down there at the cemetery, poor kid.

Flavia, like all mothers, and even more than others, some of whom were capable of alarming comments ("Just think, Martina and he might get together, a perfect son in law!"), Flavia adored Anand Gupta, she trusted Anand Gupta, she was grateful to the fates that had united—yes, united—Andy and her son. But understanding, that was beyond her.

What made their house so attractive to Andy, a house so much smaller, messier and old-fashioned than his own, with fewer interesting games and toys apart from the basketball hoop on the terrace, and yet at times used by him like a real haven? The only explanation she had been able to come up with over the years was that the kid found their house a sort of intermediary terrain between his own environment and this place he happened to be growing up: Rome, Italy. That the Bielinskis were like one of those magic doors in a fairy tale that you could go in and out of without the risk of being stranded in another world. But even this theory, if she thought about it, did not quite convince her.

And so she was pleased when around 9:30 that evening she called Edoardo and he answered immediately and not in monosyllables as he had before, and when asked how it was going shouted "Great! We're having mussels and *frittura mista* in a little place in front of the sea at Scauri! We even went swimming. Andy, the genius, organized everything."

"Can I speak to him a moment?" she ventured.

"Okay, here's my partner, Ma."

"Very good idea, Anand. Are you having a nice time?"

"Yes, Flavia, very pretty places here, a beautiful landscape. Maybe we'll go and see the abbey tomorrow; it looks very impressive from where we are. It's supposed to be such an important site, so it must be worth a visit."

"Oh, do that!" said Flavia, but meanwhile Edo had taken possession of his phone "before you start asking Andy how our research is going."

"I wouldn't dream of it. Now listen, Grandfather Radek wants to know if you have consulted his precious books."

"What books are those?"

"The ones about the battle, Edoardo. Don't tell me you didn't even bring them along?"

"I brought them, I brought them, but only to make sure you didn't sniff them out somewhere in the house. You do know, however, that that's not exactly what I'm interested in. But hey, maybe I'll have a look, just so he doesn't feel bad. In any case, I have them, Ma, right on the table in the bed and breakfast."

And there they would have remained, unmoving and untouched, if Anand (when Edoardo fell asleep as sweetly as a baby and began to snore loudly) having switched off the computer after various communications with cousins from Australia to California, had not begun to peruse the spines of that pile of books on the table.

Among those written in the incomprehensible Polish language, there was one in English, *An Army in Exile,* whose author was even familiar: he was the one with all the flowers and ribbons on his tomb, Lt. General W. Anders C.B. Whatever C.B. meant. He drew the book out of the pile cautiously so the ones above it didn't fall and disturb his friend who was snorting and flailing about in his sleep, although as he opened it he thought maybe he should wake him, give him a shake so he would quiet down and he himself could go to sleep, and while he considered that move and possibly buying some ear plugs, he gazed at the portrait of the Lt. General next to the title page. A man with a dark cap bearing decorations, a beige or khaki-colored military shirt, a moustache on his upper lip. More Polish moustaches! But this moustache was quite different from those he'd seen on Anders' compatriots here in Italy and those missing, different too from what some of Andy's relatives back in India wore, the kind that—although you often see them in Bollywood films—he liked to call "a Paki moustache." This moustache was more like what Clark Gable wore in *Gone with the Wind,* or George Clooney in the film where he was supposed to imitate him. No, it was still different. It was a military moustache worn by a high ranking officer of another time. There was nothing oily about it, no hint of the would-be Lothario, the aging, second-rate Latin Lover. And so, drawn by that miraculously proud and perfect moustache, Andy stayed up late for nights reading a memoir of war, prison and exile by General Władysław Anders, commander of the Second Polish Corps.

Going to Meet Irka

"Tell me the real reason. Why are you going to Israel?" My mother is on the phone. It's 8 a.m. the day before I leave.

"I've told you why. But I can't talk now. I have to take the kid to school."

She must have woken in a confused state and she does not want to hang up while still in the grip of that unease generated by plans to her incomprehensible, plans that might conceal other purposes. I will call her back, therefore as soon as I am home alone.

We go over it again: I'm off for three days to speak with her cousin Zygmunt's wife about how they came to be part of the Polish army.

"Haven't I told you everything already? Everything that Irka told me. I gave you her phone number and you talked to her too."

"Yes, but only to ask if she was willing to meet me. These are not things you can discuss on the phone, when you don't know what language you want to speak and whether you understand each other sufficiently."

"But are you writing a history, or a novel?"

It wasn't the first time my mother had asked me this. A question that wasn't quite rhetorical but certainly delivered an opinion: I was going much too far. I had told her that precision was important to me; told her that it's just because I am *not* a historian that I needed to see the place where Irka lives, her house, pick up those details that I can't even guess I need, look this woman in the face and compare her with what I remember from my childhood.

"But have you ever met Irka?"

If only I had the albums full of photos she always snapped with such zeal, I could have shown her the evidence, the documentary

proof of those perhaps two times we went to visit our relatives in
Israel and their visits to Munich in turn. But just now, on the phone,
I don't really wish to triumph over my mother's memory, an archive that is beginning to crumble, and brushing off my fright, I
face the fact she doesn't believe me. Memory against memory: it
is never enough, even when you're not dealing with someone near
ninety years old. As for the person I'm going to see, I can only hope
the layers of life's terrain deposited in her mind have been better
preserved from erosion. That was my impression when I spoke to
her and when I put together what my mother had said afterwards,
that "haven't I told you everything already?" which amounted to a
brief account punctured by various unlikely details.

Irka, she told me, came from Wilno, that is Vilnius, then part
of Poland, and she came (and it was typical of my mother to say
so) from a very good family. She had met her cousins in the lager,
and from the lager they had been able to escape and join the Polish
Army, "the one you're interested in, Anders' Army."

She and Zygmunt had stayed in Palestine while Dolek, the eldest of the Szer brothers, who had been a doctor before the war and
was an officer, continued on with the Poles to Italy. "To Monteca-
tini, no, Monte Cassino, I mean the one your book's about."

"Right, Mamma, excellent. But just a moment now, which lager? Russian or German?"

No reply. I had pressed her with questions like "In Siberia, or
somewhere else?" and she had replied somewhat annoyed, "I don't
know, in the lager." A lager was a lager and that was that; why in
God's name did I need to know more? As if the lager were a place
in absolute, where anything could happen, even things against lager rules, even the impossible.

"Did you say they *escaped*?" I tried to ask, and she repeated
the same story, perhaps saying "got out" instead of "escaped" but
without being aware there was a difference. To be in a lager was utterly normal; to meet someone in a lager was equally normal. "They
met in such and such lager" was the same as to say "they met at
university" and if getting out, and in a group, was all the more unlikely, it is still the case that every story of survival is so unimpeach-
able that we take it for good no questions asked, as if this too were
governed by a law that is no less than a miracle.

It seems that the largest percentage of Polish Jews who escaped the Shoah were saved because they were deported to Soviet gulag camps, but my mother doesn't know that and I doubt that Irka, whom I called just after speaking to my mother to remind her I'm arriving, knows either.

"I can't walk," she told me in her English, which was rather better than I'd expected, and I assured her that I knew that, no problem, I would get a taxi to her apartment.

"Very well, I look forward to see you."

The woman I recalled was all in that voice: calm, composed but in no way sweet; a lovely voice that matched her blue eyes, blue-grey like a turtledove, but the turtledove came to mind because of her voice. Irka's eyes came back to me later that day as I cast about for a present for her, a scarf, a necklace, something plausible for a person who had undergone various operations from the pelvis on downward, had pins and implants that meant she had to walk with a brace, and was now disabled because of the immobility.

"A wreck," my mother had said, as always rather quick to point out she was superior to her age-mates in physical and motor terms. In the end I hadn't the nerve to buy one particular necklace of a very frivolous blue, but that labored search of mine, all that painstaking effort to procure the shopping bag that would show I had made the purchase in a fancy Milan boutique—it all came to nothing because I left the bag in the taxi. I had the wrong street name and so the taxi driver got the right address via speaker phone, in his rough Hebrew, and Irka, I couldn't tell what she understood, and didn't know how nervous she was, and so when he told me "It's here," all I could think about was getting out quickly.

It was late Saturday morning, Shabbat, and even downtown Tel Aviv was almost deserted. I stood in front of a newly built complex on that suburban main street: a bank, a shopping center, both closed, and that tall building, it must have been ten floors, that supposing it was a residence for the elderly looked utterly incongruous. Luckily there was a café open where in the worst case, I could call another taxi. That semicircular shaped door with the Israeli flag above it, star of David flapping in a hot wind I assumed was *hamsin*; could that entranceway worthy of some city government office be the one I wanted? I didn't know Hebrew, that was the trouble; I was even less able to read it than to decipher a few spoken words or say I was unable to speak it. *Ani lo m'daberet ivri:* inside the door I was once again forced to admit it after saying "Irena Sher?" to the doorman. He spoke to a coworker in dreadlocks, and she spelled out "Three-Four-Five" in her Ethiopian English. It was only when I was inside the elevator pressing the button for the third floor, that I realized I had lost the present brought with me from Milan.

Irka opened the door; she was without the leg brace. She said "Hel-looo" and then "Shalom;" we embraced, or rather I gently joined my arms around her soft old woman's torso. I'd seen some recent photos snapped by my mother, but she looked less well than in those pictures, her turtle-dove eyes squeezed small by the pain of standing on her two legs. Still, she didn't look shaky and her pace wasn't halting as she led me to the long table dividing kitchen and living room, and had me sit, while she, standing, offered me break-fast which I said I was sorry but I'd already eaten.

"But I haven't."

"Sit, sit," I said, "Let me do it." And then I thought, why not reiterate that in a more familiar language? "Usiądź, Irka, proszę", I said, and her reply, in Polish, was, why didn't I have some fruit to keep her company?

"My back is all out of place," she said, now finally sitting down, her hand making a wavy motion. "Not a good day today."

Now I've learned that for many older people, talking about aches and pains can be the least personal subject of conversation, just a way of gaining that attention that is their right by age. But there in her apartment, even with the air conditioner on, I could see beads of sweat on Irka's forehead.

"You tell me when you've had enough, and I'll go," I said. "I can also come back tomorrow, if you like."

Her reply was a slight nod no, and a small smile, regal in its hint of nonchalance, and I recognized her in that. The wife of my mother's cousin did have that quality: a slightly detached courtesy that childish instinct suggested was not merely formal, a calm air of superiority that was difficult to put your finger on, but which became tangible in her sober, fair beauty. From the minute I set foot in her apartment I had recognized the paintings above the sofa, her oil paintings, post-impressionist or inspired by the Flemish masters, paintings I had known nothing of when she first showed them to us in her studio in the house at Rishon LeZion, city founded by the pioneers and today a satellite of Tel Aviv. Her daughter Michal, now married and a mother, also painted—pictures that were more abstract and brightly colored—but only Irka was a "real painter", her pictures having been acquired by several museums and put up in various shows both collective and individual. "Too modern for me," she said of several of Michal's works that hung in her house. It was the 1970s, and Irka, wife of one of the founders of Maccabee beer (he had been an advanced chemist even before the war) made that remark as if to say that jeans and Abstract Expressionism should be left to the young. How I saw this then and now remembered it, I cannot say.

I wanted to tell her right off that I recognized her paintings, but feared it might seem I was just flattering her, and then Irka oddly became quite agitated about her English and I was unable to reassure her that it seemed excellent to me, and she began searching for her grandaughter's number so she could come and help us.

"She speaks very good English, I forgot, I forgot," she kept saying, flipping over and over through her address book, and though I would have liked to help her I couldn't, because the numbers were in Hebrew. Meanwhile I noticed, in an open cabinet of her kitchen in pale wood, some art books—Matisse, Cezanne, Rembrandt, Vermeer—and then it occurred to me they were written in the Roman alphabet, the same in which she signed her paintings Irena Sher, with a name in parentheses that I was unable to make out.

"Your maiden name?" I asked, pointing to the script at the lower left, the western corner of a landscape that likened the hills near Jerusalem to Cezanne's Mont Sainte Victoire, and for the first time she really did not seem to understand a word.

"Dein Mädchenname?"

"Ja, mein Mädchenname."

"Das ist?"

"Levick, Irena Levick."

Now that we had hit on a language in which she easily understood what "maiden name" meant, everything was simpler. I had already asked her on the phone which of the languages we had in common did she know best and which would she feel most at ease speaking, but all I got from her was "as you like" and after we had exchanged some pointless courtesies—"no, as you prefer"—it had been left to me to choose English, the lingua franca in which street signs are still written in Israel, and the language of the army into which Anders' Army was incorporated. I had assumed she knew German as Poles of her generation did, and for that reason it seemed doubtful it was the right language to piece together her past. I was mistaken.

"Mein Vater," she went on, "hat mit mir deutsch gesprochen."

I was still standing in front of the painting, with Irka behind me beginning to talk of her father the doctor who had spoken German with her, her father who had died when she was ten, eleven years old, died because he had cut himself shaving and had not long before operated on a man who had lost a hand in a press; he had been forced to amputate.

"Mein Vater hat in der Schweiz studiert." He had studied in Switzerland.

We sat down and began to speak the language of her father. Not the instrument by which the exterminators had delivered orders, but the perfectly respectable language acquired in Switzerland thanks to the limits placed on Jewish students in Polish universities, which often transformed those destined to be marginalized into full cosmopolitans with excellent educations.

The accident had happened in a factory in Kaunas, or Kovno, then the temporary capital of independent Lithuania. The worker had six children and was saved; her father, no; her father was carried off by *Blutvergiftung*, "blood poisoning," septicemia. I was astonished to hear that cruelly precise term and even more so to hear her say it with no hesitatation, just as I was to hear her say *Flecktyphus, Lungenentzündung* and other such terms. This faithfully preserved German medical lexicon was certainly a form of love as resistant as any of the microbes that took her father's life.

"Six children to maintain," she told me her father repeated before he died. "Me, no," he went on, "thank Heaven, no."

"You had no siblings?"

"No, I was an only child. In those days, you know, that was the fashion."

Her reply startled me, despite the hint of irony in it. The fashion? Where?

"In Kaunas?" I ask. "In Vilna?" I place her there because it was a metropolis, although not large, with its crucible of languages and nations: Lithuanians, Russians, Bielorussians, Ukrainians and Germans living alongside the Jewish and Polish majority.

"No, no, we moved to Vilna after my father died; before that we were in a town called…"

She told me the name of the town but later I would find no trace of it except in the name of a street in Kaunas: Giedraiciu gatvé. Was the town so small that it did not appear on maps I could consult online, or, given that the only references I could find seemed to be tied to the extermination, had it perhaps been swept away with its inhabitants?

The next day, when I came back to see her along with her granddaughter, who had managed to find a photo album, we looked at one that showed the whole Levick family standing in a field of fresh hay, the adults in their shirtsleeves or cotton dresses, some with pitchforks in hand. There were paternal uncles too, but in that *plein air* portrait, Irka's parents were smiling far more naturally than you see in the usual period photograph. They were young and handsome and looked rumpled and healthy despite the dark exoticism of their Jewish faces, but then, considering the real coloring of the youngest Levick, that may simply have been a distortion of black and white photography.

"This was at Giedraičai, in Lithuania."

What I sensed in that photograph was something more than a world that is lost. A world that is lost is one you know very well existed, whose loss can be measured. A world like Vilna, Jewish Vilnius, the city of Rabbi Eliyahu, founder of the 18th century Orthodox Enlightenment. Vilna, where the best Yiddish was spoken, where the Jews were more than a third of the population, where there were more than one hundred synagogues and ten yeshivas; Vilna celebrated as "city of spirit and innocence"; Vilna, that "sewed the first thread in our flag of freedom," "our hometown, our longing and desire," already reborn in the 1930s on the banks of the Hudson, in Lower East Side theaters in New York. They had called it the "Jerusalem of Lituania" when Napoleon appeared, a brief moment of hope for a people under the Tsar's yoke. But even when those prohibitions were restored after emancipation, Vilna still offered space for every secular aspiration, from socialism to the Bund to Zionist books and newspapers written in Hebrew, a Yiddish research institute, and all the places where the peoples of Vilna came together, the parks, cafés, concert halls, theaters, museums, cinemas. The beauty contests for children.

"That was when they crowned me *queen*," said Irka, flirtatious and self-ironic, pointing to a portrait somewhat larger than the others.

She must have been three or four years old, and was wearing a light-colored dress with embroidery, hair in a pageboy with neat bangs, her face round, eyes wide, serious, and sparkling. Written below the portrait, the word *Wilno*. Curiously, there's a similar photograph of my mother, who is the same age as Irka, although she was in fact was a few years older than Irka in the picture when her cousin Jósek, the sweetest of the Szer brothers, seeing how pretty she was, packed her into his thrilling automobile and took her to the photographer in Katowice. And my mother too had won a beauty contest for that photo.

The lost world I'm able to put together, then, is one in which girls from good families were photographed in their prettiest dresses, a world where you learned to play tennis, and the piano, where you didn't always go to synagogue on Saturday but had birthday parties with cakes and candles and presents. The traces of that lost world are infinitely more fleeting than the other: the one with the narrow lanes and workshops, the Hassidim with their *shtreimel*; the poor, devout shtetl, a few little houses and a wooden synagogue in the midst of fields and woods.

But Irena Levick's native town, was that also a shtetl? Was she brought up in some isolated village, this girl who was an only child by her parents' choice, whose father spoke German and her mother Russian (and they never spoke Yiddish at home, only later with her grandparents when her golden age had already come to an end)? Was it in such a village with a mere sprinkling of souls that she was given a violin so early in life that she gave her first concert at age seven, something she told me even as she was recounting the story of the fatal septicemia, proud as only a child prodigy can be, her father's little darling, her attitude just slightly disguised but this time without the least ironic distance. Where would she have given that concert? At Giedraičai? Vilna? Kaunas? I didn't ask, in part to permit the tenderest and most terrible memories to flow, in part because I was struggling to put together all I was hearing. Two parents and a little girl who played Mozart, her head, with its braids, bent toward her violin, and at the same time ran through the fields, even, perhaps, barefoot. I have no idea whether they had any political ideals, but that young couple radiated an air of *pioneers*: that humanistic upbringing amid forests, fields and lakes was utopia made real. A bourgeois utopia preserved in the flesh and polyglot mind of an octogenarian daughter, a living fossil inside thirty square meters of an Israeli old people's residence.

Irka was calmer after she began to speak about her father. She seemed to have forgotten she meant to call her granddaughter, and she had already laid the table herself by the time that the woman appeared who lent a hand when Raissa wasn't around. Raissa had been helping out since her arrival from Minsk with the great wave of post-Soviet emigration. It had been about 15 years, since Irka had the first operation on her pelvis. She took her out every day for a walk, cooked the things she liked, but she lived too far away to come on Saturdays. Later they would talk on the phone in Russian, as if they were family.

Shoshana, in her fifties, nicely coiffed and made up, came with home-made sweets which I promised I would try later "mais pas tout de suite, madame, excusez moi." Irka had introduced us ("vous pouvez parler français") and sat down to eat. Shoshana was Egyptian.

"D'ou, si je peux demander?"

"Du Caïre!" Cairo.

She told me she had travelled all around Italy from Capri to Lake Como, but she didn't like Naples; "c'est trop caotique"; it was too Arab. "Ben oui," she said with a laugh, pointing to her huge dark eyes and her large hooked nose with a theatrical wave of her hand. Even her granddaughter called her an Arab. True, she did speak Arabic, "mais c'est normal, n'est ce pas?"

"She's not uncivilized," said Irka after she had gone, calling her *Arabička* as Raissa probably did.

"That's evident," said I, adding that Egyptian Jews were mostly cultivated people, educated.

How much courtesy learned in the diaspora ran through that tiny apartment on the third floor! How many worlds communicated effortlessly there, while beyond, where they were reduced to stereotypes, they seemed distant and irreconcilable. But this was cosmopolitan Judaism—whether of Vilnius, Lviv, Alexandria or Cairo—that indefinable and untenable identity destined to be absorbed or eradicated. The dessert Shoshana had brought was a soft cheesecake that had nothing to do with French patisserie, nor with that of the Middle East.

After I'd eaten, I cleared the table, ignoring Irka's "leave it, leave it" and sat down at my little white portable computer, which didn't seem to bother her. With apparent ease she resumed her tale where she had left off.

Irka and her mother were illegals when they arrived in Vilna, although it was only some fifty km from their town, because they were Lithuanian citizens. Her uncle took them in; from there they would travel most of the way across Poland to settle with her maternal grandparents at Łódź, where Irka attended the Jewish lyceum and obtained her *mala matura*, her "little baccalaureate," before the city was occupied.

Her mother had meanwhile remarried a man who was himself a widower with a son a few years younger than Irka. When the Germans arrived, father and son had fled to Lviv and her mother wanted Irka to join them, promising that she too would come, but not immediately, only when she had figured out how to bring her aged parents with her.

"Meine Mutter," said Irka, putting down a glass, her hands beginning to tremble, "man hat sie gebracht wo man hat lebendige Menschen begraben." *They took her where they buried men alive.* She couldn't think of the name, and she said again: in a pit, where they buried men alive, and she looked at me, blankly, imploring.But I did not know the reply she sought, and then, to the relief of both of us, she muttered, "to Treblinka." And both of us were silent.

"Sie war sehr jung, meine Mutter, nicht viel mehr als dreissig."

She wasn't much more than thirty years old? For the first time I wondered whether Irka was confused, whether an image guarded inside for more than half a century now led her to exaggerate. A monstrous image, the reflection of her own helplessness, her guilt for not having been able to protect her young mother. I did not recall that anyone had been buried alive in pits, if not for that percentage of error inevitable in large scale murder; or at least I did not recall it happening in a functioning death camp. But asking her anything was unthinkable, even how and when and from whom she had learned of her mother's fate. I could not do it; it was not important. I would try to verify what I could without interrogating her. The survivor's truth would be another: her nightmares, spectres, the petrified shape of her trauma.

The following day I went to Jerusalem for the first time, headed mainly to the archives of the Yad Vashem museum and memorial. On my first try I found more than I had hoped in the data base: the file dedicated to Irka's mother, complete with—and this was rare—a photo from some document showing a face with high cheekbones, of a dark, wild, Gypsy-like beauty that resembled her daughter not at all:

> *Master of Pharmacy. Riva Levick nee Fridman was born in Dokshitse in 1904 to Mendel and Rakhel. She was married to Yosef. Prior to WWII she lived in Giedraicai, Lithuania. During the war she was in Lodz, Poland. Master of Pharmacy Levick perished in 1942 in Treblinka, Poland at the age of 38. This information is based on a Page of Testimony (displayed at left) submitted on 01-May-1999 by her daughter, a Shoah survivor.*

Therefore, even if the rest remained obscure, like some wild nocturnal truth, her age at least was accurate.

Something told me that Riva Levick nee Fridman, the thirty year old widow with a child to look after, forced to drift from relative to relative, and despite her degree in Pharmacy, to marry a second time, might be a figure one would not want to investigate too deeply, and that put the pain for her death even further out of reach. Perhaps the fact that Irena Sher registered her mother's existence and death in the archive of the victims under the name of her first husband, that is of Irena's father, is significant. But beyond that, there was the story of a violin.

"I had bought myself a valuable one, a concert violin, but when I left my mother told me I had to leave it behind, that they would take it away, confiscate it."

As she tells me about her years in Łodź, she speaks of almost nothing else but the trio and the quartet she played in, the private lessons she gave, the aunt and uncle who had emigrated to Johannesburg who'd promised to help her embark on a career as a soloist. Behind all this, one could read the sacrifice and the discipline of a girl of spirit and intelligence dedicated to a single cause, in the service of her instrument. At that age, my own mother, who from the days in which they had both been "beauty queens" had lost that indefinable quality that distinguishes a very attractive girl from one who's beautiful—as Irka must have been, even rather intimidatingly beautiful—my mother had other things on her mind. Listening to swing, dancing the foxtrot; she even had a boyfriend, Polish, to boot.

A child left alone with a mother too young, a child who knew she had only herself to count on, who crossed Poland alone with a violin, rather than a doll or a teddybear, and its case in hand, that child became a woman.

"At Lviv, however, I sold my good dress, and bought another violin."

To get to Lviv, travel alone for 500 km, of which only the last 100 were not occupied by the Nazis, was no mean feat for a girl of sixteen. She protected herself as best she could, with some money hidden away, perhaps a family jewel or two. But above all she relied on her blue eyes, her manners, those of a well-brought-up young lady, her excellent knowledge of German, Russian and Polish, things that made it seem perfectly plausible that she was not Jewish, but Christian. To take shelter on the Soviet side of the border seemed the shortest and easiest path to safety, although the Russians and the Germans were allies, and the secret promises between Stalin and Hitler did not end with the partition of Poland, but included sharing out its inhabitants.

And so beginning in September 1939, young Jews from the northern suburbs of Warsaw and from the Jewish quarters of small towns occupied by the Germans "set out like a cloud of birds in the direction of the River Bug"—so wrote Gustaw Herling in *A World Apart*— thinking only of how to escape and get to the frontier safe and sound. And there, miraculously, the Germans did not try to prevent the crowds escaping, "but with clubs and rifle butts gave

them a last practical lesson in their philosophy of the *race myth*."
While on the other side, "the Russian guardians of the *class myth*,"
in their long greatcoats and bearing fixed bayonets, interrupted
their flight to the Promised Land with dogs and guns.

Had they known? Did they expect this? What did the Jews
in those territories the Russians had invaded know of what was
happening to their people, what did they foresee, imagine? They
had become outlaws in the space of just one or two weeks. Both in
Będzin, declared Slesia, that is Germany, from which my mother's
cousins fled, and in Łódź, which remained part of the Generalgouvernement Polen, but was renamed Litzmannstadt in honor of the
German general. Yes, they did know, but the situation was never
static, it just kept getting worse. It was something you had to face
day by day, with new anxieties every day, and new illusions that
the worst, perhaps, had already come and gone. And while minds
debated these matters, sometimes legs would reply almost on their
own that no, the worst had not yet come.

In Łódź, a large industrial city where the synagogues and shops
had already been smashed in September, the raids were recurrent, with assaults that could, and did, end in death, arrests, firing
squads in the public squares and jails, killing both individuals and
groups. On November 9, 1939, with the racial laws already in effect,
Jews were further obliged to wear the yellow star, on pain of death.
Property seizures kept lockstep pace with the owners's deportations. On December 10, 1939, the first ghetto was ordered into place,
a collection point to allow the city to be made *Judenrein* in less than
a year. On February 6, 1940, all Jews were forced to move into the
ghetto and on April 30, the gates were locked. More than 200,000
people were massed inside, making this the largest ghetto short of
that of Warsaw. Yet by March, 1940, 60,000 Jews had already been
deported, or had escaped, some to Warsaw itself, or to where, according to those rumors that spun wildly as people grew ever more
desperate, the persecutions were slightly less deadly. And some of
them, like Irka, her step-father and step-brother, fled east toward
the land of the Soviets, the land that promised the end of every dis-
crimination, equality for all human beings.

But that was no reason why Germany's new ally need be more
welcoming to those refugees than neutral Switzerland was with

Austrian or German Jews. In Poland, the Jews existed as such only for the Germans. For the Soviets, they were like all the rest: citizens of a nation that had been cancelled, according to a secret clause of the Molotov-Ribbentrop Pact:

> Both parties will tolerate no Polish agitation in their territories which affects the territories of the other party. They will suppress in their territories all beginnings of such agitation and inform each other concerning suitable measures for this purpose.

At the frontier, that clause was applied, no questions asked. By now people knew it, Irka herself probably knew it when her mother said "Go", but the swarms driven by fear and by hope kept coming.

"During the months of December, January, February and March," recalled Herling, crowds of Jews camped on the neutral no man's land that extended about a mile onto the Soviet bank of the Bug, "sleeping under the open sky, covered with red eiderdowns, lighting fires at night or knocking at the doors of nearby peasants' huts to beg for help or shelter." Barter markets appeared in the farmyards; clothing, jewelry, and dollars were exchanged for food or help in getting across the river. "Every cottage was besieged by a crowd of shadows, peering in through the windows and tapping on the glass, then returning, shriveled and empty of hope, to their family camp fires." Once in a while, at night, one of those shadows would break away and dash across the snow-covered plain, where "caught in the beam of a Soviet searchlight," it fell, struck by machine-gun fire.

According to Herling many, perhaps most, of those refugees in time lost hope or the means to keep it alive, and retreated back under Nazi domination where they would end up being annihilated. Some could probably not bear the wait. They had left behind others who couldn't or wouldn't make a journey so chancy: parents above all, and grandparents, relatives in poor health, siblings, sometimes children so small they didn't want to expose them to danger or privations. They believed, they chose to believe, they had departed as an advance guard, and that once they were organized, they would find a way to bring the others along, just as Irka and her mother had believed. They had fled, in any event, deciding in haste and taking along as little as possible, careful to avoid any contact with the Germans, disguising themselves if possible, sleeping in fear as victims sleep, or not sleeping at all, traveling in terror always. And now they had halted, just a few yards from their destination. Now that their flight had ended, anxiety surrendered. It surrendered to nervous collapse, to desperation, to unease, remorse, even homesickness. They were not in America, not ready to board some steamship in some great European port. They were still in Poland, although on the verge of a frontier very difficult to cross. They merely had to turn around, go back and in no time at all they would be back home, for whatever room they ended up in together, that place would be their home. *Home is where the heart is.*

That was what happened to Jósek, the cousin who once took my mother to Katowice so she could take part in a beauty contest. He went back to Będzin "because he'd always been a good son and wanted to go back to his father and his mother," my mother told me, in those words. Dr. Jósek Szer stood by his parents right up to the *Selektion* by the rail tracks at Auschwitz, where all were exterminated, one sooner, one later. If my mother is not mistaken, this prodigal son decided to return after the Szer brothers had already reached Soviet territory.

He was not the only one, according to Gustaw Herling. At a certain point "an extraordinary thing happened — the same crowds who only a few months ago had risked their lives to enter the Promised Land now started a mass exodus in the opposite direction, back to the land of the Pharaohs." What was this, collective insanity? Or did the gulag survivor exaggerate here? It was clear he meant to show that even those who hoped the Russians would save their skins, were by then so disillusioned as to prefer returning to a ghetto rather than taking out a passport in a new state. A passport on which, it must be added, the ethnic identity *evreij*, Jewish, had been noted down from the time of the Tsars. Was that the reason why (as historians confirm) most of those who lined up at the improvised counters of the German Commission on Repatriation were Jewish?

So it happened in all the cities of eastern Poland, and in Lviv too, where the Commission arrived in May 1940. The refugees were bitterly disappointed when they learned that practically no one but the *Volksdeutsche*, the ethnic Germans, were entititled to repatriate. And so among the many who turned back, few had their papers in order when they returned where certain death awaited them. They didn't know death awaited, just as the Nazis themselves didn't know, and would need another year before they determined that the final solution to the Jewish question was systematic genocide. The refugees had no way of knowing how much worse the situation at home had become. And even when they did hear rumors of what was going on in the ghettos and all the rest, they could only choose between what they were living and what they were hearing.

What had become of their loved ones at home? In no time at all, magnificent, prosperous cities like Lviv, the Lemberg that had once been a jewel in the Austro-Hungarian crown, had been reduced to starvation by the greed with which the Red Army soldiers swept away the last goods to be found on the free market, a plague of locusts. Those once proud cities were now filthy, ruined, overcrowded like the cities of the east. The exodus for Lviv, preferred destination because of its reputation, size and nearness to the frontier, had doubled the Jewish population to 200,000 in a macabre imitation of a giant ghetto, in addition to the Polish refugees who were in any case tens of thousands. All of those illegals could never find work, let alone reunite their families. The only certain prospect awaiting observant Jews was to find themselves forbidden to practice their religion for life; the rest found only new dangers and threats. Dangers now looming because they were Polish citizens and bourgeois, for the professional restrictions that had vexed them for centuries had the paradoxical result of making them "capitalists."

How many rabbis and community leaders, how many doctors, lawyers, writers, even poets jailed, forced under torture to declare themselves "enemies of the people," "exploiters," "agents of a foreign power," taken away at night by the secret police, and their families too, vanished, deported? How many tailors, cobblers, small shopkeepers and traveling salesmen? In May of 1940, beyond the everyday terror that courtesy of criminal informers and occasional spies could strike anyone anytime, two of four waves of mass deportation of Poles to the Soviet interior had already taken place. This was what people knew in Lviv, in Bialystok, in Grodno, in Vilnius. Perhaps it was not so crazy to think it was preferable to go back and suffer with one's family, rather than risk in any case ending up in Siberia. And yet the multitudes that asked to return to the land of the Pharaohs could never have imagined how close the German-Soviet friendship was in those times. The lists collected by the German Commission for Repatriation, the only ones that had the real names and addresses of the refugees, were handed over directly to the NKVD, the People's Commissariat for Internal Affairs. And on the basis of those lists Stalin's secret police prepared the third deportation, carried out in June, 1940. And then the final one, in June 1941, in which as always the refugees were the primary targets.

The only thing I know about Irka from the period before she was deported is that she sold a good dress in Lviv to buy herself a lousy violin. In other words she used one of her last resources— having sold the dress she probably had few other valuables left—to take possession of something that was neither bread nor butter nor coal. And she risked arrest not once but twice, for anyone who turned to the black market, even for food, was guilty of speculation, and therefore a sworn enemy of the new order. And then a pretty girl who owned valuable clothing and was in a position to exchange it for an instrument that procured luxurious calluses on one hand alone, was by definition suspect. The new Soviet man needed no violin, but Miss Irena Levick needed one so badly she risked her life to acquire it. A fact that makes it clear she felt free to decide for herself how to dispose of her things and make her choices, although by now she had joined her stepfather. The flip side of that autonomy was solitude. Irka never left that violin behind, unlike the mother for whom by now she had lost all hope.

I have no way of knowing how her stepfather and stepbrother ended up on that deportation list, but from what I know Irka, when the NKVD agent appeared to take them away, told him, "I'm going with them." In that excellent Russian of hers, with those Nordic eyes, that air of almost-womanhood, quiet and serious.

"Ty sumasšešaja!" it seems the Russian said to her. *You are crazy.*

It seems he even pointed out to her that because she was as a Lithuanian, not a Polish, citizen, she could return to Vilnius or to Kaunas, and finish her studies, resume a normal life.

"Yes, but this is my family," Irka insisted, "what would I do all alone in Lithuania?"

"Niet, eto nie vozmožno." It was impossible. The Soviet state knew who must be transferred, and if you were not on on the list, you could not be deported.

To pick a quarrel with an officer of the secret police in the middle of the night, pretend to be more helpless than she really was, conceal that one of her plans from the beginning had been to reach some remaining relative still in Lithuania: what was this if not madness? Why didn't she simply give a rapid hand to that poor kid forced by the Russians to pack their bags in half an hour while they held his father at gunpoint, hands on the wall, kneeling in his pyjamas?

Yet I have before me another remark that Irka was supposed to have said to the NKVD man, a sentence that when I reread my notes and looked at the dates, I first discarded thinking I had misunderstood, or that she had remembered wrong.

"Anyway, there are Germans in Lithuania."

Still, she had repeated it more than once. And since nothing gave me the impression Irka was in any way confused about her memories, I decided to pursue the matter. Here is what I learned: the final Soviet deportation began on June 20, 1941, just two days before the German assault, which was probably why it was hastier, more partial and arbitrary than the earlier ones. There, not very far from the frontier where huge numbers of tanks and men were massing, it was likely that war was considered certain, as was its outcome for those, crushed by the Soviet regime, who were counting heavily on the Russians losing. Perhaps that deportation was still going on while the first German bombs were falling—although at that point the NKVD would have been busy killing off the political detainees.

In the heavily overcrowded prisons of Lviv, the massacre of as many people as inhabit a small city occupied nearly a week. Still, the Wehrmacht in Lithuania moved rapidly: Kaunas fell on June 25, Vilnius the 26, Lviv only on June 30.

If it was really the very last Soviet deportation that Irka, so polite and so stubborn, was able to join, then perhaps she was less mad than she seemed. The Lviv prisons had become slaughter houses in the heat, epidemics perhaps brewing in the corpses soaking in their own blood, and when they were opened, the new occupiers and the Ukrainian nationalists spread the word that the villains were Jews enrolled in the NKVD, or in any case Russian collaborators. During the entire month of July, a further retaliation deprived Lviv of the population of another town, although this time solely Jewish. Unlike the Nazi *cleansing* that would follow, the Ukranian pogroms did not confine themselves to plunder and murder, but included mass rape and mutilation, violence the victims would be forced to live with afterwards, never fully recovering. In Lithuania too—despite its nearness to the Russian border and the fact that persecution only began in 1941—collaboration with the Nazis would be such that the number of exterminated Jews would slightly outnumber those anywhere else in the Nazi-conquered world, including in the Generalgouvernement Polen and under the smokestacks of the death camps.

How did the girl with the violin, that young lady of good family, ever guess that the Russians were her only route to salvation, even if she were to end up in the gulag? Was it a survival instinct, or was it resignation, had she lost all interest in everything but to avoid being left alone again, or avoid leaving alone those her mother could no longer care for? Whatever, it was in a sealed freight train waiting to leave Lviv station that Irena Levick met the three cousins of my mother who had remained in Soviet territory: Dolek, the eldest, a doctor like Jósek (now imprisoned in the ghetto of the family house in Będzin); Benno, a lawyer, with his wife and her two brothers; and Zygmunt, the youngest. From then on, out of all that the Szer brothers had studied at the University of Montpellier, the only useful expertise would be that of Dolek.

A doctor is always useful. Even when all he can do is to certify the deaths of children and the elderly by hunger, thirst or heat, supplying the cold dignity of names like *dehydration* and *malnutrition* before their corpses were heaved out the window of the moving train, the only way they were permitted to dispose of dead bodies during the journey. A doctor, if he had been able to bring along a few medicines, and above all if he had the courage to maintain the state of mind his oath demanded, was an anchor for all those tossed about in a dark and foul-smelling railroad car, a sturdy alternative to prayers, of any and all confessions, that could become indistinguishable from laments. But then, too, a girl who understood Russian as if it were her native tongue, who knew how to judge which of the guards was approachable, could also be useful. She could wait for the right moment, stare at him with gentle indifference. "Nemnožko vody, požalusta, dolžny vypit' rebiata" she would say holding out another keepsake as a sacrificial offer. *The children are thirsty, some water, please.* Or maybe not, maybe no Russians were willing to sell their mercy. Then she would shake her head, but only slightly, because her desolation was great, and because any excessive motion seemed to steal air, subtract space, from the others.

"Bardzo mi przykro proszę panì," she would say to the child's mother. *I am mortified.* And then she would hunch down making herself as small as possible, pulling up her knees with the violin in its case wedged in between. Even a violin, perhaps, might be of use during a deportation.

"Look," said the mother to the child, who was coughing and gasping like a frog out of water and kept raking his tongue over his cracked lips, "ta piękna panienka gran a skrzypcach." *This pretty young lady plays the violin.* "You'll play us a concert when we arrive, won't you?"

"Of course," said Irka. *Oczywiście.* Luckily there wasn't much light.

But even if the narrow band coming through the window had fallen right on her face, the slight welling behind her lashes would not have been easy to detect in those velvety, immutable grey-blue eyes.

Divided by an Abbey

The following morning when they got to the gates of the cemetery, it was already past 9:30. Usually it was Andy who dragged Edoardo out of bed, and he was getting less polite about it: opening the shutters, flushing the toilet, playing music at high volume on the computer, laying hands on him and hissing "wake up!" in his ear. But that day, had grandmother Dorka's call not come through ("what time is it, *babcia*?" "Eight-thirty, Edek") both of them would still be sleeping. They washed and dressed sloppily, ate breakfast without opening their mouths except to pour in litres of coffee and homemade cake, cereal, bread, butter, jam and fruit juice. Their first words were uttered by Andy in the car when they were already taking the switchbacks. "What did your grandmother want?"

"She said they might come down one of these days because some of their friends, people who live in England, veterans, are coming here."

"You mean veterans from the Second Corps, guys who fought with General Anders?" the question came out in English.

"Of course. Yes. Why, are you too out of it to speak Italian?"

For a while Anand drove in silence, staring straight ahead, and had the road not demanded his attention, you'd have thought he was offended, which seemed strange.

"Hey partner, I didn't mean to annoy you."

"Don't worry about it. But tomorrow, I'm setting the alarm."

"You sleep badly? The mussels giving you problems? Something else?"

"No, no. Except for the fact that you snore like…a walrus!"

"A walrus? This is not good news you're giving me. You mean always, or just last night?"

"No idea; I think I fell asleep before you the other nights and didn't hear anything."

"Hey, I'm sorry, partner."

And so the moment passed, and Andy, who was about to tell Edoardo about the book he'd begun to read at night, didn't; and even he had no idea why he didn't mention it later when they were sitting on their folding chairs doing nothing (tardy though they had been), because for most of that morning the cemetery was empty. They talked about other things, beginning with the fact they hadn't even had time to buy the newspapers and a bottle of water; they shared the same old memories which, in that place, on those chairs sitting next to each other, made them seem like two old guys on a bench in the park, memories both celebrated in their way and others less so, and recalling them made them feel grown-up, united.

"You know, walruses," said Anand although there was no connection, "have you noticed that many Poles wear, you know, walrus moustaches? You see, here," he said, pointing at the tiny faces on the flier kept in readiness on his lap.

"And so?"

"Nothing. I'm just saying."

Edoardo stared at those faces he'd looked at so many times before, and told Andy that okay, even Lech Wałęsa had a moustache like that, "and if you don't know who he is, he's the head of Solidarność and he got the Nobel peace prize," but so did that cousin of theirs who had organized a boat trip on Lake Masuria, one of those vacations when the Bielinskis had celebrated their newfound opportunity to reunite the entire family. But the missing Poles whose portraits had been stamped on his retina from the first time he connected to the Polish police website had boyish faces. Michał Serbinowski and Rafał Zarczycki, one dark, one blond, both looking like normal kids you might find anywhere in the world. Clicking on the clean, childish face of Michał Serbinowski, Edoardo saw he was just seven years older than himself, and Rafał was eight years older. Two young men with the names of archangels who had left home when they were his own age and had vanished into the thin air of Italy. A lump in his throat had seized him when he learned that, and it returned every time he went back to look at their faces.

* * *

Edoardo Bielinski had learned about the missing Poles one winter evening, returning from a movie he'd gone to with a girl he'd met at the demonstration against budget cuts to public education, the so-called "clash of extremists" at Piazza Navona. That's what they had called it on TV and in the newspapers backing the government, trying to make it look like the kids of the Onda, the protesters, had unleashed the violence, which was false.

Edoardo and the kids in the upper classes of the Liceo Tasso had been up ahead when his younger sister Marta, with some other girls came running up, some struck dumb, some screaming "they're slaughtering us!" There were gangs of fascists, all male, adults, armed with baseball bats and chains and metal bars and wearing motorbike helmets, going after whoever they could hit, when you could see—couldn't you?—that they were only fourteen or fifteen years old. Marta then burst into tears and Edoardo hugged her hard, his sister the top of whose head came up to his chin, and began to whisper "uspokój się" though he himself had no idea why in Polish. *Calm down.* And between them, that private language had its effect. There were kids on the ground, beaten and bleeding; two had blood pouring from their heads when they'd tried to fend off the blows with their hands; one of them was from another school.

When they heard this, not even the teachers who had joined the march were able to bring calm to the older kids. And that was when Edoardo Bielinski had lost. He had tried to say, "hey, let's keep cool" but he was too upset, too enraged, and when Lorenzo Pascucci snapped, "Bianco, but don't you get it that the fascists and the cops are in this together? This is like Genoa in 2001, it's like the Battle of Valle Giulia in 1968 that my father's told me about so many times" Edoardo had not known what to say and the others, too, were silent. And so Pascucci, son of a big shot at the public television RAI, kept haranguing them about legitimate self-defense, and finally, swelled by what seemed to him the tacit approval of the others, had contacted a comrade in the university branch.

Throughout the school occupation, Edoardo Bielinski had been the student rep everyone listened to at his liceo. He was passionate about the cause, yet not willing to screw around, and whenever he spoke his language was clear and direct ("We catch anyone writing on the walls or stuff like that, first he cleans up, and then he's out, get it?") so that even the parents and the teachers held him in high esteem. He matched the very profile of the protest ("not on the left, not on the right, the public schools belong to all") so effortlessly that everyone followed him. He even found himself with a new nickname, a real nom de guerre: in truth it was a name the kids in his class already called him although nobody remembered where it had come from. Maybe because some silly girl had overstepped the line and called out "Ciao Biondo," *blondy*, and he had snapped back, "You can call your brother Biondo," and then "try Bianco, that's what Bielinski means anyway." *White*. Or maybe it was as Pascucci said, that Edoardo was a White and Lorenzo and his friends were Reds; Whites and Reds as in the Russian Revolution said dear Lorenzo who thought he was pretty awesome to have come up with that historical reference.

He hadn't had problems with Pascucci up until then. Two years before, when there was a brawl with the fascists who showed up at the Tasso bearing leaflets and truncheons, Il Bianco had already displayed true grit and good sense, but our Lorenzo could still consider him a mere acolyte who had no intention of stepping on his toes. True enough. Edoardo had never aspired to be a student boss, and it was precisely that which gnawed at Pascucci, the way that he had been passed over by popular acclaim in just a few days and without trying at all.

And so matters stood, until such time as Lorenzo was able to take his revenge by calling in reinforcements, although afterwards he would swear he was not the one to have contacted those fellows who in turn showed up wearing helmets and ski masks.

In any event, Piazza Navona seemed to have cooled down, so far as any piazza crammed with protesting students could be cool. It was just in that false interregnum that Edoardo began to talk to that girl who'd appeared with the first university students. This time it was quite clear that Il Bianco was a high school student, admittedly in his last year, while Sara, from Magliano in Sabina, was studying modern literature at university, yet after they had commented on the bloodshed, they began to talk of other things. Edoardo produced some chewing gum, then some mints. "Want one of these, or do you want a Mentos?" Sara in turn offered what was left of her bottle of water. "If it doesn't turn you off to drink it."

"Are you kidding?" said Edo, putting the bottle to his lips and taking a long, long sip while he gazed at Sara who had black curly hair, greenish eyes and a tiny diamond stud in her right nostril.

"Hey, no fear, I left you a swallow," he said smiling as he returned the bottle, and between one remark and another they exchanged cell numbers and then Sara went off saying, "Okay, I think I gotta get back to the guys in my department, but we'll talk, okay?" And she gave him a quick peck on each cheek.

What happened next were scenes of war televised in all the news programs that evening, and then uploaded and commented upon on the web, where blame was reciprocally charged by one side and the other. Bar chairs in front of Bernini's fountain piled up in barricades, chairs flying, elegant yellow wooden chairs with fabric seats, more aerodynamic, thank heavens, and less lethal than the old-style chairs with metal frames. Bottles, tables (few) and other more or less blunt objects; then the fascists struck back, and they had baseball bats, those same bats with the flag wrapped around them they had used against the high school students before, but the students were long gone, along with just about all the other peaceful protesters, and when Edoardo stopped to ask himself what he was still doing there, he didn't have an answer.

Had he been detained by the thought that Sara might be there somewhere in the fray, or was he just so gaga with euphoria that he hadn't caught the scent of danger? Il Bianco remained pacific, but he was not at all calm; he howled and shrieked desperate things he didn't recall later, waving his arms and sometimes advancing toward the front line like a kamikaze, or no, more like a Viking beserker, in any case like someone going bonkers. "Enough!!" "We're destroying everything here!" "Fascist shitheads, filthy bastards!" "Fuck you too, dickhead! Who do you think you are, assholes; who gives a shit about you?"

And then finally came the police charge, the riot police who swung their truncheons and beat everyone up a bit, well, no: the fascists succeeded in being disarmed and made to board the police vans without the cops ever laying a hand on them, because the officer in charge knew them, they were "his boys" and he could vouch for them, while those arrested on the other side were treated rather less politely.

In the end Edoardo wasn't surprised he was one of those taken down to the station to be checked out; he wasn't even all that scandalized that the cops called them "faggot communists." No, at first, riding in the back of the van, he was even able to calm down, and think what an ass he'd been, and hope that someone or something would be able to testify that yes, he had gotten far too agitated, okay, but hadn't taken part in any violence.

And in fact that was what happened, and there were street cams ready to confirm it, but when down at police headquarters they asked for his identity card, Il Bianco suddenly discovered he was just a guy named Edoardo Radosław Bielinski.

"Oh right, you came all this way just to commit murder and mayhem, you scumbag of a Slav? That's all we need, for you to come here and cause trouble!"

"I had nothing to do with it, you can ask the other kids; I went there as a peaceful protester."

"Oh, no, don't even try. This is not your country and your job is to keep your mouth shut!"

"But I was born in Rome; it says so right here. I'm a student at the Liceo Tasso like all the other demonstrators here today."

"Oh, did you get that, Vincenzo? So now we got this kind of scum in our best schools. Okay, let's see: born March 21, 1991. So a minor. Perfect. You know what? Right now we're going to see how your parents are fixed for residence permits; we're going to your house and if we find one thing—one thing—that's out of order, know what you can do? You can pack your bags, the whole family. You can go back to your own country."

"No, no, you see…"

"No, no? Yessiree, you can count on it!"

"We're Italians, Italian citizens. My mother's Neapolitan, and my father…let me give you the phone number, you can check it out."

"You do not tell me what to do, understand? You just prepare yourself to spend the night inside here, and then we'll see. And keep your mouth shut, if you don't want us to do it for you. Understand?"

And so Edoardo Bielinski ended up in a cell full of right- and left-wing thugs, and had no clue why, as night was falling, he was let out along with most of the kids who'd been taken in by mistake.

Everyone was outside police headquarters. Marta began to cry when she saw him, his mother hugged him hard like the time he got lost taking a shortcut during an outing to the Gran Sasso, his father was catatonically calm in a way he'd never seen him before. It had been hours since Edoardo said anything. He had hunkered down in the corner of the cell and wrapped his arms around his knees, ignoring the fascists and the hard-lefties who were trashing each other, letting their voices boom back and forth over his head, head empty like a pumpkin, invisibly dented far worse than if he'd been beaten with a nightstick. Now he was pressed against the back seat of the Lancia, and never had the inside of a car left under the later autumn sun been so nice, the way the stored-up heat flowed into him like some life-giving sap from the upholstery. No one said a word. At a certain point, his sister blew her nose.

There hadn't been time to cook and so Flavia sent Giorgio out to get pizzas, which were eaten in front of the TV while they flipped through the channels in search of news.

"Nobody's saying anything about what happened to us," said Marta. "Or did they say something before, Mamma?"

"I don't know, I was working," said Flavia with a sigh, turning to look at the TV.

"They'll do an investigation to determine what happened. Let's hope."

"Sure, Papà, sure. You could see the cops were going by a double standard. And it's not the first time; you know that, don't you?"

"Yes, and that's why I said 'let's hope.' Until otherwise proved the judiciary is still independent and able to expose improper behavior on the part of the executive."

"Right, let's hope. Can we change the channel? I'd like to think about something else."

"Fair enough, Edek. What about if we watch a nice film?"

"Okay, Let's let Marta choose."

Edoardo didn't know why he had let his sister decide, but she had the smart idea to go right for one of the classics of their childhood. And so the Bielinskis emptied their pizza boxes watching the antics of a mammoth, a sloth and a saber-toothed tiger, cracking up each time the squirrel with the bug eyes tried and failed to grab an acorn. A normal, happy family in front of the TV. If they laughed a bit too loud, what did it matter? Edoardo was still very grateful for all of it. Yes, keep the Bielinski name flying high. Ask nothing and say the minimum necessary in response to any questions. Reticence and self-censorship among the Bielinskis? Yes, stuff that was supposed to have disappeared with the end of the Communist Ice Age. Edoardo let the cops' racism pour out on his pillow before going to sleep. *Where is this country headed?* Giorgio and Flavia, behind the closed door of their bedroom, decided that Grandfather Radek and Grandmother Dorka must hear no word about the fact the kids were in Piazza Navona. The family was united, and after all, nothing had really happened. After all, they had even been fortunate that Flavia was home all day and so was able to comfort Marta and then, about 3 pm, begin to worry about her son. After all, the hours during which she'd been in real distress, if not worse, when she understood that Edoardo must have been detained, were not so very many. And the thought that her son might have been drawn into some foolish action ("He's a good kid, but he can be hotheaded"; "Come on, let's not exaggerate, it doesn't take much to be more hotheaded than you are.") quickly dispersed when a phone call arrived telling Flavia to come and come down and get him.

"Signora, are you the mother of Edoardo Rad-o-sław Bielinski, born in Rome on March 21, 1991?"

"Yes, of course."

"And your husband is a certain Giorgio Tadeusz Bielinski, born in Warsaw on November 6, 1953 and an Italian citizen as of his 18th birthday on November 6, 1971? Residing in Rome, via Bellinzona 14, professor of international law at La Sapienza University?"

"Precisely. Pardon me, but may I ask...

"Signora, we are calling to inform you that your son has been detained, and we have ascertained he is extraneous to the acts of violence perpetuated today. We therefore invite you to appear, in the company of your husband, to present both your sets of documents, which are needed, the detainee being a minor, before he can be released."

"Okay, we'll come right away."

Later, Flavia would ask herself if anything about that conversation or in the procedures to release Edoardo had seemed strange. Later: meaning much, much later. It was one evening near the end of January, when her son returned after a movie with Sara and flung himself on the sofa to watch the end of a public affairs program on TV. Giorgio was in Budapest at a conference; Marta sleeping over at a friend's. Flavia had just finished going over a doctoral thesis and had turned on the TV in part to distract herself, in part to hide the fact she was waiting up for her son. Most of the program had been about the island of Lampedusa, where both the would-be immigrants just off their flimsy boats and detained in Reception Centers, and the local population of Italians, had recently staged revolts. Among the guests on the program was MP Roberto Cota, but Flavia wasn't sure she wanted to hear him make his nasty political points on the backs of those poor immigrants. But Cota, the Northern League's just appointed floor leader, a man of utterly unruffled self-assurance, was hypnotizing to watch.

"Want to change channels?" she asked, almost hoping Edoardo would release her from the spell.

"No, no, let's hear what the crackpot has to say for himself."

"He may be that, but he's a presentable one, a smart one. He knows that what he's saying, and the way he says it, is very popular."

"And so?"

"These people are changing their skins at the speed of light, while on the other side of the political spectrum nothing changes, it's all hopelessly blocked. Hey, I'm hungry, I'm going to get something to eat. What about you?"

Edoardo nodded and then he was alone in the living room when a guy named Alessandro Leogrande, who had recently published a book about modern day slavery in the southern region of Puglia, appeared. Behind the politicians in the studio, the young man, in jacket and shirt but no tie, stood up in the cone of a spotlight that picked him out clearly from the rest of the audience. What he had to say before the credits came up made an impression on both Edoardo and his mother, who had just returned with a packet of biscuits and a pitcher of water.

He spoke, Leogrande, without losing his train of thought or his calm, and when he addressed the anti-immigrationist MP, he didn't seek the complicity of the audience. He used no rhetoric in his counter-arguments, and his composure, his ability to stick to the concrete, his round face, glasses and beard, made Flavia think more of a old-fashioned union organizer from the south, than a journalist or a writer. Edoardo, meanwhile, was struck by what he had to say, about a shadowy universe of slaves, some of them blacks, undocumented; some white, thousands of Poles and Romanians press-ganged into illegal jobs in the fields. "New Europeans" Leogrande had called those Poles and Romanians, just as his father would have defined them, but Prof. Bielinksi had never dealt with or probably even come across such human cases.

Flavia turned off the TV and carried the pitcher and biscuits into the kitchen. Edoardo, unexpectedly, followed her, slamming the glasses down in the sink.

"You see that? We've become slaves again, their white slaves."

"We who? Sorry, I was just trying to think whether to prepare the small coffee pot or the large one for the morning."

"Us Poles. They treat us like shit, but we can't say that in this house, because everything is great since Communism ended."

"Under Communism they didn't just treat you badly, and you know it, Edoardo. And anyway, those folks never had a very high opinion of us *terroni*, us southerners. As for the Neapolitans, we're the pits. In other words, you have the wrong ancestors, my boy," said Flavia, stroking the peak of his blond mop.

"Don't joke about it," hissed Edoardo, backing away from her, and coming to a halt, shouting: "You want to know how those thugs at police headquarters treated me, you want to hear what they said?"

Yes, Flavia wanted to know. And shaking her head while she listened, putting her hand back in his hair from where she'd withdrawn it in fear, standing up there in the kitchen beside the dirty plates from her supper of left-overs, she wondered what she should do.

"Can I ask you please not to talk about this to Papà?" said Edoardo, surprising her again.

"No, wait. First you complain that some things can't be mentioned around here, and then you don't want your father to know what happened. Apart from the fact he has the right to know. Apart from the fact that he knows much better than I do what can be done."

"Listen, Mamma. What do you think he could do? Three months have gone by; three months exactly today."

"I don't know. Convince someone to testify. Anyway, it's you who should have told us right off what happened."

"Oh, now it's my fault!"

"Don't shout, Edoardo. Sorry, maybe I didn't explain myself well. I understand. I guess that now, effectively, it would be difficult…"

"What the hell do you understand? What the hell are you talking about? Nobody here wants to go against the cops, nobody wanted to do it then, so go figure how much they want to do it now that they're back home with mamma and papà."

"Well, but it's worth asking, it costs you nothing."

"Mamma, I don't want to turn this stuff into a major case. I don't want to, get it? I'm not the problem. The problem is this country, that wouldn't move an inch if it came out that the son of a professor at the Sapienza was—"oh, we're very sorry!"—treated like a subhuman Polack. I don't want justice for the privileged; stuff like this happens every day."

"Okay. Let me think about it. Now let's try to get some sleep because we have to wake up early. You have a test tomorrow, if I'm not mistaken."

"But you will tell me, when you decide?"

"Of course. And now, can I give you a good night kiss?"

"Yeah. Night, Mamma."

The next day Edoardo came back from school with a red bag from the Arion bookstore in Piazza Fiume containing Alessandro Leogrande's *Uomini e caporali*. Of slaves and slave-drivers.

Reading it, Edoardo grew indignant, then excited ("it's good stuff, Ma', and the writing is great, I swear you'll like it too") offering his mother a sort of live radio broadcast that would seal, without either one of them being aware of it, a pact of silence. The book, Flavia saw, permitted him to get to the bottom of what had happened with the police. He could speak of the Poles in Puglia and be silent about himself. One evening at supper Edoardo summarized the book for all of them, even underlining the fact he had learned about something like this watching a TV program his father sometimes followed, while detesting it.

"Did you know about this? What about the Polish association, all of Grandfather Radek's friends, what do they say? Have they done anything?"

"Look Edek. I did know some things, yes. I knew about the trial against those criminal farm bosses, the *caporali*. It's true, though, that I didn't know of every single person missing or dead in suspicious circumstances. You are probably right; the Polish community should pay more attention to these matters. But in the end, the fact that an Italian has investigated is the best thing that could have happened, no? It becomes a matter of Polish and Italian public opinion, not one to be treated within a very narrow circle."

"You may be right, Papà. But it's time you woke up."

"Okay. You try to write a review of the book, I'll translate it in Polish and we'll send it to *Polska Włoska*. That way you can give the wake-up call."

Edoardo didn't write the review and he seemed to have forgotten all about the matter. He was deep in his last few months of study, and with the *maturità*, the school-leaving exam, fast approaching, that was his first priority.

Sometimes Flavia wondered if she had been wrong not to speak to Giorgio. It was an unprecedented lapse on her part for something as grave as the threats Edoardo had received, and when she thought about them as threats it still upset her. It was wrong, she was behaving like the typical Italian mother, protecting her own and to hell with the community or the society, but damn it, she simply couldn't help placing Edoardo's well-being before anything else, although he seemed to have gotten his balance by identifying with others who had received far worse treatment.

And so in July when he passed his *maturità* with unexpectedly high marks, and some of the pain for his breakup with Sara had worn off, and Edoardo announced his plan to post himself in front of the Polish cemetery at Monte Cassino to try to find the missing, Flavia stood behind him. Not that Giorgio was openly critical. Sure, the kid, if he really wanted to, could even go and do that sort of thing, but privately he remarked to his wife that it was pointless, a useless waste of time, Edoardo would do better "to find a job or take a real holiday."

It was not just Giorgio, though, who was mistaken, thinking this was a fanciful, idealist adventure; Flavia, who believed she alone was party to what had led Edoardo on this search, also failed to see that her son's interest in the matter was no longer just a pretext.

It was no one's fault, and no one could do anything about it if Edoardo continued to feel as he had since that afternoon in police headquarters on October 29: alone. Maybe he was exaggerating, that would be typical for his age and his character, but sometimes things happen, a person gets hit on the head, and his perceptions of the world change irreversibly. The most painful part was his hearing: to discover that Slavic languages are so much alike that he was able to understand the construction workers on the bus, the home-help ladies eating lunch at McDonalds, even those blond-headed young women with long legs exposed, almost phosphorescent white in the headlights, where they stood on the side of the Via Salaria.

They were legion, a hidden army, like extraterrestrials who had landed on earth in some teen film; and only Edoardo seemed able to perceive them as they moved around in a parallel dimension. He watched as they were swallowed up into call centers, kebab counters, shops that sold okra and bags of rice next to bottles of vodka and jars of pickled cucumbers. He found an apartheid in practice, not of color particularly: there were blacks, whites, Asians and every shade of brown. This was the capital, Rome: no, not really Rome, only those parts that Edoardo happened to pass through. Was it surprising that just beyond them lay territories of genuine invisibility? A veil of invisibility slashed open only in those moments when something sensational happened—a rape, mass eviction, a beating—but immediately those ghost people would disappear once again. It was simple to make young men like Michał and Rafał disappear from the Italian face of the earth.

The first time he showed their photos to the kid who would become his associate, Andy said "nice-looking guy" and that was that. That brief statement was enough for Edoardo. He had hardly ever spoken to him about things at the Liceo Tasso, nor about what had happened after the demo at Piazza Navona. For a long time they had barely seen each other, and they had been in touch less often, first because of the school protest, and then because their rhapsodic texted conversations were mainly about Sara who was three years older, who shared an apartment at Piramide where Edo hung out a lot at first, Sara in attached photos ("U no I don't like piercing, but hr eyes are ++ and she has big b-bs 2!!") in a kind of epistolary soap opera.

Il Bianco thought that the politics that joined him to his eternal love had alienated the prince of Kashmir, but when eternal love came to an end ("I feel like shit. Want to go to hr house and tell hr what an assh- she is in front of hr friends!" "Edo, don't be a dick-hd. Hold on til yr exam and then U can get all the girls U want.") he found that in talking about Sara, their friendship was restored. That, and the comment "nice-looking guy" in front of the photo of Michał Serbinowski, made him decide to ask Andy to join his cemetery honor guard for the missing. But maybe it was also because none of his new friends who were concerned about immigration and racism would ever find themselves being treated like he had, while his friend, although he had never exposed himself politically and was the son of a Bulgari executive, risked the same treatment. All that had to happen was a minor accident in that car owned by Shrila Gupta, mother of a kid with an Indian passport (and a Belgian one, too, for he had been born in the shadow of the Antwerp diamond market), in any case a kid who was barely 18 and whose driver's license was the only thing Italian about him.

This first came to Edo's mind while his associate, next to him on the striped camp chair, yawned and stretched, or rather, Edo watched him awkwardly aim the long arms that stuck out of his white polo shirt toward the heavens. The polo shirt was perfectly clean and white and bore a genuine crocodile on the front; the stainless steel watch with the rubber watch-band was worth about $6,000. Edoardo studied Andy from his light-colored moccasins right up to his hair cut: neither long nor short, and just slightly trendy, a "nice-looking kid" himself, a well-off "nice-looking kid," sure, but what cop or carabiniere would think that, when he had the wrong-colored skin, skin that now stretched and crinkled around his eyes as he yawned again.

"I'm sleepy."

Edoardo was thinking he needed to find a way to warn him before it was too late, although it was probable everything would continue on just fine for him as it always had. And anyway he was sure Andy wouldn't understand, he'd laugh in his face and say something like "come on, are you getting paranoid?" End of argument. But just then it occurred to Edo that maybe he was not paranoid at all, but a real fool, a reckless fool to have dragged Andy along with him on this unauthorized quest. Jesus! And if they stopped them and wanted to see their papers? Two hours away from home and from anyone who could help them. And just a few days before the new security decree was to take effect. He didn't have the slightest idea whether Anand Gupta had a proper residency permit. There was no need to wait until they had an accident; all that had to happen was for someone to spread the word that every day two kids, one of them certainly a foreigner, were down at the cemetery bothering the tourists.

Il Bianco—that student who had led the march from the Liceo Tasso down to Piazza Navona—would have dealt with the problem. Edoardo, the kid who had emerged from five hours at police headquarters, Edoardo Radosław Bielinski, no. He no longer believed there was any way to guarantee his own safety. And that was a hundred times truer for Andy, now curling up in his seat all sleepily unaware, deep in that gilded innocence Edo didn't ever wish to drag him out of. What could he do to protect him?

"You've been yawning and saying you're sleepy for an hour now, can I say something? If you're bored out of your skull here, you could go back to Rome, you know."

"But why? I'm just tired, I'm relaxing. I was thinking that soon we could go have a look at the abbey and then have lunch."

"The abbey? But do you really care, or do you just want to do something? Come on, confess, you're bored."

"It's a stone's throw away. It's the abbey of St. Benedict, it's one of the oldest in the West."

"Andy, it's not one of the oldest monasteries in the West. It was reconstructed stone by stone after the war; the Fascist-era building I live in is older. There's absolutely nothing left of the original that the good tourist must dutifully go and see."

"So what? You've seen it and I haven't. Can I go?"

"But what do you care about the abbey? Can you tell me that in your own words, not in phrases that sound like they come from the Touring Guide? Why do you always have to play the star pupil, why don't you go and pay your respects to the Indian soldiers who took a bullet here, like I've been suggesting for days?"

"Because I'm more interested in the abbey, okay? Because quite honestly just to look at somebody's gravestone just because he was born in India, who cares?"

"So, you couldn't care less?"

"Not much."

"In other words, you're telling me you're more interested in this super-Catholic restored stuff than in people who came from your own country? Do I have to tell you, Anand Gupta, that you're from India? Meaning you'll be lucky if they get that and don't confuse you with some Arab or fucking black guy?"

"What the hell's wrong with you today? I know I'm Indian, okay, but that doesn't mean I feel obliged to go and visit those fucking graves. I don't believe I saw you walking round and round the Polish ones. Even there in front of General Anders' tomb, all you said was, hey, what a drag."

"But they've been bringing me here my whole life, I've had it up to here!"

"Don't you get it…"

"Listen. What is it that I don't get, while you—you who've practically never been outside the Villa Borghese and Via Condotti—do get?"

This time Andy was truly offended. He had been about to tell Edoardo something he wasn't sure he understood himself: how great it was that there was a place where the commander of an army wanted to be buried just a few feet away from his soldiers, and how fascinating that man's story was, more incredible than the war films they both liked. But now he was certainly not even going to try.

"Edo, you're such a self-righteous dick sometimes," he muttered. "Such an asshole," he said, keeping his eyes fixed on his Tod suede moccasins.

"Sorry. Really, I apologize. Shall we go and see the abbey?"

Edoardo was now on his feet facing his associate, waving a hand toward the huge white walls behind them, shifting his weight from one foot to the other, little steps that didn't help at all, not even to discharge his nervousness.

"No. Today, no. I don't feel like it any more."

"Do you want to go back to Rome, partner?"

"I just want to be by myself for a little while."

"Okay. Go. You can go right now."

Andy studied his Bulgari Diagono, according to which it was close to 11:30, and did not look up. Edoardo didn't know whether to sit down again or stand there without moving, waiting for him to make some sign.

"I'm going to sleep for a while. I'll be back in the early afternoon."

Edo began to walk, relieved he could finally move his legs forward. The uphill path was just fine, the effort, the motion, liberating. They walked up leaving the fliers on the chairs, one behind the other, along the border where the trees were, in the shade. Half-way up, they began to hear the voices. When things go wrong, they go really wrong, thought Edoardo, who was about to speed up so he could see how many visitors were arriving, but then felt ashamed in front of Andy. He didn't want him to plod on behind him, confirmed in the impression that what mattered most to Edoardo were the fliers, the missing, the Poles. And yet he was relieved to think he would need to run back, and even more relieved when he saw the parking lot and they were all still there. Amazing how all this silence could distort you perception of distances.

"There's a lot of them," said Anand, "do you want me to come back with you?"

"No, don't worry, you go. I'll manage somehow."

Now Edoardo couldn't wait to get down to work. "See ya!" he yelled through the car window, and began to run.

Andy sat there with the key in the ignition without starting the car, maybe to let some air in, or because he was tired and yes, disappointed, dejected. He yawned again and it was such a basic reaction that he relaxed, turning to look toward the road that led to the cemetery, where he didn't expect to see Edoardo. He was there, though, standing still and looking at the group approaching behind a wreath and a cross. And maybe keeping an eye on him too, so at that point he started the car and drove off.

When he got to the room he went to the bathroom and filled the toothbrush glass twice with water. A shower might be a good idea, but he didn't feel like it. He hadn't really sweated much. You can see I'm Indian, he thought to himself bitterly, with no desire to pursue the thought further. It was pointless, Edoardo wouldn't get it. He had his mission, his *dharma*, and I, mine. And he wouldn't have any idea what I'm talking about.

There were no incoming calls on his cell phone, especially none from Edoardo, which meant he was still occupied with the crowd of visitors. Afterward, he was almost certain, he'd send a message repeating that Andy was free to go if he wished, or to stay, and excusing himself again.

But Andy was not actually free to do as he pleased because he had the car, without which it was difficult to get around, and because he had committed himself. He could therefore take off his shoes and his jeans, lie down on his side of the queen-size bed, and dedicate himself to what made sense right then, which was to get some sleep. But no, he couldn't sleep. He might as well turn on the computer, he thought, but then another idea came to him. He drew his legs up on the bed, crossed them and closed his eyes, concentrating on the Gayatri Mantra, as he'd been doing since last year when he had his *upanayam*, his coming of age ceremony, in New Delhi. He was a man now, and could even recite the mantra in his head, but he preferred to say it aloud. *Om bhūr bhuvah svah tat savitur varenyam bhargo devasya dhīmahi dhiyo yo nah pracodayāt.* He went on chanting the sacred verses until the croaking noise that emerged from his throat settled into a normal-sounding voice. When he breathed out the final *om*, he felt calm.

He hadn't heard the beep announcing Edoardo's text. He replied that he'd be back at 2:30 or 3:00, and Edo immediately messaged back, "Thanks, partner!"

Anand wasn't hungry, or thirsty, or sleepy. He decided he would have lunch with Edoardo, sitting side by side on their camp chairs, as they had the other days. Later he would get some food to take to the cemetery. Later. He still had time. He lay back on the bed and picked up General Anders' *An Army in Exile*, sitting on the bedside table since last night. He decided to start at the beginning again, because there were a bunch of things he hadn't understood, or knew little about. For example, he hadn't remembered that there had been a Russian invasion of Poland along with the Nazi one.

Edoardo would say he was acting like the usual show-off, but Andy had begun to write his questions down in a notebook. What was General Rommel, who gave General Anders orders, doing on the side of the Poles? What did he mean, before that, when he wrote about the long years of "the other war" fighting under the command of the Khan of Nakhchivan, until Tsar Nicholas, "surrounded by his family" conferred on him the diploma of the Military Academy of St. Petersburg? Strange that he had begun his career in the Russian Army, but not impossible to comprehend. He could also just follow the passage in which Anders donned the cap with the Polish eagle but as for the rest, he was lost. So far as Andy knew, there was supposed to have been peace between the two wars, but Anders is racing from front to front: German, Russian, Ukrainian, revolutions, coups d'état, wounded, medals, apart from "two happy years" at the École Supérieure de Guerre in Paris.

Later, consulting Wikipedia, Andy was able to distinguish Juliusz Rommel ("Polish General") from Erwin Rommel ("German Field Marshal") and he would learn that Władysław Anders was the son of Germans from the Baltic and had been baptized a Protestant, but that he had made a vow to convert to Catholicism if destiny allowed him to get out of the Russian prison alive. This information too was disconcerting, because from the general's memoirs his Polish identity seemed to run deep in his soul and his blood. *His* Poland, his men, an affront by some Bolshevik toward a medal of the Virgin that seemed to injure him more than all the wounds and the beatings. It was this foreign world, of unpronounceable names, unfamiliar places, unheard of events, that fascinated Anand Gupta. It was the mystery of a man who had come through here and was now buried just a few steps away from where he, Andy, had been spending his days. And even more, it was the mystery of this piece of history that once again drew him in, so that while he continued reading chapter one, the Moleskin slipped between his pillow and that of Edoardo on that queen-size bed, and Andy just kept reading.

"The shadow of disaster had already begun to loom" wrote Anders of downcast refugees fleeing with all their household goods on every imaginable kind of vehicle, their livestock behind them. He had ordered fortifications to be put up near Płock to protect their crossing of the Vistola, his only possible line of retreat. The town of Mława resisted magnificently despite the enemy's superiority but now its defenders were ordered to withdraw to the rear at dawn. Passing through burning villages, Anders saw the bodies of civilians in the streets, many of them children. He saw a group of children being led by their teacher to shelter in the woods. Suddenly an airplane appeared, dropped to about 50 meters, circled, and began bombing and firing. "The children scattered like sparrows. The airplane disappeared as quickly as it had come, but on the field some crumpled and lifeless bundles of bright clothing remained." It was clear what this new war would mean.

Rivers to defend, rivers to cross, bridges destroyed, bridges to blow up, order, counter-orders, orders that came too late, orders ignorant of the real situation on the front, communication lines cut, high commands that had to scatter when Warsaw fell. The situation had grown critical, Anders knew. Advance, retreat, take refuge in the forest at night; roads destroyed by bombing, roads blocked by columns of refugees, German troops, air power capable of mowing down whole platoons, having to take their tanks over the fields, break through knowing they were surrounded, scrap their orders because the Russians were attacking at their backs, keep on heading southwest because that was the only direction they could go.

They continued to advance, joined by some of General Dab-Biernacki's men. Anders' orders were to attack the enemy between Zamość and Tarnawatka, having only cavalry units to deploy. "The only unit of mine with good morale and decent supplies was my old Nowogrodek Brigade." The Volinia Brigade was also capable of fighting but there was little left of the other units. Those were the only real troops under his orders.

They had to break through the enemy lines at all costs. On September 22, 1939 they attacked, and they made it through the next day, having first destroyed all their vehicles both armored and otherwise because they had no more fuel, nor could the petrol trucks get through because they had to drive across the fields. The remains of the artillery were mounted on the backs of four teams of horses, but the ground was very hard and the horses very, very tired. General Anders and his staff, on horseback, led the advance troops, stopping to watch as the Cavalry Brigade Volinia brought down the German reserve troops in a bayonet charge.

They went forward. They fought at the Krasnobrod crossroads. The "magnificent and indomitable" Greater Poland Uhlans broke through with a cavalry charge, but nearly an entire squadron perished there. They took prisoners and freed hundreds of their own who had been captured by the enemy, but the Germans were breathing down their necks on all sides. They had to defend their flanks even as they could hear the guns echoing behind them. Still, they held out despite everything, and for a long time.

The Russians, however, were moving deeper into Poland, they heard. They must hurry, try to get through in time between the Nazi troops and the Soviet forces, they must reach the frontiers of the only friendly countries, Romania and Hungary, to try to save what was left of the Polish Army and regroup abroad. It was their last hope.

But both the men and the horses were utterly exhausted. They had been marching by night and fighting by day since September 1, and they could not always find woods to hide in. "Soldiers slept in the saddle and the officers had to keep riding along the columns to wake them," Anders wrote. "We could not order a halt as the men, once dismounted, fell so soundly asleep they could not be roused." But they weren't fast enough. They began to meet Soviet troops, forces that were ever larger and well-placed in the territory. General Anders sent one of his best officer, Captain Stanisław Kuczynski to their headquarters seek a temporary truce to let the Poles pass through to Hungary. "But in vain. He was robbed of all he had, and nearly lost his life as well." Almost immediately the Russians opened fire on them.

On September 27, the Polish artillerymen and fusiliers fired their final shots. The supplies were finished. The horses were exhausted and water had run out. There was no chance they could break through.

Breaking up into small groups, they dispersed in the woods, trying to move only at night, hoping to reach Hungary piecemeal. But the area was thick with Soviet troops, and there were also armed gangs; it was dangerous to send out reconnaissance patrols, or to approach villages, houses or roads.

They hid in the woods, resting their tired horses, ready to set out at sundown. But not much later they saw that Soviet units had surrounded them on all sides, with specific orders to capture Polish troops. The woods were thick and the ground marshy, so they left their horses and hid far from the trails.

As they proceeded on foot, they were tripping over tree roots to find the thickest and best part of the forest to hide in. When the Russian search patrol, shouting and letting off their guns like a hunting party, passed by, the Poles were hunkered down in the underbrush. One by one, General Anders stared the few men still with him in the face, willing them not to pull the trigger in their nervousness. At sunset they began to walk south. Nearing a village, they were attacked by a band of soldiers and partisans. It was gunshot at close range and then, hand to hand combat. "How wonderful at that moment was this handful of Poles!" Anders was wounded once, then twice. He could feel he'd been hit in the back and that his leg was bleeding profusely. He begged his comrades to leave him there, not wanting to keep them from moving on. He was determined he would not surrender to the enemy alive. But his men absolutely refused to abandon him. With great effort, pushing themselves to the limit, they carried him forward in their arms. He was hemorrhaging from one wound, then the other. Now he issued an unconditional order—they must reach Hungary—and said farewell to his marvelous soldiers.

Anand followed the General through the next chapter, when Anders came to his senses the next morning and decided he would drag himself to the next village, Jesionska Stasiowa, and take his chances along with Captain Kuczynski and private Tomczyk who had not allowed themselves to be ordered to leave him. He read of how Anders was taken into custody and immediately driven to the Red Army headquarters, how he passed though villages already occupied, all of them, and then Anand fell asleep with his head on the page.

It was daytime sleep, light, intermittent, more a state of reverie than sleep, in which horses moved in and out, horses as dark as shadows, or white and lathered, horses and woods, dark green trees, snow-covered land and treetops, woods that looked black and white under the moon. Shapes moving though a lunar landscape, small, dark soldiers huddled in their saddles: awake, asleep, one with their animals' backs, single shapes riding ahead. The one at the head of the column must be General Anders, gripping his horse's mane, dipping his head to pass under the branches, hooves silent, no neighing, no gunfire, just the general leading his soldiers over the white ground furrowed by hoof prints; more white on black, General Anders galloping through the forests of birch and fir of this land of his that was about to be defeated and occupied; the general fulfilling his *dharma* like Arjuna, leading his soldiers thought the night, the woods, the falling snow.

When Andy awoke, it was time to go, but without hurrying. He put his jeans back on, surprised to find he was perspiring a bit, but in fact, at that hour and with the shutters drawn, heat was the only thing that could get in the window. He splashed his face in the bathroom, and washed his hands letting the water run over his wrists. His dream had been like a movie, he thought; he must have seen something like it, but certainly not about World War II. Maybe *The Last Samurai*, or maybe even *The Lord of the Rings*, but the snow he'd added himself, snow from those parts where he'd never been, snow that he'd only seen once.

From the moment General Anders went into battle until he was taken prisoner 100 km from his destination, between September 1 and September 29, 1939, not one snowflake fell (even in Europe's far east, that was normal for the season), and not a drop of rain either.

The excellent weather, so sunny and dry, had shrunk the rivers and so there was nothing to stop the advancing German tanks. Enemy aviation had perfect visibility, and the Polish air force was no more.

The snow had arrived from the pages Anand had read the night before. It had filtered in from the future.

Irka in the Gulag

Maybe not Irena Levick and the Szer brothers, whose voyage took them to a camp in Arkhangelsk Oblast, but many other Poles reached their destinations as deportees just before General Anders was released from the Lubyanka, the last stop on his tour of Soviet prisons that began on that day in late September when, badly wounded, he was taken by the Red Army. He had been listening to the bombing raids inside his Moscow jail in the palace of the secret services, and although he was hopeful of what the fighting would bring, the consequences for him personally came as a complete surprise.

At 4 pm on August 4, the door to his cell opened.

"Whose name here begins with the letter A? Quick, quick, come to be examined."

Something felt quite strange, even there in the corridor. Nobody pinioned his arms behind him, as he'd grown used to. The prison commander appeared and Anders, on crutches, was helped up the stairs. Finally "I was shown into a big, beautifully furnished study, full of carpets and soft armchairs." There were two men, not in uniform, behind the desk.

They spoke to him and he asked their names. Beria. Merkulov. When asked whether he wanted tea or a cigarette, Anders enquired whether he was still a prisoner, or a free man.

"You are free." they said. Then he would have both the tea and the cigarette, he replied.

The NKVD—the People's Commissariat for Internal Affairs, the ultimate decider of destinies for all those under Soviet dominion— informed him that a treaty had been signed with England that included an accord with the Polish government in exile in London.

They were now to live in harmony, that is, fight together against the Germans, those vile Nazi traitors. Soon there would be an amnesty for all Poles, and under the agreement, an army would be formed. And he, Władysław Anders, the most popular man among all the Poles in Russia, was to be its commander! Comrade Stalin himself had taken an interest in his case!

While the second statement might well be true, Anders had no doubt that the other one was a lie, and he asked himself what it meant, for if it was mere flattery it seemed exaggerated. In any case, a few days later he really was freed, and even conveyed to his luxurious new quarters in Laventiy Beria's limousine, still wearing NKVD trousers that sank over the bare feet inside his shoes.

All the Poles interned in the Soviet Union, not just the war prisoners but the civilians scattered around the gulag camps, their families and all the others in exile there: from that moment all were free. Free to come to him and become soldiers fighting to liberate Poland. However, many of them did not know this, or would only learn it very late, and some—who knew how many—would never learn it at all. And even when they did hear of it, the directors of the camps did not always willingly let them out, were not always inclined to do without their labor.

Whenever it was that Irka and the Szer brothers reached their lager in Arkhangelsk, an entire winter went by before they learned of the amnesty. They were free, and didn't know it. Just as they didn't know they had shared the same territory with the man set free without socks, the man who would lead them out of bondage from their arctic Egypt in the forests.

General Anders, too, was taken to Lviv when captured, and it was there that the bus about to deport him to the east with other prisoners, broke down. The general was badly wounded, and he protested that he was bleeding and could not move, could not continue traveling the next day. Finally the NKVD agents looked for a hospital, but all were full, and then the military hospital took him in.

It was to this that he owed the fact he wasn't sent to a camp, he wrote. It may also have been why, he thought, he didn't share the fate of his fellow officers at Katyn.

Less than two years later, Stalin must have thought it was his luck (no, the proof that infallible historical necessity stood at his side) to dig up from his dungeons at least one general among all those that just six months earlier he had ordered be executed. That was probably why he took an interest in Anders! Yet while he'd escaped the massacre of Polish officers, the fact that Anders was still alive at that moment was probably closer to a miracle performed by that Virgin the general so worshiped than the result of the determinism Stalin was devoted to.

While Anders was in hospital at Lviv in the autumn of '39, the NKVD tried several times to enlist him. They even proposed he become a Red Army commander. "Think about it," they said to him, "and we'll talk about it next time." He didn't like that at all. He still had a bullet in his leg and his injuries hurt enough to discourage any fantasies about a solitary escape. The only way he could think to evade what Soviet minds seemed to have in store for him was to get himself sent to Nazi-occupied Poland, wait until he recovered, and then try to flee across the border. At last, thanks to some connections he had cultivated, he got himself, along with some other wounded officers, onto a train headed into German territory. But the train came to a halt at the border town of Prsemyśl, and there it remained for several days. The NKVD guards kept reassuring them they would soon depart, but their reassurances rang ever more hollow. It must have been humiliating for Anders to know he was trapped, his physical condition making a fool of him with his destination so close at hand, within reach for anyone who could walk. And was it not an even crueler joke, an even more macabre twist of fate, that he, the general of German origin hankering to fight for Poland, stood blocked, while perhaps right in those very days, the young doctor Jósef Szer of Będzin had managed to re-cross the border?

The train did not move. Anders and the other wounded officers were transferred to a bus and sent back to Lviv. During the winter months of 1940, when Miss Irena Levick was defying the Soviet order for a violin, Władysław Anders was in the Brygidki prison, where a massacre would take place when the Germans neared, but by that time the general was already in Moscow. First in a cell so crowded the other prisoners ate up all the air, sleeping twisted up on the floor practically one on top of the other, often getting no water for days on end. And then, pushed and kicked on his crutches, made to tumble down the stairs more than once, bruised and scraped, he was locked up in solitary confinement in a cell with a broken stove and a window with bars but no panes.

They hadn't returned his uniform and he was only wearing an undershirt. It was a cold winter, with temperatures that went down to -30 C. "A warden brought in a bucket of water, which immediately froze, and another bucket for excrement."

Every two or three days, he got a murky soup and a crust of bread. No doctor. No clothing. The window still without glass. He was let out of his cell just once. After six weeks his hands and feet were frost-bitten, his face covered with sores oozing pus.

His end was near, he thought. He had become so thin and so weak that his wounds and the cold no longer hurt. He was convinced he could not hold out another two weeks.

His only visitors were the men of the NKVD, who came to search him. A scrupulous exam of his cell and bodily cavities was carried out with great skill and brutality. They even searched "the long beard which had grown during my imprisonment and which was stiff with pus that had run into it from my frostbitten face." He was beaten repeatedly on such occasions.

After eight weeks in that tiny, private white hell, on February 29, 1940, General Anders was transferred to Lubyanka, the political prison in Moscow. The first trains bearing deportees had left for that great outdoor collective, that gulag universe so gigantic it will never be mapped, all the camps, the colonies, the prison towns, and all of those who disappeared inside them. In the occupied cities these were mainly those who had served in the Polish state bureaucracy, whether in high positions or low: policemen and judges, mayors and deputies and also teachers, railway workers, postal workers, right down to the postmen. In the countryside, whole villages disappeared: farmers and woodsmen, and not just Poles but Belarusians and Ukrainians. The February cold was so harsh that even before they arrived at the trains, at the gathering points or on the trucks to the stations, small children literally froze.

Irka, too, who despite the air conditioning turned high in her tiny apartment had beads of sweat on her brow, told me over and over again how cold it was.

"In Arkchangelsk Region, we were cutting wood in the forests, and it was 40 below zero, *minus vierzig!*"

Wood-cutting. In the forest. There was no other work there, just that. And nothing all around but forest. There in Arkhangelsk Oblast, west of Siberia, south of the Arctic Circle. Where the earth had been able to cover itself with virgin forests, tall trees that had never been downed except by wind, or age or some disease corroding them from within. And where now, thanks to the prisoners' toil, and to the vast supply of labor furnished by the gulag system, those trees were ready to become planks, houses, furniture, even toys for the children of some apparatchik or prizes for some exemplary Socialist child. Arkhangelsk Oblast is larger than Poland both before and after the war. But those who were tossed into it had no idea. They could not see "the forest for the trees," as the saying goes.

Needless to say, Irka was not cut out to be a lumberjack, dragging tree trunks through deep snow and piling them up on sleds to be drawn by horses back to camp. Tree-cutting was one of the hardest jobs in the gulag. Gustaw Herling understood that immediately, and when he arrived at Yertsevo he right away sold his boots to one of those criminals who count in the lager hierarchy, in order to be chosen for his company and not sent out into the forest. It may well be that Herlings's lager and that of Irka, both in Arkhangelsk Oblast, both devoted to lumber and sawmills, fell under the Kargopol'lag, the group of "corrective labor camps" headquartered at Kargopol. Or perhaps not, but it is curious that Herling recalls the "clouds of Jews" who tried to cross into Soviet territory across the River Bug taking off from one of them: Zelik Leyman, a barber in Warsaw as he was in Yertsevo, a privilege that according to the old camp barber he owed to his status as a spy, which to Herling "seemed probable, because Leyman had miraculously avoided the fate of other Jews from Poland," who were sent to "a slow death in the forest."

Irka, too, might have died of exhaustion in the woods. Or rather, she might have fallen into the vicious cycle of fatigue, which meant her production fell, and therefore her rations were reduced, so that the next day her production was further reduced, and so her rations further cut. But she had met Zygmunt on the train to the camp, and Zygmunt Szer was part of her work brigade. He had been courting her from the start. He courted her in a way that he couldn't have done had they met as refugees in Lviv, not to mention before the war, when they were bright young Jews of the day. He courted her by helping her load logs on her sled.

"My horse didn't like him one bit; he even tried to bite him once."

"Seriously? The horse was jealous of Zygmunt?"

"Well, maybe," said Irka, laughing and growing tender. "He was handsome, that horse of mine, huge and all white."

And I too felt tender, thinking of that poor horse: he, too, deported to a wilderness of snow and trees, reduced to biting poor Zygmunt. In Irka's photo albums and in my memory, my mother's cousin Zygmunt always looked the same. Not much taller than his wife, his hair combed back and stuck to his head first with Brillantine, and later with water, always a pair of thick glasses with dark frames before his eyes. Unlike the white horse, he was neither large nor handsome. Zygmunt Szer, chemist specialized in beer-making, incarnation of the slight, studious Jew: was it not already a miracle that he too hadn't succumbed to the cold, the waist-high snow, the weight of those gigantic trees, and instead with constancy, with devotion, risking the ire of a horse even, had taken it upon himself to help Irka. Love, at times, is a great and amazing thing.

In the camp, too, Irena Levick and Zygmunt Szer were neighbors. The hut where Irka slept with her step-father and step-brother along with an entire Polish family was right next to that of the Szer brothers, with Benno the lawyer's wife, and her brothers. And that suggests this was not quite a lager but rather a village of forced residency, along the lines of those that began with the deportation of the Kulaks, who were dragged from their lands as a class to be liquidated during collectivization in the Thirties.

In the "corrective labor camps," men and women were housed in separate barracks, children too, until they were old enough to be sent to orphanages. But when entire populations began to be deported—Poles, Ukrainians, Balts, Finns, Volga Germans, Crimean Tatars, Chechens, Uzbeks, Kalmuks, Ingush, and all the other Central Asian and Caucasus nomads—not all ended up in true camps. They merely had to be sent somewhere and set to forced labor, and with the help of that space and that time the great Soviet fatherland was rich in, they would be decimated.

But when Irka spoke of the place she was deported to, she simply called it a lager. Lager: the word is the same in both German and Russian, and there is a similar gamut of double-barreled neologisms created by both regimes that employed them, to distinguish one camp from the other. In everyday speech in those languages, just one of those compound names is familiar: *Vernichtungslager*, "extermination camp," the one equipped for, and aimed at, exterminating human beings. Certainly, between a Nazi forced labor camp and a concentration camp whose prisoners were mostly Jews, between a "soft" Soviet camp and one north of the Arctic circle, there were measurable differences in terms of the numbers of dead, an unambiguous criterion. But both were places where there was nothing beyond the lager. A world where you were imprisoned, inspected, forced to work like a slave, deprived of all rights like a slave, subjugated by hunger like a slave. A world apart. Where spiritual destruction intensified with every further day you spent there, and your physical death, if not actually an aim, was part of the equation, like the depreciation of a machine. A *lager*, from the deportee's point of view, is something that cannot be called by any other name. From the point of view of the person who gives a name to the world she has landed in, it is one of the very last things she's still free to do there inside.

Did Irka's lager had a name of its own? That minimal lager, just Polish and Polish Jewish deportees, rules laid done under an economic plan, work brigades sent out to the woods to fulfill their objectives, accountants to register the results, a few NKVD guards and a commander. Perhaps it was not even enclosed by barbed wire, in any case the virgin forest served as a fence along with the ice and snow that covered it nearly all year long. Where could you possibly escape to?

A tiny lager, where at night the prisoners took turns standing guard. What did they guard against, considering there was no human presence for miles and miles? Against the Germans, said Irka. Out there, somewhere, the Wehrmacht continued to advance, had perhaps already besieged Leningrad, and Arkhangelsk, remember, is not in Siberia, but west of the Urals. It's possible however, that with hindsight the Germans threaten even her Russian memories, that the map has shrunk between Treblinka and Arkhangelsk Oblast.

And so it happened that she, too, was called to guard duty one night. Alone, with a stick, right at the edge of the woods, among the first trees, even. This time Zygmunt couldn't help her.

"A big stick, wood," said Irka, and she pulled herself up on her legs to show me how she held it with two hands.

"Wie ein ganzer Mann," said Irka, "I had to be a real man." She winced a little, whether in pain at some vertebra half-crushed in standing up, or just half mocking herself.

The stick was not for Germans, but for wolves. There were many wolves in the forest.

"Eine ganze Kompagnie," said Irka. A "whole pack" of wolves appeared. Some were small, but two of them were quite large.

"I was horribly afraid, but if you run, that's it. If you try to get away, they jump you. My fear was awful."

Luckily the night was not dark; rather it was a white night. In the dusky light Irka kept her stick out in front of her and began to move backward, guessing where to step, her feet trembling. She kept going backward slowly, keeping an eye on the pack, until she reached the clearing. Only when she had seen them stop and then slip back into the forest behind one of the big ones, did she turn and run for the huts.

It was after that night that Irka gave in. "I was on good terms with the camp commander because I spoke Russian well. But I didn't want to profit from it. I wanted to do the same job that everyone else did."

But her terror at having to go back out into the forest with the wolves was too great. "Don't make me go out there again, Komandant," she begged. "I was so afraid that the wolf would swallow me up."

That's how she said it: *verschlucken*, to send down, swallow. Was it because she couldn't think of the word for *slaughter* or *devour*, or did she choose the word on purpose? Having seen the way she just raised one eyebrow, and considering that the wolf had now been reduced from a pack to just one, the second is not improbable.

A few months before, in the winter, she had contracted pneuomonia. *Lungenentzündung*. She had no trouble recalling that scrap of her father's lexicon, but no one there spoke German and pneumonia could be fatal in any kind of lager. Luckily there was Dolek, Zygmunt's brother, who was camp medic, and he looked after her.

"Do you know how easy it is to catch pneumonia in the woods and snow, wearing wet rags at minus 40?"

Minus 40. Forty degrees below zero Celsius: it was the only element of her story she repeated, it was almost a refrain as she told me about her time in the lager, never repeating anything or getting confused in her effort to recall. No, it was clear she enjoyed telling her tale, including the wolves, perhaps the wolves above all, and the horrible fear they inspired. It was fine to be in a pleasantly air-conditioned room on the third floor looking out on the main street, near the end of your life which has begun to bore you a little, telling your story to someone else like a fairytale. But 40 degrees below zero was inconceivable, indescribable, unspeakable to someone who has never touched that temperature, especially when outside at midday on a Saturday in Tel Aviv, it was about that much above zero.

"You can't even breathe at 40 below," she said at one point. It was a stab, some lame words left in the air as she held her hand over her mouth to show you what your breath was like at that temperature. As if your breath were there in front of you, frozen, shrunken into something solid and extraneous.

I nodded and smiled, for she made me think of Varlam Shalamov when he wrote how the prisoners at Kolyma could guess from their exhaled breath how many degrees below zero it was. When the fog froze, it was -40; if your breathing was noisy but you could still exhale, that meant it was -50; when your breathing became noisy and laborious, that was -60. Beyond that, "spit froze in mid-air."

Miss Irena Levick, sent to cut down a forest, probably suffered the extremes of cold at 10 degrees above that which punished the veterans of Kolyma. Maybe the reason she asked the camp commander to be transferred to the accounting office was the fear of that minus 40, not the fear of wolves—those villains both real and denizens of fairytales. Despite the implicit nod at Little Red Riding Hood, I don't doubt those wolves were real, both them and the terror they inspired. But there are stories that turn unreal, almost deceitful, in the telling, even for those who have lived them, making them lighter and easier to exorcize. That body of hers that was first damaged at minus 40 when she was seventeen, had survived beyond the age of eighty-six, and now it hurt her all the time. Inside her, in the tissues of her lungs rent like those of a careless diver, were the things that could not be told.

However Irka arrived at the safe haven of office work, what she now had to do was keep count of the production achieved by each brigade. Not the easiest task for a girl who had studied at the *gymnazium*, but a prisoner who did know how, a Pole with an accountancy diploma, was patient enough to give her a hand.

"I learned quickly. I was always good in mathematics."

It was not such an innocent job, for the transubstantiation of lumber in rations of soup and bread was based on her calculations. Someone among the prisoners had to do it, though, and someone, one hoped, would be good enough to close an eye—blue or not—on the cheating necessary to reach the production quotas.

Now Zygmunt didn't have to break his back and split his hands lifting extra tree trunks. But he didn't need to, in any case. It seems Zygmunt Szer had proposed marriage to Irena and she had said she was very happy to accept. Who can say whether Zygmunt might ever have won a woman as beautiful as Irka, as intelligent as Irka, as full of talent as she, and even a bit mysterious, like all those who wear an air of solitary independence, except by courting her as he did in the lager.

For Irka, though, the value of that love measured in trees must have been quite clear, and she never forgot it for the rest of her life. She spoke of her husband with a knowing irony that left no doubt, not even one, that her veiled affection was not mere gratitude.

It seems she understood right off, Irena Levick, what he meant to her—that man with his ever more spindly legs, his ever more chafed and callused hands, those glasses of his that fell in the snow and were a catastrophe to recover—that person who just kept saying "I'm here." If there was any advantage, just one, to being in the lager, it was that you didn't err about people: about what they were worth and who they were, at their best and at their worst. From the day her father had died of blood poisoning, it was the first time Irena knew there was someone she could count on. That she had not only her violin, but Zygmunt Szer to hold onto. And she was still serenely aware of it when we spoke, telling me her story, glancing toward the wall where a photograph of the two of them hung:

Irena, blond hair regally back-combed in the manner of the Sixties; Zygmunt in jacket and tie, looking the same as ever. It must have been why the story of her deportation unfolded so smoothly, and even had the faint cadence of a fairytale.

And so Irena Levick and Zygmunt Szer were married in the lager.

"What? That old Jew?" the camp commander said when he learned about it. Perhaps not only the white horse was jealous.

"I'm also Jewish," she recalled telling the Komandant and apparently that was enough for him.

Okay, Zygmunt was Jewish, and not very handsome, but old?

I wondered if that "old Jew" was the remembered version of a far worse insult, as if memory itself could exert a sort of delicacy.

If the not-long-to-be Miss Levick did indeed have that kind of hold on the camp commander, perhaps we should not be so very surprised that in the end, they were wed in that lager. And not just married in on paper, or in bed: married in a proper Jewish wedding.

For the chuppah, you need a strip of cloth and four sticks, and of sticks, however crooked and unfinished, there were many. The synagogue itself is not indispensable, and with the relatives of the bride on one side and the brothers of her betrothed on the other, one hut or the other was quite sufficient. There were many Jews in the lager, though, and the family of Poles in her hut, the accountant and quite a few others who really ought to be invited. The hardest part was the rabbi. In that small lager in the forest there was only the Hassidic Talmud scholar who hadn't yet finished his studies and become a rabbi. However, he had learned to write up a *ketubah*, a marriage contract. And if the bride would steal a pen and a sheet of paper without columns on it from the office, a sheet of paper blank on one side at least, with the aid of HaShem, blessed be his name, he could and would write one up. They were a nomadic people, after all, and with the consent of the Most High, a temporary exception from the law could be made, both in the desert and in the forest.

Finally all was ready: the wedding canopy for Irka and Zygmunt, an old scarf to serve as a veil, even the glass to shatter by stamping on it, precious as a glass was. It wasn't every day that someone in a lager got married.

Then someone, perhaps the Polish woman, the mother, with whom Irka shared her hut, took her aside one evening just before the wedding.

"Słuchaj Irusiu, look: we didn't even know you were Jewish. We think of you as one of us. I mean this with all my heart, z całym sercem. We too would like to celebrate your marriage!"

"Of course, of course, thank you. You too, have come to be like family for me, and I would be very pleased if you came."

"No, wait, Irka, that's not what I meant. We would like to celebrate your wedding in our way."

"You mean with a priest? Quite honestly, we couldn't do that, and anyway there isn't…"

"Oh heavens, no; I understand. However, if you don't mind we would like to celebrate a nice Polish wedding. In addition. Afterward."

And so on a single day Irka and Zygmunt became man and wife twice: first under a chuppah of sticks and rags, then blessed with sprinkles of water that became holy, with the Poles making the sign of the cross, and bringing the couple bread and salt, an offering both exceedingly generous, and auspicious.

"I was married twice in one day," said Irka. "In the lager," she repeated punctiliously, apparently still quite proud of it.

If that was not the best day of her life, it must still have been one of the very best of all those they all spent in that camp. Almost as good as the day when they learned they were free to go.

It was quite unbelievable, this story of Irka's: more so than the wolves, more than the horse that was jealous when Zygmunt piled logs on her sled. True, the gulag was full of clerics of every sort of faith, and what was forbidden wasn't belief, it was the practice of a religion. It was not forbidden to be a Christian, but just about every monastery and church had been seized, deconsecrated, very often turned into a lager or a prison. It was not forbidden to be a Jew, but the Hebrew language was outlawed. Nevertheless, there in Arkhangelsk Oblast, with the camp commander's knowledge and possibly even the light of the Arctic day, two religious ceremonies, two sacred unions, were consecrated in a single day!

Perhaps it isn't right to keep on using the word *lager* for this village—okay, there were wolves, and it was terribly cold, and they had to go out into the forest and cut wood—where, all in all, compared to other camps, things were not terrible, however. Or is it?

There was one episode that Irka told me later, almost by chance. Emil Goldwag, her stepbrother, she said, had joined the Polish Army and then transferred to the British Army, and because he was a minor they had given him the chance to finish his studies in England and become an engineer.

"And your step-father?" I asked. It seemed he had been heard making the remark, "Stalin doesn't go around wearing rags like this," and then, said Irka, "they arrested him and took him to another lager, a penal camp."

"Stalin geht nicht herum in solchen shmatn," she said again, and in those *schmattas*, those rags, the only Yiddish word she spoke, was all the horror she preferred not to remember. *The good ones to the pot, the bad ones in the crop*: memory selects like the doves in Grimm's tale of Aschenputtel, and who can say it shouldn't? At that point I ceased to ask myself why (never mind the joy she must have felt on one particular day) she continued to call the place a lager.

Liberation day. Was there really such a thing? A day on which only the commander, guards, NKVD were left in the camp—and maybe, but this would be too good to be true, the bastard spy who reported the comment about Stalin? A day on which all the agents of the counter-revolutionary forces were suddenly once again citizens of an allied nation, a state represented by a legitimate government, albeit in exile? Did they—double file as they had gone out to their work in the forest in that incommensurably distant time of a few days before—now proceed slowly with their papers and old suitcases in hand or on their backs, toward freedom, out?

This is probably the matter about which I most regret not interrupting Irka's flow of memory. Why did I ask her so few questions? No dates, for example ("Now do you remember when you were deported?"), no precise details ("Can you describe what your lager looked like?"); why didn't I at least try? Was it because of those beads of sweat on her forehead, signals that while she was speaking to me her back was hurting her; my uncertainty how long her spinal column would support this tale of hers? Was it because of the way the spectres of her father and mother had come forth immediately—and now I was going to call up more dead, will them from the lamp entire and then leave them with her in her tiny apartment? You mustn't wake the somnambulist while he's walking: perhaps that would be the best way to describe the instinct that guided me. I was afraid to take Irka onto a terrain where some nebulous memory would leave her shaky and insecure, like those prisoners struck with malnutrition-caused night blindness that Herling writes about, who when dusk was coming on, would try to get back to camp as quickly as possible. Afraid that some similar discovery she hadn't been in control of her past life would make her not want to talk about it. I feared she might be humiliated by the absurd circumstance in which the one asking the questions seemed to know more than she who had lived through it—and this I did not want.

I wanted her to be the craftsman of her own story, the one lending it tones and colors; I wanted her to be free to contradict herself or jump around, free to choose what to tell me and what not. Because—yes, my mother was right—I am not a historian. My material can be full of gaps, vagueness, things not said, things transfigured, but also chasms that open up in a phrase or even half of one. What's more, the truth itself, the one I am trying to make emerge through her, is made that way, and risks being distorted if it does not belong completely to the teller. If, among all the violations suffered by one who has survived the totalitarian grindstone, the worst is the loss of innocence, what right can there be to question someone in the name of truth that isn't also a kind of violence? Ask me no questions, I will tell you no lies.

But it was not just this. Irka did not speak to me of things that ought to have been remote from acute pain, or even embarrassment. True, at 11:00 am she ate an Israeli breakfast with bread, fresh cheese and salad, and around 2:00 she offered lunch prepared by Raissa—soup, followed by chicken—and then Shoshana's dessert, which it seemed she ate because eating was a habit that filled her days. But in all her war memories, including the lager, the word *hunger* never came up once. Could she be so much the well bought-up young lady still, that hunger was for her like money, something that good manners prevented you from mentioning? The cold, the fear, even the harsh remorse for her mother's fate were all things that could be spoken of or shown, while the hunger no, hunger remained veiled by what—shame?

Then I thought about something said by a friend of Polish origins, with whom I'd gone to the 65th anniversary commemoration of the battle of Monte Cassino. Paolo Morawski is a historian who has made radio documentaries, and he had interviewed Gustaw Herling several times along with other veterans of the Second Army Corps.

"You know," said Paolo, "whenever I go around interviewing people about the war, I always hear about the hunger people suffered. But the Poles I know never speak of it. Does it seem likely to you that people in Italy suffered more from hunger than Poles did?"

We agreed that no, it was unlikely. That in Italy the memory of hunger came first, while in Poland it was so far down the list—after the carpet bombing, the summary executions, the lagers of the one side and the other, the very cancellation of the national state—as to be forgettable. If in Poland after the war every family had to count its dead and its members lopped off by the frontiers of the new blocs, what difference could it possibly make that they had gone hungry in wartime? Why would a Polish Jew like my mother, who survived Auschwitz, or Irka, a Russian lager, indulge in recollections of hunger? Were they still alive? What more could they ask? To speak of hunger, even just to mention crusts of dry bread and stinking soup, was gross ingratitude, or simple indecency. The others died, and you were merely hungry. You were so merely hungry as not to notice it. That was the obscenity kept silent, with a silence rent only by those who had the courage and the specific will to recount everything.

And yet, if this story could be told from the point of view of hunger, some things would be immediately clear. It would be clear that the count of the drowned and the saved did not end just the other side of the lager gates. Hunger did not end there, or rather, as happened in Nazi camps when they were liberated, the end of hunger sometimes meant the end of life. To die with a full stomach! That desire came true for many a skeletal body that had resisted up until that day. But not in the Soviet Union. In the Soviet Union, hunger did not end, period. In the Soviet Union, freed prisoners were also mouths that didn't have to be fed. And it seems that this was often the grounds upon which prisoners were released. Who costs us more than they produce? Old people, women, children, orphans, and among the men, the exhausted ones, the ones least useful in the huge wartime effort the Soviet fatherland was carrying out in those invisible Arctic trenches.

General Anders had reason to complain about it, five months after they had begun to appear at the transit camp, those men with their feet wrapped in rags, and their stories. On December 3, 1941, the head of the Polish government in exile General Sikorski went to Moscow on mission for the first time, after the Red Army, the anti-aircraft weapons and the cold had finally pushed the Germans back. From October until the end of the counter-offensive that was in the works, a million Soviet soldiers would be in the field, but reasons of state demanded that the tiny Polish forces also be counted.

SIKORSKI informed Stalin that the amnesty he had ordered had not been implemented. "A great number of our most valuable people are still in labor camps and prisons."

STALIN, taking notes: "It is impossible, because the amnesty applied to all Poles and all Poles were released." His words were directed at Molotov, who nodded his head.

ANDERS, providing details at General Sikorski's behest, told them that was not how matters effectively stood. The useful people had been detained and only a few had been given their freedom. There were men in his Army who had informed him that there were "hundreds, even thousands of our countrymen in various camps." The camp commanders didn't comply because "they could not fulfill their production plans if they lost their best workers."

MOLOTOV, smiling, nodded.

Already in the autumn, when Leningrad was under siege and the hunt for rats, crows and every other crawling, flying thing had begun, prisoner Gustaw Herling could not understand why the amnesty "passed me by as if with some inexplicable obstinacy." Each night he went to inspect the the transit barracks, "where parties of Poles, leaving other camp sections for freedom, would spend the night before their final release." This went on until the end of November when, only six of the 200 Poles at Yertsevo remained, and

Herling asked himself whether he had been "by mistake crossed off the list of the living." Now certain he would not survive until the spring and having lost any hope he would be freed, he decided to go on a hunger strike in protest.

Why were they not freed, those six Poles, one of them a woman who'd been a teacher? Who can say? In Herling's case, there was an informer who stood in the way, he later learned, but what about the others? Yes, the gulag universe obeyed the law of the exploitation of labor, but that most monstrous face of the Soviet state was also ruled by the purely arbitrary. Decisions about freedom or slavery, about life or death, could rest in the hands of anyone: the camp commander, the NKVD, your companion in prison who denounced you for some tiny reward.

Herling's hunger strike was thus a wager hurled into that arbitrary world, a near-untenable test for a body "in the final stages of scurvy, physically exhausted" his reason intact to the extent he could imagine only three varieties of death: to be shot immediately, condemned to die for his action, or to starve to death.

On January 20, 1942, when Herling had recovered his health after months in the hospital and in "the mortuary" (where prisoners were sent to die) and was finally released, the people of Leningrad were sacrificing their domestic animals, and the death rate each month for human beings had reached 100,000. The freed Polish prisoner was given a residence permit and a list of places for which he could buy a train ticket. There was no way he could reach the Polish Army. The NKVD officer, "now all politeness" claimed not to know where that army might be, but even if he had known, Herling could never have joined it "because the route that prisoners released from Kargopol camp were allowed to take stopped at the Urals." It would be another two month odyssey—more deaths, more hunger, trains boarded with the hope he would not be discovered or denounced for transit in forbidden areas—before he finally arrived at the Polish Army transit camp in Kazakhstan.

Meanwhile, Irka and the Szer brothers? All I know is that they traveled through Tashkent and ended up in a holding camp near Samarkand. Which meant that freedom was slow to arrive for them too, because the Polish troops were only transferred to the central Asian republics from January 1942. "Somehow they were able to escape the lager": I remembered my mother's words the first time she told me her cousins' story, as it had been told to her by Irka. "Somehow they escaped." But how? And how did they reach Uzbekistan from the forests of Arkhangelsk Oblast?

"By train," Irka said, adding no more.

As if a train had been waiting outside the gates to transport them 3,000 kilometers (as the crow flies), a train with comfortable seats and carts coming by to serve food and drink.

Many Poles, some of them children deported with their mothers when their fathers were locked up in prison camps or the gulag, have testified that voyage was the worst, far worse than deportation itself. After a moment of joy, when in one way or another they learned they were free, they rapidly understood that there was no one to conduct them out of Soviet slavery. Many, considering the tender age or poor health of their family members, decided not to leave. The rest—piling their few possessions and their relatives unable to walk onto sleds—men, women and older children, dragged themselves dozens and dozens of kilometers through the snow to the nearest train station. Or they perched on rafts and let themselves be carried down the rivers, praying the water wouldn't freeze. And supposing they did get to the rail station, they had to find money to buy tickets for a train that might not even exist. Then, after maybe a week, if a train did come, the cars would be overflowing with Russians being evacuated from the fighting toward the east, and exhausted Red Army troops in transit. Freight trains, of course, which, if you were lucky, might be carrying something edible you could steal, trains that were always stopping to let others with priority pass, trains that started up without warning leaving adults behind, standing in a queue to buy bread. More hunger, more thirst, more disease; more dead of hunger, thirst and disease: grandparents, especially, and very often little brothers and sisters. Months. As many as four, sometimes just two; but the exodus of those freed slaves and their disintegrating families—even with the invention of train travel—usually exceeded the forty days of Biblical ordeal.

When I think of Irka and the Szer brothers on those trains she doesn't speak about, I can't help but think of those railcars as something like Russian dolls, made of wood from the Arctic forests.

Inside the smallest car, the solid doll that cannot be opened, are the three million Polish Jews exterminated by the Nazis. The next larger one contains the five to five and a half million Poles who died at the hands of the Germans and the Russians, and the Ukrainians, while the largest doll that contains all the others holds the twenty three million people who died during the war in the Soviet Union.

When those travelers finally escaped their matrioska, though, when they got down from their train near Samarkand and arrived in the Jizzakh camp where the Polish eagle flew, their ordeal was still not over. The rations supplied by the Soviets to feed 40,000 soldiers had been reduced to quantities for 24,000, and had to be shared with a number of civilians who were more than twice that. Malnutrition continued to pile up victims.

The transfer of freed Poles to central Asia had been the result of a hard bargain with Stalin during the Moscow meeting, in order that those arriving in the early camps in the Urals didn't go on freezing to death. Yet the mild and increasingly warm climate to the east meant that all those diseases carried on filthy trains stuffed with lice-ridden passengers exploded. Epidemics of all kinds bloomed: dysentery, scarlet fever, and above typhus.

Flecktyphus, Irka told me. "I almost died."

Again it seemed urgent to her to recall the precise medical terminology. *Fleck* plus *typhus*: my first reaction was that this was hyper-precise, almost superfluously so, but then I discovered that Irka had reason to use that particular term. The *Flecken*, as the small red spots of dried blood are called in German, distinguish typhus spread by lice from other strains. And near Samarkand, in the first months of 1942, that variety of typhus infected countless numbers of Poles collected there.

The medical staff, doctors and nurses took enormous risks, wrote General Anders. They saved soldiers from certain death in appalling conditions, without medicines, beds, sheets or adequate food. There many deaths, particularly among the young.

Many meant *many*: thousands and thousands, ten percent of all the Poles who gathered in central Asia. But to save the young wife of Zygmunt Szer, there was her brother in law.

"Dolek got me to a hospital in Samarkand, and one day he arrived with wine, red wine, to treat me. He had joined the Polish Army as a medical officer and they gave him a lot to do; he was good. 'Drink this,' he told me, 'it will clean your blood.' And I drank and felt better, and drank some more, and in my delirious state I felt better and better, and I began to sing, and I went on singing while all around me they were dying like flies. But then the nurse came and took away that excellent wine."

Fighting for her life just then meant fighting for her freedom, for now it was clear the Poles were finally going to leave the Soviet Union. The British had made an agreement to transfer the Polish Army to Iranian soil, and the civilians were to go with them. And even Stalin, who was busy pushing back the German who had occupied the Caucasus and were attacking the city named after him, had agreed to allow 40,000 not very fit soldiers, plus many other useless mouths to feed, to depart. That departure was imminent when she left the hospital still weak and in pain, raising her head to look out of the army truck toward Samarkand's mosques and madrassas, once devastated by Genghis Khan then prized by Tamerlane and rebuilt as the capital of an empire.

There was news, good news, back at the Jizzakh camp where Zygmunt awkwardly embraced his wife, brought back to life by his brother's skills. One of Irka's uncles who had gone to Białystok and was deported from there to some lager, had reappeared, and as he was capable of driving a bus, was soon to drive a load of Jewish children to Iran. There were many, many Polish orphans as well, and despite great efforts to get permission for them to leave, only a few could be evacuated with General Anders. The Soviets insisted they could look after them, and this time neither economic plans nor any mission to educate the new generation in socialism was at stake. All of those children together on a boat with news cameras aimed at them, those 50,000 infant skeletons so similar to the ones who would later be freed from Nazi camps: it would be terrible propaganda. It was already perhaps unwise to have released all those Poles who in the coming decades would be the only ones to tell the world about the gulag. But a world in pieces had other priorities, or would rather not know; so Stalin reasoned. And the world mattered little next to his alliance with Churchill and Roosevelt.

Even Irka's stepfather made it to Jizzakh one day. Somehow, somewhere—how he knew where to go or how long he wandered around remained a mystery—he had found his son.

"He was unrecognizable, all broken," she said. *Ganz zerbrochen.*

Broken, like a plate that you drop, or a cup. Her eyes narrowed, and the grey grew more opaque.

Once again, I could not speak. There was just that image, an image that didn't flash by or return to the story's main course. The experts in propaganda are right: images are more powerful than stories. More powerful because they can't be explained. I understood this the following day when she showed me a photograph of her step-brother Emil taken in Palestine, wearing his *juniaki* uniform, that of boys between 12-17 enrolled in the Army. He looked older, already an adult.

"How handsome he is," I said, and without thinking asked, "is he your step-father?"

"Er war ganz zerbrochen," she repeated the words of the day before. And then, in almost a howl, for me who didn't understand. "Er war im Kazett."

Her step-father died in the Uzbeki camp not long after he got there. He died after dragging himself there from some unknown point in the Soviet gulag, a place that more than half a century later steals the word lager from Irka's mouth.

Images are stronger than stories even when they don't exist. When they are part of another sort of album, as immutable as those we paged through at the table, Aschenputtel's "bad ones", her discards. When they are made of words: just two words. *Zerbrochen,* an adjective that pertains to china; and *Kazett,* the letters K-Z in German, shorthand for the Nazi camps.

"Who could tell one of our faces from the other?" wrote Primo Levi of the camp attendents at Auschwitz. "For them we are *Kazett,* singular neuter."

Irka had seen one who stood for all, all those who never left the Kazett. So those two words, those two history-annihilating words of hers, revealed. That he had made it to the transit camp like a stray horse, like a lost dog that drops dead after rejoining humanity, counted for nothing, it was no consolation.

Perhaps that is why Irka never called her stepfather by his name.

The dead man was buried on Uzbeki soil; maybe they were able to find ten men to say prayers for him, maybe even a rabbi to say Kaddish, and then his last live traces were put away in the album of the dead. She had to find something to eat every day, had to think about the boy Emil, had to hang on to Zygmunt. Above all, they had to keep Dolek in sight, for he was the one who had the means to free them all. It was thanks to the stethoscope, to medical science, that they could escape Egypt. A doctor is always useful. He will never go unneeded in an army that is fighting to survive in order to go to war.

The day finally came when the ships were ready in the port of Krasnovodsk — the ancient name meaning "red waters" in Russian — recently rebaptised Türkmenbaşy, "leader of Turkmen" after a post-Soviet potentate wanting to glorify both himself and his large country's only maritime outlet. They arrived at Krasnovodsk in two waves of train convoys; the ships were filled to the hilt; they crossed the Caspian Sea, that vast inland sea with its sturgeon full of black gold in their bellies; they docked at Pahlavi. That port too has changed names; today it is called Bandar-e Anzali, the tribute paid to the Shah of Iran having been abolished. The Iranian Revolution, however, did not bother to meddle with the Catholic cemetery where those who expired aboard ship or just after, in tents on the beach, were buried.

> Here lie 639 Poles, soldiers of the Polish Army in the East of General Władysław Anders, civilians, war prisoners and detainees in Soviet camps who perished in 1942 returning to their country. May they rest in peace.

It was the last such tragedy, however. Certainly, the return to life was not immediate — for the ships also carried typhus and another 2,000 were destined to die — but those who survived this time now began to recover. The new land was beautiful. It was the opposite of their Arctic Egypt; there was not one pine forest along the entire way from Pahlavi to Teheran, only clean, warm air smelling of fruit trees, thickets of scrub, and roses. Never seen so many roses. Never imagined you could smell roses from the back of a half-covered military truck that stank of fuel. What did the Iranians do with all those roses, so different from the ones remembered from pre-war films? It was hard to make out. But it was already a gift just to remember, in a flash, that roses existed. From the most devout Catho-

lics uprooted from country villages to the most secular of Jews who
had fled the cities, many of them felt that a land with so many rose
gardens must have something to do with paradise.

That thought did not occur right away, because for long stretches the landscape was dry and stony, but always bright with color,
and the people who lived there even more so. Seeing those people so unlike themselves as they walked about, halted, bowed to
each other, the children running through the streets, the markets
so thronged with crowds you could get lost, those worn-out bodies
began to sense what they had suffered beyond hunger and beyond
cold, how they had been deprived of color and of movement.

"They took us in, the Jews of Teheran, the rich ones," Irka recalled. "They took us into their own homes, and made sure we had
everything we wanted. They actually had us westerners eat at a
table, while they sat on carpets on the floor."

The head of the household where she stayed not only had the
means to equip his house with modern furniture, now of some use
for the first time, he also had a business that as Irka described it,
would have been quite a source of pride.

"He was the Shah's personal parfumeur!"

That was what all those roses were for.

It was in Teheran that the 115,000 evacuated Poles began to go
their separate ways. Some enrolled in Anders' Army, in those first
units training for battle, in the women's auxiliary and the youth
corps, continuing on their slow return to the continent where their
country was waiting to be liberated.

"They gave us uniforms, I had one too," Irka said, and it was
evident she didn't mind at all wearing the short, rather tightly-but-
toned jacket and side cap perched at an angle over her blond hair.

At last they resumed their voyage, across a land that for the first
time Irka was unable to name.

"We were in the desert," she said, and when I said "Iraq" she
nodded briskly, as if to concede that yes, that was probably it, but
it made little difference. Odd that she was unaware, and this I see
only now, that the road to Palestine led though the land of the pa-
triarchs and that of the Babilonian captivity, a sign, perhaps, that
her almost certain salvation provided the luxury of not having to
pay attention.

For Irka and Zygmunt, in fact, it was almost finished. In Palestine they stayed in the Polish army camp at first and then, still divided men from women, were housed in kibbutzim after some representatives from the Jewish Agency came to recruit them. If they almost immediately accepted the offer to stay, it was probably less out of faith in the Zionist dream, more to realize a private one. A house where they could live together, no more, no less. Thanks to an old friend they now met again, they finally went to live in Tel Aviv, in a white, Bauhaus-style building on Frishman Street, a building like those going up everywhere, with a balcony from which you could see the sea nearby.

Among those who instead stayed with General Anders were young Emil, who in Egypt would be taken under the wing of the Brtish Army, and Dolek, the officer-medic who would land at Taranto in southern Italy in September 1943 and be at the front at Cassino with the Second Army Corps the following May.

During those same months the diaspora of Polish civilians from Teheran sent many far from their native land. Quite a few ended up in India—still colonial, but not for long, and still un-partitioned with Pakistan—in places like Karachi and Quetta as well as many smaller cities in what would still be Indian territory after 1947. Poles would also end up in South Africa but above all in the British colonies of Kenya, Uganda and Tanganika. And finally, 733 orphans accompanied by about a hundred adults would disembark at the port of Wellington, New Zealand on November 1, 1944, to be sent to the Polish Children's camp at Pahiatua with immediate rights to future citizenship.

This crossing of the ways between soldiers departing for war and the stateless being offered asylum was actually less casual, and therefore less astonishing, than it might appear.All of them were history's secondary material—bodies to enlist and those to relegate to the margins—for a power like that of Great Britain which still held vast overseas territories. From the United States, where they called Stalin "Uncle Joe," no offers of asylum were forthcoming.

In one photograph, one of the first taken in Palestine, Irka still looked like someone at the threshold.

It was small, a document photo, and her gaze was captured straight on, pinioned by the camera.

"Look how thin I was," she said, evidently thinking I might not notice.

What I saw in fact, was a young woman, in a light flowered dress, hair to her shoulders, wavy and even a bit mussed, two eyes very blue, huge and dazzling as they would never be again. It was in that gaze both luminous and wide-open that you saw the moment of passage; it was only in her eyes that you saw how thin she was.

And then, the last traces of hunger and near-death disappeared from her face. There remained, however, one particular sorrow that Irka could not forget, because the gratuitous pain was what held her story together.

At the transit camp in Jizzakh her other brother in law, Benno, had also appeared. Alone. He had left his wife and her brothers, and gone off. He had abandoned her in the lager, or somewhere between the lager and Uzbekistan, and even today Irka was sick about it.

My mother tells me that unlike her cousin Jósek, who was always so good, Benek had been terrible from when he was a child, remembered for the time he leapt onto an already-moving cart on which the Szer family was moving all its belongings. "Oh and he liked women, he was a real bon vivant, but charming."

Women? In the lager?

"Do you know what he did?" said Irka. "We were at the port waiting for the transport ship, and he sold my violin for two buns and four eggs. And he was quite pleased with the deal!" She didn't raise her voice, which remained sweetly sarcastic. She could be nasty with elegance.

The violin! The one with which she had given concerts, along with a pianist, even in the lager, the one she carried with her all the way from Arkhangelsk region to Uzbekistan, the one Zygmunt had looked after for her while she battled typhus at Samarkand.

"I was enraged with Benno. About everything. Enraged."

And then Irka had gotten herself another violin and had continued to play it until she became a mother. And even today, when she no longer even painted because her back and sometimes her hands hurt, it was still a presence that anyone entering her house would notice: just above the sofa, centered over it, in the only self-portrait she had transferred to the residence for the elderly. Irka's hair, drawn back in an old-fashioned way and her face, painted in soft brushstrokes, shone in contrast to the nearly invisible strings and the body of the instrument in shadow. They made a timeless figure, a self-sufficient unity, idealized and modestly ecstatic.

It was the first time that Irka had expressed a feeling in my presence, or at any rate, called one by its name.

Rage, that was what was left of a violin bartered for two rounds of Arab bread and four eggs. Just two or three years previously, at Lviv, it had still been worth a good dress. But now, more than half a century later at Rishon LeZion (twinned with the city of Lviv in Ukraine) that violin, the memory of it, was still able to sound the voice that Irena Sher had not lost yet.

The Swallows and the Abbey

When Andy arrived at the cemetery at the appointed hour, everything seemed back to normal. Edo, when he saw him appear, clean
white shirt, knapsack on his shoulder, waved his arms wildly like
someone trying to flag down help on the highway, but really to
say, "You don't know what you missed!" It was obvious that whatever had happened in the interval had made everything simpler,
but Edoardo was glowing in that way of his, that exaggerated way
he had of getting fired up, and so Anand acquiesced to his friend's
urge to tell him right away.

"Those pilgrims, the ones before... Remember?"

"Pilgrims, before. Okay."

"You know, the Poles who were on a pilgrimage before. A trip
to religious places and to the Polish cemeteries in Italy. Roma, Monte Cassino, Loreto, and then the military cemetery at Ancona. And
Assisi, I don't know whether before or after. Have you ever been to
Assisi? It's really beautiful there, not like this place."

"Yeah, just about every time some relatives come to visit us in
the Maremma. *Take them around, darling, would you please?* San Gimi-
gnano, Siena, Volterra, Assisi, Gubbio, and of course Florence, on
its own."

"Hey, the complete tour. Not that I would expect any less from
you."

"Well, Assisi is essential, no? And we all like St. Francis."

"We who?"

"We the Gupta family, maybe even we Hindus. We Vaishyas.
St. Francis was the son of a merchant, as was Gandhi as a matter
of fact, he came from a Vaishya family. Okay, but this has nothing
to do with anything. Tell me what happened with those pilgrims."

"What happened was that on the way out, a few of them stopped and we began to talk. They asked me how the Poles were doing in Italy today. I, you know, told them what I could, and I even talked about my own case. And they liked the fact that though I was born here, and even my father had been raised here, I continued to follow what was happening in Poland. And I tried to explain that wasn't exactly true, that I was mostly interested in these poor guys who had disappeared in Puglia, but they liked that too. They said that not much came out about these guys in Poland either, except when big stuff happened."

"So they told you about some big stuff?"

"Yeah, well, the big stuff was the trial in Bari where those fucking criminals got sentenced to fifteen years. Polish TV had been there, and the newspapers, and they all remembered it."

"And did they tell you more?"

"No, but they were pissed about it. The shame of seeing Poles reduced to slavery by other Poles, those *caporali* who call each other *kapo*, joking around. And then some of them said this had happened in Italy because the mafia was here. That it must be the Italian mafia in charge of it all, and they were so powerful and so protected that no one could touch them. They asked me what I thought about that, given that I knew Italy. And I didn't know what to say. I didn't know how to tell them that this time maybe the mafia didn't have much to do with it. Anyway that's what the book says, and the judges, even though, you know, I'm not sure I'm entirely convinced. But their arguments do have a certain logic, unfortunately.

"This racket with the slaves picking tomatoes, the magistrates say, isn't all that lucrative. Now you, as a big organized crime group, have to ask yourself: what are we doing here for a handful of artichokes, broccoli and tomatoes? Okay we can take our cut, but as for the dirty work we'll let these foreigners take care of it themselves. But besides the fact that it was tough for me to explain this thing in Polish, you know what? I just hated having to say these people had disappeared from the face of the earth—or anyway that they were made to live in lagers—and that maybe there wasn't even the mafia behind it. You know what I mean?"

"Yeah, you mean that compared to the Nazis and the Soviets, this time there wasn't even some big boss on the side of the bad guys?"

"Andy, you got it! Exactly! After the Krauts and the Russkies, there wasn't even the worst that Italy has to offer. So anyway, I just said that thanks to the courage of some Poles, at least they had been able to put the foremen in jail. Somebody recalled that only one of those foremen was Polish, and the the other two were Moroccan and Ukrainian. The Ukrainians, you know, massacred us in Volhynia and Galicia; they were in the SS, at Auschwitz. But some of the others insisted there was no excuse for it, it was a shameful thing that Poles had been involved, and less than twenty years after Poland had gotten its freedom back. That people were forgetting everything, just running after prosperity. Thank heavens that someone who grew up so far away still has the fate of the Polish nation at heart, they said to me. They even invited me to the mass they're celebrating up at the abbey tomorrow, so now you see, we will be going up there after all…"

"You go ahead, if you want to. I'll stay here and then I'll go and make my visit there some other time."

"No sir. You're my partner, aren't you? You have the *Po-lysh pippyl* at heart, don't you? Christ, Andy, when my grandfather used to say stuff like that it would drive me nuts!"

Edoardo, blondish curls in his eyes because he was shaking his head so hard with laughing, was so utterly happy that Andy could only nod in agreement.

"You realize this is the first sign of real interest we've had? Tomorrow we're going to offload a whole bunch of flyers on these people, so they can take them back all over Poland. And you know, with a bit of luck, something might really turn up from there?"

Anand nodded yes again, lips pressed tightly together. He wasn't thinking about the various pathways the fliers might take to the distant provinces of Poland, but about his friend who was mocking his grandfather, or maybe their Pope, the one whose funeral he remembered so well. Rome in tears, Rome prostrate, everyone at home, even himself and his family, watching the historic moment on TV.

"What's the matter? You're not convinced?"

"Sorry, no. I was just remembering Wojtyła's funeral, the pope. Because of the way you said *Po-lysh pippyl*."

That improbable accent made Edoardo howl with laughter, reassured. But his wild mirth embarrassed Andy a little, and so he kept on talking about how that day his mother had been on the phone for an hour with his aunt in London, as the lady revisited all her grief at Lady Diana's funeral, the great event of that kind they'd had in England. His mother had raised her eyes to the heavens in high Bollywood style, and that was what had been funny, but Anand didn't get around to saying so.

"Good God, it was a madhouse at home. I had the job of taking all our relatives to pay their respects at St. Peter's. Hours and hours in the queue, I can't tell you. Like sardines, or worse, sardines on their knees. I told my parents that my good deed should earn me a bunch of free Sunday masses. And yet I have to say it was also a nice thing to be there in the middle of all those people, who had come from all around the world to say goodbye to our Karol. Anyway, come on, come with me to the mass at the abbey tomorrow."

"I think I'd rather not," said Andy right off, instinctively, without knowing why, because he had never had any problems with that kind of thing. And without skipping a beat, without Edo having repeated the question, and again having no idea why, he shot back an answer to his friend's question whether he was convinced, about the fliers that is. Sure, he said, something might well emerge if these pilgrims really took them back and spread them around Poland, because Internet was one thing, but a flier delivered by hand was another.

"Exactly! Because, you know, the missing ones often came from small towns, very provincial places."

"However, if someone did know something, why would they get in touch with you and not with the Polish police?"

The reply was not at all what Anand Gupta would have expected, although for a moment Edoardo kept his eyes on his Converse All-Stars, moving a few pebbles back and forth, and even when he looked up and met his gaze, did not look all that inspired.

"You know, partner," he said. "Maybe I don't care all that much about being the one to track down the missing people. Or rather, maybe I've understood it's not very probable. I mean, we can't work miracles, can we? And I'm okay with that. However, it matters to me that all this isn't totally useless. That somehow it serves the cause of the *Po-lysh pippyl...*" and here, as he began to laugh again, his blue eyes turned iridescent.

For the rest of the afternoon, there were few visitors, and in the down time each of them did as he pleased: one went deep into the Anders book, the other fiddled with his cellphone, bored but relieved. As soon as they were back in the car, Edoardo hung an arm out of the open window and made flying motions toward the turnoff, singing *Tutti al mare!* Everyone to the beach.

This time they made it to Scauri before seven, enjoying the water and the sun, as long as it lasted, and then they tossed around a frisbee they'd bought from the one Indian offering the assorted merchandise otherwise sold by the blacks. Another time Edoardo would have gotten the whole story of his life out of him; now he let Andy do the job, pleased to find out that someone really did come from Kashmir, and astonished when his friend raised the frisbee and saluted him with "Salam aleikum." They stayed a bit longer, chasing the green disc as it sliced though the red of the setting sun like a psychedelic knife, the air growing more and more opaque above the sand of Scauri.

Hunger, more than fatigue, finally sent them in search of somewhere, anywhere, to eat. Then, as they walked along the seafront, chance put a poster in front of them. *Kung Fu Panda* was showing that evening.

"Seen that one, partner?"

"No, I mean, a cartoon…I don't have any little brothers or cousins, at least not in Rome."

"Want to see it? It's no masterpiece, but it's a laugh. Oh, wait: do you want some fries too?"

"Sure, pizza and fries. And a mozzarella, because in America, I'm not going to find mozzarella like they have here."

"Okay, one more time: pizza, fries, one large *mozzarella di bufala* and a kiddie's film at the Eden outdoor cinema of Scauri. Is that plan okay with you?"

Yes, it seemed pretty good to his associate Anand Gupta, licking his lips with their patina of *bufala* milk and potato salt. And then, sitting out under the sky at the Eden cinema, it seemed pretty good to both of them that among all the families on holiday there were three girls who seemed to be having a fabulous time watching a cartoon in a language they didn't understand a word of. Tall girls with ash blond hair wearing flipflops and shorts or tiny skirts, Nordic by all appearances, and therefore game for the bunch of big male jerks sitting at the back, even as the fat panda Po struggled to become the Dragon Warrior, the one who would defeat ferocious Tai Lung and bring peace once again.

And given that in Italy the movies break for an interval halfway through, it was no problem for Edoardo and Anand—once the girls stood up to buy something to drink and the jerks followed, hoping to pick them up—to get there before them. It wasn't the first time they'd carried out that maneuver, but it was more thrilling when you were heading off the provincial riffraff for three Scandinavians.

"Hi there! Hello! What would you like to drink?" Edoardo pulled out his best Californian accent and smile. Magic. The girls were as friendly as if they were their official boyfriends, and the cost of the Coke and popcorn was nothing compared to the pleasure of taking their seats again with the young ladies wedged between the two of them, nibbling and grateful. When the film started up, the Vikings laughed even louder, and with a pat now and then on the thighs of their saviors, indicated it was okay to put an arm around a shoulder (as Edo did) or lay a hand on a hand (like Andy). Unfortunately, the jerks had booted out the family who'd been sitting behind them and occupied their seats. And despite their rough Campania dialect, even Anand understood that their insults were becoming quite threatening, and that their preferred target was *that monkey who needs to learn a lesson*, in other words, him. The fact it never occurred to them that their comments among themselves might be understood by that *faggot American drughead* or even by that *black piece of shit* was not much consolation.

Edoardo Bielinski's arm had begun to stick to the slightly sunburned skin of Gunnel, from Stockholm; Anand Gupta's hand dug deep in the popcorn tub and withdrew. The fat panda's final battle, in which he defeated the terrible Tai Lung with all the moves the venerable Master Shifu had taught him, taking advantage of his unappeasable appetite, was lost on Edo and Andy. When Po applied the coup de grâce, the legendary Wuxi Finger Hold, to his spotted adversary, Gunnel, Kerstin and Annika exploded in a soccer stadium cheer. Only Edo and Andy didn't raise their little fingers and repeat the magic word that marked the end of the baddie: *Skadoosh!* Because the jerks in the row behind were saying *Skadoosh* in a distinctly menacing tone aimed at the two of them.

But when you had been friends for many years, all you needed
to do was exchange a glance and you could face anything, or at
least you thought you could; it gave you that modest courage more
likely to be found in two than in one. And the situation took care
of itself, or anyway it became clear what to do next, when Annika
of the long strawberry blond hair, the prettiest and most petite of
the three, and the one who'd been in the center, said, "so, you guys
would like to have an ice cream or a drink?"

"Okay, sure, let's have a gelato," said Andy, thinking that walking toward the seafront on a crowded night in the high season could
not be a mistake. The jerks of course followed, glued to their backs,
muttering in a hostile way, so that even the Swedes noticed.

"Can't we just tell these guys to fuck off?" said Annika, who
seemed ready to take care of the matter herself right away.

"Ah, no, I wouldn't do that," said Andy, and he sounded so cool
and impassive that his friend would repeat the phrase over and
over during the rest of their trip and even afterwards when they
talked on Skype, whenever it suited the occasion. In that moment,
though, his friend's "Ah, no" gave Edoardo just the cue he needed.

"These guys could be trouble," he said loudly, "so now we'll
have our gelato and then we'll take you home, if that's okay with
you."

No, the girls did not object to being escorted back to their holiday camp, not at all. Nor did they object when, at a sign from his
partner, Andy asked for a bottle of bubbly when he went to pay for
the gelato, and raised it over his head like a trophy toward Edo,
who yelled out, "Chaaaam-pagne!"

Who knew whether, or when, they realized that their bluff had
become defiance, their fear a wish to show off, not so much for the
girls as for those maybe-real delinquents, those in any case genuine troglodytes? Who knew what it was that happened inside you,
what made you say, oh, what the fuck; how it was that the fear you
were pretending not to feel, all of a sudden you really didn't feel?
All they knew was that they were Clint Eastwood and James Bond
rolled into one at that glorious moment when the Citroën of Shrila
Gupta, architect, arrived at the gates of the Baia Domizia holiday
village, where Kerstin told the doorman he could let their friends
in. And the two of them, when they had parked and watched the

girls go back to their bungalow from where they'd meet them on the beach, had turned toward the gate where outside stood three motorbikes and two big scooters with their headlights trained on them, and if they hadn't made any obscene gestures in the direction of those bikes, it was probably because the hero, the victor, doesn't give the finger.

But the thing they were most proud of was that after finishing off the bottle of Asti Spumante, then a bottle of red supplied by the girls, and three beers (mostly drunk by the Vikings), anyway sometime after 2 a.m., having figured out who liked who (they both liked Annika, but she liked Andy, as always) and done some good-bye hugging and kissing not all that chaste or sober, they left, making a date for the following evening.

"*Stessa spiaggia, stesso mare...*"

"What?"

Same beach, same sea: the words to an oldie about summer romance. While Andy explained, Edo memorized a number on his cellphone.

"We have a heavy day tomorrow. Good night, now."

Yeah, a heavy day. Although the enemy at the village gates had vanished without need for the great Wuxi Finger Hold. It was about 3 am when Andy and Edo collapsed in their beds at the B&B, very excited, very tired and drunker than usual, but also happier than usual, or at least happier than they'd been in recent days.

"Edo?"

"What?"

"What time's the mass tomorrow?"

"Christ, at 10:30!"

"Okay, I'll get you up."

"Oh, thanks, partner; you're the greatest. Almost good enough for Miss Strawberry Locks. *Almost*, I said."

But the alarm, set by Anand for the late hour of 9:15, had yet to go off when Edoardo's ring tone began to bleat out the whining Roman voice of Antonello Venditti, his replacement for Massive Attack after he broke up with Sara from Magliano, although it wasn't much to wake up to. If Edo stretched out a ghostly hand toward the bedside table, it was only because some Swedish gold was lodged even in the deepest strata of sleep.

"Mamma?"

After that came a series of monosyllabic grunts, the most expansive of which was "okay" followed by a final effort: "Fine. Thanks. We'll talk, Ma." Edo then flipped onto his stomach and went back to sleep, while Andy was now awake. He did everything he had to do, including procure breakfast, a roll and a banana for his sleepy friend, " Thanks, Signora, so good of you." He even prepared the packs of fliers, putting rubber bands around them, and when it was 9:30, he began, without any warning, to shake Edoardo. Who promptly got up without protesting and only opened his mouth when they were in the car, to say that his grandmother had sprained her ankle and so his grandfather and Polish friends wouldn't be coming down on their outing to Monte Cassino.

"Sorry about your grandmother? She's not in the hospital, is she?"

"No, emergency room, X-rays, and now she's home again. Maybe when we're back in Rome we'll go see my grandparents, you know, you might meet some veterans, male and female, and they'll hold a big celebration for you. Especially now that you've gone nuts about this book. But first you have to give me a summary, so I don't look bad either."

"Female veterans?"

"From what I know one of the people who came from London is a friend of a certain Signora Grabowska, from the days when they served in the auxiliary of the Second Polish Corps. They did everything—they were nurses, mechanics, everything. I saw a photo in which one of them was fiddling with a military truck from above, and one from underneath. Cute!"

"So you're not totally ignorant about this whole history?"

"What do you expect, Andy? I grew up with these people. Anyway, Grabowska is a tough old lady, a music teacher who I believe even performed with the wife of your famous commander."

"The wife of General Anders?"

"Yessir! Irena Anders was an actress and a beautiful woman even when she was old, and she made a film with De Sica, and Anna Magnani, before she went to England and became a *generalessa*. Oh yeah, and the famous song about the red poppies of Monte Cassino, she sang it for the first time, and maybe at this point I should teach it to you."

"And how is it that all this comes to you just like that?"

"You know, I was thinking about this lady who often used to be at my grandparents' house when I was small, and how much I used to like the stories she told. There was one in particular, about a bear. They had brought a brown bear cub with them from Iran, and first they had to feed him with a bottle, and then he grew up and began to eat everything, even cigarettes, and he loved drinking beer. He was called Wojtek, and he was actually enrolled in some regiment or battalion, and after the war he also emigrated to Great Britain, to the Edinburgh Zoo. And he was also here at Monte Cassino; they say he helped to move crates of munitions during the battle. That, in fact, was my favorite story."

"No kidding. Awesome!"

"Wojtek the Bear, okay! If any other stories come to mind, I'll tell you."

They left the car in the usual parking lot, and began to climb toward the abbey immediately. They could already feel the heat, tired as they were and walking uphill. They were breathing heavily and the walls of the monastery loomed over them like a fortress."

"Did we bring the fliers?" asked Edo, bending over suddenly.

"They're in the knapsacks, as many as would fit. The rest are in the car."

Edo's breathing was noisy. "Thanks."

He exhaled deeply, passed a hand over his forehead, and still standing in one place, gazing up at their destination, began, a bit hesitantly, anyway, rather softly, *"Czerwone maki na Monte Cassino, Zamiast rosy piły polską krew...* And that's all I can remember."

"What does it mean?"

"The red poppies on Monte Cassino/ Drank Polish blood instead of dew." So, don't tell me you like it," he said, starting up again and now walking faster."

"Yeah, I guess it's very patriotic."

"Sure is. You're great, Andy."

When they got to the main cloister, the pilgims were still arriving, now mostly old people and those in wheelchairs. All had wooden crosses around their necks and red and white ribbons stuck to their chests with safety pins. There were a certain number of those drooping moustaches that Anand scarcely even noticed now. When he snatched a quick look at his watch he saw that the hands, miraculously, hadn't yet reached 10:15.

"I'm going to go and take a look inside the Church before mass starts, all right?"

"You want to sneak out on me immediately, you bastard? Fine, go; say hi to St. Benedict, but don't leave me alone, partner!"

"Don't be stupid," hissed Andy, heading away from the crowd of Poles, to whom he nodded politely however.

And did he go so far as to add *dzień dobry*, wondered Edoardo Bielinksi, as he watched him scale the stairs that led up to the church a couple at a time. Meanwhile he'd seen one of the Polish pilgrims of the day before, who came toward him, kissed him once on each cheek and once more, addressed him as Edek and introduced him to the others as such: Edek from Rome who was looking after their military cemetery and had been invited to their mass today.

"Pleased to meet you," said don Paweł from Cracow, who laid a cross like the pilgrims wore around his neck and gave him a little flag to pin on his t-shirt, which was one of his last clean ones, huge, bright orange and decorated with green and purple graffiti script. Maybe not perfect for the occasion; Kerstin or Gunnel might like it, though.

And in fact during the mass, especially after the sermon in Polish and the prayers he could take part in, when the Benedictines filled the church with Gregorian chant, Edoardo oscillated between tremendous sleepiness and the need to stay awake and peek at his cellphone, luckily concealed under the surfer t-shirt. Lucky too that he felt the unmistakeable buzz of an incoming message on his right thigh just as he was about to exchange the kiss of peace with Danuta from Poznań and Janusz from Lublin, that is, as the mass was ending. When everyone queued up for communion, he left the church and just outside the door, extracted the profane object.

"Sleep well, heroes?" There it was, the desired text, but Edoardo couldn't figure out which of the three girls had written it. In part it bothered him that the question was addressed in the plural, in part he wondered what had become of the other hero, who seemed to have vanished in thin air, although Edo was now standing where he could see the cloister below and the mountains to one side of the valley. "Less than U," he messaged back, seeing it was now almost noon, and added a smiley. And then he messaged Andy, "Where the hell are you?" and got an immediate reply, "Behind museum. Cool! Hurry up."

Communion was going to take a while and Edoardo was curious: what could be cool about the museum of a Benedictine monastery? Cool enough to make his friend use an exclamation mark. As soon as he spotted Andy, who seemed unsurprised at how quickly he'd obeyed his order, his friend signaled at him to slow down and be silent.

On that side, the walkway ended in a sort of colonnade, but it didn't seem there was much of a view. It was only when he got to where Andy was standing that he understood what his friend was looking at. Where the beam met the underside of the arch, there was a nest, a swallow's nest. That was it. He would have liked to say "Yeah, so?" to his friend but Anand was restraining him, holding his arm tight. Strange. Then just as the mother swallow slipped out of the nest, swooping down into the courtyard and then soaring high, he saw the heads of the little ones with their still pinkish beaks, declaring they were hungry. Edo had never seen Anand so happy. He was radiant, his eyes were misty, his voice a little throaty as his own had been when he came out of the church. Finally Andy said something, one word.

"Nice?"

"Yeah, um…"

"Okay, we can go. She won't be back for a while."

"You mean to say you've been here all this time watching the mother swallow feed her babies?"

"Yeah, about an hour. I mean, it doesn't take long to see everything here. The museum, well, I saw this from the window while I visiting it, and came out."

"In other words, you came to the cradle of western monasticism to do some birdwatching?"

"Yeah, I like it."

"I can see that. You seem to like that swallow better than Annika, damn you!"

"Naah. Don't jump to conclusions. Let's just say this is an older passion."

"What? Swallows? Birds? How come I never knew about this before? How come you never pestered your parents to get you a parrot, or a canary or something, when all of us were driving ours nuts for a cat or dog?"

"Well, I liked my aquarium better than a bird in a cage. Remember my aquarium?"

"Sure. You had that weird fish, flat and black with a white stripe as I remember, that would stand still in the water and even swim backwards. That was awesome."

"The black ghost knifefish. But that was the only one I really cared about."

"True. I never thought you were all that wild about any type of animal."

"Yeah, but swallows are different. They once made a nest in our house in the Maremma, and one time when I was really bored I discovered it, and I couldn't stop watching them. Like now. I was probably around ten then. You know, too old to go around telling people I'd made friends with some swallows."

"You could have told me, dummy. I mean I wasn't going to mock you or go around telling Chad or some of those other idiots: hey, Andy Gupta really likes *birds*! Who do you think I am?"

"Well, probably I had already forgotten about it at the end of the summer vacation."

"Doubt it."

As they came down the hall Edoardo picked up his pace, maybe because there were voices coming from the church, but he held his head down in an unmistakeable way and when Anand caught up with him, running after him with that light stride of his, he just brushed his arm.

"Hey, you're not pissed off, are you?"

"A little. I mean, you're such a good person and all, but you don't even trust your best friend. That's how it is, I know, and there's no time to talk about it right now. Anway, you're leaving for America soon, and you can start all over again there."

"Edo, it's time to do your work now."

"*Our* work! How do I get this across, Anand: if I asked you to come here with me, it meant something."

Andy gave him a little smile and pointed his index finger at his friend's arm. "Let's just try not to act too weird in front of these Polish people," he whispered nicely.

"We are weird, who cares!" said Edo, who had spotted Janusz

and was heading toward him. He introduced his friend in Polish and gave a summary translation in English, both to be polite, and to convey how to communicate with his friend.

"Dzień dobry," said Andy with that Stan Laurel stage accent he had in every language except for Italian, where a slight Roman inflection prevailed. "Nice to meet you."

They were invited to lunch. At the restaurant of the hotel from which the Poles were to leave for Rome that afternoon, Edo dispensed advice about cheap trattorias, shops and markets in the capital, and Andy kept up with him, pulling out his Moleskine, and given that he could pick out the Roman names and addresses, writing them down in capital letters and passing the torn-out pages to Danuta.

"Dzjękuję."

"Proszę."

The hotel was out on the Cassino ring road, and it was a sort of Rex that looked as if it had been flown in from Rimini, or maybe, said Anand, from Miami. But the parking lot where they were to wait for the buses was deserted, or nearly so. While they waited, they took the fliers out of their knapsacks and filled the box they had brought, then began to drag it to the door. Edo was repelled by how plush and new the place was, the mirror floors and huge blocks of sofas in the entrance hall, but it wasn't the moment to wonder who or what had made this bad mirage appear next to the highway exits.

"When they're all sitting down, we'll make the rounds, okay? I'll explain, and you can help me to hand out the fliers."

"Yes sahib!"

"What?"

"Nothing, a joke. It's fine."

Between the prayer before lunch and the arrival of the antipasto, the two got rid of all the leaflets they had brought with them except for the last three stacks. Edoardo's cheeks were as red as when he came out of basketball practice, or when, even smaller, he sang in the first row at Christmas concerts. They didn't even find places at the table, but in the end, that worked to their advantage. When they stopped to talk to Father Paweł, they discovered he spoke good Italian, having spent more than a year in a seminary in Rome.

"Do you speak Italian?" he asked Andy, very politely.

"Yes, I live in Rome."

"And where do you come from, if I may ask?"

"It's complicated; let's just say my parents are from India."

"Ah, India, I thought so. Now when you've finished lunch, would you pass by because there's someone I want you to meet. Someone who speaks English well, so you can communicate."

"Really, Father, there's no need. Thank you."

"No, no, I think this lady will be pleased to talk to you."

Obviously Edoardo couldn't help muttering "Christ, I can't believe this!" when the lady was introduced by Father Paweł, but she gave Anand a hug and a big "So pleased to meet you!" and dragged him off. She was a great big lady, somewhat mangy-haired, who must have been at least seventy.

Edo sent him an ironic grin but in fact Andy was rather pleased to be taken under someone's wing, even this aging Polish matron as energetic as she was huge. The only thing he couldn't figure out was how she managed to polish off everything on her plate from antipasto through dessert scarcely pausing to interrupt her story, while he, just listening, often found himself with a forkful in mid-air and his plate still half full when the waiter came to take it away. For the story that Hanka ("just call me Hanka") Kowalska had to tell was wonderful.

These were very special days for her, she began, because she would be going to Ancona to visit the grave of an uncle who had fought with General Anders.

"You know a little bit of the story of General Anders and his army?" she asked Andy, downing a gulp of red wine.

Andy nodded, and without knowing why, timid but proud too, he bent down and took the book from his knapsack.

"Oh, wonderful!" said Hanka, and warbling something in her language held up the copy of *An Army in Exile* toward the others, who approved with big smiles and vigorous nodding of heads.

"Dziękuję," said Anand blushing, although luckily it wasn't visible.

"So you know!" said Hanka Kowalska. "But not everything."

What Anand Gupta in fact did not know and could never have guessed, was that while Hanka's uncle enlisted in Anders' Army and ended up fighting and dying in Italy, his wife and two children, deported to Kazakhstan, had continued their odyssey going east. And arriving, after a very long voyage on every means of transportation—trucks, trains, ships—in the land of his forefathers, India. And because her cousin had contracted tuberculosis, the family was transferred from a refugee camp in Maharashtra state to Panchgani, one of the hill stations where the climate was mild and there were many sanatoria. When the little girl had recovered, her aunt continued to work in the sanatorium while both of her cousins were given the chance to enroll without paying fees at one of the English boarding schools that were another reason why the place was famous, at least in those days. Had Anand ever heard of Panchgani, Hanka wanted to know.

"I'm not sure," said Andy, explaining he had never lived in India and that his family came from another part of the subcontinent.

"Aha," said Hanke, somewhat disappointed; had he known of the school, you see, he would have been aware that at the very institution, St. Peter's School, where her cousin had studied, one of the most famous rock stars of all times had boarded a few decades later.

"Can you guess who?" she said.

Anand didn't feel like guessing, and he said he wasn't a great rock fan or of any kind of music, that he just listened to whatever, which was true.

"But you know who Freddy Mercury was?"

"Sure," said Anand, who couldn't suppress a broad smile. First, because it really was an absurd coincidence, and secondly because he was amused, touched, almost, that this elderly Polish lady with her pilgrim's cross was so hugely proud her cousin had gone to the same school as Freddy Mercury, the rock star who came out of the closet, not at first, but when he did, asserting his homosexuality right through disease and death.

"Amazing!"

For the rest of the war, and even after the unhappy news of their father's death at Ancona, Hanka's cousins stayed in Panchgani, where they were part of the Polish community and friends with other refugee students, most of them orphans. But not only refugees; even today her cousins kept in touch with their former Indian classmates. One of the orphan girls had even met her future husband at a tea at St. Peter's attended also by young ladies fom St. Joseph's convent, and he was nothing less than a maharaja! In other words, one of her cousin Julka's friends had become a—what was it called?—a maharani?

"Yes, maharani," said Anand, who was now somewhat woozy from the wine that Signora Hanka had made him to drink with her repeated toasts to Polish-Indian friendship. Those three years had been such a peaceful time for her poor cousins after everything they'd gone though, although they had been relatively fortunate in not having lost their mother or a younger sibling, as so many had. Yes, Julka often talked about how their British education had been a blessing. And of course you can imagine how many times she repeated that real life fairytale about the Polish orphan who became a princess. That was years later, though. Because, after the war, when Poland became communist and India was about to become independent, her relatives had moved to Australia. Many years went by before her cousins, who by then had established delightful Australian families and achieved a certain standard of living, came to visit her. It was so incredibly moving to be reunited with those people she'd played with as a child—they were tiny children then—before, shall we say, the world caved in. Only her aunt, who already from India had begun to send them the odd package and who helped them all her life, had sadly died without seeing her native land and her loved ones again.

Hanka Kowalska's eyes, reddened with the wine, filled with tears, and her chin trembled, doubled. She rested her fork on a tablecloth for a while.

"Sorry," she said, drying her eyes on her napkin. But maybe Anand was aware they, the Poles, were sentimental, "not like the English-speaking, no, we're very romantic."

Andy nodded, and downed another sip of wine, which burned even before reaching his stomach, but in his own way he was enchanted by this large woman who seemed the very antithesis of romantic: enchanted by the way she ate, the way she told stories, the way her vigorous bulk seemed to be well-planted in the here and now. In short, he was very pleased to have met Mrs Hanka Kowalska, to take down her address and promise to send her a postcard from the United States as soon as he got there.

"Oh, America!" she said, ready to launch into tales of her relatives who'd ended up there after many other peregrinations, but just then Edoardo appeared and said it was time to be getting back.

Okay, the coffee had arrived, also grappa and limoncello, but the Poles were still seated around the table.

Edo, too, to judge by the fumes that accompanied his brusque "Hey partner, we gotta go", had downed some after-dinner alcohol. But it was a look at his face that made Anand get up immediately.

"Feeling like shit. Gotta sleep or I'll die."

"Okay, let's go."

But being Andy, he had to let himself be heavily kissed and squeezed by Hanka Kowalska and say goodbye to everyone before catching up with Edoardo, who was waiting for him like an upturned mop propped against the door of the restaurant. Andy, too, had drunk too much and felt tired and nauseous, and he didn't realize the bad state his friend was in.

"Air!" he said, when they got outside the hotel, and stood there, just outside the door, breathing deeply with his eyes closed.

If there was a time they risked having a car accident, this was it; however they made it back to their queen-sized bed without problems, and collapsed on it. They didn't even look at their cell phones or turn them off. And once again, it would be Antonello Venditti to wake them. This time Andy responded, because Edoardo didn't budge.

"Hey, your sweetheart called. She's worried. And sends you many kisses."

"Yeah."

"Edo, what's the matter? Have you got a headache? Need to throw up, or something? I already told them after dinner, and I really don't want to stand them up, our Swedes."

"No, I'm feeling better. The worst of the hangover's passed."

Anand thought that Edo would turn over then or at least ask for an aspirin, but he didn't. And so he went into the bathroom to take an aspirin himself, but as he turned the water off he heard an explosion of sobbing. Now what? He sat for a moment on the toilet seat, in his hand the glass with the soluble aspirin fizzing in it, hoping the sobbing would stop. But it didn't, no; it got worse. Something, compassion or disbelief, drove him out of the bathroom but then he froze in his tracks, for the sight of Edoardo Bielinski head down, clutching his pillow and convulsed like an electrified frog in his oversize orange t-shirt, was fearsome.

"Edoardo, what's wrong?"

"I found someone who's missing, that's what's wrong." Finally he turned over and looked at him with his large blue eyes, blurred by alcohol and hurt.

"Close the shutters some, and I'll tell you."

Anand sat down on the chair in front of the desk and for the second time that day listened to a story, a Polish story.

"I was talking with Janusz and this old guy came over and asked if he could talk to me. Thank me. He took both my hands in his and held them. 'You know,' he said, 'I also fought, but with the Russians, with General Berling. I earned a lot of medals.' Know who Berling was, partner?"

"Yeah, Anders considered him a traitor, a mercenary, if I'm not mistaken."

"I don't know much myself, I can only tell you he was a Pole who commanded a division under the Red Army. And that many of the Poles who were deported ended up fighting with him because they no longer had a choice. Anyway, this old guy came from a little town in Masuria, and he had a granddaughter named Ania. As early as elementary school they knew she was a talented dancer, but while in Communist days she could have had a place in the state ballet school, now they had to find money to pay for it. So he and his wife took their savings out to pay for her dream, and she went to study at the best classical ballet school in Warsaw, but she didn't accomplish much, except to appear on a few TV shows. She wasn't just good, she was beautiful; her grandfather showed me a photo. Too beautiful, the model type, forbidding, unapproachable. At some point she met a certain Tomek who promised her there were many opportunities in Italy, because of the fashion industry. Her grandparents heard about the matter when she and her mother came home for Christmas. The old man was somewhat doubtful, because, he told his daughter, he didn't like 'these young men who you don't know where and how they got their money'. But she just laughed at him and told him he was old-fashioned and probably jealous too."

"I can guess, Edoardo."

"Okay, but listen. It seems this Ania was not all that convinced herself, because she wanted to be a dancer, not a model. But then she learned she'd been accepted at an American school that according to the old man was like the one in the TV series, but even more prestigious. And so to pay her trip and stay in New York, she decided to go to Italy."

"You mean Julliard?"

"How did you know the name? You have relatives there too?"

"Yep. My cousin Deva studied music there. It's true, it's a very prestigious school for music and dance."

"Okay. The rest is what you feared. Ania came to Italy with Tomek. She sent presents, she sent money, she sent photos. Many photos to her mother, by email, and her mother had some printed up and gave them to the grandparents. Pictures taken in expensive places, and not just in Italy. Her grandfather told me about one in which Alain Delon had his arm around his Ania, and he said there were many others with famous people too. She sent him a lot of postcards, including one with the Statue of Liberty, and wrote on it, 'Soon I'll be here! Thanks grandfather, thanks grandmother!'

But then at a certain point, Ania disappeared. She didn't reply. Tomek didn't reply. Finally her mother went to the police and reported her missing. They told her they would do their best, but they couldn't investigate all over the place. From the end of summer, the months went by, and then it was winter. What happened, her grandparents only learned later. Ania's mother went to Olbia, in Sardinia, and they took her to a morgue. There was a body that might be her daughter; it had been there for months. Drowned, floating off the Costa Smeralda. They showed her the jewelry, looked at the photos the mother had brought, and recognized two rings. At this point, the old man touched his chest. You know, he was wearing one of those wallets tourists have to hide stuff somebody might steal. He opened it up, took out a ring, and insisted on putting it in my hand. It was there in the palm of my hand and he was staring down at it, saying, 'Ania, Anusia.' I couldn't take it, Andy. I stood there holding that damn hand of mine open, feeling like Frodo Baggins. That fucking ring was just like one your mother wears, the one that spins around."

"The one with our logo around the edge? God, that's so freaky!"

"It was awful, let me tell you. But that wasn't the thing that got me. And maybe not even the fact they don't know how she died, because pretty soon the grandmother died, of heartbreak, probably, and then the old man moved to Warsaw. You said to me right off: I can guess. But he can't. The old man told me the whole story as if it were a terrible, senseless misfortune. How could this have happened to his granddaughter just now? He kept on saying, 'But we don't want it back, the money we gave to Anusia.' God, it was pitiful, Andy, to see him like that, that old Pole that grandfather Wladek would probably have said was a party member."

"But you think he hadn't understood, or was ashamed?"

"I don't know. Maybe he didn't want to understand, or Ania's mother didn't want to. He told me he had lost his parents in the war, that he had been deported and was injured twice. He had to go through various operations for complications of his wounds. He never saw his brother, who stayed in the west, again. 'But I was young then,' he told me. 'Now that I'm old, I must look after my daughter. I'm a jack of all trades; I'm even a pretty good housewife'."

"That's heartbreaking."

"I know. Tragic. Here was a guy who was riddled with guilt for something he hadn't had anything at all to do with. What was I supposed to do: try to track down this filthy Tomek? It might not even be impossible. And when that shithead went to jail for procurement, at the very least, what would the old man get out of it?"

"Nothing. More sorrow"

"You know, while I was holding that evil ring in my hand, it occurred to me for the first time that sometimes the missing were better off if they remained missing. Meanwhile the old man kept thanking me for what I was doing, kept telling me that out of tragedy, at least we have earned the right to know the truth, and so forth. What a rip-off, Andy."

"So what will you do now?"

"Nothing. First I'm going to take a long, hot shower, and then we'll go see the Swedes, and that should take care of it. Which one called?"

"Gunnel."

"I'm going for Gunnel, then, God willing."

While Edoardo was closed in the bathroom, Anand went down-stairs to tell the B&B lady they were leaving in the morning and paid the bill with his new credit card, recently acquired for his move to the United States. He said nothing to his partner, except the following day when everything was already settled.

It wasn't all that early, but everyone was still asleep among the Swedes at Baia Domizia when Andy drove back to Cassino to pack their bags and take them away. When he returned to the holiday camp the doorman refused to let him in, and so they had to wake Annika.

"This is my boyfriend," she said as she flip-flopped toward him in her blue plastic thongs and messy hair, and sealed her affidavit with a sleepy kiss. She didn't even ask where he had been as she pulled him into bed, lifting off his polo shirt, while Edoardo snored loudly in the other room of the bungalow.

"Like a walrus," said Andy, and that was the last word he said.

Anand and Edoardo stayed at La Serra holiday village for the last days of Annika and Gunnel's vacation, while Kerstin, the one who'd brought them there in the first place, had been made to move out by her parents the very first night. Andy, of course, apologized to her father, attorney Per Tore Svensson, for the bother, and of-fered to pay their part of the bill. It was another of those occasions on which it was handy that you couldn't see him blushing.

But they were such nice, charming boys, and anyway, you had to expect things of this kind if you wanted to have your grown-up daughter come along on your holidays.

"Just let me know if you have some nice friend to introduce to our Kerstin," said attorney Svensson, who didn't take Andy up on anything except his offer to drive the girls to the airport.

In the end, waiting in the check-in queue at Fiumicino, Edoardo was the more heartsick of the two for their departure. Gunnel had turned out to be a soccer enthusiast; not only did she know about it, she could knock a ball around. As goalkeeper, she was tougher than you'd have expected, and he only pretended to be annoyed that she adored Zlatan Ibrahimovic ("he's all they've got" he kept saying to his partner, who couldn't care less) and when she nick-named Edo "Francesco-Totti." The fact was he really liked this girl,

who had already decided she would study jurisprudence, and spe-
cialize in international law. She too, although she teased him merci-
lessly, was quite enthusiastic about what Edoardo had been doing
at the Polish cemetery of Monte Cassino, and said she was going to
pin up that last flier they'd found under the seat of the Citroën on
the door of her room.

"For my Zlatana. Who I found while searching for the lost!
Love, Edoardo" so he'd written on it in green marker pen.

When the summer came to an end he told his parents he hadn't
decided what he wanted to study, but he did know where: Stockholm. He intended to sign up for a language course and find himself some kind of job. And even Professor Bielinski thought that
learning Swedish might be worth losing a semester or a year for.

One morning, as Edoardo was getting up and outside, the first
snow of the year was falling, he found an email that Andy had sent
from Cambridge, Massachusetts while in Sweden it was still dark-
est night.

Dear partner,

I've been thinking about you a lot. First because I recently took General Anders' book out of the library; I never actually finished reading it, you know. In fact I couldn't have
given you a summary if we had gone to visit your grandparents. Partly, I had a lot of things to do in those last few
days, but it wasn't just that. At first, the book got me really
excited, because of all the amazing things the man had done
and lived through, his escape on horseback, the inhuman
conditions in prison, the job of building an army and of saving as many women and children as possible. And his story
was full of crazy things, like all the ways to fly from one
place to another passing through points you'd never think
of: Russia to England with a layover in Egypt, a leg across
Lake Tanganyika, landing in the Congo and then in Gibralter; crazy routes, airplanes that were falling apart, one that
totally froze and could have crashed, but this the general
only learned when they woke him later. Or when they were
supposed to meet with Stalin, and he and the other Polish
delegates were bombarded with phone calls from uniden-

tified young Russian ladies who pretended to have gotten the wrong number. Or even when they were talking among themselves in their room, keeping their voices down and simultaneously beating on the table with a spoon. Like in a film—better than a film—and yet this stuff really happened.

But then I lost interest, and not just because of Annika. I began to realize that I couldn't really get to the bottom of Anders' story. And that the reason it had fascinated me so much at the beginning was precisely that. It's hard to explain. Remember *Kung Fu Panda*? Remember in one of the early scenes, when the fat panda dreams of becoming the Dragon Warrior, but he tells his father his dream was about noodles. His father is thrilled about such an auspicious sign, for his family has been making noodle soup for generations. Maybe I also needed to dream of something different from my own mundane noodles; I wanted to dream of being heroic. But it's not my thing, you know. That way *you* have of being in history up to your neck, engaged in a fight to the death, from grandfather on down to grandson, I just don't get it in the end. I like it, just as I really liked the thing you did at the cemetery, but it's not me. And now that I've looked at the book again and compared it with the impressions I had then, the feeling's even stronger.

Maybe I should explain this better. It's that I understand stuff too, but by another route. For example, the swallows. When I was at the abbey, standing there looking at that nest under the colonnade, it occurred to me that it wouldn't have been there at the time of the battle. Although, when General Anders' soldiers were fighting there it was May, and so the swallows should have been back from their migrations. But they couldn't nest there, for the abbey had been razed to the ground. And they couldn't build their nests anywhere else either, because everything around there had been destroyed. Even flying was dangerous, because they were shooting in the air on the front and bombing on all sides. And so I asked myself: where did the swallows go during the war? And I thought about all the fronts of World War II, at least the ones we studied in school: Europe, North Africa, Russia, Indochina, the Pacific. I could see these black swarms of poor, maddened birds, all over the world. For me to understand fully what your general was telling me, I had to go through swallows. And so—this is the hot news, my friend—I'm thinking about how to pursue this interest of mine along with what I'm studying. To begin with, I've discovered the Museum of Comparative Zoology, which has various things going on. Little Andy Gupta really likes *birds*, as you so rightly put it.

So don't get too drunk up there in Viking land, and give Gunnel a big kiss.

Yours forever,
Anand

The Last Battle

May 11-18, 1944

Milan, September-October 2009
Lviv, September 1939—Milan, January 1965

MILITES V PEDESTRIS LIMITUM POLONIAE
LEGIONIS QUOS VIS EXULES FECIT
PER CARCERES CASTRA SIBERIAE PALUDES
PER DESERTAM MARIQUE POLONIAM PETENTES
HIC PER DIES SEMPTUM PUGNAVERUNT DIII
VITAM DEDERUNT MDXXII VULNA ACCEPERUNT

—*Inscription, monument to the 5ᵗʰ Kresowa Division,
Point 569, Cassino*

Samuel Steinwurzel, 1943. Next to the photograph there is nothing but these words, picked out on a typewriter. The words and the photocopied image float off-center in the space of a large sheet of paper, fine paper of a color you would call "champagne," letter paper. The man in the photograph wears a dark jacket and his dark hair is combed back, he wears the look of an adult man at an age that today would make him an adolescent, his face is composed in a way that both accentuates the length of his nose and contains it, a Pierrot face without the makeup. I have never seen him so serious: it is a kind of ceremonial seriousness that lends his features an involuntary melancholy, yet I recognize him easily.

"Samuel," I say to his son. "I didn't know that. Was that his real name?"

"Yes, but…as you know he was called Milek, but here…"

Here means in Italy; they must have said to him, 'Hey soldier, what's your name? Milek? Huh? Emilio!! We say Emilio; that's your name, Emilio, in Italian'."

The man in the photo was where it all began. He was the rill from the spring that led me to all those torrents gushing forth from the continents that came together in the river of this book and followed its windings until it reached the Valley of the Liri and flowed into the battle. But then, as often happens with a spring, that first source seemed to disappear, to founder.

Some time ago I asked my mother: "Is it true that Emilio Steinwurzel came to Italy with Anders' Army and fought at Monte Cassino?"

"No, no, that was my cousin Dolek. He was the one with the Poles. Emilio, you know, he came from Lviv, from Galicia."

"But mother, if he came from Lviv, then it's even more likely he was with Anders. Most of those people came from the eastern parts; they were deported by the Russians and then released."

"I don't know. No." She said it with a tiny grin that confirmed a total void.

My mother knew little of what had happened in that part of Poland, and as yet I knew nothing of Irka and the Szer brothers. It's even possible I would never have learned anything had she not come up with that cousin I never knew in place of the family friend I'd seen every summer since I was a child. Of course I knew that her memory was becoming unreliable. But without any evidence to back me up, I began to doubt my own. Who had told me that Emilio was a soldier in Italy? And when? Why did I remember that, and Monte Cassino and the fact there had been a Polish army? Why was it that "Anders' Army" had sprung to mind when I still knew almost nothing about the Second World War, either the experience of my own family or any others?

And so I began following my mother's lead, confusing one story with another, pursuing the Szer brothers and discarding Emilio Steinwurzel, whose tale seemed to have ended with him in the Jewish section of the Musocco cemetery in Milan. And when, many months later, I looked up his son's phone number, found it immediately, and saw from the web directory that he had moved into the apartment on via Bramante, I let a whole summer go by before I called him. Part of it was embarrassment at telephoning someone I'd lost touch with twenty years before, out of the blue. But even more I feared he might say, "No, sorry, you're mistaken, you've got it wrong."

When I finally did call Gianni Steinwurzel, he was out on a mountain hike on a sunny Sunday. "Yes, sure," he said in answer to my question whether his father had arrived in Italy with General Anders, his voice intermittently breathy from talking and climbing. We spoke for a while and before he climbed too high to get a signal, we agreed to meet one evening the following week.

That the memory I myself had discredited was so instantly confirmed might have seemed an unreal stroke of luck if the voice of Gianni, who didn't slow his pace as we talked, hadn't brought Emilio back so forcefully. He was a son who resembled his father both physically and in the difficulty he had keeping those long, skinny legs of his still on a sofa or under a table. Even their features were restless: smallish, oval heads, longish noses, they looked like the bird-people drawn by Bruno Schulz, the Galician Jew, painter and writer, who was murdered by a Gestapo officer to spite the SS who had arbitrarily put Schulz under his protection. The building on Via Bramante that held the family apartment, its façade of brown tiles further darkened by the smog, a few of them missing, seemed to pertain somehow to that twisted darkness. The only new thing was a bank of door-bells. Not even the Chinese had come to rent out the ground floor shops.

All around, though, the Chinese had settled in. The first of them had arrived here in the 1930s, and when as a child I used to walk up Via Paolo Sarpi with my mother and we passed three or four restaurants with red lanterns outside and shops called "Hu" or "Wong" selling leather goods, I would try to imagine myself in another world. "Chinatown" was what Emilio Steinwurzel called these stretches of exoticism just beyond his home turf. Chinatown: a hyperbolic term that suggested Milan was a city that mattered; it was almost a point of honor to have a Chinatown. While the nice thing about Via Paolo Sarpi was something else entirely. A street that ran ever so slightly uphill from city's flat center, just beyond the Bastioni di Porta Volta, it was like the main street in some small town where there was nothing you couldn't find: genuine Tyrolese jackets, wineshops, milk bars, linens, a huge variety of Florentine hand embroidery, and a little boutique selling flowered skirts and dresses, which I craved above all. Everything cost loss on Via Paolo Sarpi, and the quality was good, good as merchandise can be when it is chosen directly by the proprietor, a proprietor in his shop day in, day out, a shop that could still be called an atelier in many cases.

Did Milek maybe feel something of the armosphere of home here? Something of the Lviv of his childhood to which he couldn't return, even if the workshops and ateliers were mostly very Milanese, and not Jewish. Today Chinatown really is Chinatown, and has spread well beyond Via Paolo Sarpi, which has become a distribution center for Chinese merchandise to street stalls and shops up and down Italy. The sidewalks swarm with Chinese unloading crates from trucks and moving them into wholesale shops on forklifts. The things on display are all the the same, and nauseating to contemplate; in winter, the pretend wool clothes make your throat itch just to look at them. But the problem is mostly quantity: there is so much merchandise it would look like dead rags even if everything were made of cashmere.

I'd been back several times since the neighborhood was transformed, but never to Via Bramante. I never had reason to, although perhaps my not venturing there wasn't entirely casual. But the new Chinatown, wholesale aside, appealed to me, more than any nostalgia I might have felt for the Via Paolo Sarpi of my childhood. This far China, this China for the Chinese inside a perimeter of Italian streets—inside, indeed, those very streets that were my first reference point on the map of Milan—thrilled me.

Fresh tofu, Chinese pastries, medicines, doctors, travel agencies, supermarkets, hairdressers, hardware stores, restaurants and dives that only Chinese patronized, TVs showing Chinese videos, solitary customers waiting to be served while reading Chinese newspapers, specials of the day scratched out on blackboards in Chinese only, something you'd never see in Chinese restaurants elsewhere in Italy. The Italians remaining in the neighborhood were unhappy, they had sent petitions to the mayor asking to remove the newcomers or at least limit the invasion, and yes, there had even been shootouts between young men who wore the rapper uniform favored by globalized young criminals, people killed, and still, every time I came through there, I thought I wouldn't mind living there at all.

Until the day I went back to Via Bramante. I went there on foot, on a stifling hot evening in early September, dragging behind me a new red trolley bag from a shop in Porta Garibaldi Station to replace the cheap Chinese trolley bag that had broken down. With my Italian-brand purchase—made in China, of course—in hand, I had rolled along past the gym-toned Happy Hour drinkers of Corso Como, past the plaque to the memory of Ho Chi Minh on the corner of the building on Via Pasubio. I rolled past the point where the Bastioni di Porta Volta meet Via Farini and Via Ceresio as the latter swings toward the Cimitero Monumentale, the cemetery: a space so wide it is like a bend in a river to be crossed, marking a frontier. Then as so many other times I walked down Via Paolo Sarpi, still crowded with Chinese coming and going in their own world, but this time I didn't look around me. A dark cross street that came to an end at the high cemetery wall, Via Bramante, unlike lively, busy Paolo Sarpi, was littered with industrial ruins, garages and mechanic shops. But now, with the Chinese wholesalers spreading out where once there had been nothing, the Serafino restaurant with its heavy red drapes and name spelled out in neon script, a place that had already seen better times years ago, now the street had become squalid. Or not so much squalid as violated: afflicted, an ever thicker layer of dirt smudging the façade of the large apartment building that had been home to Emilio Steinwurzel and where his son now lived. That ungainly building of the years of Italy's economic boom had never appealed to me to me much, and so it wasn't my own memories that upset me, it was his memory. What remained of a Polish Jew in this strip of territory annexed to China, on a map where huge new migrations were marked by erasing smaller and more remote ones? The future was Chinese, and we belonged to the past. Even our survivors were almost all dead, and no amount of cultivating memory, individual or collective, could change that.

Now it was just us, the children, in Via Bramante. Gianni Steinwurzel came downstairs to meet me, kissed me lightly on both cheeks like someone he always greeted that way, then turned quickly and led the way with long, somewhat asymmetrical strides, my red trolley bag rolling behind him. There was no time to calculate how long it had been since we last met, although later he would recall: not since my father's funeral, about a year after that of his own father. December 1984, twenty-five years before.

And yet everything seemed pretty much the same. There was still no mezuzah on the door post where there had never been one, and if the dining table now stood where the sofas once had, that was the only significant change I could see in the entire house. Nor had we changed more than what was inevitable. We didn't wear glasses, we hadn't lost too much hair, turned very grey, nor been remade by new hair styles or colors. We hadn't grown too fat, our faces weren't lined with age, we hadn't radically changed the way we dressed or spoke, not even our ideas about politics and the world. If Gianni had a little more belly, it was disguised by a button-down shirt that he kept neatly tucked in a pair of jeans. I appeared in wide, loose pants much like those I'd worn thirty years before.

"You're becoming the spit image of your mother," was his only comment, while he in turn seemed to settle more and more into his father's likeness. As if the only possible mutation was backward, toward the physical footprints of our parents. As if this finding ourselves so little aged, this illusion of youth that spirited us back to the years when we were young, and felt powerful enough to perhaps be true, was just a trick to disguise what had really frozen us in time: the fact of being children. We were not, as we had thought, projected forward beyond some breaking point, but quite the opposite. We had been good children, had done all that was expected of us, found a decent job, had a family. But rather than inherited furniture, crystal and silver to cope with, our only real endowment was an invisible one that had shaped us from within, and late, when the traces we'd begun to follow were scarce and hard to read.

The first thing Gianni pointed out to me as I entered the house were two binders put together after the trip he'd made a few years before to Ukraine, a trip he'd mentioned to me on the phone. That pilgrimage to the origins of his father's side of the family, back to his great-grandparents, was not just an important experience for him, it was a common grammer that now lay open on the table where we sat. It was now easy for me to ask about his father. Had the Russians had deported him because he came from Lviv, from the territories the Soviets had occupied?

"No, he was a soldier. He was in the Polish army during the invasion; he had some rank, sergeant, or something. They took him prisoner and they even sent him to Siberia. From there he was able to reach the army Anders was putting together and that was how he came to Italy."

I was nodding enthusiastically, gazing at Gianni triumphantly. "This all makes sense you know, the Polish prisoners of war sent to the gulag, and so forth. Forgive me if I put it that way, but I've been researching this history for more than a year."

Gianni seemed pleased that his father fitted into the historical reconstruction, mine and the greater one, and he tapped his finger on one of the binders to indicate that it held all that he could contribute to the story.

"Shall we look at them now or later?"

"Later. Let's take our time. First, I suggest we have something to eat."

"I hope you'll find something useful in there," he said jumping to his feet and stuffing his wallet in his jeans pocket, "because my father never said shit about it, not even to my mother, from what I know."

"How is your mother?"

"Well, so far as her health goes, not bad, but you know…"

I was nodding as we went out the door. We walked fast, taking the same route I had arrived by, to a pizzeria beyond the Chinese territory. From what Gianni said, none of the women in his family wanted to move away from there. Cecelia, the second of his three daughters, the only one then in Milan because she had to take university entrance exams, had come along, she too a good daughter, and considering that she was just the same age as Edoardo and Anand, I asked her about her *maturità* exam while we ate. Gianni filled me in on what had happened to them in the last decades, but he also spoke as much, and far more passionately, about his visit to Ukraine, explaining that the idea had come to him during a trip to Israel when he went to Yad Vashem and searched the archive for the names of family members who had perished.

"They must have been put in by my aunt, who lives down there."

The third time I walked by the stall selling fresh tofu, still open, it began to dawn on me that it was maybe surprising that someone like Gianni Steinwurzel might undertake what has come to be called a "remembrance tour." A manager for a large company always on the go, father of three grown children, a man who rather than sprawl on the sofa went hiking in the mountains on weekends, he was what he had always been, a Steinwurzel who wanted to be done with whatever he was doing and move on, never pause. Yet he too had felt the need to dedicate his time—time that by definition travels forward—to the past. Gianni Steinwurzel digging into what he could find on the web, sitting at computer of Yad Vashem, came up with a guy who from Poland sent him an old handbook on pre-1939 Lviv. He found a Ukrainian home-help worker in the town of Vercelli nearby who could act as his interpreter on the trip; he took photo after photo of old ladies in the countryside, wooden houses, street signs and markers, all done, as I would see later, in that way of his, in a great hurry, don't fuss about it, and so a number of the pictures were somewhat out of focus.

All this came to me while walking back along Via Paolo Sarpi, extraterritorial China, open day and night, although there weren't many people, Chinese or otherwise around now, and matters began to seem not just odd, but problematic. If even someone like Gianni Steinwurzel was turning backward, the match with the Chinese was already lost. Memory is sacrosanct, of course, but also a ball and chain; and a people ground into 100,000 acts of witness on videos and tapes, into three million names of the dead out of six million because more than that have not been recorded even at Yad Vashem, may be as tenacious a weed but will always be a bunch of scattered tribes, of children and the children of children of individual survivors. The Chinese did not need memory and did not seem to suffer from their dispersion, their diaspora. It was enough for them to be many, capable, hardworking, adaptable. And at the same time, not to alter, not one inch, their Chinese nature, considered as basic as the fact that grass was green and the sun, hot. That too was a sense of belonging—perhaps even a sense of being chosen—that dispensed with any need to tell their story and count up their numbers, and that apart from their demographic and economic strength meant the future was in their hands.

And what if they were to become like us—us meaning not just us Jews but us Old World, old and weighed down by the past; or us, the descendents of every people that from new continents return to the native towns of their ancestors or pay, with a credit card at best, for the dubious genealogies supplied by the web—what would happen then? What if citizens of Chinese origin born in California or in Via Paolo Sarpi were to wish to go back, what if each one of them wanted to know where they came from and from whom in order to understand what they had become? It would not even be possible, not entirely. Even the undocumented Chinese of Milan, had they been sent back just after arrival, might no longer have found their houses, their quarter, their village. After the Revolution, the past was for a long time, like the imperial palace in Beijing, forbidden. Then the Forbidden City became a museum and anyone who could afford the price of a ticket could tour the emperor's gardens and palaces. But if the Chinese continued to be the future, maybe that was because they could come here, scatter themselves on every continent, unload boxes full of the same shoes and track suits in every corner of the world, and yet were still forbidden to enter parts of the Forbidden City, were unable to move freely through the meanders of their own history. And supposing one day, one by one, then many of them, demanded to see inside the hundreds of buildings in there still closed to the public, the ones that haven't been restored and the ones that housed the Party headquarters: perhaps those same walls that still enclose the empire would begin to crumble?

Maybe it was also for those in the queue at the tofu stall, the ones in the restaurant kitchens, the young men in fake RayBans hunkered down smoking on the corner of Via Bramante, that the son and the daughter of family friends were returning to the fourth floor of a Milan apartment building to put their files together: the five or six documents, the few sentences uttered by a dead man who "never said shit." And mix them with others—maps, tables, sources, statements—to try to call up the man in the 1943 photograph. Samuel Steinwurzel, Milek, soldier in the Polish army who became Emilio in peacetime.

He was born July 2, 1914 at Radziechów, today called Radekhiv, a town about 70 km northeast of Lviv, not far from Brody where in June 1941 Red Army tanks sought to arrest the German advance in a last battle. Even before the war most of the inhabitants were Ukrainian; Jews being the most numerous minority, but the city retained a strong Polish and Austro-Hungarian stamp. In the past a Polish count had built a Catholic church and on the edge of his vast estate, a palace, and his successor had given over part of the palace gardens as a public park. There were primary and secondary schools, a court of law, town hall, public baths, a Ukrainian church, a synagogue, and various brick buildings around the market square where many Jewish workshops were clustered. But as the residential areas inhabited by various ethnic groups spread out from the center, brick houses gave way to wooden ones, the roads turned to dirt, and the town became a large village, something that to judge by Gianni Steinwurzel's photographs, it still was. A large village that came to a halt in fields and pastures, with a river nearby and woods all around. It was because of the woods that Samuel Steinwurzel's parents had moved to Radziechów. Mojzesz and Fania Steinwurzel came from a place yet further east, an even smaller town in the midst of the forest. Hrycowoła, or Grystsovolya or Hrystevolia or Khrytsovolya: the first being the Polish name and the other three, possible transcriptions of the Ukrainian. Life among a few hundred Ukrainian woodsmen in the middle of the forest had been good for Samuel's grandfather. There were very few Jews in Hrycowoła and Nechemia Steinwurzel had become the Jew who sold the wood. But some years later, his son Mojszez began to find the forest of Hrycowoła, although a family monopoly and a source of income, too small. He needed a base in a larger town to expand the business, in Radziechów, in fact, where beyond wood, the road led to Lviv. When the business continued to prosper he took a further leap, and moved the whole family, wife and children, to Lviv.

Steinwurzel, Mojzsez, kup., Glinianska 17: so said the pre-war handbook on Lviv that Gianni got a Polish man to send him. *Kup*, short for *kupiec*, meant merchant. His father, who came to Lviv while still a child, grew up near the outskirts of the city, on a large road that continued east, passing out through the fields. A road that led out in the direction from which Mojszez Steinwurzel had come, so perhaps the location was connected to the logistics of the business. The family home, in which a baby girl named Hela was born, was perforce in a building that was one of the newer, but to judge by Gianni's photos, still today quite solid and bourgeois. Growing up to learn his father's business was not only natural for the sole male heir, it was easy. In the meantime the kid could go to school, probably a Jewish school but probably not Orthodox, for there was no earthly need for a son who only knew how to pray. I say *probably* not only because that was the usual choice for most Polish Jews and because there were many such schools in Lviv, but because I'm trying to use the four cards I've been dealt, the few bits of information I have. For he was named Samuel, Nechemia's grandson and Mojzsez's son. Not Emil like Irka's stepbrother, or as I had imagined he was, having known him as Emilio. Not even Samuel followed by Emil, or Emil Samuel, or just Emil for the registry (for his Jewish name, the name given by the rabbi, would have been Samuel in any case). Many, once they had established a respectable home outside the Jewish quarter, would have wanted to furnish their improved position with a nimbler, more worldly, above all less Jewish, name for their son. They might have begun with the Greek and Roman repertoire, perhaps even risked some Catholic name, especially those like Anna or Józef that spanned Old and New Testaments, while modesty, good taste or fear of treading on national pride would have made them hesitate before Slavic names, or anyway excessively Slavic ones. Names like that *Władysław* with which Albert Anders and Elżbieta had sealed their loyalty to Poland and perhaps marked their son out as a future commander, well before there was an independent Polish state.

But while bestowing such a name on a German nobleman might be an act of free patriotism, it was not so for the offspring of a Jew. Therefore the fashionable names for males in somewhat assimilated Jewish families, the names considered most modern and manly were mostly of German origin (and as it happened, almost identical in Yiddish): Herman, Gustaw, Ludwik, Teodor, Artur, Edward, Henryk, Zygmunt, Emil, and even the one that became Dolek in the diminutive. Adolf, in other words.

But the Steinwurzels were down to earth people, like that material on which their prosperity was based, people who didn't forget the effort of pulling those carts from the woods, the poverty of Hrycowła, or their identity. And thus the name they registered for their only male heir was that of a Biblical prophet.

Yet Lviv was a large city, and a Polish city: Polish because its growth was a source of pride for the entire nation; Polish because almost two-thirds of its inhabitants were Polish, although the Jews made up another third. A place where a young man, even as he looked after loads of wood and went to Jewish schools, might find something of the city had stuck to him. The name Milek stuck to Samuel Steinwurzel. And given that in Poland, full names were never used except in official records, he would henceforth be Milek for his schoolmates and teachers, for clients, suppliers, even his father's workmen to whom he gave a hand when necessary; he would be Milek for the entire outside world. Even at home he was called Milek, not the Yiddish diminutive of Samuel, Shmulik. It was a sweeter name, Milek, and indeed you could hear the Slavic *miły* in it: "nice, dear," but it had nothing at all to do with Samuel.

Maybe they no longer spoke Yiddish at home; whatever the case the Steinwurzels were apparently susceptible to the desire to be ordinary, respectable Polish citizens. Was it only this, and not all those bourgeois affectations—the seats at the theater, the non-Kosher delicacies for the table, the tennis and piano lessons, the beauty contests—that they really wanted for themselves and their children? Simply to be acknowledged as citizens? Citizens for the taxes they paid, for the employment they provided, for the work they did, for work itself was more important than anything, as they taught Milek too. For the entrepreneurial spirit with which they had transformed the forests of Galicia into Polish economic growth?

And so Milek, with his sweet name and the city of Lviv around him, became somewhat Polish. He was Polish in the company of workers and lumberyard men, builders and carpenters, less so in the mixed company that met in the Austro-Hungarian cafés in the town center. He became Polish without ever ceasing to be a good Jewish son.

That's how I imagine him at twenty-five, when he was called up by the Polish army, and went to the lumber yard to say goodbye to those left behind, and goodbye to the trees of Galicia, a land never again to be Polish. He then went home to say farewell to his mother and sister, who loaded him up with provisions, chased away their tears, said senseless things like "but please, I beg you, be careful," and embraced him while Mojzesz murmured that he had to go, that even on a day like this, work and the wood couldn't wait. He left Glinianska 17 and departed the very same day—or the day before—that Poland was invaded by the Germans and then by the Russians. Where he went we don't know; perhaps to a regiment to the east, because he succeeded in reaching it, and because soon, the Red Army would capture him. But this much is clear: Milek Steinwurzel was captured defending the independence of the republic, and he was sent to Russian territory.

And then, between September and October 1939, his imprisonment began, and nothing more was known. A dark, muddled chapter begins, in which the only light, refracted and speckled as when light filters through trees, would fall in the middle of a forest. The forest of Katyn near the city of Smolensk, where the Germans would find what the Poles had been looking for from the time their agreement with Stalin was supposed to make them free.

General Anders was still in Lubjanka prison when he first learned from a Polish captain in which camps their officers were being held: in Kozielsk, Starobielsk, and Ostaškov. But after Anders became commander, when in all his back and forth between Moscow and his headquarters at Buzuluk in the Urals he never saw a single one of his officers appear, the question of what had happened to them became pressing. On August 16, 1941 at the first conference to organize the Polish Army, Soviet officials offered a disturbing reply to his question. The total number of war prisoners amounted to 20,000 soldiers and non-commissioned officers in two camps and "one hundred officers in Gryasovietz camp," he was told. What had become of the rest of them, the "prime of the Polish officer class" that had been imprisoned at Kozielsk and Starobielsk, he wanted to know. Where were they? He appointed Captain Józef Czapski, a painter and sculptor who had himself been detained in one of those Soviet camps to investigate, but when the time came for Anders to meet Stalin on December 2, 1941, he was still without any reliable information.

Sikorski had brought with him a list of some 4,000 officers deported by force and still in prison or labor camps. The list, he said, was incomplete because it was made up of names supplied from memory. "These men are here in Russia," he said, "and none of them have been returned to us."

STALIN: "That is impossible; they must have escaped."
ANDERS: "Where could they escape to?"
STALIN: "Well, to Manchuria."

With few illusions now, the pointless searches continued, and the lists of the missing grew longer and longer as the missing officers' wives, who had been deported separately with their families, arrived in the transit camps.

When on April 13, 1943 Radio Berlin announced that thousands of corpses had been discovered in the forest of Katyn, Anders and his soldiers were already in the Middle East. Joseph Goebbels, in Berlin, followed intently as those Polish prisoners were exhumed, prisoners whom "the Bolsheviks simply shot down and then shoveled into mass graves" he noted in his diary on April 9. "Gruesome aberrations of the human soul were thus revealed."

It was a shocking statement. So was Goebbels' subsequent remark, when he observed that now the world could understand what was in store if the Bolsheviks won—although maybe that was a bit less shocking. Those *gruesome aberrations* suggested his total lack of any political reference points, his frightening air of harmlessness, of sincerity. At any rate, an air of sincerity that the diary writer could believe in, although a Minister for Propaganda will always be a propagandist even in his most intimate confessions. Gruesome aberrations of the human soul were thus revealed. Gruesome. Human soul.

Had Joseph Goebbels forgotten that just before the Polish invasion Hitler had warned his closest aides that he was getting ready to destroy Poland, and that his goal was the "elimination of living forces, not the arrival at a certain line" Was Goebbels unaware as he wrote that millions of Poles had been deported to forced labor in Germany? That a number of corpses infinitely beyond those found in the mass grave of Katyn had already been killed in German concentration and death camps: Polish Christians, not Jews? Guilty, most of them, of having been the best of that conquered nation, as were the officers murdered by the Russians. Had he forgotten that the professors of the University of Cracow and of Lviv had been deliberately eliminated? That the universities had been trashed or closed down, along with high schools and libraries, while the children in Polish elementary schools were supposed learn only "simple arithmetic, nothing above the number 500, writing their own names, and the doctrine that it is divine law to obey the Germans," as Himmler directed, adding he did not think it desirable they learn to read. Did Goebbels not agree with the doctrine that classified Poles, and more generally Slavs, as *Untermenschen*? Had he forgotten the *Generalplan Ost* that foresaw that the Poles, once they belonged to Germany, be deported to the Urals and Siberia so as to free up *Lebensraum* for the Aryans?

True, the Germans were never responsible for a massacre of officers. But Goebbels was further outraged that priests were among the dead at Katyn, as if the Germans had not gone after the Catholic clergy, sending priests to concentration camps or executing them on the spot. But no, he saw no likeness between them. Other people are always responsible for gruesome aberrations.

Yet the day after Katyn was announced on German radio, he wrote in another mood entirely:

> We are now using the discovery of 12,000 Polish officers, murdered by the GPU, for anti-Bolshevik propaganda on a grand scale. We sent neutral journalists and Polish intellectuals to the spot where they were found...The Führer has also given permission for us to hand out a dramatic news item to the German press. I gave instructions to make the widest possible use of the propaganda material. We shall be able to live on it for a couple of weeks.

The Germans, and the Poles with even more desperate energy, called for a Red Cross Commission to be established, and with that, the Soviet Union broke off diplomatic ties with the Polish government in exile in London. Once again Poland was overwhelmed by the equal and opposite reactions of the powers that had dismembered it. There would be a commission, but following Soviet pressure, it would not be under the Red Cross aegis. Among the twelve medical men of various nationalities who visited the site at the end of April, Vincenzo Maria Palmieri of Naples was recognizable in the Deutsche Wochenschau footage for his black wide-brimmed hat and tailored overcoat, the young pathologist's Italian elegance at odds with the place and the circumstances.

Back in Italy, he wrote up a report under his own name which was published in July:

> On concluding its examination, the Commission drew up a report, whose conclusions I transcribe word for word here:
> "The cause of death of all the victims was a shot in the nape of the neck. From eye witness reports and from correspondence, diaries and newspapers found with the bodies it is concluded that the shootings took place in the months of March and April 1940. We are all in complete agreement with the findings written in the transcript regarding the mass graves and the individual corpses of Polish officers."
> I may add that these conclusions were unanimously

agreed upon and subscribed and that even during prelimi-
nary discussions no disagreement was expressed among
the members of the Commission.

But Churchill and Roosevelt did not want to put their relationship
with Stalin at risk for several thousand dead Poles, and they would
find a way to make the best of a bad situation. More important than
any mass graves at Katyn was the fact that the Red Army had been
able to retake Ukraine in January 1944 and was pushing westward.
In the end, the heads of the free and democratic world perhaps reasoned, they knew these guys. Whether it was the Germans or the
Russians, when both were absolutely capable of it, was a mere detail.

   After the war, however, a university professor in Naples risked
his academic career for the report he'd signed on examining those
corpses, a report that left him looking like a fascist reactionary. And
thus when a Pole, an ex-deportee and ex-soldier under General Anders who had recently settled in Naples, asked to meet him, Vincenzo Maria Palmieri replied politely that although he understood
Gustaw Herling's interest, he "would rather not dig up the graves
of Katyn again" or unearth any doleful ghosts of the past. Many
years went by before Palmieri himself asked to meet Herling.

   What does he want with me now, wondered Herling as headed
out for his appointment on a rainy January day in 1978, the wind "so
gusty that it almost flew me to the old university quarter hanging
from my ballooning umbrella like the pensioner in Bruno Schulz's
story." As he contemplated what he was about to hear, the alley-
ways of the city center made Herling feel "a solitude and a void"
that only someone who had emigrated to an utterly foreign place
that he "superficially loved, but in reality detested," could understand, he felt. It was like visiting a Polish cemetery, like the lump
that always came to his throat on the motorway to Rome, when he
caught sight of the Abbey of Monte Cassino.

   But the emeritus director of the Institute for Forensic Medicine,
Herling soon found, had no wish to confess "teary-eyed secrets" to
someone who would *understand*. He merely took down from a shelf
a box full of photographs, and calmly, just slightly moved, began
to talk about them.

There was "a reek, a terrible reek that I will never forget," Palmieri told him. It had been hard to work, although the corpses were well-preserved in dry soil. In the pockets of their uniforms were identity papers, letters, newspaper cuttings, family photographs. "Look at these photos, they are heads in a block of earth; they look like reliefs on the façade of some temple that's been excavated."

Professor Palmieri was unruffled, feeling he had the support of scientific truth. He was convinced that one day the Russians would recognize it too.

But when that happened, Palmieri would already be long in his grave. Only with the glasnost of the Gorbachev years, that "transparency" that was the prelude to the empire's collapse, would there be acknowledgements and apologies to Poland from the Soviet side. They would reveal that Beria and Stalin were directly responsible, and the exact number of the victims, more than 20,000 between military and civilian, not only from those interned in prison camps, but those in jail too. They were executed in the forest as well as in various Russian and Ukrainian prisons, dug up in places that had never been identified before. They were, most of them, that is the officers, not only men prepared to lead an army, they were a select portion of the Polish elite—or they would have been. For anyone who had finished university, once he had done his military service, became an officer in the Republican army. As would be the case in Anders' Army, where Dr. Adolf Szer would hold the rank of captain. And given that there were many Jewish university graduates before the war, even when there were quotas and even when the universities were closed to Jews, their numbers in the mass graves of Katyn and elsewhere were by no means negligible.

Which means that if all my mother's cousins with degrees from the University of Montpellier had been deported as military men rather than as refugees, they might have ended up as their brother Jósek did at Auschwitz, only before him. Paradoxically, luck may have been with them because when the war began, they were so close to the frontier that it was impossible to obey orders to enlist, and easy to imagine trying to flee from the Germans. Every story of survival contains countless others of near-death, both real and probable.

The death Samuel Steinwurzel dodged was written in his demobilization certificate from the Polish Amed Forces, issued on April 18, 1947 at Predappio, Italy and shown to me by Gianni with other documents. It read: Rank: *Corporal 1ˢᵗ class (pending)*. Civilian Profession a/o Degrees: *Master Craftsman, Lumber/Wood*. Whether he wasn't cut out for school, or whether his father had preferred he get some useful training and begin to assist him right away, the fact is that Milek's salvation lay in having no higher education.

Katyn was the fate awaiting officers. When it came to ordinary soldiers who were prisoners of war, the story was confused, and the outcome subject to chance. That story is less documented, perhaps because the Katyn scandal and its truth long-denied have over-shadowed the deaths of other military personnel. From what we know the reply given to General Anders in August 1941 that there were just 20,000 soldiers in Soviet prisons and camps was not a lie, at least not formally. What became of the others? Disappeared, vanished, no one knew where. The Poles knew that some had been released immediately and others, especially those who lived in the western occupation zone, were handed over to the Germans. If Milek Steinwurzel had belonged to either of those two groups he would have ended up trapped in Poland.

But instead he ended up in a third group that also included the many who, having been freed as war prisoners were rearrested by the NKVD. It was certainly counter-revolutionary activity to have fought against the Red Army, and since the Geneva Convention did not ap-ply to political prisoners, they could be sent wherever. Samuel Stein-wurzel escaped the extermination of the Jews by being sent to Siberia.

To Siberia, but where or when we do not know. That Siberia, a word merely mentioned to his wife without saying anything more, was not a place on the map. Siberia was prison, freezing tempera-tures, forced labor. Siberia was the gulag.

The Poles, both civilians and soldiers, who arrived to join An-ders' Army came from far and wide: from the roadworks and rail-ways in Ukraine, from Arkhangelsk, from Siberia itself, even from the mines of Kolyma. They included a group of 171 men who de-parted from Kolyma on July 8, 1942, one year after the Soviet-Polish accord, men who were alive only by a miracle. Almost all of them had lost fingers or toes and had large black marks on their skin, symptoms of scurvy, General Anders recalled.

The General spoke with almost of all them, took down their stories, and in time those fingerless men produced 62 written reports. Selections from them were cited in his book, each identified solely by an initial to protect their families who remained in Poland, but linked to precise references in the archives.

Now, the reader in London or Milan who came across those pages in 1949 or 1950—pages that for many years were the first reports on the gulag—what did he think? It is not difficult to imagine the typical buyer of *An Army in Exile:* conservative, anti-Communist, interested in political and military history, perhaps he himself (it almost went without saying he would be male) a veteran. He would sympathize with the poor Poles and perfectly understand the commander's hatred for the usurpers of his country, for whose liberty he had shed and ordered shed useless blood, a hatred that seeped through every sentence. Yes, Anders was right to open people's eyes to what communism meant, but parts of his account were excessive. Probably the good general had simply read too much Dante. You could see the man had an excellent education, no doubt about that.

"I saw such a camp at Magadan," his book testified. "It was occupied exclusively by cripples without hands or feet. All were crippled by frostbite in the mines," and even they were not given food for nothing; they had to sew sacks and make baskets. Even those who had lost both hands had to work, shifting huge logs with their legs and feet, while others, missing feet, split wood. "The most extraordinary sight was when these cripples made their way in fives to the *bania*," a primitive sort of Turkish bath.

Samuel Steinwurzel was not interned at Koylma and we can only hope not in the most terrible camps of the Siberian far north. But he was a healthy male, as well as a soldier in an enemy army, and perhaps had even been revealed to be the son of a genuine capitalist under interrogation by the NKVD, for whom torture was routine. It was unlikely he was sent anywhere better than one of the ordinary labor camps. His only lifeline might have been, once again, his qualification as "master craftsman" in wood. The entire Arctic forest was there to be cut down and sawed up, and the great machine of the gulag needed expert labor. The secret police, however, did not answer to any productive or industrial imperatives. In any case, if Milek was able to turn his experience with lumber and wood to his benefit in the lager, he must have given thanks to his father Mojzsez and all his forebears.

Another clue suggests he was probably interned somewhere not at the far fringe, but very much within the gulag system, where the order to release the Poles arrived early and was relatively quickly realized. Milek's demob sheet shows he enlisted with General Anders on September 15, 1941.

The very day before, Anders had made his first visit to the Tock camp, where earliest arrivals in the 5th Division were waiting for him. It was the division in which Milek Steinwurzel would serve. The camp was nothing but a cluster of little tents in the forest. He would never forget his first impression of his future soldiers, wrote Anders. "Most of them had no boots or shirts and all were in rags, often the tattered relics of their old Polish uniforms." Their bodies were emaciated, practically skeletal, festering with ulcers due to a lack of vitamins. He had never before seen barefoot soldiers parade before him, and he hoped never to see it again.

Did Milek watch that parade, still too exhausted from his travels to understand that those skeletons standing to attention would soon be his comrades in arms? Whatever, he was once again deep in a forest, where it was bitterly cold and just about everthing was lacking: nails, trucks, spades and shovels, soap, stoves to heat the soldiers' tents. The rations coming in were not enough for the men, nor for the poor woebegone horses (so the former general of a cavalry brigade complained to Stalin). Once again, only the lice were abundant, and they brought the first typhus epidemics.

And yet, despite hunger, cold and disease, Samuel Steinwurzel was fortunate once again.

As time went by, it became more difficult for Jews to be accepted in the ranks of the Polish Army. At the beginning, at the time when Milek arrived, there were many, about half of those enrolled. And this seemed strange to the other men camped in the forest, and the tents began to buzz with discontent and bad feeling. They had no way of knowing that a third of those deported had been Jews, but they did recall those who had sung the praises of the Red Army. What were they going to do with all these people who had rushed into Soviet arms? What kind of Polish Army would this be if Jews made up the majority of it?

The political and military leadership was also suspicious, con-cerned. Two Polish Jews, Henryk Ehrlich and Wiktor Alter, un-derstood this and they hastened to plead their people's case with General Anders. They were Socialists, members of the Second Inter-national, but even more to the point, they were leaders of the Bund, the Jewish labor party that was forever at odds with the Commu-nists on one side and the Zionists on the other. In other words, they were patriotic Poles, and the Soviet authorities had treated them as such. Captured as they tried to cross the border into Lithuania, they were condemned to death as spies, a sentence then commuted to ten years in the gulag. The amnesty had arrived while they were in jail waiting to begin their sentences. Now they wanted to con-vince the general that Jews would fight for Poland as fiercely as the others, or rather, more so. Who more than a Jew burned to defeat the persecutors of his very family members? Who more than a Jew yearned to see them free again; who, if not a Jew, was so willing to shed his own blood and that of the enemy in order to have revenge?

Perhaps they knew they ran a risk in this, especially in asking for word on the missing officers, but they felt secure, backed by socialist and labor organizations, both Jewish and not, and espe-cially by the Americans. On December 1, 1941, the day before Sikor-ski went to Moscow to meet Stalin, the two were re-arrested. The news sparked a chorus of protest, and petititons to Stalin signed by the likes of Albert Einstein and Eleanor Roosevelt, but no word came from the Soviet side for another two years. Stalingrad had just been liberated, proof to the world that the Russians were win-ning the war at a price and under conditions that no one else could endure. Henryk Ehrlich and Wiktor Alter were spies for Hitler, said the communique; they had been executed. The authorities were un-moved when there were protests from abroad, and the two were likened to Sacco and Vanzetti. Perhaps Ehrlich committed suicide in his cell, while Alter was murdered two days after Sikorski met with Stalin.

General Anders, too, in his way, brought up the Jewish ques-tion. During the meeting with Stalin he quickly began to complain that the Jews had been the first to be freed from the Soviet camps, followed by the Ukrainians, and only finally by the Poles, and then the least fit of them. It must have cost him an effort that was far from his nature to find a diplomatic way to say that the Russians were deliberately filling his ranks with the least able men, poor material out of which to build a good army. And there he had to stop, not giving voice to the suspicion there was an even more malicious reason to inundate their army with the Jewish element.

Yet later, when he was supplying the numbers of his forces, 150,000 soldiers, perhaps more, fearing he might be told that was his limit, he returned to the question once more during a meeting with Stalin.

Anders observed there were many Jews among his soldiers who did not want to serve in the Army. He said that on several occasions, Jews had deserted.

"Jews are bad soldiers," said Stalin.

According to Sikorski, many Jews who had volunteered were black marketeers, and had been sentenced for contraband. He did not think they would be good soldiers. He did not want them in the Polish Army.

"Yes, Jews are bad soldiers." Stalin said again

Milek was not among those who ran off; he took the weapons they were given, at last, to replace their wooden guns, and like all the other men in the 5th Division, he began to train. His morale had probably improved, although his physical conditions and the climate remained what they were. But the Polish leadership had already raised that problem. Now they had another, thornier, one to face.

When the next day Anders met Stalin again, the Poles had somehow to maintain their slim accord with the Russians while bringing up just the opposite problem. Polish citizens from labor battalions serving in Soviet occupied territory, and Poles recruited in the Red Army—systematically the minorities—were not being released, he and Sikorski complained to Stalin.

"What is the case of the White Russians, the Ukrainians, and the Jews to you?" snapped Stalin. "You want Poles, who are the best soldiers."

This time Sikorski was careful not to leave himself open to Stalin's wisecracks, and argued that citizenship derived from the territories the deported came from. But then the discussion turned to the Belarusians, and above all to the Ukrainians, who had to be kept in line because they were sympathetic to the Germans. Diplomatic quicksand once again.

"We're not concerned about the Ukrainians, but about the territory," said Sikorski brusquely.

The right to join the Polish Army could not be denied, because the Soviet Union, in recognizing Poland's borders, effectively recognized its inhabitants as citizens. *Jus soli*: anyone deported from the soil of the Polish Republic as it had existed until 1939 was a Polish citizen.

Nevertheless the Russians did exactly what the Poles feared. More and more Jews, Belarusians and Ukrainians were treated as if they were Soviet. The formal agreement would only come later, when Anders' Army was put under British command. While the Poles were in the Soviet Union, though, they faced a dilemma. As the Red Army advanced, the Russians had less and less interest in nourishing—in every sense—an independent Polish national army. As far as they were concerned, it would have been better had it just disappeared. Anders and his men saw both their numbers and their rations cut back, and they had to share those rations with women and children, which made it impossible for the Poles to step out of line. Of that 150,000 soldiers Anders spoke of in December, less than half that number were now left in the transit camps, and only 40,000 would be permitted to leave for Iran. The barrel kept shrinking, while out there, somewhere, were officers they believed were in the gulag, some even in Kolyma, and a huge number of Poles, perhaps a million or even more, some of them maybe wandering over the steppes trying to reach them. If they got there, must they be turned away?

Neither the Polish constitution nor the Soviet one permitted inequality among citizens. In practice, though, inequality there was. And whether because the army corps kept contracting, because the Soviets expropriated the minorities (maybe that was okay with the Poles), whatever, an ethnic selection took place.

As time went by it became almost impossible for Jews, Belarusians and Ukrainians to join the Army, and expedients were even found to expel a good many of those already enlisted. Jews, above all, if for no other reason that that they were numerous.

When the Szer brothers went for their medical exam in Uzbekistan, of all the university degrees that would have landed them in a mass grave at Katyn, only one served to earn the uniform with

the Polish eagle that the British were giving out on the other side
of the Caspian, along with the right to citizenship for the civilians
they were travelling with, too. Jews might be bad soldiers but they
were often good doctors. In wartime, the man who's not good at
shooting or driving a tank, especially when his patriotism is doubtful, has pretty much two ways to get into the army: as a doctor, or
as an engineer.

When the first of them to enter the Army's enlistment offices
in Tashkent identified himself as Dr. Adolf Szer, born in Będzin, a
medical degree from the University of Montpellier, France, already
in practice at home even before the war, and when he was even
approved for officer status, something they were not so eager to
extend to Jews, he must have been very, very convincing.

Despite his malnourished state he was a strong specimen, with
a squarish face and a slightly crooked nose, but crooked in a manly
way, not at all Jewish, that indicated a good character. Asked where
he came from, he replied, in a sober voice and eccellent Polish with
no trace of a Yiddish accent, that he had been deported to a rudi-
mentary lager in Arkhangelsk region where he had worked as the
camp medic.

"It is not easy to practice in such conditions, but one learns a
lot."

"Certainly. Could you supply me the name of someone you
treated, someone who might have joined our ranks?"

Dolek had many, many references among the Poles. He told the
committee that some of them were right there having passed the
medical exam, others were in the queue. By this point the committee was already convinced.

"This is no greenhorn doctor," said one of the officers as Dolek
left the room, in a low voice so that the Russian inspector didn't
hear.

"True, he's one of those Jews you just wouldn't think…"

They gave him an "A" rating and an officer's rank. And they
also approved his pretty blond sister in law with her orphaned
stepbrother, and that husband of hers, a little Jew with a useless
degree.

The fact that all the Szer brothers, including Benno who showed
up later, were accepted in the army was due to the desperate need

for doctors the Poles had just then. Dr. Szer did his first duty to the nation immediately, hurrying back and forth among camps and hospitals from Tashkent to Samarkand, trying to tame the typhus epidemic. Fighting a deadly disease on that scale is a struggle between life and death where mere professional talent is not enough, where the virtues of the battlefield are needed: strength of will, a spirit of sacrifice, a cool head. And Dolek, long before he reached the front, showed his valor on that particular field that he had before him.

Thus, when they got to Palestine, he had been asked to stay on, and not desert like his brothers and all the others, desertion that was a providential solution to the Jewish question for the Poles. (Even under pressure from the English, the Poles did little to try to find the missing Jews). But Dolek by now perhaps shared the Polish esprit de corps; perhaps all those bodies he had saved, and those that he hadn't, had made him part of the Army and the nation.

And Samuel Steinwurzel?

Why did he not stay in Palestine? His travels would have been over, and his war, too; for Milek had already been through war and prison. Yes, some Polish Jewish soldiers did join the Zionist militias and became the original nucleus of the future Israeli army, but that was a free choice. Why did Samuel Steinwurzel want to go to war?

And why, if we take a step backward, was he still among the 4-5,000 Jews in Anders' Army at the time they left for the Middle East? Why had he not been weeded out in some medical selection, assigned a "D" ("unfit") rating although, skeletal as he was, he had been enrolled as "A", a letter that corresponded to his physical condition right up until he left the army?

Was it because he had distinguished himself doing carpentry work in the Tock forest? Were there not enough Polish Catholics to saw and plane a couple of boards?

Because—here's how I imagine it—had someone dared to put down the unequivocally Jewish name of Steinwurzel, Samuel, somebody else, his captain, his lieutenant, would have shaken his head.

"No, no, take that one off. Milek is a good soldier and a good Pole."

Was Samuel Steinwurzel a good Pole?

Certainly he didn't fit the other stereotype. Neither physically, being tall, fair-skinned, with a nose that was long, yes, but straight—nor in any other way. He wasn't a Zionist, or a Communist, or Orthodox, he didn't look for reasons to speak Yiddish; in short he wasn't Jewish first and foremost, either in his own eyes or those of others. And even if he wasn't rash and daring, or endowed with amazing ballistic skills, he was still a good soldier: loyal, disciplined and yet quick-witted, able to grit his teeth, fast, rapid on the uptake. Little did his superiors know that his restless nature had been shaped to their advantage by the bourgeois patriarch of a family business. If Jews were bad soldiers then it stood to reason that anyone who wasn't must in some way be a good Pole. If not, if Milek hadn't proved himself the exception to the rule, and if he hadn't been integrated in his battalion as a Pole, in confirmation of the rule, it's hard to think he wouldn't have taken the opportunity to skip out.

Israel Gutman, one of the most important scholars of the Shoah, made it his business to study anti-Semitism in Anders' Army, from the commander through the hierarchy down to the daily life of the troops. The Jewish soldiers who stayed on nearly all said that yes, the problem existed, but it hadn't touched them personally. Perhaps they held back out of gratitude, or because they were accustomed to think that a certain degree of anti-Semitism was normal, and could therefore be overlooked. They were assimilated Polish Jews, most of them bourgeois, like Milek.

Some had even enrolled after the Army had endured Soviet efforts to hobble it, in Palestine or even later, when enlisting was fully spontaneous, and when they could instead have signed up for a Jewish unit in the British army, or later, in the Jewish Brigade. Those men, or many of them, wanted to fight alongside the Poles for their native land and their people.

And Milek?

After the war, from what I know, he didn't keep up contact with Poland, nor see other Poles in Italy, not even those fellow soldiers who were still alive. If the first was not surprising, the second might be explained by the fact Milek/Emilio was constantly busy, always ready to leap up and charge off, a neurotic version of his father Mojzsez. One way or the other, he kept no ties with Poland.

Samuel Steinwurzel chose to fight for Poland's freedom because his family was there and they were dying. And he knew it.
The Jewish newspapers said so, and the Poles in contact with the
Armia Krajowa, the clandestine Home Army fighting the Germans
on occupied soil that was the best source of information for the government in exile in London and for the British government itself,
knew it better than anyone.

Samuel knew that Jews had been closed in the ghetto at Lviv;
he knew that the Germans had begun to select and deport them en
masse from there; he almost certainly knew of the Nazi camps that
meant death for a Jew. Perhaps he was spared knowing about the
initial Ukrainian slaughter, in which he could only hope that Glinianska, in an outlying neighborhood, might not have been touched,
along with the lives of his family, and his sister and mother.

In any event, they died. When he was in Iraq or Palestine with
what today is called the Polish Army in the East, it was the youngest of them, Hela, who unlike Milek had taken a degree and become
a pharmacist.

The following year, 1943, when soldier Steinwurzel was finishing up his training in Egypt, his father Mojzsez died in the Lviv
ghetto, while his mother Fania and his older sister Ella, married
to Emil Zelcer and mother of a four year old son Abraham, were
deported to Majdanek.

But Milek did not know that. He didn't know, when he landed
in Italy in March, 1944 and finally the real war began, that they
were probably already dead, all of them. And even had he known
that the ghettos had been emptied, including that of Lviv, he would
still have been ready to fight to avenge them, and perhaps even
more, for hope, prospects, a future.

Anyway, Glinianska, where they lived, was far from the Jewish part of town, and perhaps they hadn't been sent to the ghetto.
Among all his father's clients and employees, it was hard to imagine there wasn't even one willing, for money or whatever reason, to
help them. Mojzsez, it was true, might be too proud to ask for help,
maybe even too ready to obey the rules, but Hela, with all those
Polish friends she'd made at university, might she not be hidden
away somewhere?

These may have been his thoughts when at night, the Poles

around him discussed the news from home: who had been captured, who shot on the spot, who sent to a concentration camp as a member, or backer, of the Resistance. Often they were people he knew, and the voices came and went with a start when, from cot to cot the names of those who were fighting the Germans, every day more of them, bounced back and forth. Milek tried to remove himself from that hum of voices, which so often came to the same conclusion: when would it be their turn to help liberate their country? He thought about his family, eyes closed. And he felt alone. But when one of his Jewish fellow soldiers tried to interrupt, "Milek, where do you think they are now? Do you think they'll make it?" he would sit there unmoving like a kid pretending to sleep, something that was utterly unnatural for him.

Yes, it is possible that Samuel Steinwurzel tried to keep hope at bay, so it would not spill over into its opposite, just as he tried to scotch extravagant desires for revenge. But even when he was able to think of nothing for days on end, while he was learning to leap over scrolls of barbed wire, to recognize a mine, even while repacking his knapsack and polishing his army-issue boots, his jittery, nervy body sensed where he was heading. To die, maybe, but at least to die properly, as a Jew and a Pole, as a free man—no, as a man, period.

That is how I see Milek, corporal of the Second Polish Army Corps, 5th Kresowa Infantry Division under the command of General Nikodem Sulik, 5th Wilno Infantry Brigade, 15th Fusiliers Battalion, as he was about to land on the southern Adriatic, on his way to the well-known battle front.

Samuel Steinwurzel, the man so many Polish Jews, their entire lifetimes, have regretted they were not. He would never have to suffer because he had fled under a false identity, hidden in woods and caves like some prehistoric creature, in dog's hutches, or dropholes under the floor made to store coal or potatoes, like things stuffed in a cupboard or at the bottom of a wardrobe. Or because he had the undeserved good fortune to survive among the slaves, the worse than slaves, the envelopes of skin and bones that answered the rules of the ghetto and the law of the lager. For whom there was always a worm of doubt, the worm of their impotence and their humiliation as men, young men unable to do anything to defend their wives and their mothers, their children, their younger siblings, the old.

What could you have done, they said to themselves, you all by yourself against the Germans? How could you, just for a start, have procured a gun with the SS encircling the ghetto? If they'd caught you, they would have shot all of you together, immediately, don't you remember?

Each time coming to the conclusion there had been no alternative between escape, and certain death. But it was only a way, every time the same way, to end the debate, without ever really making peace with themselves.

And in fact, it wasn't true.

"Milek, are you asleep? Listen, Milek, this is important. Did you hear there's been a revolt in the Warsaw ghetto?"

"I heard, Leon."

"They're dug in, they have weapons, Milek. The Armia Krajowa supplied them. And don't say it's pointless. We know it is."

"Why should I say that? Let's hope they kill a lot of them before…"

"Let's hope so, Milek, let's hope so. Shall we say a prayer for our brothers in arms in Warsaw?"

"Okay, but no prayer. Let's make a toast, a *brachà*, in benediction, but tomorrow."

"You are right, Milek. They're fighting, and we're being taken around to see the Sphinx and the Pyramids."

Before the Second Army Corps had ever faced a single scuffle in Puglia or at the Sangro River, there had been uprisings in a hundred Polish ghettos, including Łachwa, Minsk-Mazowieczki, Białystok, Częstochowa, not to mention Będzin, home of the Szer brothers. There were armed resistance groups at Lviv, Łódź and Vilnius; Jewish partisan formations in the woods of Galicia, Belorussia and Lithuania; even an insurrection in the Sobibor death camp and one at Treblinka. In Warsaw the uprising had broken out on the eve of Passover, April 19, 1943, and would go on until fire spread house to house by the Germans brought defeat on May 16. The quantity and quality of the weapons brought into Poland's largest ghetto were only a little better than symbolic. There were more combatants and they were better organized, better connected to the Poles. And it would be the only revolt in which a few survived, going through the sewers to emerge beyond the ghetto, and later taking part with the Armia Krajowa in the Warsaw Uprising, along with many other

Jews hidden behind false identities. The first in all of Europe to take part in an armed revolt against the Nazis were young people, many of them minors when the German arrived, and often still minors when they began to fight, and not even their commanders were more than twenty-five years old.

Israel Gutman was just twenty when he took part. In the ghetto, he had seen his father die, then in short order his older sister who had kidney disease, and a few months later his mother. He was left with a younger sister, and decided it was best to entrust her to the orphanage run by the esteemed pediatrician Janusz Korczak. But on August 5, 1942 the good doctor had no choice, if he wished to be loyal to his charges, but to accompany them to Treblinka. Israel now had nothing left but his grief and his Zionist youth organization, which for once had found common ground in socialism and the desire to fight the Germans and joined the Communists and above all the young people of the Bund, who had circulated home-made letters signed "Henryk Wiktor," encouragement, as it were, from Henryk Erlich and Wiktor Alter in their Soviet graves. Gutman, injured close to an eye, was forced to come out of his bunker, and so was deported, first to Majdanek, then to Auschwitz.

He took part in the resistance at Birkenau, too, helping to supply explosives to the Sonderkommando, the prisoners charged with removing bodies from the gas chambers and transporting them to the crematoria. He was not among those discovered or executed after Crematorium IV was blown up on October 7, 1944. After he was freed from Mauthausen, he hastened to Italy to join the Jewish Brigade, by then assisting Jewish refugees and helping them to reach Palestine. Gutman himself went to the British Mandate Palestine shortly before independence. In 1961 he would testify at the Eichmann trial; he took a university degree and became a historian in 1975, after having lived on a kibbutz in Galilee for 25 years. For years Gutman was the director of research at Yad Vashem, editor of the *Encyclopedia of the Holocaust*, consultant to the Polish government on Jewish matters.

In the one video interview with Israel Gutman I came across, I saw a white-haired gentleman, slightly heavy, round-faced, his eyes small, sad, shy, behind a pair of outsized glasses stuck on a large bulbous nose.

I sensed something that seemed to trascend the exclusive perspective of his own people when he wrote, in detail, about anti-Semitism in Anders' Army, for the issue had been one I struggled with. There was this problem of history writing: not only did it reflect the historian's identity and views, but somehow inevitably also coincided with the writer's national interest, at least insofar as that was compatible with modern historical practice. And inside modern historical practice, the problem touched just about everyone: the English historians who gave more space to the British role in winning the battle of Monte Cassino than to the French, and denied that the Poles had been of any importance. The French historians who underemphasized the crimes committed by Moroccan troops, and undervalued the role of soldiers from the colonies in liberating France. The Indian historians who absolved Gandhi of any responsibility in the tragedy of Partition, which divided and set against each other soldiers who had been comrades in arms in the Indian Division. Each one assigning all possible merit to his own side and understating any mistakes or blame, often assigning the blame and the mistakes to others. Each time (and I could hear my mother saying, "you're not a historian") I had to try to listen to the missing side, and in the case of the Indian accounts, actually ask myself: who is providing this reconstruction here; is he Hindu, Muslim, or something else? At the end I understood that even the numbers of the victims were part of the game, especially the innocent victims. More when the victims were yours, less when you inflicted death on others. The more tragic the circumstance, the more your own memory of horror expanded at the expense of others. History became trauma-telling, the handing down of one's own, irreconcilable wounds.

It was clear what to expect from Israel Gutman, expert on the Shoah, Israeli historian, even without knowing exactly who he was. And yet behind his pages I sensed something that eluded every attempt to pin him exclusively to an identity of Jew, Israeli, Zionist. Something that *came before,* like an even more searing rage, something in which to channel a suffering without any meaning or any limits. You drove us out again, you forbid us to fight our executioners, you deprived us of the right to pay the price, to be citizens: this was what Gutman seemed to say between the lines. How could we show we were not all cowards and traitors when *you, too*, excluded us because of your prejudice?

That was why I went to find his story.

And yet Samuel Steinwurzel, along with the last thousand Polish Jews remaining in the Second Polish Corps, was wearing the green uniform and the cap with the eagle when the time came to show the world the price Poland was prepared to pay for its freedom and its independence. For at that point, Poland had a desperate need for the world to see it.

On July 4, 1943, returning to London from a visit to the troops in the Middle East, a plane with the head of the Polish government in exile aboard crashed into the sea just after takeoff from Gibralter. The Poles abroad were overwhelmed at Sikorski's death. "It was a profound shock to the whole army," said Anders. General Sikorski, he believed, would have been extremely cautious when dealing with Russia, and no other Pole had so much prestige with the Allies. The American and English leaders who met with Sikorski had made him significant promises. There was every reason to think that the Polish cause would have been far better defended in the final phase of the war had Sikorski survived, Anders believed.

Perhaps General Anders overestimated what Sikorski might have accomplished, for the Polish cause had already begun to falter from the days when the graves at Katyn were discovered, when the Poles' alienation from Soviet power brought no consequences, except their isolation.

And so on November 28, 1943, Churchill, Roosevelt and Stalin met for the first time to agree on how to proceed with the Second World War and begin to think what they would do with the world. They decided the date of the Normandy landing, the tri-partition of Germany, the creation of the United Nations. But for the absent Poles—and even Sikorski most probably would have been absent— they negotiated the shifting of frontiers, above all. Stalin would take the Eastern territories, swapping them for a piece of those belonging to the Germans: from Slesia, more or less, to Danzig.

But this their Polish ally—valuable perhaps more for intelligence services than for the heroic- Romantic presence from Norway to North Africa of Poland's ever more numerous soldiers in exile, including the fearless pilots of the Battle of Britain—must only be made to understand little by little.

For now, from the Tehran Conference, all that was required was a joint statement from the Three Powers. They looked with confidence, they declared, "to the day when all peoples of the world may live free lives, untouched by tyranny, and according to their varying desires and their own consciences."

The suspicions, the rumors, finally became a public and unequivocal statement on February 22, 1944, when Prime Minister Winston Churchill appeared before the House of Commons:

> [T]the fate of the Polish nation holds a prime place in the thoughts and policies of His Majesty's Government and of the British Parliament. It was with great pleasure that I heard from Marshal Stalin that he, too, was resolved upon the creation and maintenance of a strong integral independent Poland... I have an intense sympathy with the Poles, that heroic race whose national spirit centuries of misfortune cannot quench, but I also have sympathy with the Russian standpoint... The liberation of Poland may presently be achieved by the Russian armies after these armies have suffered millions of casualties in breaking the German military machine. I cannot feel that the Russian demand for a reassurance about her Western frontiers goes beyond the limits of what is reasonable or just. Marshal Stalin and I also spoke and agreed upon the need for Poland to obtain compensation at the expense of Germany both in the North and in the West.

For the men of the Second Army Corps this was no consolation, nor was it for Samuel Steinwurzel. Was there a radio able to receive the BBC on the ship transporting the 5th Kresowa Division to Italy—that division named for Kresy, those eastern lands from which most of its soldiers came? If by any chance there was, Milek too, along with all the others, must have felt turmoil far worse than the usual sea sickness in his soul, and in his gut.

"They betrayed us, they sold us out to that evil Georgian, may he roast in hell!"

"Are you kidding? Hell is too hot; he should be sent to the depths of Siberia, where he sent us, and kept out there as long as he lives."

"If General Sikorski were still alive, maybe this wouldn't have happened."

"It was them, somebody fiddled with his airplane; they killed him, those Russian bastards!"

"No, no, it was our dear English friends; don't forget the plane took off from Gibraltar."

"What do we care about that now? We need to understand if what Churchill seems to have said is really true."

"If it is, it's the end. No, it can't be!"

Some of them vomiting, others clinging to their fellow soldiers like drunks, they tried to strike up the national anthem. "Poland has not yet perished, as long as we shall live!" But the chain fell apart as some began to sob with the refrain: "March, march Dąbrowski/ From the Italian land to Poland" and Milek, pale and gaunt as a lunar Pierrot, leaned against the railing.

If that was how things were, how could he go back to Lviv to search for those left alive? At the best, they wouldn't let him out; at the worst, they'd be waiting for him at the border to arrest him and send him back to some part of the gulag. And even if all went well, he would now have nothing: not the house on Glinianska, or the warehouse, or the sawmill. Nothing with which to begin again, supposing someone in the family was still alive. But chances were it would not go well, because he was the son of an entrepreneur, he was actually a capitalist himself, although the Germans had taken everything away from him.

"Milek?"

"Lucky you; you're from Warsaw, Franiek."

"What can I say?"

"Sometimes I think it would be easier if I knew they were all dead..."

"No, Milek, don't! We must fight; it's the only way we can show the English and the Americans that they cannot make such decisions without consulting us."

"Let's hope. Anyway, we have no choice at this point."

If that was how the troops reasoned, what could General Anders say when General Leese, the British commander, told him what they were thinking about his contingent at headquarters? It had been proposed the the Second Polish Corps take on the "far from easy" task in this first phase of the battle, to capture the heights, first of Monte Cassino, then Piedimonte San Germano.

Since he'd arrived in Italy Anders had watched the Allied forces fail one after the other as they attacked the Abbey, when it was still whole, and when it was reduced to a ghostly wall that looked like a mouthful of chipped teeth. The Gurkhas were still dug in at Rocca Janula, enduring a medieval siege. They were holding the castle but could not get out to take a position higher up, and had lost all hope. I mean, the Gurkhas. Incredibly brave and strong, especially in the mountains, nor was there anything to criticize about the Rajputana Rifles, or for that matter about the Essex Battalion, English soldiers. But most of the men the British sent to take the heights belonged to their colonial troops, and that certainly meant something. The New Zealanders, too, were burned out. And after the bloodbath in the Rapido, even Clark was reluctant to volunteer his men. He just wanted to get to Rome, from wherever.

General Anders knew that the "far from easy" task might either be an honor bestowed, or a costly favor to be done, but something snapped back in his military, Polish soul, more a reaction than a true thought.

You have the biggest and most powerful air fleet that has ever been, you have as many tanks as you want, mortars, bazookas, machine guns, smoke bombs, grenades. But you don't have my men. You have freedom but you don't have the courage, the spirit of sacrifice, the drive to fight of these soldiers, on whom I wouldn't have bet a penny when I saw them parade before me the first time, ghostly bodies that not even your taste for the macabre and the chilling could have summoned up. And you know it. You know that we may be the only ones who can do this.

His role, however, demanded he quickly contain that burst of pride and be as shrewd and calculating as possible. He had to calculate not just his estimated losses, but also the craftiest of political variables.

The Second Army Corps, even if it were assigned to another front, could sustain heavy losses, he realized. While success in the operation at Monte Cassino, a battle front now famous around the world, might be of great importance to the Polish cause. It would answer once and for all "the Soviet lie that the Poles did not want to fight the Germans. Victory would give new courage to the Polish resistance movement, and "cover Polish arms with glory." Anders added up the risks of combat, the inevitable losses, the responsibility, which would be entirely his own, if the action did not succeed. He bowed his head for a moment in thought, and then he said he would accept.

Now the commander in chief of Polish forces arrived for a meeting with General Alexander at the Reggia di Caserta near Naples, and he predicted the losses would be "oppressive" and the result, defeat. Anders argued with him. He was told he was dreaming. His superior believed it was pointless to pursue the same objective after three failures and insisted, even in Alexander's presence, they try an alternative to a direct assault, moving around the abbey. Perhaps, as he flew back to London, the Polish supreme commander may have decided Anders was reasoning too much like a politician, not that it was his fault. Actually, he had done ecceptionally well in their sessions with Churchill and with Stalin, and Poland would always be indebted to him for the many lives he'd saved and for the way he had been able to get schools, orphanages and public kitchens running in Iran and Palestine. It wasn't a question of Władysław Anders' personal courage, nor of his patriotism, but what had he been in the last war? Brigadier General. And perhaps, with that thought a sigh had drifted from the Mediterranean heavens toward those fourteen generals of theirs lost in forest graves of Katyn.

But then spring arrived, and after more than a month of very little action, the wet, muddy ground began to dry up. Where it could, and as soon as it could, both on the plain and in the hills, grass began to sprout, and weeds of all kinds, along with huge patches of red poppies.

The morale of the Polish troops was so high that the English were alarmed, although they were accustomed to comrades in arms of every race and color. Who *were* these people? They smoked their fags with cigarette holders, went around all polished and pretty, kissed the hands of the local peasant women, young and not so young, who absolutely adored them, needless to say. They were sissies, if not worse, that seemed clear—and yet they weren't. Because when you had to do some military action with them, they would lead the way as if they were marching off on a picnic. And when you said to them, "hey, you, if you don't get down the Jerries will shoot you!" and even pushed their heads down and said it again making bum-bum noises so that there was no way they didn't understand you, they still didn't react. They just didn't give a damn. So they had guts, maybe more guts than they should. These blokes really hated the Germans! However, where I come from we call being too brave just plain foolish, and so let's hope we don't find ourselves by their sides too often.

Just let an English soldier say something perfectly normal like, "let's hope we get out of his hellhole in one piece," maybe not even speaking to one of the Poles, and they would get their backs up. And even when you were all halfway drunk, the shock, the mute judgment on their faces was inescapable.

"What's up mate? Don't you people care at all about getting out of this alive? You'll see how lovely war is, when it hits you."

And you could say it to provoke, or in a spirit of camaraderie, and the Poles would react with a little less, or a little more, of their customary discipline and courtesy. Was it really worth it to pick a fight with these bastards?

The soldier whose English was the best then began to recount what they had been through since Poland was invaded. The English lads didn't seem to believe him, and they were getting bored. So the Poles ended up their list of horrors with a flourish: the latest bad news from the Resistance at home. At this point they were mostly talking to themselves. When the wine came to an end, the atmosphere had become unreal, and some skinny Italian sheep or goat bleating nearby made more sense than the failed dialogue among fellow soldiers.

But the Poles were more charged up than morose when they got back to camp. Even such silly experiences cemented them together, it seemed. Milek walked between Franciszek Kułakowski from Warsaw and Leon Simon, with whom he shared city of origin, religion and the ranks of the 15th Fusiliers. Why their battalion was so full of men from Lviv they didn't know, but they were by no means unhappy about it. So long as he and Lesek (a nickname about as related to Leon as Milek to Samuel) avoided certain questions, they got along wonderfully.

284 The Swallows of Monte Cassino

Franiek recalled a song, a popular song, very Slav, very dance-able, and began to sing it at the top of his lungs for the English, for the Italian sheep, and especially for the Germans, who couldn't have been far away. Everyone got it right off, and in the warm night air they all began howling together, barking out toward those hills soon to be a front again that song about a tipsy old lady and her naughty goat who had stolen two heads of cabbage, the refrain rumbling across the valley like thunder: "Tra-la-tra-la-tra-la-la-la, two pretty heads of cabbage!"

Milek seemed to be his old self again, his congenital nervous-ness taking on something of a canine sense of smell, and he even resembled a sort of hunting dog with a long, pointed muzzle. May-be it was spring, and this country which was the best he'd been through yet, the people most like his own, even though he wasn't a Catholic. Despite everything they were in Europe, and not so far from home, and with battle imminent, the nostalgia was bearable. It must be this, this knowledge that now it was their turn, that these bright, clear days might be their last, that made them so perceptive, so aware, and dazed, so elated and controlled at the same time, so cautious and so dreamy. Everthing was filtered through the senses, even love of country became concrete, motions repeated a thou-sand times in drills until they became automatic, until facing death, the human being became one with the soldier.

They were confident because they couldn't be anything else, be-cause they had faced snow, steppe, desert and sea before arriving here. Only they knew (but every one of them knew) how different they were from those sad wraiths that had once come together in a forest of the Urals. As for those who had died there, or along their interminable voyage, now was not the moment to think of them.

But their superiors were optimistic too, those who knew the orders and the magnitude of the offensive, this time well coordi-nated and properly planned. Their numbers were greater than ever before; they would all attack at once—Americans, the French, the English and the Poles—along a line that went from the gulf of Gae-ta up to Cassino. The weather was finally right, their preparations carefully concealed.

General Anders's only regret was that the secrecy had prevent-ed him doing any reconnaissance, but for the rest he could not complain. He had even had to decide which division would attack the Abbey and take Point 593 (also known as Mt. Calvary) by drawing lots, for neither of the two commanders was willing to step back. General Bronisław Duch, head of the 3rd Karpacka Division, won the honors; General Nikodem Sulik of the 5th Kresowa Division was left holding the short match.

Among the 15th Fusiliers scarcely anyone muttered a complaint about that arbitrary verdict, not Lesek nor Franiek of Warsaw, who merely said, "so be it," while this time Milek recalled his rank and told them that everyone must take his place and do his duty.

But things changed when they arrived at the line, in the mountains, and there had to wait for orders to attack. To wait: it sounded simple. It was all right while they were on the approach, first in vehicles, then on foot, uphill, in utter darkness. But then, they had to endure a rule of silence far tougher than that of the monks whose ruined abbey they were supposed to take. Their objective bore an all-too eloquent name: Phantom Ridge, as the English called it, just Phantom to them. Hunkered down in stone shelters and if they were lucky, behind some spindly bushes, as the days passed in waiting, they felt more and more phantoms themselves: unable to move, unable to talk unless covered by the background noise of artillery fire, unable even to wash. Which was no mean problem, because their old friends, lice, had returned. It was amazing how quickly you grew unused to the hard things as soon as matters began to improve: the bad food, the water that only came at night, the rusty soup, hot and scarce.

Everything else was new, but worse, a surprise because they thought they had already been through the worst the world could offer. There was the terrible stink of dead mules and men. On their way up, they had to step around the carcasses along the path, see parts of trunks with legs in boots attached, hold back from looking further to see if the rest of the soldier was still there. Once they had, instinctively, made that mistake, they learned not to look again. When you were walking you could concentrate on your fellow soldier ahead of you, but when you were still, and had to be silent most of the time, the stink of death was so pervasive that breathing in, you asked yourself how you could bear to breathe. You wanted to say, "I can't breathe" but that could be enough to get you killed. For the Germans were invisible, even by day: phantoms like themselves, but there. Silent like themselves, but their weapons spoke for them. Or maybe "spoke for them" was an exaggeration; weapons just spoke, they said the only thing that mattered, battered them with artillery and mortar fire, constantly, but especially at night. Those bullets and grenades hailing down on all sides—in front, around, and even behind them—said "you cannot see us but we are all around, on high, nearby and far away, everywhere."

You felt your life was all in your ears and your nose. Strange, but it was easier to fall sleep to the sound of weapons that might kill you, than with the smell of the dead in your nose. For Milek, having to stay still was torture. But if he gave in to the need to stretch his limbs or stamp those feet he could no longer feel, if by mistake he sent a single stone down the ridge, the machine guns of the "green devils" as the English called them, would ring out. Green devils: there was a kind of reverential fear in the way they referred to those enemy paratroopers, however accustomed the Brits might be to talk about Krauts and Jerries, to the point they scarcely remembered they were insulting them.

The Poles too had their terms of denigration, but during the silent immobility of waiting, even language shrank. Food, water, radio, bandages, munitions. And Germans, *niemcy*. One or two of them recalled the several meanings of that word *niemcy* ("German", but also "foreigner, deaf-and-dumb")—and used them to communicate in sign language, although at first their comrades didn't understand. Why did he hold a finger up to his mouth when they were already perfectly silent? And then point over there, when the other time...? Of course! *Niemcy:* the silent, the dumb; that is, the Germans, the enemy. Never was a word's root meaning more appropriate. Since they'd arrived, they had been trying to capture a shadow—no, too risky—at least a sound, a noise, they could understand. They don't know where the Germans were, but they were certainly very near.

In the end the 15th Fusiliers found themselves up front, which meant they would be first to move at the appointed time. "You wanted it, you got it!" they signaled silently to the one who had complained out loud when they were still permitted to speak.

And so, after they'd spent two anxious weeks as spectres, the day chosen for the attack came. May 11, 1944. Their orders came down in the afternoon with messages to the Polish troops from Generals Alexander, Leese and Anders, and their wireless operator had his ear glued to the headset so he could repeat that of their own commander at least:

Soldiers!

The moment for battle has arrived. We have long awaited the moment for revenge and retribution over our hereditary enemy.

Shoulder to shoulder with us will fight British, American, Canadian, and New Zealand divisions, together with French, Italian and Indian troops.

The task assigned to us will cover with glory the name of the Polish soldier all over the world...

Trusting in the Justice of Divine Providence we go forward with the sacred slogan in our hearts: God, Honour, Country.

Whether the entire battalion including Corp. Samuel Steinwurzel was able to hear him, we don't know. What was audible, and particularly on the front lines, was the message of arms. It was 23 hours precisely. They had 1,600 guns and mortars spread out along the front for 35 km, not to mention the Allied light artillery, with a boundless supply of munitions. No one had ever seen a hail of fire like that, especially none of those who didn't dare watch, forced to keep their heads down. Everything was flying overhead: rockets, howitzer shells, grenades, shrapnel and fragments of every shape and substance—iron, stone, split wood, flaming wood, stuff it was better not even to think about. The stones they hid behind vibrated as if electrified, the mountain beneath their flattened bodies gave a long, deep, angry groan that mounted to an indistinct roar when the enemy artillery replied.

It wasn't so surprising that the walls they'd amassed were crumbling, or that every impact made dust rain skyward, dust made of all that could be reduced to dust; but there was no way to escape the feeling that the entire mountain of granite beneath them was cracking and coming to pieces. And they had to stay there like that, clinging to the spine of that fossil whale come back to life, for what seemed an eternity. When finally someone was able to look at his watch, it was only just midnight. They would have to wait another hour, but now it seemed a real privilege to be the first to attack.

In the meantime the moon, too, reached its expected position, and was not hidden much by clouds.

When they got up they were still deaf (some even had burst ear-drums) and shaken inside and out, although their limbs were stiff. The first and second companies were to go into action, including Lesek and Franiek, who Milek hadn't seen since they were brought to the front. He had embraced them before they made the climb, silently, because they had to, but the darkness had allowed him to weep, for what reasons he couldn't say, with his eyes alone, those secondary, now useless, organs.

And Milek wept again as the third company, his own, crouched silently, alert to any sound from Phantom where their comrades were headed. Unfortunately they did not have to wait long. That barrage they thought would shatter the Apennines seemed to have been entirely useless. The Germans, their trenches intact, sent back an immediate, crushing reply, and between explosions you could hear mortars and machine guns, orders and cries for help, the screams of the wounded. Polish screams, for the *niemcy* were still silent. They had destroyed their front line no sooner than they emerged, and killed countless numbers of their men without even coming out of their holes. That was the unmistakeable message, even for those who had never before heard the sounds a man makes when he is shredded by a mixture of metal and explosive. In confir-mation, the radios of both companies were silent.

When it was Milek's turn to go for the top of Phantom, he had no idea what was in his head, bottled up in that prison too long, while his body seemed to have been reduced to a machine to keep his heart ticking. His sense of smell had been overwhelmed by the ubiquitous stink of explosives, and his hearing was half gone. From here on he would have to rely on his eyes, as much as they stung, and watch where he put his feet, up and down the stony hillside be-tween briers and bushes, practically no way to follow a path traced out by the sappers' flame-throwers. His heart, filling his whole chest, was in charge: a heart beating so hard you could no longer understand what the hell it was trying to communicate. Fear? Hatred? More one than the other, or both, or was there any difference? The only thing that was clear to Milek was that he was alive and almost certainly about to die. After that, until they were ordered to withdraw the following day (and thus avoided death on masse), his existence was much like a dark, smoky canyon, lit up by scattered streaks of fire, that is, like the landscape he found himself in.

In no time at all they, too, lost contact, first with the artillery covering them, then between one platoon and another, and when the radio too went silent, it was a miracle they didn't fall apart completely. Advancing as rapidly and low to the ground as they could, they soon met their dead and injured comrades. Lesek had a great hole in his head; Franiek was missing a leg and the left side of his groin. Where they dared try to divine with their flashlights, they saw many, many other bodies slumped around spikes of rock, sometimes rising out of the bushes. The smell of fresh death was very different indeed: it didn't stink. But it, too, was terrible, multiplying the olfactory memories of a thousand little cuts and scrapes until they became something nauseating and final. Milek recovered his senses for a moment; he removed his friends' tags and closed their eyes. He wished he could close the hole in Leon Simon's head, Leon Polish Jew of Lviv, but there is no time for such a pointless, upsetting gesture.

Instead, he went through his knapsack looking for a wallet or something that might have letters or photographs. He found Lesek's wallet only, no surprise, and while looking for Franiek's knapsack, lifted off his medal of Our Lady of Częstochowa, but his knapsack had been blasted away, and when he couldn't find it quickly decided he'd have to let it go and hope that sooner or later someone would get up there and bring back everything and everyone. Which wasn't something you could count on, considering the stink and the actual dead bodies they'd shared space with in the past two weeks. When you're lodged with a corpse, you risk his same fate if you don't have the patience to wait for the right moment to remove him.

Milek let them be; it was time he looked after the wounded. As he bandaged and applied tourniquets, his eye fell on a knapsack stuck to a clump of barbed wire; there might be a mine, too. With his rifle butt he hooked a strap, pulled it, and grabbed the bag in the air. It was the right one. As he got up and ran after his company, thoughts came to him. He had to say Kaddish for Leon, had to find some relative of his in Poland who was still alive. He had to write a letter to Franiek's family. His heart was no longer beating hard; it was smaller and higher up, where the nausea sat. Grief, it seemed, was a tranquilizer.

This went on long enough that the Germans could have wiped him out if they'd got him in their sights. Which meant there was still someone up ahead keeping their invisible enemies busy, and so all was not yet lost. All the stories of all the atrocities committed against Jews and Poles at home had less effect on Milek than the vision of the corpses of Franciszek Kułakowski and Leon Simon.

Up on Phantom, they fell under fire from a couple of nests of German that their advance guard hadn't been able to clean out. They had to figure out where they were, get covered and fire toward those bunkers, and the one who got there first had to toss in a grenade. At the first sign of ceasefire, you let off a couple of rounds just to be sure, or to blow off steam. They too were shouting insults in their language as they fired, shouting that for Poland, this was just the beginning. *Dla Polski!* Milek too yelled the words. It was good; he too would give his all for Poland. He ran and fired, unworried now that he might end up injured or dead.

And then, just before dawn, a vague allusion to a white flag, a dirty handkerchief, came poking out just as they were getting ready to clean out that bunker, American-made bazookas in hand. It was surprise, more than anything else, that made them freeze as they watched a machine-gunner come out with his hands up. *Nicht schiessen! Nicht schiessen!* Don't shoot.

Nein!

What made them, more than one of them, say that? Why did they stand there, without lowering their weapons, but at a distance? Why did the sergeant merely say, "We're taking you away" when a second man came out of the bunker?

Why were there rules to obey in war? How was it that those green devils were actually not much older than boys, and why did they resemble those who'd spent time in the gulag? Why did they themselves not feel the instinct to kill those who surrendered, or even to kill altogether?

Who knows whether it happened that day or during the second attack on Phantom? In wartime, even experiences so fresh they are hard to think of as memories can superimpose themselves one on top of the other.

This, more or less, was what remained impressed on Corporal Steinwurzel of the day that was supposed to bring glory on Poland in the eyes of the world, and instead saw the remnants of companies one and two coming down from Phantom between rocks and charred trees. The men still able to fight were very few, and they had to help transport the wounded. And so Milek and his company were back at their starting point, and curled up with bunker stones for pillows, awaiting new orders that might come any time, even right away, they finally accepted their duty to sleep.

At just about that same time, Commander Oliver Leese arrived in aid of General Anders. The Second Polish Army, although it had been defeated, had been useful, he said, in keeping the enemy occupied, and especially the German artillery, thus allowing his own 8th Army to proceed up the Liri Valley. His praise for Polish sacrifice sought and achieved was just the preamble, though, to his refusal to consider letting the Polish troups regroup for a new attack the next day. It was up to the British, up to him, in other words, to decide when to deploy the Poles, and Anders must obey!

All night long during the Polish attack until the early afternoon of the following day, General Anders had been given reports, dwindling reports, on the battle, yet continued to hope he could organize a quick counterattack. But there was nothing to be done but accept that litany of numbers: numbers of points that corresponded to positions taken or lost, numbers of losses that climbed with every new report until the final count came in at 205 dead, 1028 wounded and 384 missing.

But even the commander was not certain what had happened up there on the mountain. War was no longer what you saw in a painting, the commander on the heights following the battle's forward motion and its obstacles, giving orders, encouraging, directing. The reality was very different, thought Anders; battles were often fought out of the commanding officer's sight. The darkness and the smoke at Monte Cassino meant nothing could be seen even from few steps away. The picture had to be composed from "a collection of small epics, many of which can never be told, for their heros took to their graves the secret of their exploits." Yet the Polish soldiers, their will and spirit of sacrifice unbowed, were one in spirit, although each man had perforce to play his lonely part. "Each minute brought its dreadful experiences, and the sum of them was victory." So thought Anders.

There was, perhaps, someone who had a more tangible perception of what was happening in that battle than did the general, or the individual soldiers scattered around that canyon at night, under fire. From the early hours of the morning, before dawn, the Polish camp hospital, down in the valley they called Inferno, had been working frantically, the staff drenched in sweat, their uniforms splattered with the blood of the wounded, for there was no time to change.

Captain Dolek Szer had dealt with frostbite and pneumonia, he had faced typhus and malaria, he had probably even assisted as children were born in the camp hospital hut or the tents of Central Asia, but he had never had to saw off an arm or a leg, take out the shrapnel and bone splinters that had been hurled into every inch of a man's body, or remove a length of gut to see if something underneath had to be taken out, then put it back, sew him up. Or perhaps he had; perhaps he was already in Italy when they were fighting on the Sangro, although that was nothing compared to this. There, you had time to reflect, to see who these people were you had to operate on. This was a bloodbath: wounds to clean, suture, bind, and stop the bleeding as quickly as possible. Any words of comfort or encouragement were reduced to the formulaic; all the faces looked the same, and anyway you didn't look at faces but at wounds, searching out the eye of a bullet, the teeth of shrapnel lodged in the flesh.

It had been a massacre, and it was still happening, and who knew how long it would go on. Somehow, instructions had been given that all those wounded who could be treated by a nurse be removed elsewhere. Now there was just this howling mass calling for their mothers, God or the Virgin Mary, who railed against losing a limb, against dying, who wailed, wept, vomited in pain and because of the stench they themselves and their miserable comrades in arms were making.

You couldn't let it touch you, nothing; you mustn't think, or let the catastrophe your hands were immersed in arrive at your brain. You could only hope that, for that day and as long as it took, the enemy would let you work, let you save what could be saved.

And hope that what had happened a few days before did not repeat itself, when the German artillery fired on their main medical station killing ten wounded men as well as Don Augustyn, the chaplain, and two of Dolek's colleagues, one of them Dr. Adam Graber of Warsaw. They had played cards together in Egypt, although Dolek wasn't terribly good at card games. But Graber was an appealing man, almost too well-balanced. A man resigned to the fate of his relatives back home, who liked to say, "You know Dolek, our religion tells us that our blood is not worth more than the blood of others, and even though I'm not an observant Jew, I've always thought that was the meaning of what we doctors do."

Yes, he'd grown fond of old Dr. Graber, who wasn't even as old as he looked, maybe about fifty. Was it the Soviet lager behind him or the German one whose thought tormented him, that had aged him so? In any case it was a blow for Dolek to see that even ministers to the soul and the body could die in service. What if it had been him on May 8, 1944, in the place of his friend Adam Graber? He couldn't think about it now, though, and he wouldn't be able to for a while. When on that night of May 12 General Anders and what was left of his troops finally lay down to sleep, the battle was still raging in the camp hospital and would continue for who knew how long.

The remains of the 15th Fusiliers awaited new orders and hoped for word on the wounded and the missing, word that could raise their spirits some, although the news that did come in was often discouraging. However, it seemed that things were going better at the front. Without knowing it, they had served as the lightning rod protecting the English, who had made forward progress in the following days, progress that could be summed up in two words.

Bridge. While they had been hunting down the German paratroopers on Phantom, the sappers of the 4th Indian Division had gone out to mount the first bridge, just about where in January the 143rd Texas Regiment had tried to cross, just beyond the town of Sant'Angelo in Theodice. The bridge over the Gari, that river that had swallowed Sergeant Jacko Wilkins was ready at 7 a.m. on May 12. Did Private Jeff McVey, still with the American troops along the coast there, ever hear the names of the seven prefab steel and slat constructions that finally avenged his dead comrades? Amazon, Blackwater, Congo, Cardiff, London, Oxford, Plymouth. More likely—and like the Poles—he heard another word being muttered.

Tanks. The first convoys of armored vehicles were crossing to the enemy side. And because the bridges held and the ground was now dry, for the first time in four months the tanks of the armored brigades Ontario and Calgary, and then those of their British counterparts, were able to make for the enemy lines without ending up stuck together like a heap of giant cockroaches..

But it was not down in the valley that German defenses gave way on May 14. The Gustav Line was first breached at the toughest point, by those who stood practically on the lowest rung of the Allied ladder, below the Gurkha troops and the Indians, and well below the New Zealanders and the Poles of the Second Army Corps. Their commander General Alphonse Juin was so skilled he had scored unexpected gains right from the beginning of the campaign, but Juin and his French Expeditionary Corps had been servants of the traitor Vichy government until just two years previously. It wouldn't do for him to be too visible, although his troops were particularly adept at mountain combat. It wouldn't do for them to reap too much glory.

Milek and his comrades had encountered them right after they landed in Italy, when the 5th Kresowa Division was sent to the main front. "Go relieve the French," they'd been told. But even when they learned those French were the 2nd Moroccan Division they were unprepared for what awaited them, despite the time they'd spent in Iran, Iraq, Palestine and Egypt. They probably hadn't paid attention when their fellow Poles from the Karpacka Division talked of Tobruk and other North African battles, and mentioned that among all the strange people they were fighting with, the strangest were the French troops, largely made up of "every kind and every color of Negroes."

It wasn't their skin color or features that troubled the Poles who had just come in from Egypt, but their attire, and their manners, as well as that of their officers, most of whom were Frenchmen, it was true, but there weren't many of them.

Some of these soldiers did not even wear uniforms, just a sort of Bedouin cassock and sandals on their feet.

Now this was not Siberia, not even the Urals, but it was still unexpectedly cold in March, and from some icy remains you could see there had been snow here not long before. With those caftans the color and manufacture of a dirty old sack, the Moroccans carried American weapons and wore helmets embossed with the Cross of Lorraine, symbol of Joan of Arc and now of the Free French. The Poles frankly felt these fellows could have little to do with their just war of liberation.

And everyone had noticed that getting them into ranks and ready to attack was more like sheep-herding than what the officers of a modern army generally did.

Lesek had even watched while they wrapped turbans around heads that were shaved apart from a tail that emerged at the top. Perhaps that was why, when later a discussion arose about those disturbing barbarian warriors, when everyone said they resembled Turks, he brought out a definition they all agreed was better.

"Tartars!"

"Good God, they look like the Golden Horde!"

"But you know, my lager was full of Tartars, they sang the saddest songs at night, almost all night. They were not the most vicious by any means; the worst were the Russian criminals."

"And so, Franiek? Didn't they treat us well in Samarkand and those parts? We're not talking about Tartars of today."

While they waited to take their place on the front lines, the men of the 15th Fusiliers had their chance to test their intuition about those soldiers against the rumors that circulated among the Allies. It was said they treated their victims atrociously, slicing off what some said were ears, some noses or worse, and there were many macabre variations. Some said they came from Berber tribes, ancient warrior stock from the mountains of Morocco, and would attack with bestial war cries, invoking Allah and the Prophet. It was also said they were kept under tight curfew when not in combat, their camps surrounded by barbed wire.

The Poles, who had seen Caucasian tribes deported to the gulag, were struck by this latter rumor. Franciszek Kułakowski, in particular, was eager to understand once and for all if these were regular soldiers or if these Berbers were really more like the barbarian mercenaries used in ancient times, as their Berber-Barbar name seemed to suggest.

And so Franiek, who had studied French in school and even translated some poems by Rimbaud, found an occasion to speak to one of their officers. The French officer declared he was very proud of their battle to liberate France—and that was something a Pole could truly appreciate—and Franiek nodded.

"It was a terrible shock for all of us to learn that Paris had fallen. Etes-vous de Paris, peut-être?"

"Mais non," the officer said, "je suis de Marrakech!" And he explained that in their contingent, even many of the whites, including General Juin himself, had been born and raised in the colonies, but were certainly no less patriotic for that.

"This war will take me to France for the first time; I can't wait to march into Paris!"

"It is my good fortune to be a native of Warsaw, and every day I dream of returning. Although I cannot bear to think how the Germans have ruined it."

"Ah, ils sont terribles, les Boches!" said the Frenchman of Marrakech, and that *Boches* buzzed with more contempt than any Englishman ever put into it, and Franiek liked the man even more. And so he listened carefully while the Frenchman explained that their men, those from Algeria, included conscripts, but the *goumiers*, those Moroccan Berbers, were all volunteers. And while they had some primitive tribal habits, they had no equals in their disdain for death and the way they skipped up and down the mountains like goats.

"And why do you keep them locked up?" Franiek dared, timidly, to ask at that point.

"Parce-que ils sont des sauvages!" said the Frenchman proudly. "They are our Punic warriors, and with them we'll defeat the German Empire!" And the fact that Franiek, who knew his classics, got his quip meant they ended their conversation both of them quite happy.

However, when on May 14 the Punic or Tartar warriors of France broke through the Gustav Line and clambered up the sheer cliffs of the Aurunci mountains, Milek and his comrades, waiting to return to the front lines, probably knew nothing of it. Or if that encouraging piece of news did reach them, they paid little attention, for it didn't seem all that important even to the high command. In part, a single breakthrough was too little to count as victory; in part because Frenchmen were Frenchmen, while the designated heroes of the battle were the men under British command: the English, Welsh, Scots, Irish, Canadians, and again, those Indians and Gurkhas who were finally pushing the Germans back down toward the valley.

Even today accounts of the Battle of Monte Cassino don't necessarily make it clear that the soldiers who first broke through the Gustav Line were men of the French Expeditionary Corps. That is partly due to the usual national chauvinism, most likely, but also to the fact that the French advance was not entirely something to boast about.

While the Poles were still hunkered down in their holes, soon to go back up on Calvary and the Phantom (and then to oust the Germans from Piedimonte San Germano) the colonial Free French troops descended on Ausonia, Esperia, Campodimele, Lenola, Spigno Saturnia and many other small towns in a wave of devastation, sacking, killing, and above all, raping. The females of that rural zone, the Ciociaria, many of them adolescents but also children and old women, were raped, almost always by groups of soldiers, sometimes raped until they died. Men were not exempt either, and the fate of the parish priest of Esperia has not been forgotten.

The sole memory of French troops in Italy would be this.

After the war, something odd happened. The rapes were not forgotten, but neither were they spoken of, whether out of political convenience, or some notion of public decency. Or rather, they were spoken of only in artistic terms: Alberto Moravia wrote a novel, *La Ciociara*, Vittorio De Sica made a film of it with Sophia Loren. But the women who inspired them were neglected, forgotten. No one thought of them as the women of Ciociaria; they were the *Marocchinate*, a name that recalled the Moroccan perpetrators.

It was a dreadful term that seemed to well up out of the horror, bringing with it women screaming and men humiliated as they were made to stand by, or raped and murdered themselves if they tried to intervene.

Yet after a while the term settled in. It became a brand.

And that was above all the reason (that and the need to remove the trauma) that the actual women of Ciociaria, if they had not been marked by visible wounds, venereal disease or pregnancy, preferred to hide what had happened, and be silent. Or they left, emigrated far and wide as others from the region did, but with an extra good reason: far away no one would know what had happened to them.

The laughable reparations that first France and then the new Republic of Italy paid to civilian victims were for material and physical damages. Not for rape, a crime that in Italy would continue for decades to be an offense to public decency rather than a crime against the person, and when committed in war, just something unfortunate that happened.

It happened when the Wehrmacht invaded Poland, and Russia, and to a much lesser extent, Italy; it happened on a monstrous scale when the Red Army broke through into Germany; it happened with the American troops especially in Japan; it happened in Africa with the Fascist Army. And every time it happened, the message was the same. Contempt for the losing side, past a certain point, upturned the Tenth Commandment. You would indeed take your neighbor's house, and your neighbor's wife. It was right and fair, or in any case, inevitable. Mass rape would be considered a war crime only after the conflict in ex-Yugoslavia.

In Ciociaria, the numbers of women who went before French military tribunals to ask for justice were so few that even today, a French historian feels free to call those denunciations "wild stories" and argues that the liberators were depicted as demons in order to cancel some of the national humiliation when the Fascist regime fell. The same scholar actually suggests these women had "a morbid desire for exotic sex" and only pretended to have been raped.

In Italy, on the other hand, it was mostly the extreme right that has publicized, using the highest possible estimates, the rapes of Catholic Italian women by Muslim beasts. And so for the mass rapes of Ciociaria, like so many other horrors of the last world war, it's impossible to arrive at a definitive picture, not even of the numbers of victims. The one thing we can say for certain today is that those rapes did happen. But we do not know at what levels and to what extent the French command (sharply reprimanded by General Alexander) was responsible for the behavior of their colonial troops. Had the officers permitted their men to take it out on civilians? One of the few *goumiers* brought to trial said he would never have considered molesting French citizens, but that he considered it normal to sack or even rape Italians "because they were the enemy." Who put that in his head? How many non-*goumier* French soldiers participated? Several witnesses spoke of "not just Moroccans but some French guys too." Nor has much effort been made to understand who the *goumiers* were.

They didn't enlist for patriotic reasons but for the wages, for the prestige associated with being a warrior, out of clan loyalties, wrote the same scholar who attributed morbid sexual desires to the women of Ciociaria. Not just Moroccans, they came from all the poorest Maghreb populations, they were illiterate mountain people with whom French officers had to be "fathers, spiritual advisors and tribal chiefs" in turn, the portrait continued in best colonial tradition. Not that sources from the point of view of other armies had anything very different to say. They depicted men of ancient warrior stock, brave, if quite ferocious.

But some who have narrowed their reseach to the *goumiers* specifically paint a different picture. They came, many of them, not from the mountains but from the poorest quarters of Casablanca, some had been released from jail or had their sentences commuted if they put their X on the enlistment form. In other cases entire populations of able males from mountain villages were rounded up in police manhunts and taken off to the army, especially in those places where the French had crushed Berber insurrections.

The Moroccan historian Driss Maghraoui, publishing in an American academic journal, came to these conclusions, noting that in his own country, those last embodiments of colonialism seemed to interest no one. Others (curiously, scholars who almost always seem to live abroad, far from their country of origin) have begun to study a history in some ways similar: the Indian soldiers who behaved impeccably abroad during the war, and then during the Partition, joined paramilitary gangs that also sacked, murdered and raped, this time people who only recently had lived in their same country, same cities, next door even.

War seems to breed these poor devils, these demon genies that emerge from the lamp of battle and become tragically real. More than 7,000 soldiers from the French Expeditionary Corps died on the Cassino front. Their victims, according to the most recent likely estimates, were about the same number.

At the war's end, the *goumiers*, who had for better or worse behaved as expected, were demobilized. Morocco gained independence, and they were forgotten.

And at the triumphal victory parade in Paris, the American high command, backed by London, gave General Charles De Gaulle's troops pride of place at the head of the file, on the condition that the lead marchers look like proper Frenchmen. The people of Texas and Louisiana should not be allowed to think their sons had died just to liberate some Negroes. Of the French 2nd Armored Division, of which about one quarter were soldiers of color, all those who would have been shot under Hitler's orders had they fallen into German hands were replaced with substitutes for the occasion. Better stick in some light-skinned North African, better than a Senegalese soldier. France's Punic troops had already disappeared before they got to the Arc de Triomphe.

Quite the opposite happened to those soldiers who would somehow come to symbolize the Battle of Monte Cassino for all. There isn't a book today, not even an English or American account, that doesn't single out the *Fallschirmjäger*, the German paratroopers, the green devils, for their great military valor and esprit de corps, for their battle skills. As if to say: remember, we had to face the most elite corps of the entire Reich, the purest distillation of century upon century of Prussian militarist tradition. Which is why we, ordinary men in uniform, although numerically and technologically superior, took months and months to defeat them.

In Germany, those paratroopers dug into the ruins of the abbey (ruins produced by a vile and cowardly air war) were a legend. They were the Spartans valiantly resisting the gigantic Persian Army, composed of mercenaries of every race and breed and representing an arrogant, depraved power that was bound to be defeated. The *Fallschirmjäger* were ever present in the Führer's soul and in Goebbels' thoughts, and the master of propaganda showed them over and over again in newsreels, aware that for once, he merely had to show the truth to make German hearts burn with the faith their country was invincible. Truth, when available, served even better than lies to make propaganda. Hitler had ordered the 1st Parachute Division to hold on to the end, to fight to the last man.

Did anyone doubt they had done so?

It was thanks to them that Monte Cassino, as General Anders observed, was "famous around the world," that he and his men had to snatch victory from German fame and glory, so the world would recognize and finally repay Poland no more and no less than was deserved: her very existence. And the Polish soldiers knew this too, although they understood this could not be further from the sort of combat where armies clashed, helmets, shields and swords glittering under the sun, bards and messengers waiting by the side. They had to go back up there, to those crags and cliffs seeded with mines, and stumble on them, make this a field of glory, their blood the ink of printing presses, be captured on film by the newsreel photographers.

And that was what Milek and his comrades were about to try, even as the Germans prepared to carry out the orders received the night before, and move back to the Senger Line. The French had damaged one flank of their defenses; British tanks were pouring into the valley.

From the hill where the abbey's ruins stood, the paratroopers watched the enemy advance, literally right before their eyes. They continued to fight though, perhaps because they were being attacked, perhaps because the *Führerbefehl* — the Führer's orders — so dictated, and those orders were sacred to their general.

The Poles, back in the front lines like Greco-Roman soldiers in tortoise formation, saw nothing of this, and knew nothing, nor for that matter were General Anders or the other Allied commanders aware of the German retreat. And so they fought pretty much the same battle, sometimes better, sometimes worse, than the first time.

The Kresowa, patched up as best as possible, went first. At 7 am on May 17 they climbed Phantom, took Colle Sant'Angelo, withstood a very heavy artillery counter-attack, held their ground, saw

their munitions run out, finally got fresh supplies and reinforcements—tank drivers, anti-aircraft artillery men, mechanics and
drivers from the command—dug in there on the hill, and sat tight.

Not even those on their way to Calvary, including private Herling, were able to get past blasted Point 593. Gustaw Herling, like
Milek, was no longer watching his first comrades die; he wouldn't
have that shock to tie his memories to. Later, all he was left with
were "fragments of memory." There was the black hole of night as
they approached Point 593, their boots covered with cloth sacks;
the moment when a German rocket lit up the sky, and night became day, and half their patrol was slaughtered. How he, radio on
his back, and the artillery observer had somehow made it almost to
the top of the mountain as their comrades fell by the wayside one
by one, he didn't know. How, from a tiny hollow in the rocks where
they could have easily been hit from the German bunkers, did they
manage to direct the artillery all day long? How did they get back
down to the "Doctor's house" at sunset? There, his memories grew
less fragmentary, more vivid. It was conversations in the dark: was
the battle was won or lost they asked themselves: that was how
little they knew, on that night between May 17 and 18, just before
the flag of victory was raised on the abbey. Herling recalled "a soldier in communications with the melodious accent of Bielorussia"
who was trying to convince his superior that if he could hook up
a telephone wire to the Doctor's house (given their troubles com-
municating by radio) the wire wouldn't immediately be blown to
pieces by the incessant German shelling. "There wasn't the least
hint of bravura in this: he just kept saying over and over, 'I want to
be part of this too.'"

They had both won and lost the battle, because the night of
the 17th the paratroopers' commander had agreed to the order to
retreat, an order delivered by General Kesselring in person. The
Reich, with all due respect for *Führerbefehl* and for propaganda,
could not afford to sacrifice those heroes, who certainly amounted
to more than 300 valorous Spartans. The Reich needed its best soldiers alive, the chief of German forces in Italy insisted.

The enemy was no longer among the ruins of the abbey when,
before the eyes of the world and the eyes of Poland, the men who
had climbed Calvary prepared to run up the flag. Or rather yes, but

once again the Germans were hidden. About a dozen emerged in all. They paled when they saw the Polish eagle. Ragged uniforms crusted with dirt, unshaven, wounds covered with filthy dressings. Where had they come from? Were there more? It seemed they had come from a hole. A hole in what remained of the abbey floor, leading underground, to the crypt where the remains of St. Benedict lay unharmed. It had been joined by the corpses of paratroopers that could not be buried. Some were in caskets, others had been covered with sacks or with their now useless backpacks. It hadn't been meant to be a collective grave, but a makeshift hospital. There were even three seriously wounded men lying on gold vestments next to the altar. They had been left bread, water and canned food. Some had preferred to stay there, absent a brave King Leonidas at this Thermopylae, what with the Führer in Berlin, and not even one general of a division at the front line. The two candles providing the only light in the crypt flared brightly for an instant, and the fear on the men's faces was almost palpable. But the Poles just wanted to get away from that unbearable cadaverous stink as quickly as possible. Outside, when they got the flag up and the trumpeter sounded the Hejnal Mariaki, the anthem of Krakow, they finally began to breathe again.

The following day, May 19, 1944, General Anders went to visit the battlefield where, he would later learn, some 900 of his men had died.

It was a dreadful sight. There were enormous dumps of unused ammunition, for every type of weapon and every caliber. Blocks of cement, trench pits and forward medical bases were scattered along the mountain trails. Here and there lay heaps of land mines and "corpses of Polish and German soldiers, sometimes entangled in a deathly embrace," wrote Anders. Further on were tanks, some upturned and damaged; others frozen as if ready to attack. American tanks from the earlier battles, their guns pointing to the Abbey. The slopes of the hill were covered with an enormous number of scarlet poppies, their bright red color "weirdly appropriate," thought the general. The so-called Valley of Death was nothing but tree stumps splintered by bullets and shrapnel. Everywhere the hills were pocked with craters, shreds of Allied and German uniforms, helmets, guns, hand grenades, rolls of barbed wire, and live mines at every turn.

The Abbey towered over all. From afar, you could see the massive west wall, all that was standing, with the Polish and British flags flying from it. The Doctor's house stood on the opposite hill. The Abbey was now a great heap of ruins from which here and there a broken marble column or a piece of a stone saint emerged. Fragments of frescos and mosaics, paintings and artwork lay scattered about. From an intact corner, came the stench of German corpses that had lain there for days among the caskets of the dead monks. Masterpieces of painting and sculpture, rare books and illuminated manuscripts lay in the rubble and dust along with the trappings of war. A hurricane of fire and steel had battered that magnificent monastery, and nothing but ashes and ruins remained.

That life form that had disappeared from the landscape after the battle was now Dr. Szer's primary concern, along with the rest of the Army medical staff. And where was Milek? Had he come out unharmed once again? Did he did not even take part in the second attack? Did his "I'm not going to tell you shit" approach to his military experience perhaps conceal the fact he'd been wounded the first time around and thus avoided the repeat action? Was it possible he'd never told anyone for the rest of his life, not even his wife who'd have seen the scar?

The only thing we know for sure is that he did fight at Monte Cassino. Corporal Samuel Steinwurzel's demobilization papers attest to three "Decorations," Military Cross, level 1, War Medal, and the Monte Cassino Cross.

What are they worth, those medals, in particular the Monte Cassino Cross? Most likely it simply confirmed he had taken part; no more, but a confirmation. The only elements at my disposition to allow me to imagine soldier Milek's battle—glorious or unglorious as it might have been—are that medal and the name of his unit on his papers. Using those two hooks, I have tried to weave together a story, relying on detailed accounts of the role his battalion played and connecting them to the ranks of the fallen in the cemetery beneath the Abbey. There lies Leon Simon, fusilier, 15th Fusiliers Battalion of Wilno, born in Lviv on July 29, 1912, died May 12, 1944, buried in the Jewish section. If they were not friends, Samuel Steinwurzel would at the very least have known him. And there is Franciszek Kułakowski, fusilier first class, he too of the 15th Fusiliers Battalion, born in Warsaw on December 9, 1910, died on May 12, 1944; his link to Milek is one of chance and my own invention. And given that I know nothing of private Kułakowski beyond those two dates, I must ask his family's pardon for the license I have taken using his name. If I haven't changed that name to an invented one, it's because it seems to me that so long as even dates and names remain, anyone on earth can be certain he did exist. To create an imaginary Franciszek in tribute to the real one: isn't that what the symbolic power of invention is for?

In any case, the entire world of Milek before the war, his family and his forebears, all emerged from the data base of Yad Vashem and other such archives. Various nets, one atop the other, knotted around the names of the dead, which amount to just barely half their number. But even though the nets are woven very loosely, often something sticks to them: a brief statement, a map like that drawn by hand and annotated in Hebrew by some survivor, the map with which I was able to reconstruct the city of Radziechów, all of it, not only where the Jews who died had once lived.

In the case of the Szer brothers, too, the Web's collective memory allowed me to patch certain gaps in my mother's own recall. Dolek, a relative I never knew, and a man my mother seemed to have no special memories of, I've invented, with some caution, from where Irka's story left him. And yet, of all the things I have deduced or imagined about the battle, Dolek's shock at the death of Dr. Adam Graber (Warsaw, February 8, 1896-Monte Cassino, May 8, 1944) seems to me particularly plausible.

There was no other way to give voice to those who didn't leave a record in life, those who I never met and talked to, but to rely on those scarce facts. Thus, contrary to all expectation, it was the drowned, the dead, who helped to bring forth the saved.

I have also tried to replace lost memories with those that have been collected and preserved: accounts by the deported and by soldiers that might illuminate Milek's story where they intersect.

But none of this was enough. The stories of Milek, of Dolek, of his brothers, of Irka, are only some of the threads that come together in this battle, the ones that fell into my hands. And so I have tried to put together "a collection of small epics" as Anders had imagined, cracked and fragmented like the broken mosaics that the commander of the Second Army Corps found at the Abbey.

And I wanted to hear his voice, as I wanted to hear Gustaw Herling, two men who fought at Monte Cassino. Men who fought for a cause that was so just, so limpid, that even Anders—born of a line not very different from his German military equivalents, fervent patriot, sometimes reactionary and even anti-Semitic—could acknowledge that the battle that lent glory to his name and to his men, was one upset after another, one side ahead, then the other; the result a mass of detritus, of dead things.

Courage can be harder to achieve in peacetime than in wartime, for peacetime courage involves the truth. Gustaw Herling, still wearing the uniform of the Second Army Corps, understood that, and when he wrote something for the first anniversary of the battle, he entitled it "Civil Courage."

"Civil? But we were soldiers! It is true. But we were soldiers and no more. We were not, we are not, and we shall never be *Raubritter*, those military bandits for whom peace is a pause between wars and war a moment of vitalist fulfillment. It is said that a man has civil courage when he says or does unpopular things, even problematic things, merely because he is convinced they are utterly just. Such people are the only ones to be trusted without hesistation."

And with this I finally see again the man I knew, our family friend Emilio Steinwurzel, who every time we arrived in Milan was already at the platform at 7:00 a.m., waiting for a train that was always late, ready to bound toward the sleeping car and grab the bags from our hands, heading toward the exit with long, bird-like steps. And within him is Corporal Steinwurzel, always reliable and ready, always willing to make an effort on behalf of someone or something, in peace as he had been in war.

War that continued after the battle of Monte Cassino.

The Poles fought in Le Marche, and after another hard battle in which the Italian Liberation Corps also fought, they took the strategic port of Ancona. Between August 25 and September 2, they broke though the Gothic Line, along with the Canadian First Army Corps. At the same time, the Poles were elsewhere too. They were in Warsaw, where on August 1st the Armia Krajowa rebelled against the Germans. The entire city fought, quarter by quarter, house to house, against the German heavy artillery, tanks, and armed soldiers. They wanted to liberate the capital as the French had been allowed to do in Paris; they wanted to strike the first blows, now that Radio Moscow had urged them to "drive out the Germans!" The Red Army was at the gates. But they would remain on the banks of the Vistola, and no help would come from the Soviets.

By the end of August, the Poles—wherever they were, fighting in Warsaw, in Italy, in the armored division assigned to Normandy after the landing—had understood that the Soviet army would not move from where they were. Still hoping they might be mistaken, they had already understood they were not. They knew that Poland's freedom was more and more uncertain, all of Poland. And so, speaking to Churchill and to Roosevelt in the only language at their disposal, they asked to send the same military message they had at Monte Cassino, whatever it cost.

They were, said Herling, although far from their homeland, "comrades in arms with the Armia Krajowa." He wrote in 1969; for another twenty years it would be forbidden even to mention the struggle in Warsaw.

While private Herling was climbing the hills of Le Marche with his battalion, General Anders gave voice to the same sentiment, speaking to Winston Churchill. They met at the Allied headquarters near Fano on August 26. The Red Army had by now occupied the Praga district, but had stopped there without crossing the Vistola, while battle raged in the center of Warsaw.

The Prime Minister offered his congratulations on the magnificent victories of the Second Corps and expressed his great appreciation of its deeds. After that he asked: "What is the state of your soldiers' morale in view of the events they witness at present?"

General Anders answered that the morale of the troops was excellent, that the soldiers knew that their first task and obligation was the destruction of Germany, but that they were very anxious at the same time about the future destiny of Poland, and about all that was happening in Warsaw.

They talked about frontiers, and it was clear that the Poles alone were unwilling to see them redrawn to meet the concessions granted to Stalin. But when Anders hardened and said he would never allow the Russians to take what they wanted just because they had occupied the territory, Churchill began to plead with him. He looked him in the face, reached out a hand to touch him, promised that all would be resolved at the peace conference, once the victory was won:

> CHURCHILL: You will be present at the Conference. You must trust us. Great Britain entered this war in the defense of the principle of your independence, and I can assure you we will never desert you.
>
> ANDERS: Our soldiers have never for one moment lost faith in Great Britain. They know that first of all Germany must be beaten, and they are ready to carry out any task for this end. General Alexander could certainly confirm this, he said, and that his orders had always been and would always be carried out. But the Poles could not trust Russia, knowing her too well; they believed that all Stalin's announcements that he wanted a free and strong Poland were lies. The Russians entering Poland are arresting and deporting our wives and children to Poland as they did in 1939. They disarm the soldiers of our Home Army, shoot our officers, and imprison members of our Civil Administration, destroying those who have been fighting the Germans without interruption since 1939. Our wives and children are in Warsaw, but we prefer they should perish there rather than live under the Bolsheviks. We all prefer to perish fighting rather than live cringing.
>
> CHURCHILL (appearing deeply moved): You should trust Great Britain, who will never abandon you—never. I know that the Germans and the Russians are destroying your best elements, particularly the intellectuals. I deeply sympathize with you. But be confident, we will not desert you and Poland will be happy.

Soon after the Poles broke through the last German line of defense near Cattolica on the Adriatic, Warsaw had to give up its fight against the Germans. Nearly 200,000 people had died, almost all of them civilians, and the rest of the population was evacuated. Some ended in German labor camps, some in concentration camps and extermination camps, some were merely transferred far from the capital. For Warsaw was already a dead city, a city destroyed, but that was not enough. First, the city was thoroughly sacked, then meticulously razed to the ground using explosive charges and flame-throwers, building by building, brick by brick.

The Soviet forces once again watched from the other bank of the Vistula, from the Praga district. They crossed the river only when the Germans had finished their work.

Warsaw burned while the soldiers of the Second Army Corps should have enjoyed their well-earned relief from battle. Milek took out what he had saved from Franciszek Kułakowski's knapsack: not much, an ugly photograph with an address written on the back. He thought of the letter he'd tried to get to Franiek's family through the Armia Krajowa's network, maybe too late, and probably lost. It wasn't much, a couple of simple sentences; Milek had never had the patience for writing. In his place Franiek would have been different; Franiek, who had taken to translating from the French and who had hoped his army service would allow him to continue studying after the war. Not modern literature, but ancient history; he'd had a thing about Hannibal since he was a kid. Of course he'd seen himself rising up the university ladder in Warsaw: Warsaw, where the university, stripped bare, was now a heap of charred ruins.

"I said, 'lucky you, from Warsaw,' but I was wrong," he murmured to the photo. Then he thought, well, given the situation, it might be simpler if all Franiek's family were dead. But most likely they weren't. And so he decided he had better try again to put down those few lines and send them—how and to whom, he wasn't sure. But sooner or later, if he kept trying, someone would get them. He had better put them down on a piece of paper right away, while the ashes of Warsaw were still warm and his memory of Franiek still vivid. He had nothing else to do, and was nervous, like all his fellow soldiers. But differently too, for all this affected him; Warsaw was their capital, just as Lviv was his city. Lviv, where there was also an insurrection, where the Soviets had come to the aid of the soldiers of the Armia Krajowa, and then had arrested most of them. He might even know some of them, but it wasn't them he was thinking of when Glinianska came to mind. Oh, stop. It was time to get this damned letter on paper, do what had to be done.

Dear Kułakowski family,

Allow me to introduce myself. I am a fellow soldier of Franiek and I was with him at Monte Cassino. Unfortunately I am part of another company, and so I was not nearby when he was killed. (strike that, "when he passed on"). But I can assure that he most likely did not suffer (better, "he did not suffer") and that he was given a proper grave. They are making a cemetery for all the heroes ("heroes?" yes, heroes) who fell in that battle you've heard of. I just wanted to say that Franiek was always a loyal comrade, and a friend who told us many interesting things and made us laugh. It was an honor and a pleasure to have known him in these long years of training and combat with General Anders.

Such things permitted a soldier to go on. That, and the contrary: venting one's distress in long political discussions which in the end, someone would always say were pointless while the war was still on. Only when they were all sitting around a conference table would they understand. Until then, they must persist, and hope; it was their duty. In any case they must persist, and get back on the battlefield (in the end, the best way to drive out gloomy thoughts).

They would soon return to combat, and in terrible conditions. Autumn brought rain; rain, mud, but it wasn't only operative difficulties that made these new mountains so troubling. More and more they met Italian partisans up here, and they were very friendly yes, but for the most part they were communists, and often, in their enthusiasm at meeting their liberators, they would call them *comrades* in the communist sense. Actually, they called them *tovarish*; for them, it seemed, Polish and Russian were practically the same thing. Sometimes they even said they were envious of Poland for soon the whole country would be under Red Army control. With all due respect, what they wouldn't give to have the Soviets liberate them! The Poles were glad they didn't have time to stop and talk; anyway their Italian wasn't good enough for anything but a frustrating stab at disagreement. The Italians wouldn't believe a word they said in any case. It was strange though; these men, too, looked after their scarce and battered weapons, treating them almost as if they were living things, just as their brothers in the Warsaw resistance. And like them, when they talked about the Nazi-Fascists and about liberation, their voices lit up and so did their rough, scratched faces, unless they were out under the rain.

Therefore, they had to accept that these were their comrades, although not in the way those free communists meant it. And when on October 27, 1944 Mussolini's native town of Predappio was liberated, the revelers in the piazza climbed up on the Polish tanks.

They advanced mountain to mountain in the Romagna Apennines, flanking the progress of the British along the coast. On November 9 the Fifth Corps took Forlì and on December 16, the New Zealanders Faenza. But by now winter was underway and delays were inevitable.

It was during this pause (which they certainly deserved and surely needed, given their losses, not much less than at Monte Cassino) that catastrophe came down on them from afar.

The Big Three met for the second time on February 4, 1945. And the place chosen already seemed to indicate how matters were going to fall out. Stalin, pleading health problems that prevented him from traveling far, suggested they hold the conference at Tsar Nicholas's summer residence. What was decided at Yalta was quite simple: how to divide up post-war Europe. Stalin would have liked Italy in his sphere of influence, but Roosevelt and Churchill thought that was too much. For the first time, fears that all of Poland was doomed began to look like concrete reality. Roosevelt and Churchill had agreed that the Poles would be represented, not by their legitimate government in London, but by the one the Soviets had put up: a government being the first thing they restored once they finally decided to enter Warsaw. That the Russians had guaranteed that after the war that government would become more substantial and more democratic was one of the cheapest lies ever pronounced by Stalin, nor was it much of a fig leaf to cover the shame of the free world.

This time General Anders could not say the morale of his troops was excellent, in spite of everything. Nor could he say they had always had, and would always have, the greatest of faith in England. This time his soldiers were on the brink of mutiny, or desertion en masse. Their commander, who would have liked to roar out his dissent, who would almost rather have re-fought battle of Monte

Cassino, except that right now he couldn't bear to think about the men sacrificed on that mountain or any other, for the first time General Anders struggled to impose his authority on that army of his he had towed away from Soviet dominion.

But when the men finally calmed down, the General too calmed himself. He thought about it and decided that the situation was intolerable. And therefore he sent a telegram to the government in London and then immediately wrote a letter to Sir Harold Alexander, dated February 13, 1945.

Those hours, he wrote, were the most difficult of their lives. The decision taken at Yalta by the Big Three meant that their land and their nation was "no more than the spoils of the Bolsheviks, and renders us instantly powerless. We have left the graves of thousands of our fellow soldiers along our way—the way of our battle to return to Poland, as we thought of it." The soldiers of the Second Polish Corps believed the result of the Yalta Conference was "highly unjust and in utter contradiction with their sense of honor." Those soldiers now asked him: what is the purpose of this fight? And he was unable to reply to that question. What had happened was terribly grave: they were in a place from which he could see no way out. "I see no other choice but to withdraw that part of my men at the front, for A) their sentiments, as I have described above, and B) the fact that neither I nor my sub-commanders believe, in conscience, that we have the right to ask further sacrifices from our men."

But then the Polish government and all the Allied commanders contacted Anders and urged him not to withdraw. Alexander, on his return from Greece, called him down to Caserta and promised he would not use Polish soldiers in battle but, as the other commanders had insisted, they needed the Polish forces to maintain the lines. And further, Anders was told, if he withdrew now, it would put him in a weaker negotiating position where that remaining narrow diplomatic opening was concerned.

Nothing, therefore, happened in those days. At night, Milek would sometimes hear a sudden noise like a donkey braying, or a rusty pump, sounds that shared something with a throttled outburst of male weeping. But after a while that, too, passed. The Second Army Corps would serve the Allied cause right to the finish.

And maybe it was better that way. As time went by, the longest serving soldiers said so, the one-time inhabitants of Kresy. That was when they really became an army in exile. But exile was a state of mind, and it took a long time to get used to it. What else could they do now but remain united? Yet that they could only do by remaining in the Army, and an army, sooner or later, had to go back to the front. By now there were twice as many of them as the 40,000 who sailed across the Caspian. The new forces come directly from German capitivity, now that the Germans were being defeated on all sides: from all their lagers, especially prison lagers, but also from the Wehrmacht, whose uniforms many Poles had been forced to wear. In part because those new comrades brought with them fresh energy and fury, in part because new faces made them less willing to live with their own despair, whatever the reason, they were now ready to fight again when in April it came time for the last offensive.

They didn't know they would have to face the 1st German Parachute Division once again. Never mind; they liberated Imola on April 14 and entered Bologna, first of the Allied troops, at 6:00 a.m. on April 21. You could not but be moved by the way these Italian cities exulted; not but feel lightfooted in your heavy boots as you marched along. Not but be struck by the waves of acclamation, the hurrahs that rose and fell indicating the way to the main square. The Karpacka Division rode in with all its tanks, and sent someone to run up the Polish flag on Bologna's tallest building, the one with that stupendous name that so suited their mood, the Torre degli Asinelli, "the Little Jackass Tower." It was a beautiful day, and General Clark was speaking in Piazza Maggiore, his Adam's apple bobbing in pride, and the Poles alongside the English and the Italians (both regulars and partisans), the pennants and Allied flags and the Italian *tricolore*. And if the most vigorously waved, the most threadbare, dirtiest and best-loved were often red flags, well, they didn't even want to notice that today. Today, the war was over for them too.

What now began was a long period of getting used to the condition of exile. While they were still in service as Allied soldiers based in Italy, the Second Army Corps protected them. It opened schools,

offered courses and other leisure time activities. Milek himself participated, becoming Corporal 1st class, as a certificate from Army
Training released on January 13, 1945 attests.

Before long, the last Allied promises dissolved. The Warsaw
government was to remain under Moscow's control, but even before that was certain, the entire general staff of underground Poland was lured into a trap and arrested. And many members of
the Armia Krajowa ended up in jail, in the gulag, or were shot, or
disappeared. On June 9, 1946, when the Allied victory over the Nazis was celebrated in London with a great parade and first works,
the Poles were absent. The Warsaw delegation said they could not
participate, probably because they had Soviet orders to stay home.
Those who had fought under the British command, invited when
Warsaw declined, refused to take part.

They were victors, and yet they found themselves among the
defeated: such were the members of the free Polish armed forces.
And when demobilization came—those papers Milek signed on
April 18, 1947 at Predappio—Polish soldiers for the first time faced
collective disintegration. Anyone who didn't return to Poland by a
certain date would lose the right to return in the future. But almost
none of those who came from places that had ended up in the Soviet republics of Ukraine, Lithuania or Bielorussia even considered
the idea. Those places from which the Poles, that is, their families or
what was left of them, had been expelled.

Not even Milek—who had been made to insist on paying the
price he'd chosen to pay—had any intention of returning to Poland.
And now, just as he had proved himself to be Polish, he ended up
stateless like the rest. In the end, the English government finally
gave at least something in reparation by offering citizenship to all
those soldiers who had fought under British command, and many
of his comrades went off to settle in Great Britain.

Not Corporal 1st class Steinwurzel, who in the meantime was
becoming Emilio, because once, again Milek was a man of good luck.

He wasn't the only one who during the war or after had met
an Italian girl. That was good luck in itself, and even more so for
all those lost, solitary men. The gods be praised, the one thing that
war doesn't destroy is love and desire—anything but. And thus the
reasons why Polish soldiers settled in Italy were almost always sen-

timental. Gustaw Herling married the daughter of the leading Italian historian-philosopher Benedetto Croce. And Dolek Szer, too, spent a number of years in Rome, deep in a great love affair with an Italian princess. An unhappy love affair, of course, because her family was firmly opposed. Of all the officers in that most Catholic of armies, the one Jew had to pursue their daughter?

From the way Irka several times mentioned that affair, I understood that following it at a distance had given a touch of novelistic spice to her Israeli married life. But she couldn't remember any of the details, only that Dolek, once he gave up all hope, had moved to New York where he became hospital chief of surgery, never married, and died at an advanced age.

And so, I must confess, I'm left with some curiosity of the old fashioned Hollywood screen star variety. To all who may read this book I pose the question: was it ever rumored in the family that some noble lady of the line, probably Roman, had once fallen in love with a Polish Jewish officer and doctor?

The girl who met Milek had none of these insuperable obstacles about her. She was small, dark and cheerful as were most of the young women who got to know Polish soldiers. She was called Eliana Finzi. She was Jewish, from Mantua. Just where and how his parents had met, Gianni Steinwurzel was unable to tell me. Perhaps his father had been stationed at Mantua. Perhaps he had even met Signorina Finzi while she was accompanying some cousin of hers to the offices of a Jewish organization hoping to have word of the only member of the family who had been deported (she had died at Auschwitz). If that was what happened, or something not so very different, Milek would have been doubly lucky. At the very moment when he learned that an aunt of his had survived, and thus had the grim confirmation that all the rest of the family from Poland had perished, he met a charming young lady who could understand all he'd been through without in any way being able to really imagine. Mantua's old city was unbombed, intact, including the synagogue, which was even held to be a historical monument. In Mantua the Jews complained they had been tormented by the Fascists, but almost all of them were still alive.

Signorina Eliana Finzi did not want to waste time on bygone tragedies, however. She was eager to recover the years stolen from her when she'd had to flee to Switzerland, and here was this tall young man in his handsome Allied uniform. For Milek, things were even simpler: he no longer had a family, he no longer had a country, he no longer had an army posting. But he could manage without that demolished past of his, because he had a future, and her name was Eliana Finzi. All he had to do to hold onto that future was to marry her. He would have to forfeit British citizenship, because Polish soldiers with Italian wives could not settle in Great Britain. But Emilio now cared less and less about his fellow soldiers. They annoyed him, the way they only frequented other Poles and only thought about their home country. Maybe the feeling was even mutual, now that the days were over in which they had all been equal before the German enemy. Maybe one of them even said something like, "you don't understand, Milek; you are a Jew and you can go to your own country whenever you want." And in fact that was true. Samuel Steinwurzel, who had not wanted to stay in Palestine and did not want to live in Israel, thought a country like Italy, where the Jews hadn't been viciously persecuted and where he met more sympathy than prejudice, was an excellent place to settle down. What did he care that the place was so full of communists that a man like himself was quickly classed as reactionary, usually modified by the epithet "Fascist." In the worst case, all he had to do was mention what had become of his family, and they would shut up. Or better, he could simply give them a wide berth.

And so, with a permit from the Polish ambassador to the Holy See dated October 25, 1951, the almost Corporal 1st class Samuel Steinwurzel and the Signorina Eliana Finzi were married in the Norsa synagogue on Via Govi in Mantua. In time they would move to Milan, because outside of the big cities, there was no work for a Polish refugee no matter how eager he was to employ his technical skills to rebuild Italy, how ready to work hard.

Their first child was born before his parents were legally wed before the Italian state, while Emilio was awaiting the citizenship he would be granted on January 28, 1965. They called him Giovanni and then Mosé, Moses, in memory of grandfather Mojzesz. The second-born, once again following the Jewish custom of naming children for the departed, was called Anna, a variation on Fania that was also appropriate in Italian.

Settled in their new apartment on Via Bramante, fruit of his labor and their savings, the new Italian citizen Emilio acquired a title that would come to define him more than corporal. Engineer. It fit him so perfectly that I could hardly believe it when his son told me it was merely an honorific. I realized I had no idea what Emilio did except that it corresponded to the work of an engineer. When I went back the second time to get the papers Gianni had prepared for me, I noticed that on the nameplate by the doorbell—the only new feature in the building in 30 years—the name MIGLIAVACCA, Emilio's partner, he too an engineer, was still visible.

On long dull afternoons after lunch, while the adults talked Polish in the living room and Eliana, who didn't know Polish, tidied up the kitchen, and I had nothing else to think about, the names Steinwurzel-Migliavacca, Migliavacca-Steinwurzel, repeated until their meaning dissolved, melted into absurdity. Emilio's, which ended in something that came out sounding like *wurstel* (hot dog), and even more ridiculous, meant *stone-root*.

Today, those names that once just sounded strange to me have a certain literary resonance. I hear the imprint of the great Milanese writer Gadda, who really was an engineer and really was called Emilio, Carlo Emilio; and there is that stone-root, a word that seems to have been coined by the great Jewish poet Paul Celan, also born in one-time Austro-Hungarian lands, who wrote the line, "It is time the stone made an effort to flower."

Sorry, a scholar friend tells me, but among the works of Celan, there are many stones and many roots but no *Steinwurzel*.

The name Stone-root is still on the bell at Via Bramante, and those who bear it—Gianni and his three daughters—still smile as it's mispronounced, but after them it will cease to exist. The root will be gone, it will flower no more.

We can only share our sadness for never having asked our parents, our fathers, these questions of ours while they were still alive. Maybe if we had insisted, they might even have told us something.

Maybe we were too young, and they were too busy just getting on, working and building without stopping, behaving just like the Chinese who from Via Paolo Sarpi have begun to trickle over toward Via Bramante. They too were people of the future, and they could not be anything else: those, at least, among the saved, who didn't later end among the drowned.

My parents in Munich were such people, and "Engineer" Emilio Steinwurzel in Milan, and the future historian of the Shoah Israel Gutman in Israel, and even Marek Edelman in Warsaw, last commander of the Bundists in the ghetto uprising, who having decided to remain in Poland chose to honor the dead by working as a cardiologist among the living, waiting for the wind to change, politically.

If I ask myself why even Milek, who never fled, never spent as much as one day hidden away in a cupboard or a coal bin, who fought for the nation that made him a citizen, why even Milek "never said shit," I suppose it has to do with this.

To have taken up arms against your destiny was not enough to make you feel protected from what happened to the others, to hold back the horror that for every survivor is the choice between powerful guilt and utter meaninglessness. You didn't get a discount on the horror just because you fought in the war. And war itself was no less horrible because it was just and necessary.

Irka would forever be visited by a vision of her mother dead at Treblinka, "where they buried men alive." My mother, by the news she had somehow heard that her brother, at the *Judenrampe* at Auschwitz, was already missing his shoes. Milek, by what someone had told him, that his father Mojzsez, before they came to eradicate the ghetto of Lviv, had jumped to his death from a window.

Not even Israel Gutman, who embraced the Zionist cause as an adolescent, was able to build more than a fragile bridge over that void you must not get too close to.

I think I understood that when I looked into who Gutman was, especially two articles he wrote that spoke of the Shoah indirectly. In one, Gutman said it was right that Yad Vashem should have the paintings Bruno Shultz made for the house of the German who protected him, the man whose factotum he was. Those paintings, he argued, ought to be in Israel, even if scarcely anyone knew who the artist was. They must be there because Israel was the place where the greatest number of survivors were, the ones who had the right.

The other view expressed by Gutman was much more of a surprise. Asked about the memoirs of Binjamin Wilkomirski, revealed—a great scandal—to have been written by a Swiss author who had not been interned at Auschwitz as a child, Gutman defended the book.

"It's not that important," he said, whether Wilkomirski's book was a fraud. "He is not a fake. He is someone who lives this story very deeply in his soul. The pain is authentic."

An entire life devoted to the cause of Israel and the Jewish people was not enough to still that pain. On the contrary, it made no difference. The rage, the desire for justice, all of it, even having resisted the Germans in every possible circumstance, was useless.

Perhaps it was possible to escape feeling guilt, but that never-ending senseless pain was inescapable. Pain like a great, invisible bellows at the level of the heart that prods and pushes forward, always forward.

Having taken up arms was maybe useful in just one way: it was a brake on the perception that you had lived through horror, and horror alone. Gutman remembered every gesture of help and protection from his fellow prisoners at Majdanek; he remembered loaves of bread thrown from a train toward a column of detainees marching toward Mauthausen; he remembered the Warsaw ghetto during its few days of freedom. *And There Was Love in the Ghetto*: so Marek Edelman titled his book, published after his death.

In some ways both the young Zionist soldier and the Socialist commander who came back to fight during the Warsaw uprising, had the same thing to say about that first armed revolt against the Nazis, the ghetto uprising. They said there was no hope of victory, that they didn't even see themselves as doing anything particularly heroic, that they simply fought in order to breathe: not to breathe deeper, just to breathe. I cannot find, among my notes, the exact citation, but I believe it was Edelman who said that it took less courage to fire on the Germans than to step up and die, as most Polish Jews did: fully aware of what faced them, and yet composed, disciplined, silent, no wild screaming, tears and pleas for mercy.

I see my father again, that day when I opened the door early in the morning, knowing only that he had come back on the train from Milan. I hadn't been told what he had gone there to do by himself, something urgent, down and back, meanwhile you must study. My school-leaving exams were about to begin, and I had to concentrate and study. And yet, as much as my head was stuffed with notions, the face of my father in his threadbare loden coat, his sagging tweed hat, was so grim that I began to wail at him.

"Why did you go to Milan? I need to know: the truth. Tell me what happened. Why didn't you take me along?"

He hadn't yet come inside, and had a dark look on his face. "Emilio Steinwurzel died. I went to his funeral."

But for me, who didn't even know that Emilio had liver cancer, a condition that according to Gianni was connected to the malaria he contracted as a soldier, my father's reply was not enough. Once again, I'd been cheated. Once again, I felt the bubble of silence descend, that "I'm never going to say shit" that was supposed to protect me (and probably did) but also deprived me of my legitimate portion of pain, pain that could also be the invisible bellows keeping a person going.

The year after Emilio, it was my father's turn, a fatal heart attack while my mother and I were in Milan, where I had just moved. It had never really dawned on me, as daughter denied or as daughter in mourning, that my father, that morning when I forced him to tell me the truth, had lost the only Polish Jewish friend he ever had in the years after the war.

Maybe it was he who told me that Emilio Steinwurzel had fought with Anders' Army, maybe my father didn't accept the rule you weren't supposed to talk about it; maybe it was he in fact who forced Milek to tell him his story.

Because my father envied that story. Because my father told his other Italian friends who had fought in Yugoslavia, or even in Val d'Ossola with the partisans, that he also had been in the woods somewhere, fighting against the Nazis with the Russians and the Poles.

It wasn't true, however. I learned this one day, when he was already dead, just as I learned right before his funeral that his identity was all false: name and surname, his date of birth, the one we'd always celebrated as his birthday.

Milek, or Emilio, was what my father would have liked to have been, his imaginary double to whom this book is dedicated.

Strange, though: it is only at the end that I see how difficult it would have been for my father to take any other path. When he fled, he went with all his younger brothers and the small children of an older brother, hoping to save them. When they were found by the Germans (and after he'd persuaded a Polish family to hide his nephew Beniek in a dog hutch) my father was alone. By now Soviet-controlled Poland, where most of the Jewish resistance was active, had become almost unreachable, and the ghettos were closed. What was there to do but keep on fleeing?

Another strange thing: when I went to Via Bramante a second time, I realized that I had invented that striking photograph of Samuel Steinwurzel in 1943. There was only a photograph from 1932, Milek's passport photo from when he left Lviv, and you can see his face was that of a boy, in spite of the slicked-back hair and good suit. There is no trace of suffering in that picture. I see that I must have superimposed a photo of my father, taken sometime after 1939 and before 1945. It is my father who in that sepia passport photo has the Pierrot face, the ears that stick out, a pointed nose, a gaunt and troubled face like he never had again.

And so I also see that the truth can sometimes be disguised as fabrication, as Israel Gutman suggested, and I think I was right never to ask my father anything, and I know I will always do all that is in my power not to reveal how he really managed to survive and become the father I loved and love for all that he was, as well as for all that he would have liked to be.

This book is for him, my father, my imaginary soldier, and for Emilio Steinwurzel, who although he did really fight never said anything about it to his wife or his children, for Milek who died of cancer and maybe of that spectre of his father leaping from a window in the ghetto of Lviv, a spectre he took with him to the Musocco cemetery so that we could be free of it.

We can no longer ask anything of our fathers. We can only record their lives and their truths, even when these come forth as tales that can never be verified, or when they clothe themselves in the mercy—never large enough, never sturdy enough—of fabrications.

Thanks

To Irena Sher and Gianni Steinwurzel; to Paolo Morawski, Camilla Miglio and their family; to Laura Bosio; to Chiara Valerio and Federica Manzon; to Roberto Saviano; to Kay de Lautour Scott, Roberto Molle, Livio Cavallaro and all those who work for the Associazione Battaglia di Cassino and at the Italian website "Dal Volturno a Cassino"; to Fabio Santopietro, to Laila Wadia, and to Sergio Altieri.

Thanks also to Gustaw Herling and Władysław Anders, whose words are cited in this book :
Gustaw Herling, *A World Apart* (London: Heineman, 1951) and
Władysław Anders, *An Army in Exile* (London: Macmillan, 1949).

CPSIA information can be obtained at www.ICGtesting.com
Printed in the USA
BVOW07s0506271113

337479BV00002B/375/P